BRENDAN WOLF

ALSO BY BRIAN MALLOY

The Year of Ice

BRENDAN WOLF

Brian Malloy

St. Martin's Press New York

This is a work of fiction. All of the characters, organizations, and events portrayed in this novel are either productions of the author's imagination or are used fictitiously.

www.stmartins.com

Book design by Philip Mazzone

Library of Congress Cataloging-in-Publication Data

Malloy, Brian.
    Brendan Wolf / Brian Malloy.—1st ed.
        p.   cm.
    ISBN-13: 978-0-312-35976-8
    ISBN-10: 0-312-35976-4
        1. Gay men—Fiction.   2. Brothers—Fiction.   3. Minneapolis (Minn.)—Fiction.
    I. Title.

    PS3613.A454B74 2007
    813'.6—dc22

                                                                2006051193

First Edition: April 2007

10 9 8 7 6 5 4 3 2 1

For my sister, Dorothy Anne Malloy,
the smart, pretty, funny, generous, and compassionate one,
and (let's be honest) Dad's favorite

Acknowledgments

FOR THEIR HELP WITH THE MANY and varied drafts, sincere thanks to Charles Baxter, Julie Schumacher, Patricia Hampl, Anne Ursu, Keith Kahla, Lisa Tucker, Simon Lipskar, Laura Flynn, Don Sommers, Bonnie MacDougal, Jennine Crucet, Caroline Leavitt, Katharine Weber, and Dan Lazar.

For their financial support, sincere thanks to the Atheists for Human Rights Award Fund of the Philanthrofund Foundation, the Linde-Ostrander Leadership Award Fund of the Philanthrofund Foundation, and the Travel Study Grant Program for Minnesota and New York Artists supported by the Jerome Foundation and the General Mills Foundation.

I am deeply grateful for the love and support of Terrence Straub. Heartfelt thanks to all my family, and in particular to Dorothy McRee, Robert Bader, John and Lisa Rogers, James and Holly McRee, Corrie Alicea, Art and Barb Straub, Michael Malloy, Phyllis Malloy, and Denise Malloy Hubbard.

Thanks, too, to my friends Deb Leavitt and Anne Phibbs, John Flanigan and Michele Zurakowski, Nick Mattera, Dan Stringfield, Gerry

Tyrrell and Kevin Reuther, Peter Farstad and Paul Melbloom, Sherrie and Brad Beal, Norajean Flanagan, Terri Foley, Scott Cantor, Chris Forbes, Marge Barrett, Patrick Troska, Nancy Gaschot, Linda Myers, Antay Bilgutay, Vickie Lettman, Carol Skay, Pat Malone, Pat Cummings, Karen Kelley-Ariwoola, Kirby Bennett, Bunny and Earl Anderson, John Blaylock and Karen Nickel, Joan Nichols, Joan Drury, Tyree Hilkert, Beverly Sky, and, of course, Cat Thompson and the members of the 611 Alumni Association.

My love from this side of the veil to Thomas Joseph Malloy, Thomas Michael Malloy, Hugh McRee, Jim Smith, Jeff Scott, and Paul Illies, gone too soon.

An extra-special dog kiss right on the lips to Pepper, Cerberus, Max, Maggie, Lucy, and Tippie Moo Cow, good dogs all.

Someone or something is leaning close to me now
trying to tell me the one true story of my life. . . .

Marie Howe, "Prayer"

BRENDAN WOLF

Prologue

BRENDAN IS IN THE PARK on what those assembled are calling a glorious day: the sky is clear blue without even the wisp of a cloud, the temperature is hot but not oppressive, and there is a soft breeze that gently sways the branches of the trees overhead, creating an agreeable rustling sound. It's May, it's Minneapolis, it's the day of the annual Walk for the Unborn, and it is glorious.

The coordinator of his little group of volunteers opens a bible as he announces that he'll be reading from Luke 23, verses 28–30: "Jesus turned to them and said; 'Daughters of Jerusalem, do not weep for me. Weep for yourselves and for your children. The days are coming when they will say, Happy are the sterile, the wombs that never bore and the breasts that never nursed.'"

Brendan whispers "Amen" along with the rest of the volunteers in the little prayer circle. Around them, families eat picnic lunches of fried chicken and potato salad as vendors sell corn-dogs and cheeseburgers and ice cream and foot-longs. The event's organizers rush back and forth, shouting into walkie-talkies, eager to estimate the crowd's size, which is large, perhaps a record setter for this event. Brendan hears one of them yell, "There must be over fifteen thousand people!" Brendan doubts it as he scans the park, but then he understands that his indifference allows him a degree of honesty that for the faithful, in their enthusiasm, is unobtainable.

In the parking lot, the small fleet of rental trucks has been prepared to transport the donations from the park to the accounting office. Assuming that five thousand walkers from Minnesota and surrounding states have each collected at least $350 in pledges (an individual can't participate unless he or she brings a minimum of $300 in pledges to the park the day of the Walk), *and* assuming that one quarter of contributions are in cash, *and* assuming that the contributions will be distributed equally among the five trucks as they make their deliveries, Brendan should make off with just under $30,000 in legal tender by the Walk's end.

If everything goes according to the plan.

He's been told, promised, assured, and reassured that the plan is a sure thing. But today, here in this park, where he is surrounded by preachers and priests and politicians, the plan seems based on a lot of assumptions—too many, in fact—layered one on top of the other, like snow before an avalanche. As his doubts multiply, the pain in his side sharpens. He pops four aspirin in his mouth, washing them down with spring water donated by one of the Walk for the Unborn's many corporate sponsors.

Brendan tells himself it's not too late to back out of the plan. He could simply deliver the donations in their entirety to the accountants as the other drivers will do. With this thought, though, comes an agonizing throbbing in his side, almost unbearable. If he were a believer, he would take this as a sign that God actually wants him to steal the money. He looks around, wondering whether anyone has seen him wince.

A fair number of the walkers have brought dogs with them. A few of the dogs are burdened with small sandwich boards that have been strapped on their backs, pro-life slogans dangling along their sides. It's a surreal experience to have a golden retriever proclaim that abortion stops a beating heart, but what he's about to do feels just as bizarre.

He spots a pay phone by the pavilion. He makes his move, trying to decide what to say, and how to say it, when one of the other volunteer truck drivers, the young, friendly one, taps him on the shoulder, murmuring, "Take a look at that." A group of teenage girls are sunbathing in the midst of this event—victims of poor planning, who refuse to give up their prime location in the park. They turn on their boom box and play rap music loudly, insolently; they're enjoying the little spectacle they're making of themselves. The driver mutters, "Aw, yeah, work it all over," as one of the girls spreads suntan lotion over her friend's back. This is the only form of homoeroticism that Brendan has ever found heterosexual men to approve of, even encourage, this *hot chick-on-chick action*. A dog walks by the girls with its signs as its owner averts her eyes, horrified.

Brendan asks the driver, "Haven't you read Leviticus?"

The man smiles, says, "That's about faggots. Leviticus never said nothing about babes."

Brendan leaves him there, ogling, as the man ad-libs the dialogue these girls say to each other when skin touches skin. Each step Brendan takes toward the pavilion rewards him with a fresh bit of misery, but he is careful to keep a neutral expression on his face. He's only a few yards from the phone when he hears voices shouting his name. His truck is already full; it's time to make his first delivery. He stares at the telephone receiver, the small buttons on which single digits are printed, numbers that, like words in a poem, can be arranged together, can connect him to something much larger than himself.

The team captain hollers now, his tone demanding, "Brendan, you're all set to go!"

Of course he is.

1

Into the Wild

In April 1992 a young man from a well-to-do family hitchhiked to Alaska and walked alone in the wilderness north of Mt. McKinley. His name was Christopher Johnson McCandless. Four months later, his decomposed body was found by a party of moose hunters.

BRENDAN CLOSES HIS EYES, hugs his worn copy of *Into the Wild*, the book he loves better than any other. He opens it again, stares at the haunting self-portrait of Christopher McCandless, the handsome and enigmatic young man who had renamed himself Alexander Supertramp before he abandoned society and wandered alone into the Alaskan wilderness. How Brendan fell in love with him during the first breathless read, convinced that if only he had known Alex Supertramp, he could have saved him, and together they'd live in their north woods cabin, surrounded by books.

There are works like *Into the Wild* that Brendan revisits regularly, and while, like sex, the first time is usually the most memorable, the second and third and fourth times bring pleasures all their own. When he reads a story, it's like osmosis; he absorbs it at the cellular level. It lets him spend time in places he's never been, and with characters whose company he prefers to the crazy man who takes the seat next to him on the bus, loudly muttering obscenities.

Books open up new worlds. That's why when he visits his brother Ian he always brings him at least one book as a gift. It's the only little piece of freedom Brendan can offer him; Ian's been in jail for several years now. In fact, for most of the time Brendan has known him, Ian's been an inmate at Rush City, a men's correctional facility north of the Twin Cities.

Brendan thinks that his own life is a lot like the books he reads; he has two or three different stories in progress at any given time. Ian's wife wonders how Brendan manages to switch from one book to the next and then to the next one after that, only to return to the first. She has a hard enough time keeping the characters straight in the romance novels that she reads like recipe cards.

Brendan's particularly excited by the book he'll present Ian today. Unlike the weathered copy of *Into the Wild*, which sits on his lap, the book he will give Ian is brand-new and safely stowed in the backpack. The backpack itself sits snugly next to Brendan as the bus to Rush City begins its journey.

The bus is a service of a nonprofit organization in the Twin Cities that provides families of inmates with free transportation to Rush City each week. Wives and girlfriends and sons and daughters catch the bus downtown, and it takes them all the way out to the prison for visiting hours and then brings them back to Minneapolis. It's much nicer than the regular city buses: there's a bathroom on board and the seats are up-holstered. It's mostly full of women and children, and there's even a sto-rybook for kids to read during the trip called *Visiting the Big House*. In honor of the season, the bus driver has given each child a candy cane. Some slurp theirs noisily while others hoard, stealing and bartering more.

There's a woman on the bus with three children. She's Asian, per-haps Hmong or Laotian, and what catches Brendan's attention is the fact that she's embarrassed by her children's behavior. Compared to the other boys and girls on the bus, hers are relatively compliant, but that's not good enough for her. Brendan feels sorry for her, surrounded by white and black and Mexican and Indian and other Asian women and children who've taken this trip a hundred times or more. He can tell this is her maiden voyage. As he studies her—her stiff posture on con-stant alert, like a sentry at his post—he understands that she wishes she were somewhere else, anywhere but here, on this bus.

One of her boys runs over to Brendan's seat. This he's used to. Brendan's often the only adult male on the bus, and the boys, no matter what color they are, all wind up next to him, wanting to roughhouse or talk or pretend that he's their father. The stray smiles at him and says, "Who you gonna see?"

The boy's mother whispers violently at him in her native language, but the boy doesn't seem to be bothered. Brendan tells him, "I'm going to visit my brother."

The boy climbs up on the seat next to Brendan, a minor feat for one so small, and says, "My daddy killed a communist."

Brendan looks at him, skeptically. "Really?"

The boy, whose little legs don't even reach the edge of the bench, pulls his socks up over his rubber boots. "Yes. He knew him from seminar camp. He tried to make my daddy *pasason*."

"What does *pasason* mean?"

The boy laughs, like Brendan had asked what color the sky is. The boy says, "People."

Before he can say anything else, the boy's mother arrives, and with one eye still trained on her other two, who sit obediently in their seats, she sweeps him up in her arms. As she carries him back to their little post near the front of the bus, the boy knows that she's furious with him, but he smiles at Brendan anyway, thrilled to have talked to a grown-up man.

Soon the bus stops next to the visitors' entrance, which is outfitted with a large evergreen wreath. Passengers gather up their layers: sweaters, coats, overcoats, scarves, hats, and gloves. It's ten degrees outside and Brendan's reminded of a book he read as a boy, *One Day in the Life of Ivan Denisovich*. His seventh-grade class saw the movie version after they read the novel, which chronicled twenty-four hours in the life of a Russian prisoner interned at a Siberian work camp. They were having a particularly brutal winter themselves that year, so a few of Brendan's classmates failed to understand what all the fuss was about.

After the metal detection and the pat-down he's granted admission to the visiting room where Ian sits, waiting for him. Ian is Brendan's older brother by five years, which places him squarely at forty, an age that doesn't suit him particularly well. Still, he's attractive for his age.

Brendan puts his backpack—his x-rayed and thoroughly searched backpack—on the table and unzips a flap. "I've got a couple of presents for you. A pack of Camels to begin with, and a book."

Ian reaches for the cigarettes and sighs. "You always bring me a book. You know I can't read anymore, it gives me a headache. Are you trying to kill me?"

"You should give this one a try." Brendan has gotten him what's called a graphic novel, in other words, a really long comic book.

Ian squints at the cover. "What's that?"

Brendan passes it to him. "It's a collected set of comic-book stories bound in a single volume."

Ian laughs. "Batman?"

Brendan nods.

Another sigh. "Let's have a look, then."

Ian flips through the pages, his eyebrows arching at the violence or at Catwoman's breasts, each one as large as her head.

Brendan smiles. "You like it?"

Ian's eyes never leave the book. "You finally picked a winner . . ." He calls Brendan by the name given him by their parents. Brendan gently corrects him, reminds him yet again of the name that he has chosen for himself: Brendan Wolf. The renaming was inspired by Christopher Mc-Candless, the hero of *Into the Wild*, who changed his own. Brendan Wolf is not Brendan's legal name, but his name in every other way. He thinks his name's intriguing. The Wolf adds a bit of *The Call of the Wild* (Jack London having been one of Alexander Supertramp's favorite writers). And Brendan is an old name making a comeback. To him it means charting one's own course into the new, the unexplored, just as the Irishman called Saint Brendan the Navigator did when he took his small crew across the unknown horizon to North America. Choosing that first name was also his much-delayed act of childhood rebellion; his father had emigrated from England and couldn't abide the Irish.

Brendan says, "I'm glad you like the book."

Ian stares at a page and asks, "Do you think Catwoman would be a tight fuck or what?"

Most people would be offended by Ian's question, and in some ways Brendan is most people, but of course in other, more fundamental ways, he's not. "I'd prefer Batman."

"You can still imagine sex with a woman, though, can't you?"

Brendan gives him the look their mother used to, the *amused warning.*

Ian laughs softly, says, "How's work?"

"Fine," Brendan says.

"Still at Wal-Mart?"

Brendan looks at the floor. "I got a new job at—"

"Jesus Christ, Brendan! *Another* new job?"

"It's a better one, I think . . ."

Ian shakes his head sadly as he asks, "Still living in da hood, then?"

"It's not so bad."

"It's dangerous. Half the guys in here grew up there." Ian slips him a torn piece of paper with a name and a phone number on it. Ian says, "There's this new kid, Frankie Thompson, just in. Remember that name: Frankie Thompson. Before he ended up here, he had a very tidy arrangement with some rich old man. I'm doing him and he tells me that his old man's lonely. So it occurred to me that if you introduced yourself to the old man as a friend of Frankie's, perhaps you could come to some sort of agreement. You know, move in with the guy."

Brendan's learned not to judge Ian's life behind bars too harshly. He knows that to Ian's way of thinking, jailhouse infidelities don't count as cheating on his wife, as no woman is involved. Brendan tells him, "Just because I'm gay doesn't mean I want to work as a concubine for an old man."

Ian seems genuinely surprised. "Just move in. Do some chores around the house. If he puts the moves on you, tell him you'll call the cops. Come on, Brendan, I don't want to spend all my time worrying about you getting shot. You have to get out of that neighborhood."

To please his older brother, Brendan puts the slip of paper in his pocket.

Bewildered, Langdon looked at the image. The close-up photo revealed the glowing message on the parquet floor. The final line hit Langdon like a kick in the gut.

"Brendan, read on your own time, please."

He puts *The Da Vinci Code* back on its display case, along with the other bestsellers the store stocks, mostly popular diet and self-help books. Like Ian, Brendan has his own term to serve: the morning shift at Target. He's late for a team meeting and as he walks down the aisle to join the other team members, he recalls one of his elementary school teachers, Miss Carlson, who had punished him for reading when he should have been coloring in a map of Minnesota. Then there was Miss Olsen, who shook her head wearily when she caught him with his face stuck in a book during show and tell. And, of course, there were the long bus rides home to the small mansion by the lake, when he would solve mysteries with the Hardy Boys, those devoted brothers, while the other children were laughing or fighting. Now he sees his mother as she sets the table for tea, saying, *Put that book down, little prince, it's time to eat.*

The team meeting is held in a main aisle that separates watches and jewelry from women's clothing. There are no tables for team members to sit around, no chairs to sit in. This is a brief, efficient meeting, one of many that are called in the early-morning hours just before or just after the store opens for the day. Brendan's Team Leader is young, short, and white, and the dark roots of her blond hair preside over a manner that is productively cheerful.

"How's everyone today?" she asks with a broad smile, and most team members mutter their innocuous responses. Depending upon their age and whether English is their first language or not, they are *good* or *fine* or *okay* or *well* or *cool*. From a distance—say looking down the aisle from the vantage point of men's clothing—they truly resemble a team in their red Target shirts, their white-and-red name tags like numbers on a jersey. But from where Brendan stands the differences are readily apparent: two Somali women conceal their hair beneath scarves, one large white woman has a teardrop tattoo just beneath an eye, an older Hmong man who matches their Team Leader smile for smile is missing all but three of his teeth.

They are the Tuesday-morning shift, their store located on a busy thoroughfare in a part of St. Paul that has never been particularly desirable, even less so in recent decades. Their Target is popularly known as "Targhetto" though they are forbidden to refer to it as such, and women like Brendan's Team Leader are anxious to transfer to more profitable locations.

The Team Leader says, "Christmas is almost here, so I think we better review the team lift. Let's head on over to home furnishings."

Team members squeeze in a small aisle. On either side of them are shelves displaying models of bedside tables, bookcases, and coffee tables. On shelves below the models are stacked boxes of the unassembled units.

"Can I get a couple of volunteers?" the Team Leader asks.

The Hmong man and a scrawny white man, who wears a hearing aid, join her. She directs them, has them stand next to a shelf, facing each other. In perfect coordination, they firmly grab either end of a boxed, unassembled unit, and using their legs, not their backs, place it in a shopping cart.

The Team Leader says, "Good work!"

The Hmong man nods but the scrawny white man with the hearing aid looks at his feet as he rejoins the small crowd of team members.

The Team Leader looks at Brendan and says, "Yesterday, I saw a team member walk right by a guest who was trying to get a heavy box in her cart." Brendan feels the heat on his face. "If that happens, you tell the guest that you'll do it for them and you get a team member to help you. It's good guest service, and it's good for you, too. You can really hurt your back working with the heavier merchandise."

She nods at Brendan and says, "Let's give it a try."

Brendan joins her next to a shelving unit that contains boxes of unassembled bookcases. She positions him at one end of a box and, facing him, places herself at the other. "It's important," she tells her team, "to communicate with your partner. The best way to lift is to look directly at each other and say 'Lift on the count of three.' Brendan, let's lift on the count of three. One, two, three."

They lift, but there is no empty cart to put the box in. "Okay," she huffs, "lets put 'er back on the shelf." She catches her breath and says to no one but Brendan, "Never let guests try to do that by themselves."

He nods slightly, wondering what the other team members are thinking.

"Okay, everybody, thanks." She places a hand on Brendan's arm, says, "Can I see you for a minute?"

Team members disperse, leaving them alone in the aisle. She looks up at him, a sympathetic expression on her face. "Did I embarrass you, just then?"

Brendan shakes his head.

"Is there something bothering you, Brendan? Something I should know about?"

He examines the floor beneath their feet. It's linoleum, not parquet, and while there's a crack between two tiles, just like in *The Da Vinci Code*, it contains no messages. He says, "I'm fine."

"I'm just a little concerned because, to be honest, you don't *look* fine."

He says nothing for a while, but then the silence grows too uncomfortable. "I guess I'm not happy here."

She sighs knowingly. "I thought that might be the problem. Sometimes the job and the person in the job just aren't a good match; it's nobody's fault. I really want you to find a job where you can be happy. Life's too short, after all. What do you say?"

He nods out of habit, unsure of what's just happened.

"Good."

He stops in the men's room before he leaves for—what is now clear—the last time. He's in luck: the stalls have been freshly cleaned; there's the strong sting of bleach in the air. At this time of day he has the men's room to himself, he can be alone. He chooses a stall, sits on its toilet, but his pants remain buckled around his waist. He reads *The Da Vinci Code* with one hand as he quietly unrolls toilet paper with the other. Occasionally he sets the book on his lap and tightly winds the toilet paper around an index finger before he stuffs it in a pocket. Some he shoves under his shirt, other bits go in his socks, lumps that are concealed by pant cuffs.

He's out of toilet paper and can't afford the packaged rolls on display without showing up empty-handed at Rush City.

Brendan has no Christmas tree, no stocking hung by the chimney with care, no chimney. It's just as well, since he has only until mid-January to vacate; he's being evicted. Again. He had hoped that the job at Target would pay enough to get him up to date on his rent, but . . .

He guesses he won't really miss this apartment complex too much. His efficiency is surrounded on four sides by the sounds of crying babies, feuding couples, and pounding bass lines that make his crates of books tremble. He could complain, but that would be taking his life in his hands. The sirens that come so often to his building leave him little doubt that the other tenants wouldn't hesitate to attack him—or do worse—if he knocked on their doors, pleading with them to keep the noise down.

Tonight is one of those rare nights; the building's quiet. The sounds of the street still pass by, soft, then louder, until they fade into silence again. He hears the voices of drunks, of rap music being broadcast to the world from the stereos of SUVs, but these noises come and go swiftly; they don't spend the night in the apartment next door. It's then, when silence returns, when he hears his own breath as he inhales and exhales, that he feels a little more at peace.

When he was a boy, his parents would take him and his brothers up north every summer, to the cabin. The sun would blaze in the early afternoons and he and his brothers would escape its punishing rays in the spring-fed lake, so chilly that you'd be a fool to try to wade in slowly. It was always easier to simply jump off the dock and splash furiously until the body acclimated itself. The outdoors was dense with green trees, tall pines that whispered in the winds, the voices of ghosts, of pioneers and Natives, at least according to his brother Ian. Ian would say, *Dare you to spend tonight outside in the woods.*

He'd say, *Okay.*

But as the sounds of living things, restless in the night, seemed to surround his tent, he would tiptoe, the beam of his flashlight in front of him, back to the cabin, forging a bed out of pillows and couch cushions, hoping to awaken first so he might make it back to the tent before the others got up, impressing his brothers and parents with his small-boy courage.

He misses it. Even in the worst summer heat those were mild times, the annual visits to a world of lily pads and water, cold, alive with fish and frogs and turtles. He misses the sun, the way it shone up there, its bright rays traveling a zigzag path through the branches of the pines to softly land on the brush. It was a time of bare feet, armored with calluses from the long days outside.

There were moments—mostly in the early evenings when his mother was in the cabin, mixing cocktails for his father and herself—when the lake seemed as smooth as carved marble. It was those times, when he would test the surface of the water with feet dangling off the dock, that he thought he might, like Jesus, step onto the lake and walk across it to the far shore.

It's not quite dusk as he sits on the light-rail train from the Mall of America, where more than ten thousand people work each day. Beneath his coat Brendan wears khakis, hiking boots, and a dress denim shirt, his best outfit, the one he wears when he's looking for a job. The shirt's a bit wrinkled; he needs an ironing board, an iron, and the skill to use them well.

The train stops, he exits with a group of loud and foul-mouthed teenagers who carry huge bags outfitted in holiday colors. Brendan has searched for a new job without filling out a single application: there were either no openings or positions that wouldn't cover the cost of the commute and an apartment, or the store was so packed with Christmas shoppers that he couldn't bring himself to search for the personnel office.

All told, he's quit—and more recently been fired from—quite a few jobs, starting with the one at McDonald's. His current record for shortest tenure is at Wal-Mart, where he gave up during his orientation. As a lover of words, he has a hard time working in the retail world—about the only sector that will still hire him—where Spending is Saving, Debt is Credit, a Sale is an Event. Sometimes he thinks we are all slowly going insane, only we don't realize it, because in our brave new world, insane is now sane.

He enters his apartment building with its plain, utilitarian, blank face on a block of blank faces, remarkable only for the number of boarded-up windows. In the hallways he hears English, Spanish, Somali; he smells cigarette smoke and dirty diapers. Of course his little efficiency is not conducive to reading. Yes, the place is tiny, the building noisy, but neither of these things are really the problem. He can read while couples fight, he doesn't need one room to sleep in, a second to live in, a third to eat in, a fourth to piss in. What he would like, though, is a soft chair, large, over-stuffed, wear-worn, perhaps the sort of thing that college students rescue from the curb in order to furnish first apartments. He's seen likely candidates facing the street on garbage day, but retrieving them, carrying them up to his apartment, this would require an extra set of hands, a brother or partner who would look him in the eye as he said, *Let's lift on the count of three.*

His books are organized in crates, the crates themselves found in alleys or purchased with staff discounts from Home Depot or K-Mart or Menard's. Lying next to them on the scratched wooden floor are three couch cushions, their pattern an odd mixture of plaid and polka dots. This is it then, the cushions and the crates and the books, of course the books, some bought by the pound when the library sheds parts of its collection that are no longer in demand. Many of the titles have small black dots at the top or bottom of their pages, a remainder mark. These books have been heavily discounted; a copy that originally retailed for nearly twenty-five dollars can be bought for less than five once the spot has been applied. It's a small flaw, a little imperfection, hardly noticeable.

In spite of the missing reading chair, he does love the Spartan décor, inspired as it was by the last known college residence of Alex Supertramp.

He pours water in the sink; washes the day off his face. He stares at himself in the mirror, half expecting to discover a black dot on his skin, that little indicator that something is not as valuable as it once was, or that it hasn't lived up to expectations, or perhaps has never received its proper due. The mark isn't there, though, and his overall reflection pleases him: the soft crow's feet are new, acquired just this year when he turned thirty-five, along with a few strands of gray that hide among the maple brown.

He lies on the hard wood floor. Before he permits himself even one page of a book, on odd days (the first, the third, the fifth . . .) he must do four hundred sit-ups, one hundred push-ups, a hundred squats. When he ventures out in the world, he wants to look as large as he can: on the bus or the streets, in the store or a bar. He wants to look like someone you would leave alone if you passed him on a corner, someone you would pursue if you saw him standing by the dance floor. His father believed strongly in the mind-body connection and it was from him that Brendan learned this routine. Before his father would have dinner with a client he would exercise to the point of exhaustion, reviving himself in a steamy shower and a clean suit. It engendered a confidence that was contagious; he would say that he could gain the trust of men and women simply by the way he glowed after pushing himself to the point of exhaustion.

When Brendan's finished, he pours himself a bowl of bran cereal, arranges the cushions as comfortably as he can, and opens *The Perfect Storm*. (He finished *Into the Wild* yet again during the ride back from the Mall of America.) Words fill a page like colors on a canvas and tonight he rejoins the crew of the *Andrea Gail* as they battle waves ten stories high and winds of 120 miles per hour. He tastes the freezing salt water in his mouth and shivers in cold terror as the ocean rises and falls. He dreams of those on shore, the men and women and children who hold vigil in the churches and the bars, the ones he will never see again.

2

The Call of the Wild

HE WORKS FOR IAN'S WIFE, Cynthia, when he's between jobs, which he frequently is. Ian thinks holding down a position is difficult for his younger brother because Brendan's not a team player, a condition Ian attributes to Brendan's sexual orientation. Cynthia has never offered an opinion on the subject; she simply greets him when he shows up at her office as if he had never left.

When he works for his sister-in-law, Brendan's job is to call people during dinnertime and ask them to donate money to her firm's clients, which range from pro-life groups to police benevolent societies. The operation is archaic: there are no headsets for staff, just ancient Princess phones, which must be cradled on their necks; there are no computer monitors, just pads of charge slips that must be filled out by hand. By and large the people he calls fall into two broad categories: the ones who hang up on him and the ones he hangs up on. The latter group is usually composed of elderly people who donate a dollar or two in order to talk to someone at length. Much cheaper than dialing a 900 number at $2.99 a minute to talk to a real, live person. He expresses his gratitude to these donors for their meager contributions but if they don't take the hint, he says: "I'm sorry, I have an important call holding. Thank you and good night." He disconnects halfway through the second syllable of *good night*. When it's too late to make calls, he processes credit card charges, both the ones he's taken as well as the ones Cynthia occasionally leaves on his desk.

Tonight his stack of slips is fairly small. With Christmas just a week behind them, revenues are down; the people they phone have already maxed out their credit and need time to recover from their holiday binge. So the charge slip in the amount of five hundred dollars startles him. Even more surprising is that the charge is not for payment to "Good Works," the name of the telemarketing firm, but rather for a personal account that bears Cynthia's name.

He studies the slip for a moment and sets it apart from the others.

Cynthia's in the office she shares with the other shift supervisors. All of them smoke and the entire floor reeks of their spent tobacco, the generic brands they buy by the carton. When Cynthia emerges, she travels from cube to cube, picking up the evening's receipts and telling her ragtag staff to punch out and go home. She can't abide dawdlers; they make her late for wherever it is that she rushes off to every night. And occasionally they set off the security alarm she had activated in the belief that she would be the last one to leave.

Brendan hears Cynthia from across a partition. A pleasant Mexican employee, who always shares her dinner with him, has no receipts to offer; hasn't successfully solicited a single donation all night. Cynthia clucks her tongue, telling her, "You need to learn English, honey, if you're ever gonna make us a dime. People don't understand you when you talk and even if they do, they don't trust that accent."

Next, Cynthia's at his desk. He hands her his paperwork, save the five-hundred-dollar charge.

He holds it up and asks, "Is this correct?"

She looks at the slip and then at him. Her expression is matter-of-fact as she says, "Yeah, that's right."

"Why would a ten-dollar donor to Babies First give you five hundred dollars?"

"She's my aunt. It's a loan. She can't spare the cash, so I told her she could call it in on her card tonight. Relax."

"What's your aunt's name? I couldn't quite make it out."

She grabs the receipt, shoves it in her pocket, cursing. "For Christ's sake, I'll do it myself. Go home."

"I'm supposed to work late tonight cleaning the offices—"

Her broad face coils in irritation or embarrassment (he doesn't think it could be shame) as she says, "Don't worry about the cleaning money, I'll punch out for you. Go home."

This is the beginning of their little arrangement. In exchange for his silence, she pays him for hours not worked. It's a considerate gesture, though not particularly lucrative, and nowhere near the scale of what his parents used to pull off.

A vast silence reigned over the land. The land itself was desolation, lifeless, without movement, so lone and cold that the spirit of it was not even that of sadness. There was a hint in it of laughter, but of laughter more terrible than any sadness—a laughter that was mirthless as the smile of the Sphinx, a laughter cold as the frost and partaking of the grimness of infallibility. It was the masterful and incommunicable wisdom of eternity laughing at the futility of life and the effort of life.

He closes his copy of *White Fang*, sets it on the little crate next to the couch cushions. After he had read *Into the Wild* for the sixth time, he decided to read all the books that Alex Supertramp had loved so. In addition to *White Fang* there are *War and Peace*, *The Call of the Wild*, *Doctor Zhivago*, *Walden*, among others. He's never been able to find a used copy of *Education of a Wandering Man*, perhaps the last book that Supertramp read before dying his solitary death in the Alaskan wilderness.

Outside his window the sun sets, one of just a couple of sunsets left to him in this efficiency. He's late for his shift at Good Works, but he cannot seem to help it, the world outside frightens him. Perhaps he's only a visitor to this world, ill equipped for his stay, a tourist alarmed to discover that his passport and all his important papers are missing. He feels like a foreigner, tentatively saying out loud words from a language everyone else speaks fluently. He's often genuinely surprised by the reactions he gets from other people; it's as if he's mispronounced something that gave his words an entirely different meaning than what he'd intended.

When he finally arrives at Good Works, Cynthia does not reprimand him for being late. Instead she waves from her open office, lights a cigarette with the stub of a dying one, and flips a page in her romance novel.

Brendan's Mexican co-worker has left a ham and cheese sandwich on his desk for him, along with a note, explaining that she had quit and how nice it was to have met him. In shy, tiny script, she has carefully written her phone number.

He opens the White Pages, picks up a Princess phone, and begins dialing. He studies his sister-in-law as best he can through the open door of her office as she reads intently from her book. As the busy signal fills his ears, he recalls the first time he met Cynthia, in the Rush City visiting room. Over the years, she has remained tolerant of Brendan, but aloof. His sexual orientation was an enigma to her, a slightly unnerving one. If she thought about it too much, her expression would change from one of benign confusion to mild revulsion. Fortunately for both of them, she rarely thought about it too much. Her charity extended only as far as offering him one of the ever-vacant positions at the telemarketing firm. He expected nothing from Cynthia, and that is what she delivered, with a dependability that was mind-numbing.

Tonight, however, she asks him out for a drink as he heads toward the gated front door of Good Works. He's worked maybe half a shift, if that, and her tone is neither friendly nor accusing, just matter-of-fact.

"Now?" he asks her.

"I got someone to cover for me. You got something better to do?"

"No, not really. Where would you like to go?"

She says, "Why not the Coliseum? They got them male strippers, right? With Ian up the river, I could do with seeing some skin."

"Yeah, but the Coliseum's a hike."

"I just got a new van. Well, a used van, but it's new to me. I'll even take you home."

The snow's coming down hard and fast so they have to inch along Hennepin Avenue to the Coliseum, a sort of shopping mall for gay men. In the Coliseum complex there's a leather bar, a disco, a restaurant, a piano bar, strippers, a drag show lounge, and a regular-Joe happy-hour bar. It's become popular with straight people who like to gawk and with bridal parties who want to see the only male strippers in town. Fights break out more often now that gay men and straight men are under the same roof and it's not unusual for the cops to be called. It isn't like the old days, when the fights were between gay men competing for the same man.

As his adoptive mother used to say, *You can't have anything nice.*

They park in a ramp and make their way to the Coliseum in silence, the winds driving the snow, making it difficult to speak. Cynthia's expression is like his, frowning, and she swallows deeply so as not to gasp at the wind chill, at the feeling of frigid air in her lungs. They trudge, one foot in front of the other, until they arrive at the front door of the bar, where a white mountain of a man with a shaved, tattooed head asks Brendan for two forms of I.D. before he will let him join Cynthia, who's already inside. He doesn't have a driver's license, a passport, credit cards, a student I.D. He hands the man the only piece of identification he has.

The tattooed man smiles and in a voice like a broken nose, says, "You don't look underage, but you do look good." He hands Brendan back the state identification card, adding, "Now that I know where you live, maybe we could hook up sometime."

Brendan blushes. "I'm being evicted."

"Where you movin' to?"

"Don't know yet."

Brendan turns to enter the bar, but the man grabs him by the arm. He pulls off Brendan's coat, says, "Look, we ban handguns so I gotta pat you down." With a hint of laughter, he says, "Lift your arms."

Brendan does as he says. The man squeezes Brendan's biceps, cups Brendan's pecs in his hands, lets out a low whistle. Next he slides his hands over Brendan's buttocks, Brendan's crotch, whistles again. The man whispers, "You gotta fine ass, man, you know that? Anyone ever told you that before? 'Cause if it were mine . . ."

Brendan holds out a hand for his coat, which the man gives him reluctantly, saying, "Watch out for the bitches in there, they can get nasty."

He finds Cynthia at the stripper bar. "Thanks for waiting for me."

She keeps trying to catch the bartender's eye as she says, "You're welcome. What can I get you?"

"Double scotch, straight up."

She surprises him. "Single malt?"

"I doubt they carry single malts here. Thanks for asking, though."

He takes a stool further down the bar and checks out the stripper. The dancer is a young man, early twenties, and a wad of bills is sticking out of his G-string, all singles. Brendan's intrigued by the possibilities the New Year holds, and raises his hand, a five-dollar bill between his fingers.

The young man glances his way, but he doesn't move. He's all over an older man in a tailor-made suit.

Cynthia joins Brendan, a double scotch in one hand, a wine cooler in the other. She hands him his drink and says, "Cheers."

He tells her, "Cheers."

She looks over at the stripper, says, "He's too busy to pick up five bucks?"

He nods.

She shakes her head and asks him, "What would you do with thirty thousand dollars?"

He raises an eyebrow to convey interest with a splash of shock tossed in. He makes her wait a few seconds before he says, "I suppose I'd move away. Start over again somewhere new."

She says, "Me too, me too."

They take a table in the back and Cynthia begins to open up. "Well, you've passed the first test with flying colors."

"I don't understand."

"You didn't turn me in. About the charges I made on them old folks' cards."

He shrugs.

"So, I'm thinking I can trust you. So does Ian."

"I'm not going to turn in my brother's wife. But you're taking a hell of a chance, Cynthia. Ian gets out soon; do you want to get the both of you in trouble?"

Cynthia shakes her head. "I could use a smoke. This fucking smoking ban pisses me off."

"Promise me you'll stop your credit card scam. For Ian's sake."

She laughs, says, "Whose idea do you think it was? You sure you two are related?"

He sighs, disappointed but not surprised. Too abruptly, he asks, "Can I move in with you?"

She stares at him. "You crazy?"

"I'm being evicted. It would only be until I got back on my feet."

Cynthia shakes her head. "I'm sorry, really I am. You'll find a place."

"Maybe a loan? Landlords always make you pay the first month's rent and deposit in cash or a money order after an eviction."

She shakes her head sadly. "Something will come up."

He takes a long drink of scotch, and then another. Is it because he's gay? Does she imagine a revolving door of one-night stands in and out of her apartment? He hears Cynthia's voice vaguely as he tries to devise a Plan B. Gradually her words get his attention. There is something in the works, something very big, and she'll need his help to carry it off. He asks her for details, but she closes their conversation with a quiet *When the time's right.*

It's the fifteenth of January, his last day in the efficiency. He must vacate by midnight. He retrieves the scrap of paper from a pair of dirty jeans that lies on the battered floor. He's decided to apply for the position as a—he guesses the term would be *houseboy* for the old man Ian told him about before the holidays. He puts on his coat and leaves.

Out on the street, he finds a working pay phone, a relief in a neighborhood where most pay phones are out of service. The number is a bit
hard to read, it's not written with the bold strokes of his brother.

"Hello?"

Brendan's voice cracks, he realizes he hasn't said anything the entire day. "Ahem . . . excuse me. Sorry. Mr. Fletcher?"

"Yes."

"Hi, my name's Brendan. I'm a friend of . . ." The name. What the
hell was the name he was supposed to remember? Finally, it comes to
him. ". . . Frankie."

Silence.

Brendan continues, unnerved. "I was just up at Rush City and he
said you might be looking for some help. You know, around the house."

A long pause. "You're a friend of Frankie's?"

"Yes, sir."

"I don't recall him ever mentioning a Brendan." The words sound a
bit slurred.

"I'm only just back in town."

Another pause. "Well, why don't you come on over for a drink, anyway."

"I'd like that."

Brendan returns to the efficiency, packs. He leaves the couch cushions behind. He takes two suitcases full of clothes along with his backpack, full of his favorite books, the ones that he couldn't bear to put in
the rented storage locker with the rest. As he rides the bus over to the
old man's house, he already understands that this is a bad idea, probably one of the worst he's had in a while. It's depressing, living life on
the verge of becoming a street person, and he wishes he could discover
whatever path, hidden from him, that other people follow to buy cars
and houses and some measure of stability. Before the breakup with Jeff
(what was that, five years ago now?—almost as long as they had been
together) he didn't worry, he could come and go from jobs without a
care, confident that Jeff 's career would sustain them both as he fal-
tered. What he hadn't counted on was the resentment that would

build each time he announced over dinner that he had quit: because the job was boring, or the people he worked with were annoying, or because he simply couldn't bring himself to show up for his shift. He always thought that there was plenty of time to sort himself out and catch up to Jeff, whose promotions seemed so routine as to be preordained.

The old man's house is not all that far from the home of Brendan's adoptive parents; that is, if they still live in the neighborhood—if they still live at all. Mr. Fletcher lives in a Dutch Colonial on an unusually large lot facing exclusive Lake Calhoun. Brendan places his suitcases and backpack in a discreet corner of the huge front porch; he doesn't want to seem presumptive. When the front door opens he discovers Fletcher is a proper little man, maybe five feet five if that, as wide as he is tall, and what's left of his hair is combed over his big pink skull.

"I have no illusions that I'm attractive to others," Fletcher says once they've finished the house tour, the old man's uneven steps having led them first to the bedroom.

Brendan smiles at him. "You look fine, Mr. Fletcher."

Fletcher finally smiles. "Please, call me Marv."

Marv ushers him into the sitting room now, where flames rage in a huge fireplace, like something out of a medieval castle. Brendan sits on real leather, a deep chestnut brown, almost too hot for the skin thanks to the heat thrown off by the pyre.

"Name your poison," the old man says.

Brendan looks at him. Is he in his eighties? Older? Brendan can't tell. He's an ugly man, and it's not the fault of his advanced years. He has a face that tells you he was born homely; it was genetically encoded. He's looking at Brendan, too, from head to toe, and Brendan knows he's drawing comparisons to his Frankie, the young man whose company Ian's now keeping at Rush City. Brendan says, "Double scotch, straight up. Single malt, if you have it."

He can tell the old man's impressed. "Well, that's an acquired taste. Not at all what I'd expect from one so young."

This is flattery, of course; he has the feeling that at thirty-five years of age he is, in fact, too old for Marv. The push-ups and sit-ups and squats have kept him firm, though, big, and the curves of his biceps seem to interest the old man. Marv pours a scotch for Brendan, another for himself. He carefully hands Brendan a large glass and then sits in a chair directly across from him. Marv swirls the scotch, sniffs at it. "This is a Highland blend I'm particularly fond of." He adds to impress Brendan: "I bought a case during my last trip to Scotland. I go each spring, when the heather's in bloom." After a pause he asks, "Have you ever visited Scotland?"

Although his parents emigrated from England, Brendan has never been anywhere in the United Kingdom. He shakes his head.

"I try to get over at least once a year; you'd love it. What do you think of the scotch?"

Brendan takes a sip. When he doesn't comment, Marv studies his own glass and says, "So, you're a friend of Frankie's?"

Brendan hesitates. "More like a friend of a friend."

Marv frowns. "What friend is that? Where did your friend meet Frankie?"

"Rush City."

"I see, I see . . . well, well. How did your friend ever wind up in there?"

Ian was sent up for robbing seniors of their life savings with a Canadian lottery scam. This would only put the old man off, so Brendan says, "He stole some stock from a store he worked at. Stupid mistake."

Marv exhales deeply, his way of showing Brendan that he's a wise man, experienced in the ways of the world. In spite of his wealth, or perhaps because of it, he understands all too well what people are capable of. He wants Brendan to know that he could learn a lot from him, if Brendan's lucky, if the old man's interested, if Brendan conducts himself well. Marv says, "We all make mistakes, son. The test is whether we learn from them."

"Why's Frankie in Rush City?"

Marv's eyes mist, he frowns. "Frankie has a history of driving while under the influence."

They sit a while longer in silence. The fire casts comforting shadows in the darkness of the room, it feels like a safe place, a sanctuary. Brendan savors the scotch and it must be working its magic on Marv; he savors Brendan from a respectful distance. Marv gets up, pours himself another big helping, and says, "Well, I'm looking for someone to help around the house."

"I'm your man," Brendan tells him.

He stands in front of the fireplace, his wide frame nearly blocking out the orange and red hues. He takes a slow sip of his drink, closes his eyes. "There are various duties, of course. What I'm really looking for is a personal assistant. Someone who performed all the tasks that Frankie did so well."

Brendan looks at his glass, nearly empty. Marv fills it up again, and staring directly at him, says, "To your health." Brendan takes a little swig, and the old man shakes his head. "When your health is toasted, you're supposed to empty your glass. It's a tradition where I come from."

"Where's that?"

"Minneapolis."

They laugh, and Brendan drinks the rest of the scotch from his glass. Marv immediately tops off Brendan's glass, saying, "Let's do it right this time. When I say 'to your health . . . '"

"I down my drink."

The old man smiles warmly. "Exactly!" Now he winks as he says, "To your health!"

Brendan puts the glass to his lips, empties it. He hears the neck of the scotch bottle clink against his glass as Marv pours more in. Now the old man puts the bottle directly to his withered lips, sips a small bit. He says, "So, you see, I need someone to replace Frankie. Not that anyone could replace Frankie"—here his eyes mist again—"but there are things that just can't wait until he's a free man again." He looks Brendan over slowly, and when he's finished, he asks, "Do you understand what I'm saying?"

Perhaps it's the scotch or the way he looks at Brendan or maybe it's both, but Brendan feels his face turn red under Marv's gaze. Brendan nods tentatively.

The old man smiles sympathetically. He makes a speech that Brendan can tell he's made before: "I wish there was something more I could offer you than money and a beautiful place to live, but that's all there is. I've no delusions that you would ever find me attractive physically. But I would hope that at a minimum you could think of me as a mentor, perhaps even a friend."

Brendan nods again, but Marv isn't buying it. He says, "I can't help the fact that I have needs that can only be met through this sort of arrangement. I wish I was young again, I wish that someone would fall in love with me, but that's not the hand I've been dealt, now is it?"

Brendan shakes his head.

Marv frowns, setting his glass on the mantle. He folds his arms over his belly, says gravely, "There's one thing I need to ask you to do to ensure that you're right for the job."

Brendan watches, waits.

"I'd like you to take off your clothes and stretch out, right here on the carpet in front of the fire, where it's nice and warm. Then I want you to take a deep, relaxing breath and close your eyes. You'll enjoy yourself. Trust me, I know what I'm doing."

How bad could it be? Brendan thinks of his favorite books freezing in the backpack that sits on Marv's porch.

Brendan stands.

But then he sits back down.

Marv approaches with the bottle, tells Brendan to empty his glass. "To your health," Marv says. Brendan drinks some of the scotch but it goes down the wrong pipe and he coughs uncontrollably. Marv pats him on the back. When Brendan can speak again, he says, "I'm happy to clean your house, but I won't do that."

Marv stands in front of him now. He blushes, a deep purplish red. "I beg your pardon?"

The words come to Brendan slowly, uncertainly. "I can take care of the yard in the summer and the walk and driveway in winter. I don't know how to drive, but I can run errands to the local shops for you. I'm learning how to cook. Please, I really need somewhere to live. And this place is too big for just one person, after all."

Marv clears his throat. "I thought you understood—"

"I do." Brendan leans in toward him. "I need a place to live. I'll work really hard, I'll keep your home a showcase. I could set up a little bedroom in the basement, all I need is a mattress and some crates. You'd have your privacy. Entertain guests if you want."

Marv studies him for a long moment, or at least it feels to Brendan like a long moment. Marv's waiting for him to crack up, to tell Marv he was only kidding as he pulls his shirt over his head. When Brendan doesn't, Marv says, "I need to make it an early evening. I'll see you out."

Brendan whines, "Come on. They're going to throw me out on the street in a few hours."

Now Marv smiles condescendingly, washing away the harmless old gent in need of a little affection and bringing forth the worldly, no-nonsense look of a hard-nose. "I'm afraid you've misunderstood. There's no offer on the table. I don't think we're well suited for each other, temperamentally speaking, that is. From what you'll let me see, you're reasonably attractive for someone in his what—mid-thirties? But I'm afraid what you're proposing is a deal breaker."

Brendan gets up and helps himself to the bottle of scotch that sits on the little coffee table. "You talk like an announcer on public radio."

"Excuse me, but put that bottle down right now. I've asked you politely, but now I must insist that you leave. Frankie had no business referring you to me."

Brendan pours the scotch, only to discover his glass is already full. A tiny puddle of liquor forms on the carpet.

Marv shouts, "Now look what you've done!"

He heads toward the kitchen but stops abruptly when Brendan says, "Frankie didn't refer me."

Alarmed now, Marv repeats himself, his confidence thin: "I want you to leave. Do yourself a big favor, and get out of my house now. Trust me, you don't want to take me on, young man."

Brendan can't stand it when people talk down to him. It takes him back to his case worker, three sets of foster parents, and, of course, his adoptive parents. It reminds him, it puts him back in his place, the one he never deserved or wanted.

He takes a generous gulp of single malt and feels himself growing ever warmer, the lovely buzz allowing him to say what he does. "I know your name. I know where you live. I know Frankie wasn't even . . . old enough to vote when he moved in." He takes a quick drink, trying to think of the term he wants. It comes to him: "That's statutory rape!" He giggles slightly. "I'd bet the clock hasn't run out on . . ." On what? It's another legal term—what, what, he knows he knows this. It's not statutory, but kind of like it. It comes to him: "the statute of limitations, either."

Marv examines each word that comes out of Brendan's mouth as if from a distance. Like they're images transmitted to him by a robot's remote camera, the kind the police use to take a first look at a bomb. He says, "You can't stay here."

"I swear, you won't even know I'm here."

"Go."

"Come on. Just till I get back on my feet."

"I'll call the police."

Jesus, Brendan's drunk. "And *I'll* tell 'em you tried to pay me for sex. I'll tell 'em Frankie was seventeen when he moved in. I won't even have to lie. It's all true."

Marv's frustration grows. True, Brendan's bigger, stronger, and younger; but these things Marv has overcome in the past with other young men, men like Frankie. The threat Brendan presents is new, unfamiliar. Brendan watches as Marv weighs it in his mind. The old man sits down. He stands up again. He pours himself another drink. He sits down.

He says, "Let's try and make this work. I'm willing to try and make this work, how about you?"

Now Brendan's so drunk he can't believe it. Has he had anything to eat today? He says, "You know I am."

Marv rubs his mouth with his hand. "Good, good. We just got off to a bad start, that's all. Sometimes first meetings go poorly."

"It's going okay."

Marv smiles weakly. "That's a joke, isn't it? Your little joke on me. . . . Well, let's try this again. Brendan, would you please be so kind as to stand up and remove your clothes?"

"No."

"Then you must leave."

"No."

Marv pants. "Think you're clever, don't you, you miserable little punk?"

Brendan shrugs.

Marv heaves an old-man breath at him, almost a death rattle, before he says, his words a jumbled rush, "Well, you've really made something of yourself, haven't you? Look at you, homeless and threatening a senior citizen. *You must make your parents very proud.*"

The blood rushes to Brendan's head, his hands shake, his breathing shallows.

He stands up. He kicks the coffee table out of his way, knocking over Marv's imported single-malt scotch. Marv jumps up out of his chair but Brendan grabs his droopy shoulders, forces him back down. He looks at Marv's terrified face, and like a man in love he says: "Don't you ever . . . *ever* speak of my family again if you don't want to be hurt. 'Cause I will. I'll fucking hurt you."

Brendan stares into the eyes Marv averts. He looks at the old man's lips, which tremble. Marv whispers, "I won't do it again, I promise."

Brendan lets him go. Marv's head slumps, he rubs a shoulder that maybe Brendan squeezed a little too hard. Brendan looks at him. What kind of life has Marv lived that brought him to this moment? Brendan says, "I left a few things on the porch. I'll just bring them in now."

The old man softly nods his big pink head.

————

It's his first night in his new bedroom. He left Marv downstairs by the fire, finishing off a fresh bottle of scotch. His own buzz is fading and the reality of what he's done is beginning to sink in. He should leave. He should apologize and leave. If only he had somewhere to go.

Hours pass and he can't sleep. He goes downstairs and finds the embers glowing in the fireplace, Marv, slouched over in a chair, his mouth open as he snores softly. Brendan wanders past; he considers putting on his coat and walking out the front door. But he has nowhere to go. He's allowed himself to become the sort of person who has nowhere to go.

Maybe he and Marv will make their peace in the morning. Perhaps then things will seem lighter, manageable.

He enters the TV room with its huge screen and a DVD collection as large as any of those stocked by the discount stores he's worked at. It takes time, but he finds the correct remote and turns on the television. The hours pass, he spends them watching commercials. People are at their happiest in commercials. Or perhaps they are sad or annoyed in the beginning, but happy, even dancing, by the end. He enjoys these tiny narratives; he gravitates to the idea that one small intervention, a pill or a low-calorie snack, can change a life.

He turns off the set and makes his way to the kitchen.

As he surveys the cabinets, the drawers, the gas oven, and extra-large refrigerator, he hears the timid footsteps of Marv behind him. He turns to look at the old man. Marv's face is drooped, ravaged from too much alcohol and fitful sleep. Still, in some ways, he looks like a little boy awakened early from his nap.

"Good morning," Brendan says, a smile on his face, a hangover raging in his skull. "Would you like me to make us some coffee?"

Marv stares at him, recalling the events of last night. He nods, turns back around, and resumes his place in front of the spent fire.

Brendan's pretty sure that he's reached an understanding with Marv.

Now that Brendan lives by Lake Calhoun, his job at Good Works is two bus rides away, too far, in his opinion, to travel. There are plenty of

little shops near the lake that need someone like him to scoop up spe-
cialty ice creams or serve double lattes with half skim and half whole
milk. He makes himself a promise: at the next job, whatever it is, he'll
be reliable, he'll work hard. Thirty-five isn't too late to start over. He
begins this journey with small steps, starting with reporting for his shift
at Good Works. He'll work the shift in full, and then give Cynthia his
notice in person, as a professional would.

There's a twenty-dollar bill on the kitchen counter. He decides to
treat himself to a cab.

At a stoplight they sit in silence, the Somali cab driver and Brendan, and the sound of the engine and the glow of the streetlamps in the
early dusk of January make Brendan recall another cab ride, years ago.
Not a word was said during that trip either, but unlike tonight Jeff was
with him, holding his hand in the back of the taxi. They were heading
to a hotel in Minnetonka to meet Jeff's father and his new wife. Jeff
and Brendan had been together almost a year, and Jeff had told him
that he loved him and wanted to spend the rest of his life with him. In
a suburban hotel room, Brendan was the one Jeff's father and stepmother were preparing for, the only boyfriend their son had ever
wanted them to meet since Jeff had told them that he was a gay man.

He was near panic as Jeff introduced him. Jeff's stepmother was
warm and welcoming, undoubtedly relieved that the family's baton of
controversy had been handed from her to Brendan. Jeff's father was
cautious but friendly, doing his very best to accept the fact that his son
was a homosexual, not only in theory, but also, as Brendan's presence
attested to, in practice. Brendan told them only a little about his life;
mostly he talked about books, the state of the world—everything, it
seemed, except the fact that he had fallen in love with their son.

It was a stiff, cordial, but not entirely unpleasant evening and there
is one memory that stands out above all the others. Brendan was in a debate with Jeff's father. The subject was football, and Brendan insisted
that the first Super Bowl was between the Kansas City Chiefs and the
Green Bay Packers. Jeff's father shook his head; he *knew* that it was the
Oakland Raiders and the Green Bay Packers. It was then that Brendan

glimpsed Jeff, his face glowing, delighted that the two men who meant the most to him in the world had something in common, even something to rib each other about. This image is the one Brendan's held on to over the years, because he'd never seen Jeff as happy as he was at that moment. As if his world was complete, integrated, whole. That night, Brendan finally knew exactly what he wanted from life, and it was what Jeff had: a family—a true family—a lover, and the confidence to love both of them.

When Brendan walks into the supervisors' office, Cynthia's reading a paperback, *Seize the Night*. The cover features a handsome young man who's failed to button his shirt. The deep cleavage of his large pectorals is in dark shadow. When Brendan tells Cynthia that he's quitting, she smirks, sets down her book, and slaps a pack of cigarettes against an open palm. She says, "We need to talk."

"About?"

She shakes her head. "About the future. You know Ian and me have our hearts set on Mexico. And I doubt you wanna live in a goddamn efficiency the rest of your life."

"I've already moved on. I have a place on Lake Calhoun."

She puts a cigarette between her lips, which are the color of blueberries thanks to her unusual taste in makeup. She lights the cigarette, pauses for effect. Every once in a while her dark eyes have the faraway look of an accident victim, a woman who staggers bruised and bloodied among the shattered glass and crumpled bumpers. These are the eyes she looks at him with as she quietly asks, "How long will that last? He's gonna get tired of you sooner or later."

So Ian must have told her about Marv during her last visit to Rush City. He tells Cynthia, "I'll be fine."

She takes a deep, rich drag off the cigarette. Her eyes almost roll back in her head. She holds the smoke in her lungs, lets it linger there before she releases it, like a tire's slow leak, creating a ghostlike cloud between them. "But you'd be a lot finer if you had some money, wouldn't you? Then you wouldn't have to depend on some nasty old man; you could do what you want. You haven't really thought about what you would do with thirty grand. That kind of money can do a lot for a person. Maybe it could help get you and what's-his-face back together again."

He ignores the reference to Jeff. "No, I haven't thought much about it. I've had no reason to. Give me a reason, Cynthia."

"I told you, when the time is right."

"At this rate, it'll never be."

She stares at him and he can tell she wonders whether he's the right person for whatever job she has in mind. She weighs him, measures him, reviews her options. From her desk drawer she pulls out a bottle of blackberry brandy and two Dixie cups. "You're still young enough, maybe you can find yourself another old man after this one throws you out on your ass."

She should have gone in the army; she can identify a target, blast it out of the sky with a single shot. He says, "You think that's what I want?"

She doesn't answer. Instead, she gets up, closes the door to the office, and the quiet murmur of the telemarketers fades away. Initially she's slow to share the details, but the impassive look on his face—or perhaps her cup of brandy, always topped off before it can become empty— inspires the confidence she needs. When she finally shares her plan it's as if she's stripping, one piece of clothing at a time. With each article removed her shyness gives way to the thrill of exhibition.

Her plan will require a lot of his time. She'll keep him on the payroll at Good Works while he volunteers for one of their clients, a nonprofit organization called Babies First. The Babies First Annual Pledge Walk for the Unborn is held each May. Cynthia says he's got about four months to prove to them that he's loyal, trustworthy, and sincere. When he asks why, she says that on the day of the Walk for the Unborn he'll be a volunteer. The one who delivers the donations from the site of the event to the Babies First office, where the accounting temps will add up the day's receipts and prepare the bank deposits.

Cynthia's familiar with the Babies First operations, having been an administrative temp for the Walk two years ago and having surveyed the event last year as a volunteer at the park. He admires her patience, but he's surprised that she has recruited him so late in the game. That is, until she admits first that it's taken her this long to work up the nerve to implement her plan, and second that her ideal partner, Ian, is in jail. Though Ian will be released soon, his record disqualifies him for the role she needs filled. After careful consultation with her husband, she decided that Brendan was the best candidate for the job.

And besides, she tells him, Babies First is composed primarily of women of a certain age who will adore the attentions of a younger man. All he has to do is work conscientiously and flirt innocently. Validate them, titillate them, feed their private fantasies. Or, as Cynthia, warm from the brandy, so directly puts it: "Make them think of you when they shove the handles of their hairbrushes up their twats."

His mother had an expression: *Now there's an image I won't easily forget.*

"We don't know each other," Cynthia tells him. "You don't know me, I don't know you."

He nods respectfully, impressed by how much time and effort have gone into her plans. He could learn something from Cynthia; apply it to his own life.

She chain-smokes as she lays out the finer points. "I'm gonna be working registration. The pledge walkers check in there; they turn over the money they've collected to the volunteers working the tables. There are maybe a hundred of us. They divide the registration volunteers into teams of two, so I'll be paired up with a stranger. I'll be adding up the checks and cash, and my teammate will check my math. Next, we stick the checks in a brown envelope; cash in a white one. We seal both envelopes and sign on the seals. From there they go to one of the team captains who oversees everything. She sticks 'em in a brown garbage can or a white garbage can. When the cans are filled, another team loads 'em up in the trucks."

Brendan considers this. "Why do they separate the cash from the checks?"

"They never finish all the accounting on the day of the Walk, so they work on the cash deposits first. The checks usually take a couple of weeks to process, there's way more of 'em."

"They just leave the checks in their offices?"

"They figure the checks won't get stolen, they're locked up in the safe. And besides, it'd be hard to get somebody to cash a check made out to Babies First."

He frowns. "Wouldn't it be simpler if we were in charge of taking the cash deposits from the offices to the bank?"

Cynthia pulls another cigarette out of her pack and lights it with the remnants of the dying one. "Yeah, but by then somebody has counted the money, made out a deposit slip, so when the money doesn't show up at the bank, they know they've been screwed. I don't want them to know they've been screwed. And anyway, only the executive director and the board treasurer are allowed to take the cash deposits. Nobody else touches 'em."

"So I take a quick detour with the truck, grab as many white envelopes as I can carry, hide them somewhere, and then deliver the rest?"

"Not quite, but close enough. I only want the big bills, we can give them all the ones and fives. And they don't know they got ripped off."

"Of course they will. Jeff and I did the AIDS Walk every year. Along with the checks and cash, we turned in a pledge form. When the money doesn't add up to the pledges, they'll know something's wrong."

She savors the blue smoke as it slides down her throat and into the depths of her lungs. She forms an O with her lips and blows ephemeral rings around him. "Number one, if somebody does start getting suspicious, the first place it'll play out is at the registration tables. If I were them and knew the deliveries were coming up short, I wouldn't suspect the drivers. I'd figure a crooked driver would just keep on driving and not look back. I'd figure he wouldn't have the balls to keep making deliveries.

"And number two, they wait a while before comparing figures. No walker has collected every pledge by the day of the Walk. Thousands of dollars are sent weeks, even months, late. Thousands more never show up; some of the people who pledged renege. It'll take them a long time to sort it all out. Time enough for us to pack up and leave."

She's proud of herself, very proud, and he's a little ashamed of himself. How wrong first impressions can be. Now, he *really* can't say that he knows her all that well, but what little he does know impresses him: she's a woman in need of a change, a break, and she's not like him, passively waiting for one to present itself; she's created it all on her own. He admires this. And he wonders whether she resents that fact that she needs someone like him to help her pull it off.

She says, "So, will you do it?"

He stares at the floor, its carpet blotched with dark stains and ashes. He thinks of Marv, their precarious arrangement. He says, "Let me think about it," then adds, "If I say yes, can I move in with you until the Walk?"

She sighs. "Brendan, I'm sorry, I can't have you living with me and my mom. It just wouldn't work."

"An advance, at least?"

Cynthia looks up at the ceiling, and then back at him. "I'll raise your salary at Good Works. How 'bout that?"

Rather than love, than money, than fame, give me truth. I sat at a table where were rich food and wine in abundance, an obsequious attendance, but sincerity and truth were not; and I went away hungry from the inhospitable board. The hospitality was as cold as the ices.

Brendan closes the book, a copy of Henry David Thoreau's *Walden*. It was a favorite of Alex Supertramp's, one of several books found with his remains. Before Supertramp died in Alaska, alone, emaciated, he had highlighted the passage about wanting truth more than love, money, or fame. In large block letters, he had written TRUTH at the top of the page.

Brendan rides the bus, mulling over his options, which are few. When he arrives back at the Dutch Colonial by Lake Calhoun, he exhales deeply, his breath a frozen cloud in front of him, as he discovers that Marv has put his suitcases out on the sidewalk for the garbage collectors. He rescues his bags from the curb, alarmed to find his backpack not among them. It must still be inside, along with his favorite books, the ones he can't bear to be without. He puts the key he took from Marv in the front door's lock. Somehow, Marv has already managed to have the lock changed. Then Brendan notes that thick bars, a jail cell's, have been installed on all the first-floor windows.

That was fast.

Brendan had assumed that Marv would at least take the day and think things over before he did anything rash. All this must have set the old man back plenty. But then, he has it. Brendan considers ringing the bell, pounding on the door, but Marv would never answer. He might even call the police.

If he hasn't already.

Brendan cannot—he refuses—to leave his favorite books behind. He wanders to a side of the house, and backing up to take it all in, he studies it carefully, searching for an entrance. Just when he thinks that Marv's fatal mistake was in not barring the second-floor windows he discovers the old man's master stroke, a private security guard who emerges from the front door.

Brendan ducks behind a large oak, hoping the guard doesn't notice his tracks in the snow.

The guard is assisted by a cane, is overweight, and appears bored. He walks slowly through the loud snow that crunches like Styrofoam. As he gradually works his way along the exterior wall and out to the white backyard, Brendan decides that he's got no choice but to play a hunch. He tiptoes to the front door, landing each foot softly in the hard snow. It pays off; the guard didn't think to secure the lock behind him.

Brendan's father used to say, *No one ever went broke underestimating the intelligence of the average American worker.*

Brendan steps lightly through the entrance hall, hugging the walls, the soft creaking of the floor making his pulse race. He hears Marv descend the stairs and enter the kitchen, where the old man must be fixing himself a victory drink. After a few minutes Marv moves on to the sitting room, where the flames in the fireplace make the wood snap and pop. Brendan imagines it's an odd little routine that Marv has, spending all day methodically carrying a single log from the stack outdoors and putting it in the fireplace. Moving one after another, piecemeal, weakly, so that he can spend all evening in an alcoholic haze in front of the fire.

But then, Brendan supposes it's not all that bad an existence.

Brendan makes it to the kitchen, where SIMON DELIVERS bags lie on countertops, empty. From the entryway he can see Marv, his back toward him, in the sitting room. He makes out a very large and very empty glass sitting on the floor beside the recliner. The air is dry and full of static; Brendan needs water, but he has only a few minutes at most. He moves as he imagines a cat burglar would, big, long steps carefully placed, his breath held tight within him. Soon, he finds himself looking down on the long, wispy strands of gray that have been pulled from one side of Marv's head over to the other.

From directly behind where the old man sits slumped on the easy chair, Brendan says in a soft, intimate whisper, "Hey, Marv."

Marv jumps up and faces him, all five alarms ringing in his head. "Oh my God! Oh my God!"

Brendan puts a finger to his lips. He says softly, "Please be quiet."

Now Marv can't make a sound; the shock of seeing Brendan is too much. He just stares, his mouth hanging like wet laundry on a muggy day. Brendan tells him, "Sorry, I didn't mean to startle you."

Marv sputters, shakes.

Aware of the time, which is quickly running out, Brendan says, "I want my backpack, it wasn't out on the curb with the bags." What does he have to lose? He adds, "And I want you to listen to what I have to say and really think about it, please, before you say no. Can you do that for me? Can you really listen? Because it's important to me."

Marv nods slightly, he's Scrooge; Brendan, Marley's ghost.

Brendan smiles softly. "Thanks. You're doing just fine. Please listen carefully. First, I'd like it if you'd sit back down."

Marv drops with a mild thud onto the soft leather of the recliner.

He scratches his scalp as he sits across the coffee table from Brendan, who says, "There, that's better. Are you comfortable?"

Another little nod. Marv's mouth is wide open, but the corners droop, and Brendan's beginning to find it irritating. A thought occurs to him. He stands. "You stay right there, I'll be back before you know it. There's something I forgot to do."

Brendan jogs to the front door, picking up Marv's cell phone on his way. A turn of the key and the deadbolt slides back into the locked position. He rushes back to the sitting room, concerned that Marv may have another phone hidden away somewhere. The old man looks like a wax sculpture of himself, lifelike but not alive.

As Brendan sits back down, he says, "You know, I'm really in over my head here. It's just the thought of not having any place to live. . . . It's impossible to buy food and pay rent when you make seven dollars an hour."

Marv's eyes water and tears form around the corners of his glassy eyes.

"Well, anyway. Here's my idea: I live here; I keep your house clean and organized. We could go out on dates, sort of. I could go with you to shows or concerts or whatever you like. It's just that there wouldn't be any sex. I promise you, if you let me move in, you won't even know I'm here. I'll live in the basement. And I'll find work; I'll finally get my bachelor's degree. And I'll do my very best to make things as pleasant for you as I can."

Marv isn't listening.

Brendan says too loudly, "And there's something in it for you, too. I've been thinking about Frankie and I'm betting that there's been other boys—underage boys. I think this could be a way for you to redeem yourself. By giving a home to someone like me, a person in need of a second chance. At your age you should really be thinking about redemption. It'd be a fresh start for both of us; we could help each other out."

A single drop winds it way down the cracks and crevices of the old man's face.

"Please don't cry. Really, I didn't mean to upset you."

The doorbell rings. The guard has finished his rounds and wants back in.

Brendan's heart's pounding. "Oh, fucking forget it! Just give me my backpack."

Marv's expression changes, the terror subsides. "He's my witness. You broke into my house."

The doorbell rings again.

Brendan forms a fist with his hand. "Where's my backpack?"

Marv smiles, like he's having his picture taken.

Brendan has to have his books. He doesn't know what else to do. He stands, hoping Marv's as predictable as he thinks he is. He says, "Send him away and you can have me." He unzips his coat quickly, throws it aside. He yanks his shirt over his head; tosses it on the chair behind him.

Marv says, "I won't send him away. And you'll go to jail for breaking and entering."

Brendan has to have his books. He touches his smooth chest lightly with his fingertips and works his hands down to the button of his jeans. He pulls it loose.

Marv doesn't say anything, just watches, daring Brendan to show him more. His eyes, now quite sharp, never make it above Brendan's shoulders.

Brendan says, "Send him away."

The doorbell rings again.

Brendan unzips his jeans and pulls them halfway down his thighs. He plays with the elastic of his underwear, clumsily stretching it out and snapping it back against his waist. "Send him away."

Now there's an urgent pounding on the door and Brendan can tell the guard's afraid that something has gone terribly wrong. Brendan feels the veins in his neck throbbing. A muffled voice shouts, "Mr. Fletcher? Mr. Fletcher, are you alright in there?"

Finally Marv looks Brendan in the eyes. He rises slowly from the chair and gradually, deliberately, makes his way to the door.

Brendan waits by the fire, a statue. He hears Marv slide the chain onto its latch and open the door a crack. He exhales.

Marv says loudly through the gap in the doorway: "I'm sorry, must have dozed off."

From the other side the guard nearly shouts: "Jeez, ya scared me half to death, Mr. Fletcher. I thought some maniac had gotta hold of ya!"

A pause.

"I apologize. Please, take the rest of the night off. I think I'll just go back to bed."

"You sure? My dispatcher said you sounded kind of freaked out when you called."

Marv makes a little *ahem* noise. "Did he? Oh, yes, well, I'm afraid that was just my insomnia talking. At my age it can make you delusional. That's my problem, not enough sleep—it was making me imagine things. Forgive me. Now that I was actually able to doze off for a few minutes, I just want to climb back in bed. I'll be sure to give you a favorable report."

"Could you let me in, it's freezing out here. Besides, it's kinda company policy that I don't leave my shift early. I needa call this in and get authorization."

Brendan inhales, holds it.

Marv says, "Of course you do. And here, just a little something to express my satisfaction."

It must be a large bill that Marv hands him; the guard, still outside by the sound of his voice, almost gushes as he says, "Oh, thank you, thank you, that's really nice of you."

"No, thank you. You finally helped me fall asleep. And while I'm still a little drowsy, I want to get back in bed or I'm afraid I'll be up all night. And you wandering around won't help."

"Yeah, okay, and thanks again. I just gotta pop in and get my lunchbox."

"I'll get it for you. Where did you leave it?"

Another pause. The guard says, with less enthusiasm, "It's in the refrigerator."

Marv yawns, says like he's not thinking clearly, "I'll be right back." There's a sound, like a door being pushed back into its frame.

Marv shuffles slowly from the entryway into the sitting room, where he sees Brendan standing in front of the fire. He stops long enough to get a good look and then he heads to the kitchen to retrieve the lunch-box. On the return trip he pauses, stands next to Brendan. He runs his free hand up and down Brendan's body as he whispers, "Does that feel good? Do you like that?"

Brendan looks at the floor, nodding.

Marv whispers, "I thought you might. Don't you dare move an inch. I'll be back before you know it." He stands on tiptoe as he tries to bring his lips up to Brendan's, but Brendan refuses to lean down. As Marv pulls away, he mocks Brendan in a hushed tone. "Not a kisser, eh? Well, we'll soon take care of that."

He grabs Brendan's ass before he waddles to the front door, ecstatic, a man renewed.

Brendan hears the chain slide off its latch and the door barely open. Then there's the old man's voice saying, "Here you are."

The guard says, "Well, if you're sure you'll be okay."

"Please, please, I'll be fine once I get a good night's sleep. If you keep wandering in and out I'll be up all night."

"Okay then, you're the boss. You have a good night, sir."

The door closes, a lock delicately turns, and the chain makes its second trip onto the latch.

Marv almost seems to have a spring in his step when he returns, but it disappears as soon as he sees Brendan, his shirt back on, his jeans buttoned tight around his waist. Brendan says, "Where's my backpack?"

Marv turns, heads back to the front door, but Brendan grabs an arm, stops him. The old man shouts, "Let go of me!"

Brendan squeezes Marv's arm as tight as he can. Brendan grunts, "Where's my backpack?"

Marv squints, gasps, "Let go of me and I'll get it for you."

Brendan releases him, follows him closely as the old man walks to the fireplace. From behind a tall pile of logs stacked alongside the chimney, Marv produces the backpack, unsteadily hands it to Brendan like a little boy caught stealing.

Brendan looks at Marv, confused. The backpack is empty. "Where are my books?"

Marv's silent.

"Where are my books?"

Marv says nothing, just moves over a few steps as he rubs his arm, which places him directly in front of the fireplace. Next, he points in the direction of the front door, as if to say the security guard may still be on the other side.

Brendan stares at Marv with wild eyes, willing the old man to speak. And then a thought—a terrible, horrible, unimaginable thought— ignites like a stick of dynamite in Brendan's head. He pants, finally saying, "Move aside."

Marv trembles, his eyes squinting at the floor beneath his feet.

Brendan says, more loudly this time, "Move aside."

The color leaves Marv's pink face.

An order now: "Move aside!"

Like a blind man, Marv places his hands against the stones and rocks of the chimney to find his way as he slowly complies.

And through the mesh spark curtain Brendan sees the small pile of ashes and dying embers beneath the grate. Most of the ashes are tiny, crumbly and black or gray, but here and there are bits and pieces of smoky white, and on these, words and fragments of words.

His eyes bulge as he drops to his knees in front of the fireplace, his hands pulling the metal mesh curtains apart. He frowns, his mouth agape. Gently, he places a small piece of charred paper in the palm of an open hand like it's a hatchling fallen from the nest. He examines it closely, holding his breath so it won't blow away. He makes out the words *half-full backpack*. He knows these words, they are part of a beloved sentence: *The heaviest item in McCandless's half-full backpack was his library . . .*

The enormity of Marv's offense numbs him at first. He looks at the ashes as if they were the debris of a home after a tornado had razed it.

He catalogs his losses: *Into the Wild* with notes Brendan made to himself, his speculations about Alex Supertramp and the life they should have lived together. His battered edition of *Walden*, with the same sections underlined that Alex had underlined in the copy that was found near his body. His secondhand hardcover edition of *Doctor Zhivago*, a title that was also found with Alex's remains. Brendan's own favorite book from childhood, old and beaten when he first read it, the 1926 edition, the *first* edition, of *Dr. Doolittle's Caravan*.

He drops his hands to his sides, lets the scrap of text land on the floor, dead.

He looks up at Marv, who grimaces like a man condemned.

Brendan slowly stands. He reaches for the fire's poker, pushes the ashes and embers back and forth but there's nothing, nothing at all, save ashes and embers. He turns, faces Marv. His eyes sting, his throat constricts. He whispers, "I just needed someone to help me."

Marv looks at the poker in Brendan's hands and then at Brendan himself. He says, "I'm sorry, you're right." Quickly he adds, "I'll help you."

Brendan swipes at a tear. "Why . . ."

"I know, I know, you're right. I'm sorry."

Brendan spits out, "You bastard! You fucking bastard!"

"I'm so sorry, please, I'll make it up to you, we'll get all the books you want."

Brendan slams the poker against the chimney, his face sunset-red. "Shut up!"

Marv pleads: "I'm sorry."

He points the poker at the old man. "You're dead. You are fucking dead."

Marv tries to say something, but all at once he falls to the floor.

3

Doctor Zhivago

BRENDAN REALLY DIDN'T WANT TO RIDE along in the ambulance, but the emergency technicians had made assumptions about him, that he was Marv's son or grandson, and they ushered him so gently and kindly through the cold night air and into the vehicle that he felt he had no choice but to join them. And truth be told, he hadn't had anyone show him that degree of respect in he didn't know how long. It felt good. One of the men working on Marv was very handsome. He had the rich eyelashes and thick black hair of a Persian and Brendan allowed himself to imagine that the concerned glances the medic shot his way were attempts at flirtation. Brendan hoped the man would place an arm around his shoulder to console him, but the handsome man and his colleagues simply deposited Brendan in the waiting room after Marv had been rushed into the emergency room.

So here Brendan sits in the early morning hours, alone, bookless, waiting, not because he's very concerned about Marv, lecherous old Marv, but rather because he has no place to go, no one waiting for him. So he reads the magazines, an odd collection of news and women's journals, or he glances at the television that's bolted onto a wall, where the

few people in the waiting room, middle-aged women mostly, learn of
the latest level of terrorist threat. This seems an ironic place to find out
such a thing: disaster has already struck all who sit in this room. The
new color that the secretary of homeland security announces as he
points to his chart seems anticlimactic—what, after all, can compare to
the shrieking, pulsating red of a siren?

Brendan wonders what he should do next. He's too afraid of shelters
to stay in one.

An older black woman enters the waiting room now, a file folder in
her hands. She wears half-glasses, a thick sweater, and a skirt the color
of ripe peaches in spite of the season. She says, not looking up from the
paperwork she examines skeptically, "Family of Marvin Fletcher?"

Brendan looks around the rows of chairs, waiting for people to
stand.

She looks up now, repeats herself. "Family of Marvin Fletcher?"

The women in the waiting room look at each other, him.

Finally, the woman stands in front of him, staring down through the
eyeglasses like crescent moons. She asks, "You rode with Mr. Fletcher,
didn't you?"

He nods, afraid she's going to tell him to move on, that he's used up
all the waiting time allotted him in this waiting room. There are new,
better waiters, waiting to wait. She says, her voice a bit higher, "You're
not family?"

He's about to say something—what, he's not entirely sure—when
she frowns, says, "Oh. Are you Franklin Thompson?"

Franklin Thompson? He nods slowly, like she's miming clues in a
game of charades.

She reassures him now. "You're listed as his domestic partner. That
makes you family in this hospital, no matter what the governor says.
Come with me, please."

He follows her to a small cubicle village, where she sits behind a
tiny desk. Pinned to the short fabric walls are pictures of young men
and women, her children undoubtedly, each one just a few pounds
overweight, as she is. From the opposite side of the dividers they hear

the conversations of others, learn of heart attacks and seizures. She says, "This is your partner's second stroke, correct?"

He mutters, "He had a stroke?"

She frowns again, says, "Didn't they tell you in the ambulance? Yes, it was a stroke. Don't worry, it was another ischemic stroke, not a hemorrhagic."

He looks at her.

"Do you remember the name of his physical therapist? I can't seem to find it."

He shakes his head, and as he does, he notices a small bowl of lemon drops on her desk. Has he eaten today? He would enjoy a lemon drop.

"Well, you should know that it might be a bumpier ride this time. The stroke was on the left side of his brain. He's experienced aphasia so his speech is severely impaired, although this could be a temporary situation. You'd be surprised, some people get their speech back just like that!" She snaps her fingers to illustrate her point, a gesture that seems too peppy for the circumstances they find themselves in. "Also, there's some paralysis on the right side of his body and you should be prepared for memory loss. We'll know more in a few days. We're waiting for a private room to open up, but for now you can visit him in the ER. No doubt he's confused and afraid, so just remember to smile and speak in simple phrases. Reassure him."

He places a hand over the candy dish. "May I?"

She smirks, says, "Help yourself. I'm on a diet."

He grabs a handful and walks in the direction she points, to a little corridor just outside the ER. Patients lie on gurneys that are lined up in single file against the wall. Some stare at the ceiling, others keep their eyes closed; still others move their heads back and forth, as if pacing the floor. Marv's awake and Brendan stands over the old man, hoping for an expression on his face that's the right mixture of sympathetic concern and sincere regret. The right side of Marv's face droops, but the left side reacts to the sudden appearance, snarling and sputtering, bits of spittle bubbling on his lips.

"I'm sorry, Marv," Brendan says softly. "Really. I just lost control; you made me so damn mad. I wasn't going to hit you."

The old man's left eyebrow descends as the eye below it squints at Brendan, furious. Brendan whispers, "I *did* call 911. I didn't just leave you there to die, you know."

Marv makes a sound, something like a cat would make, a small hiss.

The social worker finds them, her head shaking. She says, "I forgot to give you these." She hands Brendan the keys to Marv's house, Marv's wallet, some change. She looks at the old man, the dribble, the spitting, and says, "It'll be alright, Mr. Fletcher. Franklin's here."

Brendan drops the keys in his pocket as he says, feigning a look of calm reassurance, "That's right, Marv; don't you worry about a thing. Frankie's here."

He looks up at the sun that shines brightly on this morning, the seventeenth morning of the new year. It takes a bit of effort, but he places one foot in front of the other, reaches into a pocket for the set of keys a hospital social worker gave to him under the mistaken belief that he was someone else, a younger man who could hold these precisely cut pieces of metal with confidence, or perhaps contempt. He slides a silver key into Marv's front door with equal measures of fear and disbelief, and like something out of a fairy tale it opens, the hinges groaning like Atlas under the weight of the world. He understands that he's changing from the man who stands outside these walls like a victim in shock into the man who will live inside, too stupid or too careless to realize that like Jericho, all this could come crashing down at any moment. He flicks a switch, and in the far corner of the entryway a feeble bulb comes to life, its faint rays struggling to spread what light they can.

He needs to calm down.

He makes his way to the library and there he breathes a little easier when he sees the extensive array of volumes, classic novels (displayed to impress?) as well as biographies of presidents, popes, and captains of industry, cramped and bulging from the shelves. From the corner of his eye he discovers an odd, small section of a shelf ungracefully stocked with young-adult paperbacks from years ago, sold for only fifty or seventy-five cents when new. The little collection includes, of all things, *The Outsiders*.

Brendan opens the book, smiling. This was the novel that quickly became his all-time favorite when he was twelve, its largely all-male world of parentless, tough, hip, and good-looking teen boys making his heart beat a little bit faster. Yes, he had read better written books, even classic adult books by the time he first came across *The Outsiders*, but it had uniquely resonated with him. He smirks now at the idea of juvenile delinquents reading *Gone With the Wind* to each other or maybe at that tender advice offered from a dying teen: *Stay golden.*

Still, he remembers being barely able to turn the page when a member of a menacing group of Socs asked Pony Boy: *Need a haircut, greaser?* The "medium blond" who posed the question was sexy and dangerous and Brendan just knew that something awful was going to happen.

As intriguing as the boys and violence were, he thinks that what resonated most was the title: *The Outsiders*. He wasn't yet able to truly understand what it was that he felt for other boys, but he was very much aware of the fact that it made him an outsider. The Socs were the heterosexuals of his world, the ones with a privilege that he doubts he could have articulated at the time. It didn't make much difference that he was on the basketball team or that he snuck cigarettes to smoke with friends—that wall of difference was still there and getting higher every day. He longed to join a group like the greasers Pony Boy hung out with, a gang of guys who looked out for each other with a passion that seemed romantic.

He takes *The Outsiders*, along with some of the classics, works by London, Thoreau, Tolstoy, and Pasternak.

Back in control, he wanders around the place. This house is luxury layered upon luxury, but what amazes him most is all the space. There are so many rooms here, a room to watch television in, another to listen to music, one to read, one to work, as well as one whose purpose remains a bit of a mystery. And the bedrooms, each seems to have a theme to it, one outfitted with modern furniture, another, Victorian. He chooses the smallest one for himself, a tiny room, an afterthought. It's about the right size, this is all he can manage right now, nothing larger.

This place is so much more than what Marv needs that he decides it's just one more tool the old man uses to get young men into his bed. After the efficiency, it's overwhelming and he wonders what it takes to keep this place clean.

A maid.

He says out loud, "Oh shit!"

He springs into action, starts his search in the den. He runs his hands over the oak paneling, imagining that there must be a safe or some hidden compartment behind the walls where Marv keeps his important papers. But then he thinks: *Marv is no mastermind, if he were, he wouldn't be in this mess. Besides, why would the name and phone number of a cleaning service be a state secret? Calm down. Start with the most obvious suspect, the desk.*

He hesitates, his hands caressing the wood panels of the wall. If there was a safe, the contents could be worth more than what Cynthia hopes to steal from the Walk for the Unborn. It would save a lot of time and effort.

But he could never do something like that.

He looks at the desk; uncluttered, save a few souvenir paperweights collected over the years, their images of Philadelphia and San Francisco and New York set under heavy glass. First things first. He needs to find out how to get hold of the hired help, who would be suspicious of him, a man they've never seen before, living in Marv's home.

The desk's drawers are mostly full of junk: batteries, coupons, out-of-date stamps that now need another few cents before a letter can be mailed. He's surprised to find what look to be bullets in between copies of General Mills Retiree Association newsletters, a clue to Marv's past. When he does come across something of interest, it's a letter from Dun-woody Institute, a vocational school, informing Frankie that not only has he been accepted, but a full scholarship has been awarded him by a generous donor, Mr. Marvin Fletcher. Frankie may enroll immediately. The letter is dated last August. Scrawled across the bottom is a note in Marv's handwriting: *Sweetheart, the key to a better future is education.*

The bottom drawer has hanging files that hold Marv's bills. Marv proves to be very old-school; a cancelled check is stapled to its corresponding invoice, immediate proof that his accounts are up-to-date. Brendan strikes gold: statements from a cleaning service, a snowplow company, and landscapers. Based on the receipts, he reasons that the maid is due back tomorrow afternoon. He'll call and cancel. He decides to keep the snowplow and lawn-care services to lend a look of normalcy to the outside world, but he won't pay them unless he absolutely has to. Anyway, the invoices go back years, some decades, so these companies will probably cut Marv some slack when he gets behind in payments. Water and heat he'll pay with money orders.

He's late for his *caregiver's conference* at the hospital, the meeting with Marv's doctor, social worker, and discharge planner. They look at him with annoyance when he finally arrives in what is really an exam room, where they balance themselves on short stools amid the blood pressure gauges and boxes of latex gloves. The physician is an older black man, but not elderly. His thinning gray hair is neatly trimmed and there are bags under his eyes, not from age, Brendan would guess, but fatigue. The eyes themselves are bloodshot, and they move quickly as he scans Marv's chart, like a freshman cramming for a final. The discharge planner is a young, perky white woman who has her own file, an accordion file, which she opens and closes, perhaps expecting to hear a polka.

The doctor sighs. "So, Mr. Feltcher—"

"Fletcher," the social worker corrects.

He looks neutrally in her direction as he says to Brendan, "So, Mr. Fletcher has had a stroke. It appears that he's experiencing paralysis on the right side of his body, as well as problems with speech. We don't believe, based upon what he's been able to write in response to our questions, that he has lost his memory"—Brendan freezes—"although it's a bit hard to make out his writing since he has to use his left hand." The doctor rubs his eyes as he continues. "The good news is that many people recover from these conditions as a result of rehabilitative services. We can't reverse the effects of the stroke, but we can build Mr. Fletcher's strength and confidence so he can live as normal a life as possible."

Normal? Marv?

Looking at Brendan now, the doctor asks, "Do you have any questions?"

"Will he be able to walk again?"

"With therapy, perhaps."

"Will he be able to speak again?"

"With therapy, perhaps."

The social worker says, "In your partner's case,"—the doctor raises his eyebrows, surprised by the term *partner*, or Brendan's age, or Brendan's gender, or all three—"we think a transfer to a rehabilitative facility would be the best option. Mr. Fletcher needs assistance with feeding, hygiene, and dressing, but more important, he needs to learn how to do these things for himself again. To the best of his ability. You should also learn how to do these things for your partner."

Brendan cringes.

She finishes by saying, "And the rehab specialists will work on mobility and speech. They'll also teach you some exercises you can do with your partner on your own time, too."

Brendan says, "So basically people will teach him how to walk and talk again."

She nods, says, "Basically, yes."

"Who's going to pay for that?"

"Mr. Fletcher has a long-term care policy, of course. You see, he was looking out for you. This shouldn't cost you a dime."

"When will he be transferred?"

The discharge planner speaks now. "With your consent, as soon as possible. I highly recommend Northstar Presbyterian Home. I have a friend over at admissions; she'd be happy to give you a tour of the facility and answer any ques—"

"No, let's just move him over."

The doctor and the social worker exchange looks. The social worker says, "We want you to be comforta—"

"Northstar sounds fine."

Nothing is said for a moment or two until finally, the discharge planner says, "I'll call Northstar right now."

When he arrives in Marv's room, the old man's asleep. There are no flowers or cards, just Styrofoam cups with plastic straws popping out and an empty chair next to the bed, the place where a visitor could sit and talk to Marv, had Marv any visitors. Someone should have sent him a card, at least. This is an odd little space, clean, cold, temporary. The linoleum beneath Brendan's feet displays the ghosts of a mop's suds, inanimate swirls of tiny dead hurricanes that have fossilized. Brendan's pushed enough mops in his life to recognize the work of a novice.

He looks down at Marv, sees the heavy stomach slowly rise and fall, follows the line of the old man's lips as they end in a small droop on his right side. The IV drip is gone and Marv's arm is bandaged: today's the day he's being moved to Northstar Presbyterian. Downstairs an ambulance is being readied for the trip.

Brendan touches Marv on the left shoulder, the good one. "Marv?"

Another touch of his hand, less gentle, more demanding. "Marv, wake up."

The eyes open slowly, revealing their wateriness, their confusion. His left brow frowns as Brendan comes into focus, and he begins the muttering and sputtering to which Brendan's now accustomed. Brendan tells him, "Relax, please. I'm not going to hurt you. We're going to take you to a new place where they can better help you."

Marv takes this information in slowly. Brendan says encouragingly, "They'll help you get back on your feet. Literally."

The old face contorts, happy, suspicious.

"You see, I'm helping you, just like we agreed before all this happened."

Brendan watches as Marv searches his memory. It may be functional or it may not; he might trust it, he might doubt it. Brendan can almost hear him say, *I don't believe I agreed to anything.* What Brendan does hear is a series of *ffftts* and *ssssss.*

Two men in white pants and blue smocks join them now, rolling a stretcher behind them, which they place next to the bed. They are large men, not friendly but not unkind, a bit hardened to human suffering perhaps, if their expressions are any indication. One says, "Okay, sir, we're going to move you onto the stretcher." He looks at his companion, says, "Let's lift on three. One, two, three."

They groan, Marv is heavy, dead weight and he cannot help them by keeping his arms at his sides. He splutters and moans until, at last, he's in position, the straps of the stretcher snug across his legs, his chest. They roll him down the hall as Brendan follows at a respectful distance, the Muslim wife of a holy man. In the elevator others join them, elderly people in wheelchairs, their middle-aged daughters by their side, orderlies, nurses, couples with bouquets. It's crowded, quiet, but for the occasional sound of Marv, who recites little half-words from a language only he can speak. People stare straight ahead at the elevator's doors, as if they were the open pages of a book.

Brendan is a bad person doing a wrong thing.

No. If he takes care of Marv, takes *really* good care of him, he can make this right. Marv has no one, after all. The old man needs him. And he needs the old man's home, its walls, its roof, its tiny bedroom that keeps out the wind and the snow. Eventually Brendan will make other living arrangements, once he has enough money, a steady job.

As if on cue, a chime rings, the doors open, and they make their exit, the well and the sick, the strong and the frail. Marv takes in the changing landscape of the ceiling until they find themselves outdoors in the cold, noisy South Minneapolis afternoon. Brendan watches as Marv is loaded in the ambulance. As Marv disappears behind its slamming doors, Brendan waves good-bye as Frankie would, or more to the point, as Marv's social worker might imagine Frankie would.

Everything had changed suddenly—the tone, the moral climate; you didn't know what to think, whom to listen to. As if all your life you had been led by the hand like a small child and suddenly you were on your own, you had to learn to walk by yourself. There was no one around, neither family nor people whose judgment you respected.

One of Alex Supertramp's favorite passages from *Doctor Zhivago*. Brendan closes the book, returns it to its shelf in the library. He has been at Marv's for just one week and has already reread half a dozen favorite volumes. But they have failed to comfort him like they used to.

He wanted to make a fresh start.

When he first showed up at Marv's doorstep he had naively hoped the old man would provide him with one. But like everything else, it's turned into a disaster. Instead of walking these halls confidently, securely, he lurks like a frightened cat in front of the windows, peering at the world outside this house. He's convinced himself that at any moment Marv will regain his speech, and with his memory quite intact, alert the police to his deception. They'll surround the house with guns drawn.

It really makes him wonder just how he could have been so stupid.

He needs money, lots of it. He needs yet another new address, one far from Minneapolis. For that he needs Cynthia and her plan. He calls to tell her to count him in, and her voice doesn't rise or fall, she matter-of-factly asks him to meet her at Good Works after she closes up, there are things they need to discuss. He's not happy about this: Good Works is two bus rides away, one on a tough route that he doesn't like to take so late at night. But he agrees because he has no choice. On the bus, a scrawny, bearded white man sits near the driver, a heavy black woman, asking her what makes her holler, promising he can make her scream. She says nothing to the man, stares out the enormous windshield. Brendan gets up from his seat, walks down the aisle to the front, and even though his stop is blocks away, he grabs the overhead rail, positioning himself between the driver and the man. He spreads out his shoulders, obstructing the man's view.

The man mutters, "What, she your fucking bitch?"

Brendan turns, looks impassively in the man's direction, letting him know that he's heard him. The man gets up, heads to the back of the bus.

The driver, seemingly oblivious to what was happening, turns her head Brendan's way, says, "Thank you."

Brendan sits down. "I don't know how you put up with it."

She sighs, "Me neither."

When she drops Brendan off, she thanks him again, a bright smile on her face, and then she tells him to have a good night. He looks up from the curb and he sees one of his foster mothers, the one who fed him until he couldn't eat another bite. He says, "You're welcome."

Cynthia's standing under a streetlamp in front of the building as he emerges from bus number two. A fog materializes in front of her face, a combination of cigarette smoke and the steam of her warm breath in the frigid air. She says, "Took you long enough."

"The buses are running late."

She smiles now, says, "Let's go. Franklin Avenue's no place for a lady this time of night."

Her van starts up on the third try and she pulls them out into the sporadic late-night traffic. He assumes they're heading to the Coliseum again, but Cynthia takes them across the border into St. Paul, where they pull up to one of the flashing meters on the curb of a large industrial boulevard, the same street that farther east is home to "Targhetto." She turns off the van's headlamps, and with the engine softly idling, points in the direction of a squat office building, its glory days well behind it. She looks at him and says, "That's Babies First."

He studies it, frowning. "Doesn't look like much."

"Don't be fooled, they're swimming in it. They're just cheap is all."

"So I walk in there tomorrow and volunteer?"

Cynthia finds her pack of cigarettes on the dash, puts a fresh one to her lips, but she doesn't light it. It dangles as she says, "No, you just can't walk in till we get your story straight."

"My story?"

"Look, they do criminal background checks on everyone, so you'll have to give 'em your legal name when you fill out your volunteer application."

He says, "No problem. But I still want them to call me Brendan."

Cynthia rolls her eyes. "Fine, whatever. Now, you're being straight with me, right? You've never been arrested for nothing?"

"Never."

"Swear to God, never?"

"If it will make you feel better, I *swear to God*."

She turns back to the building. "Good. When you walk in, I want you to have a story you can stick with. These people are always praising Jesus and praying for shit, so you have to, too."

"I'll try, but I'm not sure I can be convincing."

"Try hard."

"So why am I volunteering for Babies First?"

Cynthia removes the cigarette from her lips, considers it. "'Cause you believe abortion is murder."

"Besides that?"

"What do you mean?"

"People all have opinions on things, but what is it that makes me *volunteer* for Babies First?"

Cynthia *hmmmms*. "It should be something good, something they'll buy right away."

"My girlfriend aborted our baby and I never got over it?"

Cynthia shakes her head. "I don't know. Why would you want to be around pictures of aborted fetuses then? They got 'em all over the place."

"What if I'm volunteering as penance for something I did that I'm ashamed of?"

"Nah, they have to trust you enough to let you drive one of the trucks. We can't give them any reason to think it might not be such a good idea. We need something that'll make them like you a lot."

He thinks about this as the hot air from the vents blows on him. He asks, "What if I played on their sympathies?"

"Like how?"

"Say my wife died recently."

Cynthia's face lights up. "And she was pro-life!"

He swears that a light bulb appears above his head, just like in the cartoons. "And she died during a miscarriage!"

Cynthia one-ups him: "And you're volunteering in her memory!"

They look at each other, laughing, impressed by their own brilliance. Maybe he doesn't believe everything Babies First believes, but HIS POOR DEAD WIFE DID! Cynthia leans over, kisses him on the cheek. She puts the van in gear, saying, "There's a Wendy's that's still open a few blocks from here. Whatever you want, my treat!"

He works up his nerve to visit Marv at the Northstar Presbyterian Home. He needs to see for himself how much progress, if any, the old man's made, how much longer he can stay in Marv's house before the old man learns how to talk again. At the nurse's station a thin woman sighs loudly when he asks after Marv. The first week isn't even half over and it has not gone well. But Marv has stopped his garbled screaming, the shaking, the slapping of personal care attendants with his good arm, the struggling to get out of bed to learn yet again that he cannot walk. She tells Brendan that the thick coat of sweat that covered Marv like wax paper those first few days has vanished. By way of conclusion she says crisply, "Wish we'd known that he was going through alcohol withdrawal on top of everything else."

Like his hospital room, Marv's little cell at the home is devoid of flowers and cards. Unlike the other residents' quarters Brendan passed on the way, there are no photos of family and friends decorating the walls. A television is bolted overhead; its remote lies next to Marv's good hand, but the set is not on.

Brendan slides a chair next to the bed and sits down, smiling. "Hello, Marv."

Marv looks at him, the good eyebrow frowning.

"Are they treating you well?"

Marv shifts his attention to the television's blank screen.

"You're very quiet." After days alone, idle in his bed, Brendan thinks Marv will try to say something to him, make the grunts and sputters that now constitute his version of talking.

Brendan should just leave, but he has nearly an hour before his shift at Babies First, where he now volunteers, stuffing envelopes and sorting bulk mailings. To pass the time he makes conversation. "Did I tell you I'm rereading *Doctor Zhivago*? I got a few other rereads going right now, including *War and Peace* and *Family Happiness*. I guess you could say I'm in my Russian phase."

He hears Marv choke and then clear his throat. The old man croaks in a voice that doesn't sound like it's been used in days.

Brendan leans in, frowning, trying to identify words, but it's hopeless.

Because Marv can't talk, he can't tell Brendan where the keys to the Oldsmobile are, the perfectly good car that sits alone in the three-car garage. Brendan could really put the car to good use; he needs to learn how to drive before the Walk. That, plus the fact that he's tired of busing all the way to Babies First. Brendan sighs, leaves Marv in the crisp white bed.

Brendan heads to a bus stop and for once he's in luck, a bus arrives immediately. He takes his place on the first bus before he transfers downtown to another one that'll deliver him to the Midway section of St. Paul, home of Babies First. He has a seat toward the center, behind the old black and white women in their knit hats and the Somali women whose faces peek out from behind yards of fabric, but ahead of the hooded teens of all races who sit sullenly in the back. Like most of the other midsection passengers, he creates a hole in this universe: a book that occupies an affordable percentage of his attention and helps him create a less threatening space among these strangers. This strategy serves him well on the bus, his book a No Trespassing sign that declares both his sovereignty and his neutrality, a human Switzerland landlocked by potential enemies.

After he takes his usual place on the second bus, he pushes his shoulders up and back to make himself appear bigger than he is. The dull routine of people getting on and off the number sixteen deadens him to his surroundings as the vehicle slowly moves a few yards forward before stopping at another red light. A younger white woman works her way toward his row, looks at a black man dressed workday casual across the aisle from him, and decides to take her chances in Brendan's territory. She's wearing too many layers and she's carrying too many things: a briefcase, a tote with her office shoes in it, a paperback, and a big blue Marshall Field's shopping bag. She struggles to make herself and her possessions as small as he is large and he hears her mutter "sorry" as she attempts to get her half of the double seat organized. She glances at his copy of *Doctor Zhivago*. Now she's an awkward pile of arms and legs and snow boots as she opens her own book, *In Cold Blood*, to its very first page.

They ride together in silence and as she flips a page he knows that he's ceased to exist for her, cast off into open space a short distance behind the black man seated across from them.

He looks out the window at the sidewalks covered with the hard, dirty snow pack that comes from salt and sand and thawings and freezings. He doubts there's anything uglier than these cities when the branches are empty, the sky gray, and the ground a filthy, slick mess.

By page 107 the bus nears his stop, and he reaches for the cord above his head. The woman next to him, seemingly engrossed in reading her own book, is nonetheless alert to the rustling of his coat as he extends his arm, her cue to clear a path for him and claim this turf as her own. She puts her bags on her lap and shifts her hips so her knees face the aisle, pointed at the black man, who turns a page in his own paperback. Sometimes Brendan wonders what the odds would be of all the midsection passengers reading the same book on the same route on the same day. Would they even notice? Or would they form a mobile book club, and ride past their stops because they so enjoyed listening to the discussion about the book or because they felt so passionate about expressing their opinions?

The doors fold open and he emerges onto an ice bank littered with McDonald's cups and dog shit. One-half block north, on the other side of University Avenue, is Babies First. Even though he's relatively new to their group, they always seem happy to see him.

"Well, look who's here!" This is Gail, a brand-new grandmother from Bloomington, home of the Mall of America. She's one of the volunteers who buzz people in and out from behind the ancient reception desk, a gift from the owner of a Christian business.

He smiles warmly. "I'd rather look at the beautiful creature who was kind enough to open the door for me."

She blushes and giggles. "Oh, *you!*"

The first thing he told the staff and volunteers at Babies First—as he and Cynthia had decided—was that he had recently lost his wife, Laura. Cynthia chose the name, telling him it's easier to stick with your lie when you have an easy way to remember it, in this case, the old song "Tell Laura I Love Her." Just as Cynthia predicted, most of the Babies First crew found his status as a young widower intriguing and liked the little human tragedy he brought to their rather pure, dull work. Some of the volunteers watch him closely for any sign of grief in need of consolation; others praise their God and him for honoring Laura's memory by contributing his time to the cause. Both groups occasionally flirt, and one obese woman always brings in Tupperware containers full of meals that only require him to *reheat and eat!*

He walks up the stairs, on the industrial carpet that's worn and stained, to the second-floor conference room that's crowded with folding tables and boxes of appeal letters, each photocopied onto Babies First letterhead, every one to be compiled with pledge cards, return envelopes, and mailing envelopes. Once assembled, the little piles must be counted and sorted by zip codes. The *gals*, as they prefer to be called, are already stationed in groups of three or more around the tables. Bowls of water and small sponges for sealing envelopes sit next to their homemade cookies and bars.

Just like the grandmother downstairs, they say, nearly in unison, "Well, look who's here!"

He says, "Yes, it's me, you lucky, lucky devils."

They titter, charmed by his brazenness. He said *lucky* (evoking gambling) and *devils* (evoking hell).

He's risen like a rocket through the ranks, thanks to his gender, so he "floats," not tying himself down to a single table or one group of gals. Rather, he moves among them, checking the accuracy of their stuffing and sorting and helping himself to the small treats they offer him. They coo when he compliments their cooking, delighted that a young man is paying them the type of attention that their own sons and husbands will not.

In between mouthfuls of a lemon bar he says to the chef, "Ann, you're going to make me so fat I won't be able to fit through the doorways."

"Oh, *you!*"

The gals' conversations are about God, scripture, and the women who aren't here tonight. They talk about their children and their grandchildren, hoping to impress or garner sympathy. There are aches and pains and operations to be scheduled. As the chats run their course a new subject emerges that gets the attention of all in the room. According to Judy, baker of tollhouse cookies, the Babies First board of directors met last night to devise a response to a gay pro-life group that wants to participate in the Walk for the Unborn.

Ann's adamant as she dips her sponge into the sticky water to seal an envelope. "I hope they told them to stay far away. It's the Walk for the Unborn, not a homosexual day parade!"

Judy nods her head knowingly. "Can you imagine what would happen? My church group screened that video, *The Gay Agenda*. I wouldn't dare repeat the things those animals do to each other."

Another woman, counting envelopes with the 55412 zip code to see if she has enough for a direct bundle, shakes her head. "You know what I say? The more the merrier. If they want to support our cause, then I say, let he who is without sin cast the first stone."

Judy says, "Oh, Linda, you can't be serious. Do you want little boys walking right next to homosexuals? Do you want to take that kind of risk with innocents? I know I don't."

Linda says, "Well, if you put it that way . . . maybe they could have their own part of the Walk where it's just them."

Judy considers this. "Maybe. I mean, I hear they have lots of money. We could put it to good use."

Brendan asks, "Really? They have lots of money?"

Judy's eyes bulge knowingly. "Oh, *yes*. They don't have children of their own to raise so they just spend it all on themselves. Big stereos and televisions and they all go on homosexual cruise ships. They always get the best jobs, the really high-paying ones, because they all look out for each other."

A gal says, "Now, Judy, my hairdresser can hardly be considered rich."

Another gal says, "I just love our regular waiter at the club. If he wanted to walk with us, I think he should be able to. He's a lovely boy, just lovely."

A debate on what constitutes the greater good follows. Some women speak of how Jesus walked among the lepers; others quote Leviticus, chapter and verse. Brendan just smiles, humbly soaking up the wisdom of the gals as they come to the conclusion that homo-money would be blood money, thirty pieces of silver.

It's easy, when he's away from Marv's house, to imagine that none of it happened, that he didn't lose control and scare an old man so badly that a blood vessel carrying oxygen to his brain burst open, that he didn't take advantage of the situation to install himself in the old man's home. But he had honestly felt that he'd run out of options; it was either continue to live in Marv's house or face the brutality of life on the cold streets. He knew that he wouldn't last as a vagrant—who could? How many of the homeless ever recover from wandering the streets in search of food, shelter? How often has he been surprised to meet some capable, professional co-worker who tells him that they're in recovery from cancer, from alcoholism? A few times, at least, he thinks. How often has he met a co-worker during the course of his day who told him that they used to be homeless? Never. Or at least they never admitted to it. No, that's not right, either, a couple of them had. In fact, a few still were.

Still, there are some things most people can't recover from. Perhaps some homeless people do recover, but he doesn't have the confidence in himself to find out if he could.

The bus drops him off a few blocks from Marv's house. As he walks along the frozen sidewalk, his breath a fog in front of him, he sees a woman, an elderly woman, walking a small dog. Something about her stride strikes him as familiar and he slows his pace to get a better look. She feels his stare and turns. From the distance of nearly a block, he recognizes the face of the woman who adopted him, obscured by a hat and scarf. It changes his perception of time, this one glance when eyes lock and recognition strikes like lightning. Before she has the chance to convince herself of what she has just seen, he turns his head and quickens his pace.

He's taking stupid chances; he's being careless. Is this what his adoptive parents would call a *self-destructive tendency?*

He enters Marv's house, inspects the mail he's retrieved from the box. Perhaps he's not as careless as he thinks: he did manage to find Marv's bills, successfully canceling the maid service that would have sent a crew over here by now to find Marv gone, a stranger in his place. The rest, he's guessing, Marv has taken care of himself through years of ugly living: there are never any messages on the answering machine; no one stops by over the course of an evening to drop off a cake or some other little gift that makes life a little more bearable.

Brendan reads, makes himself something to eat, reads some more. He could spend all night in this simple routine, but he needs to sleep, or to make the attempt to sleep.

Lying on the small bed in the small bedroom, he wonders about Jeff, his ex. It's been five years since the breakup. Jeff has undoubtedly found someone new.

He wonders whatever became of his oldest brother, Steven.

And their mother.

He can still see the expression on her face.

He was just a boy, pressing the lips on two of his G.I. Joes together.

Ooh, gross! This was Steven. He was turning the television on. He told them to be quiet: he needed to concentrate; he was writing a report on the local news for school.

They heard a newscaster say, *This just in.* Their eyes opened wide as they recognized their father on the set's picture tube. He was being escorted out of his office by police officers, his wrists in handcuffs. Steven shouted, *Mom! Mom, Dad's on TV!*

Their mother joined them. Her teacup fell from her hand and onto the carpet, where the tea soaked the white fibers. And there it was on her face, that expression, the one he's never forgotten. He asked her, *Mommy, what's wrong?*

She whispered, *Nothing, little prince.* Then she exhaled deeply as she clasped her hands together. When she finally spoke, it was to say, *Get your coats and boots on! Now! Come on!* She hurried them as they got ready to go outside, and when she opened the front door, they saw two police officers standing on the porch, the older one's hand raised as if he were just about to knock.

Brendan lies on the bed and brushes the memory away. He wishes he could sleep, but he dreams while awake, alert for any sound. There's an irrational part of him, his primitive self, that fears Marv, imagines that the old man has somehow fully recovered from the stroke and is on the verge of exacting his revenge. He lies in the darkness of the bedroom, listening for the soft footsteps of the old man on tiptoe, scanning the room for any flickering of shadow along the floor or walls that may warn of impending disaster: Marv pointing a gun, Marv holding a butcher's knife, Marv with a shovel in both his hands.

There are hours to kill before he meets Cynthia for coffee. He needs time away from Marv's house so he makes his way through the slush to a bookstore, and though he's already familiar with this season's new releases, he lingers in front of the display tables that tempt shoppers with the latest titles. Signs suggest that shoppers buy books for their sweethearts this Valentine's Day, but Brendan cannot afford new books, and, besides, he has no sweetheart.

One of the things he finds so alluring about bookstores is the people who frequent them. They tend to be serious people, sometimes a bit too precious for his taste, but otherwise a solid bunch who, like him, think too much for their own good. It's rare to see one of them talking into a cell phone as they wander the store, loudly speaking to someone not present.

There's a man standing next to him, taking inventory of the new fiction table. From the surveillance Brendan conducts out of the corner of his eye he judges the man to be newly middle-aged, professional, lost. The man's dark hair is peppered with gray, the glasses he wears are in keeping with recent trends, though there's a crease in the small panes that lets Brendan know the prescription's for bifocals.

The man reaches for a slim volume from a stack that sits upon the table they share. Brendan reaches for it, too, hoping his timing is precise enough to enable skin to brush against skin.

"Sorry," the man mumbles, glancing at Brendan before he removes his hand.

"My fault," Brendan offers with a shy smile.

The man looks at him, assesses the situation correctly. "Are you a fan?" he asks as he lifts a copy of the book in the air, its cover facing Brendan.

"Huge," Brendan whispers loudly.

Yes, the double entendre is tired, and not entirely true. Still, Brendan thinks it's charming, this little code that he transmits, even more charming how the man translates the signals into something else, into the words Brendan would have said, had he the courage.

The man in the bifocals smiles, says, "I've read it."

Brendan follows his lead: "So have I."

So they stand there, the two of them, one newly middle-aged, one nearly so. It's time for boldness; it's up to Brendan.

And that's when the man in bifocals smiles, moves on. He leaves Brendan standing there alone, staring at the book by a writer he is not a huge fan of, wondering why the moment came and went, its arrival unexpected, its departure devastating.

Cynthia's late. He's been sitting at the Starbucks on Riverside Avenue for nearly twenty minutes, listening to the Somali cab drivers discussing in their native tongue what he assumes to be life, fares, and the people back home.

When Cynthia does arrive, Brendan watches as the Somali men glance at her, this American woman, thick with blueberry-colored makeup, her hair exposed for the entire world to see. They're probably wondering which of her parents was black, which white. She returns their looks, confident, indifferent. It's her face that shouts at them: *Take a look around, assholes. This ain't fucking Somalia.*

She says, as she sits in a huff, "Sorry to keep you waiting. Trust me, you don't wanna know."

He says, "I trust you."

She stops tugging at the zipper of her coat and looks up at him. "Thank you. I trust you, too, Brendan."

He blushes as he watches her pull her arms free of the sleeves. She moves economically, as if conserving her energy. It's the new, efficient walk, her sense of purpose, that builds his own confidence; she's not the woman he first met at Rush City, the one waiting for someone on shore to notice her flailing in the water, to toss her a life preserver. When she's free of the coat she eyes his double-mocha. "I'll be right back."

As she takes her place in line, he wonders how a woman like her ever came up with an idea like this. She seemed normal enough, in a mildly disaffected way, hardly the type of person who would go to such an extreme without a good reason. Ian hasn't been of much use in helping him figure out his sister-in-law. When he asked Ian why he married her, his brother simply said, *If you were straight, you'd have married her, too. She's Cynthia.*

She sits down again, blows cool breaths on a triple-mocha, no whipped cream.

He says, "What is it I don't want to know?"

She sniffs her drink for heat. "I thought you trusted me."

"I do. I'm curious, not suspicious."

She decides her mocha is too hot to attempt just now. "My mom kicked me out of my own apartment."

"Why'd she kick you out?"

She rotates her head over her neck, willing the stress away. "She found some weed in my room."

He can't help but laugh. "That's all?"

She frowns, blows on her mocha again. "She's a Jehovah's Witness, Brendan."

He apologizes and says, "Has she kicked you out before?"

"Oh, *yeah.*"

"What can I do?"

Cynthia regards him sweetly and at that moment she looks as if she could be anyone, anyone at all, she's a woman with options. She says, "Help me get my shit."

He nods and she reaches for her key chain. There's a faraway look in her brown eyes, and he imagines she's seeing the sand and water of a Mexican beach from their little perch in this Minneapolis coffee shop. She says, "Let's go."

On the ride over to the apartment, Cynthia tells him she has been living out of her office at Good Works for a few days but now she's found a month-to-month rental on the south side. They arrive at the place she has been sharing with her mother, not far from downtown, on the city's north side. The small living room smells strongly of Lysol and it nearly brings tears to his eyes. Cynthia tells him that her mother doesn't smoke, and that she deodorized the apartment every day when Cynthia lived there. The little pressed-wood coffee table has neat stacks of *The*

Watchtower on it, along with several romance novels and a candy dish full of individually wrapped butterscotches. Cynthia's mother turns out to be a lean woman, slightly darker in complexion than her daughter. Cynthia had told him on the ride over that her mother's half German, the result of a disastrous union between a black American GI and a blond Munich shop assistant. Her father was mixed race, too; it was the central fact of his life and had attracted him to her mother.

Cynthia's mother stands as they enter, her arms folded tightly across her chest. Her coarse hair's short, with tidy little curls. She refuses to color the gray, attributing each and every silver strand to Cynthia. She looks at her daughter carefully, and then spends just as much time inspecting him. When she finally speaks, it's: "I hope you've come to apologize for bringing drugs into my home."

Cynthia laughs, disgusted. "This is *my* home. You're the one who left Chicago and followed me up here. No one made you do it."

"It's not right for so many miles to separate mother and child."

"So you're kicking me out of my own apartment. That makes sense."

She shakes her head and says, "I've packed two bags for you. You can take one or the other, but not both." To Brendan she says, "I don't believe I know you. Did you sell my Cynthia the drugs I found?"

He looks at Cynthia for guidance. He's about to offer that he's Cynthia's brother-in-law, but he suspects that would only make matters worse. Cynthia finally says, "Yeah, that's him. He's been keeping my ass higher than a kite for years."

He says, "I don't sell drugs!"

Her mother's eyes narrow. Staring through him like he's an X-ray, the one that brings an unwelcome lump into the light of day, she says, "Get out of my home. Leave, now!"

He really hates it when people talk down to him. He tries to mind his own business, but people just go out of their way to be cruel. Cynthia touches his arm, says, "Come on, let's get my shit and get outta here before she really blows a gasket."

Her mother blocks the path to what must be Cynthia's bedroom.

"Oh, no, you don't. You take the little bag if you're near ready to apologize, the big one if you're gonna be stubborn. You don't take anything else out of my home."

Cynthia throws her hands up in the air and says, "This is *my* apartment! I'm letting you keep it because you're my mother and I'm not gonna kick your ass out on the street even if that's how you do me. Now get out of my way."

Her mother's eyes fill as she steps aside. Once Brendan and Cynthia are in the bedroom, Cynthia puts both suitcases in his hands and pulls a plastic garbage bag out of her purse. She stuffs the bag full of clothes, makeup, and CDs. She drags it behind her as they re-enter the living room, where her mother sits on the plain little couch, legs crossed, the hands in her lap fondling a Kleenex. Cynthia stops and he waits by the door with the bags. He hears Cynthia say, "You'll be happier here on your own."

Her mother says, "I lived on my own back in Chicago, but I wasn't happy."

"Look, I love you, but you drive me crazy. I'll call you tomorrow."

"I can't afford to keep this place on what the home pays me."

"Just make the rent through May. I'll take care of it after that."

There's an unwelcome surprise when he arrives at Marv's house: a red, blinking light. People have left messages on the answering machine. He stares at the light, willing it to stop its flashing, but then he presses PLAY as if defusing a bomb.

A woman's voice, painfully cheerful: "Happy birthday, Dad! Out celebrating, I guess. Ed and the kids send their love, they're out on the boat today. So sorry to have missed you. Happy Birthday!"

A beep, a new voice, also female, less enthusiastic. "Happy birthday, Dad. Expect a little something in the mail—sorry I didn't get it to the post office yet, but it should arrive by the end of the week. Well, I hope you have a happy birthday."

A final message, children's voices shouting in unison: "Happy birthday, Grandpa!" One on top of the other now: "How old are you?" "Guess what, we're going skiing a week from tomorrow." "Dad said we could get a dog!" "I'm gonna give out valentines with monsters on them." An adult voice, impatient and male, interrupts: "Don't talk at once, please. I did *not* say we could get a dog, I said we'd think about it. Sorry, Dad." Children chatter in the background as the voice continues: "I'm taking Suzanne and the kids to Aspen next week, so if hell freezes over and you decide to call, you can reach us at the chalet. Hope you have a happy birthday, and for the love of God, will you call every once in a while so we know you're still among the living?"

This is unexpected. There are no pictures of children or grandchildren anywhere in the house. There are no old clothes or toys in the drawers and closets, left behind as college, and then adult lives, beckoned. But then he remembers the old paperbacks in the library, *The Outsiders* and *Go Ask Alice*.

He's grateful for the distance, physical and emotional, that the children's messages convey but he's concerned that some emergency will demand the sound of Marv's voice on the other end of the telephone.

Since it's Marv's birthday, he decides to visit him at the nursing home. If the staff recognizes him, recalls his many kindnesses to the old man, then perhaps they'll attribute any charges Marv may eventually make against him to dementia. He examines the shelves and bookcases for something to wrap; he can't arrive empty-handed. He decides on a few classical CDs and an anthology of famous quotations.

He makes it to the stop just in time to see the bus pull away. He stands in the shelter, annoyed, when a tall, large black man joins him, the butt of a dank cigar dangling from his lips. "How you doin' today," he wants to know.

Brendan nods.

"Can you help me out, my brother? I need seven dollars and thirty cent. My car ran out of gas and I left my little girl sitting in the back. Now I can pay for the gas myself, but they wanna charge me seven dollars and thirty cent for the gas can. What good's gas with no can? And my little girl freezing her titties off! You got seven dollars and thirty cent?"

Brendan stares out at the street, empty save the occasional car with its single driver. It will be ten minutes until the next bus comes.

The man punches Brendan lightly on the shoulder, which surprises Brendan. The sit-ups, the push-ups, they have made him large, sturdy, but the man isn't intimidated. The man shouts, "I *know* you ain't deaf! You gonna let my little girl freeze to death?"

Brendan has seen his share of crazy people, noted how they can clear a path with their rantings. He recalls an old poem he once had to memorize in school. He says to the man in a desperate voice: "Worms feed on Hector brave!"

The man scowls, says, "Whacha talking 'bout?"

"Hell's executioner hath no ears for to hear!"

The man stares at Brendan, his jaw slack.

"Tasteth death's bitterness!"

As the man leaves he shakes his head, saying, "You crazy, man, you need to get some fuckin' help, you know what I'm sayin?"

At last, the bus arrives. It's a comfortable ride, full of quiet adults who stare grimly out the windows or talk softly on cell phones. At the Northstar Presbyterian Home Brendan displays himself freely, holds his gifts out in front of him for all the staff to see. He walks down the hall whistling "Happy Birthday." He offers a hello to the nurses and orderlies he recognizes, and even the ones he doesn't. They absently nod their responses, distracted by the fact that there are so few of them and so many patients.

He arrives at Marv's room just in time for the old man's changing. He turns his head as the personal care attendant, an older black man, removes the soiled diaper and applies a fresh one. He hears a froggy voice croak, "Fwahni . . ."

Alarmed, he asks the attendant, "He's talking?"

The man grunts. "If you can call it talking. That's all he ever says, *Fwan*. You know what it means?"

"No."

Again they hear Marv: "Fwahni . . . whuh . . . Fwahni . . ."

The man drags the waistband of Marv's pajama bottoms up Marv's fat, loose thighs and over Marv's fat, loose stomach. "He must like you. I never heard him say *whuh* before."

Marv opens his eyes and watches the doorway. "Whuh . . ."

Brendan looks over at the door and then back down at Marv, whose gray, stubby beard is starting to become a bit yellowish. "Has he had other visitors?"

The man pulls off his latex gloves, tosses them in the wastebasket. He shakes his head as he says, "Never on my shift."

Once they're alone, Brendan places a hand on Marv's pink scalp. "Marv, what are you trying to say?"

Now more of a cry than a croak and the old man's eyes mist.

"What do you want?"

Nothing.

He says to Marv, "Happy birthday."

The left eye examines the presents in Brendan's hands. Brendan places them by the good hand. "Go ahead, open them."

Marv tears at the paper weakly, and now Brendan swears there's a glint in the old man's eyes, well, the good one anyway. Marv holds a CD up to get a better look and Brendan can't tell if Marv realizes that he's simply gift-wrapped one of the old man's own CDs or if it genuinely seems new to him, an appropriate and thoughtful addition to an already extensive catalogue. Marv ignores the book of quotations completely.

Brendan takes a chair next to the bed and pulls a paperback out of his backpack. "I've brought you something else," he tells Marv. "I haven't read it myself, but it's the most popular book around. I thought we could read it together."

Marv looks at him warily.

Brendan clears his throat as he opens the book to its first page and reads: "*Mr. and Mrs. Dursley, of number four, Privet Drive, were proud to say that they were perfectly normal, thank you very much.*"

————

The gals at Babies First are throwing a party; Ann has just turned fifty and a celebration with a Valentine's Day theme is in progress. Two of the women enter the conference room carrying a sheet cake, large enough for all to have a piece. Instead of candles, there's a single sparkler in the center, firing little bursts of light in all directions. Brendan and the gals sing "Happy Birthday" and as they near the last verse, Linda cracks the group up by singing *How old are you?*

Food is everywhere. The gals cook too much and too often; there's never an occasion that doesn't call for something to eat. They display their dishes immodestly, positioning them just so, looking for that perfect presentation that sets their contribution to the party apart from the rest. There are paper plates and napkins that have little cupids on them, white cupids, clutching bows and arrows. Ann puts her hands on her cheeks, overcome by the display of affection, and says, "Oh, you shouldn't have! Oh, it's too much!"

Linda, always the card, shouts: "You heard her, gals, take back the cake and presents!"

Ann laughs, delighted. "Oh, *you!*" She wears a bright paper hat on her head with the words BEST WHEN PROPERLY AGED on it.

The room buzzes with conversation and laughter. Among the many gag gifts are an ear horn and an old pair of false teeth. There are also prayer books and inspirational placards, along with figurines of blond and blue-eyed children made of bone china. A double CD called *Songs of Praise* gets oohs and aahs as well as inquiries as to where more copies can be purchased.

After all the various dishes are sampled and the cake is cut and distributed, Ann leads them in a prayer of thanksgiving: "Oh most powerful and merciful Father, thank you for these wonderful people, for their acts of kindness, and for their commitment to life. Give courage to those who know that murdering babies is wrong, but refuse to act on their knowledge. And Lord, let this be the year that the government enacts laws to protect the rights of the unborn."

"Amen!" the room says in unison.

Gail sits next to him, passing around pictures of her grandson.

Brendan makes a fuss over the photos but it wears him out—this whole group wears him out and he's afraid he'll slip up at any moment and tip them off to who he really is. There is such camaraderie among the Babies First staff and volunteers, an unshakable certainty that they know what's right. It's seductive in its way, this warm embrace by a community so sure of itself. It provides so many basic needs: companionship, purpose, work, recreation, but most of all the sense of belonging. It reminds him of the gangs in Rush City that Ian told him about.

There are, however, in spite of all the goodwill, rules of the pack that are as rigid as those of any prison gang. There's an uncompromising conformity. Freethinking is like passing gas: best to do it in the privacy of your own home, where there's no one to offend. When a gal admitted that she had voted for Kerry instead of Bush she could no longer find anyone willing to sit and stuff envelopes with her. Her subsequent absences were noticed but not commented upon, and the ease with which the gals cut her loose surprised him.

Judy asks, "Seconds, anyone?"

Brendan looks for the little boy on the bus, the one who told him his daddy killed a communist, but the child isn't making the trip to Rush City today. Brendan does recognize the boy's mother, however; she sits near the front, alone, a vacant expression on her face, the little box of candy hearts each passenger was given as they entered lies unopened in the aisle, as if she doesn't deserve candy, doesn't deserve a husband in jail. Brendan wants to say hello, acknowledge her in some small way, perhaps offer her a paperback to distract her during the short trip north. But he lets the opportunity pass, and he rereads *Into the Wild*, the copy that he procured for a dollar from a secondhand bookstore. He sits, underlining sections, trying to re-create the annotations he had made in his own copy, the copy that Marv ignited in the fireplace. He circles the names of Alex Supertramp's favorite writers; he studies the text of a postcard Alex had written, in which he urges a friend to read *War and Peace*. This recommendation from a dead man is what sent Brendan to the secondhand bookstore years ago to find a copy of *War and Peace* for himself, to read each line carefully, hoping to discover some additional insights into Alex's character. But as he read Tolstoy's work, Alex faded into the background as he found himself in thrall to Pierre, the bastard son and misfit, whose search for meaning he took on as his own while he washed dishes at Denny's.

Once the bus has arrived at Rush City, once he has been searched, he joins Ian at a table in the noisy visiting room, the chatter of other inmates and visitors making it difficult to hear. At the table next to Ian, a large group of white women scream their greetings to a white inmate who has shaved his head. Ian smiles when he sees Brendan, stands to shake his hand. He squeezes it before he lets go, saying, "Thank you, thank you so much."

Brendan's confused. "You haven't even seen what I brought you today."

"That's not what I meant."

Brendan grunts. "Oh." Ian's talked to Cynthia. Suddenly, having someone else acknowledge his Babies First deception, even Ian, makes it seem all the more real, all the more out of control.

Ian says, "I really appreciate it, little bro."

He sits down. "We probably shouldn't talk about it here."

Ian winks, takes a seat himself. "You're right. I just wanted you to know how much it means to me."

Brendan zips open his backpack to retrieve today's gifts paid for by Good Works, where he himself does no work, good or otherwise. But he stills draws a salary, thanks to Cynthia. He presents a pack of cigarettes, of course, and another graphic novel, this time featuring the Birds of Prey, a small group of scantily clad and big-busted women who fight crime. Ian whistles as Brendan hands it to him, says, "Wow. Wish real women looked like this."

"How are you?"

Ian sets the book down, leans back in his metal folding chair. "I had a meeting with a victim this week."

"What do you mean?"

"It's part of this community-based mediation, reconciliation, something-or-other. I promised the parole board I would do it, so I'm doing it. Anyone I conned money from, they can come here and tell me all about how much I hurt them."

Brendan sighs. "Your Canadian lottery scam."

Ian nods his head. "You know, I do feel bad about it when I meet them face to face. But"—Ian forgets, calls Brendan by his given name—"if you could have only heard the excitement in their voices when I told them they'd won the Provincial Jackpot. I mean, that moment, that . . . I don't know what to call it. It was the happiest moment of their lives. With one phone call all their worries were over, and I was the one who made it happen."

"Ian, don't make it sound so noble. You lied to them. You told them you worked for the Canadian Consulate and you took them for their life's savings."

A random burst of laughter from the table next to them.

Ian folds his arms across his chest. "But it was such a high to make people's dreams come true. I can't even describe it to you, the way it made me feel, spreading such joy. I don't know, like maybe I was Santa Claus, I guess. I got a letter from one woman after I was sent up. She's probably a million years old and lives in some tiny little town in South Dakota. You know what she wanted to tell me?"

Brendan shakes his head.

"That it was almost worth it. She said that that one moment of pure joy was almost worth all her savings. And that wasn't much; I made maybe four grand off her. But still, she was so happy, and you know what else? I really liked her. I mean, I really liked her. I looked forward to talking to her, she was so enthusiastic, so grateful to me. I liked her so much I almost told her the truth, but I didn't. Because she was so happy. You see, I couldn't take that away from her."

Brendan looks at him, about to say something, but given recent events, who is he to judge? He asks, "What was it like with this week's victim?"

Ian smirks. "I told her, 'You know, what's done is done, I can't go back in time and undo it. I wish I could, but I can't.' But she didn't listen to a word I said. She's all about laying this big guilt trip on me. She said that my sentence wasn't enough to make up for what I had done. Well, let that withered old crone spend the best years of *her* life in Rush City and then tell me it wasn't enough. It's more than enough. All I took was some money, I didn't take her freedom away from her. She's the one who did that to me."

"You could have done something else."

Ian laughs softly now, says, "We've been over this a million times. What should I have done? Pump gas? It's all self-serve now, in case you hadn't noticed. Flip burgers?"

Brendan cringes.

"That's not going to pay the bills."

Brendan stares at the table. "What should I do? I mean, once we've . . . once everything's finished?"

Ian leans in. "Start over. With us. You, me, Cynthia, down in old Mexico!" He studies Brendan's face, says, "And, no, I'm not going to go down that same road that got me here, don't worry about that. I've learned something, after all."

Brendan smiles.

Ian's about to say something else when, two tables over, a fat white man grabs his wife or his girlfriend by the shoulders, pulls her toward him, and head-butts her. The dull roar of the visiting room stops dead. The woman falls to the floor, unconscious, while the guards beat the man senseless with their billy clubs. When they're through Ian says, "He's been talking about doing that for weeks. Didn't think she'd have the nerve to show her face round here."

Brendan stares at her, sprawled on the cold hard floor, a guard trying to revive her.

4

The Mass of Men

MAYBE IT'S THE STRESS of finding himself in his current situation that makes him hungry for contact with another human being. Maybe it's because for the fifth year in a row no one sent him a card or flowers or candy on Valentine's Day like Jeff used to do. Or perhaps he just can't take one more sexless minute. He's walking up Hennepin Avenue, his destination the same club where he met Jeff a decade ago. Here and there are other men like him, lonely people, in search of a companion, at least for tonight. They avoid each other's eyes as they head toward the anonymous storefront. Inside there are men, perhaps hundreds of them, packed tightly together. The dance music reverberates through both spheres of his brain, making casual conversation impossible. Some patrons orbit others like satellites; and there are small groups that huddle together in a pack for protection. The air is thick with perspiration and alcohol, and he joins the dozens of men who line the walls of the place and act as though they've found themselves here by accident. He'll soon be too old for this club, which pulsates with bass lines, youth, and arrogance. In a few years he'll find himself exiled, patronizing the piano bars favored by men of a certain age who mistakenly believed there was still plenty of time to find that someone special and settle down.

His favorite men at this club are the ones who, like him, arrive on their own, who decide that when they want to dance, they'll simply walk out onto the floor and dance, partner or no partner. What he finds so attractive about them is their disregard for convention, the unwritten rule that one must have a companion to dance with, some person other than yourself to witness your joy, validate it. He remembers the day his adoptive mother received news that an article she had written had been accepted by one of the major psychological journals. He was the only one at home and she was angry that her husband wasn't there with them; she needed to share her joy with him. He had wondered at the time: *Why? Why can't you absorb the joy on your own? Do you need to boast or be reassured?* People always want to share their wonderful news, talk about how wonderful it is, ask each other: *Isn't it wonderful?* But he doesn't, he just wants to hold a good thing close to him and relive it over and over in his mind so that he'll never forget even the tiniest detail. Like his first night with Jeff. Brendan was at this club with two acquaintances, men he had met through a discreet network at the store where he was working at the time. He was going to turn twenty-five at midnight, and he had never slept with a man before. Jeff changed all that.

May I have this dance? Jeff had asked him, as if they were in some old movie.

Brendan just grinned at him. He remembered the song that was playing, a disco/rap hybrid, and its pulsating bass guided their feet.

The music was so loud that Jeff had to shout directly in Brendan's ear: *My name's Jeff.*

He pointed at himself and yelled: *Brendan.*

Jeff smiled and they bounced around on the floor, bumping into the other couples and groups moving to the beat of the place, a rhythm that brought complete strangers together, if only for one night. Brendan was drunk in anticipation of his birthday, and thrilled to be dancing. In his entire life he had never asked anyone to dance. It was never his responsibility.

That first night with Jeff was like nothing else he's experienced be-fore or since. In some ways the memory is too painful because this night survives only in the past. The sheer intensity of it will never happen to him again; he'll never wake up in the morning so in love with the world as he was that first morning with Jeff lying next to him. He remembers looking in awe at Jeff's face. Everything about it—the eyelashes, the lips, the ears, all of it—was miraculous. But the biggest wonder of all was the fact that Jeff was with him.

When Brendan was reunited with Ian, Jeff did his best, he knows. But things slowly escalated until that final night, the night Brendan left him.

Now Brendan scans the faces of the men in the club, wondering whether one of them will turn out to be the next Jeff, a capable person, successful enough in his own life that he can help him rehabilitate his own. Wouldn't it be so much easier if people, like buildings, could un-dergo their own renovation and reconstruction, could have scaffolding encase them, long sheets of plastic to protect the work crews against the wind and rain as they went about their duties, replacing the old pieces, the rotten boards and rusted nails, the furnace that never did work properly even when new? The sidewalk traffic, those familiar pedestrians seen every day, would be temporarily diverted across the street, as they witnessed the work in progress. Once complete, the structure would stand alongside the others, as functional and efficient as any of its neighbors.

He needs someone to outfit him in scaffolding.

He's looking for a skilled man, someone who can mentor him into an adult competence, someone serious but not overbearing, who under-stands, like him, the probability of disaster, but unlike him, is prepared for it, and survives its inevitable arrivals and departures stronger for the experience.

It would also be helpful if this skilled man were well-read.

He decides to be practical, not wait for whomever this man is to spot him. He picks a face, one of the solitaries grimly staring at the dancers. The man he selects is not especially handsome, and unlike the majority of the other men in this club, he does not wear a tight shirt that outlines overdeveloped pectorals and large biceps. His dress is neat, unassuming, unmemorable; he is literally a face in the crowd. Brendan imagines he's in sales or marketing, a lawyer on the partnership track, a veterinarian with his own practice. He was bullied as a child but he got through it, his parents love him but secretly wish he were heterosexual, he donates his time and money to the Humane Society.

Brendan has to shout in his ear: "Hello!"

He startles him. The man hadn't noticed Brendan's approach; he belongs to the set of patrons who pretend that they're not here. Being caught off guard embarrasses him. He smiles, says, "Hello!"

Brendan asks, "How are you this evening?"

"I'm sorry, what did you say?"

Brendan repeats, "How are you this evening?"

Another smile. "Good. And you?"

It's Brendan's turn to smile: "Good."

Now comes the portion of this little ritual where they stand, side by side, saying nothing as they look at the men who dance. Occasionally Brendan glances at the man, occasionally the man glances at Brendan, but their looks never intersect, their timing's off. Brendan taps the man on the shoulder. "My name's Brendan."

The man shouts in his ear, "Pleased to meet you, Brandon. I'm Doug."

"Brendan. My name is Brendan."

"Sorry, it's so hard to hear in here."

Brendan takes hold of Doug's hand. "Let's dance."

He leads Doug to the dance floor, which is covered with men and the occasional woman. All club music sounds the same to Brendan. There's an omnipresent bass, a singer warbling her voice while a male raps the chorus, things like *Hell, yeah* or *Dat's right*. That the dancers can distinguish one song from the other impresses him; it's a talent, like being able to tell the difference between "eggshell" and "arctic" at the paint store. Doug dances the way he dresses, nondescript, his feet keep a respectful time with the beat, his arms move conservatively. Brendan's the less skilled of the pair; it's been years since he found himself dancing at a club and his long absence shows. At first he softly jogs in place, but realizing how absurd he must look, he varies his movements in hopes of being less conspicuous.

Hell, yeah!

Doug is gifted; he knows when one song ends and another begins. He claps his hands together, shouts, "I *love* this song!"

So they keep floating along the waves of gay men rolling across an ocean of synthesized sound. Some men drift calmly in these waters, others swim strongly, fearlessly, leaving waves of their own in their wakes. Then there are the people like Brendan, the ones waiting to be rescued, to be airlifted into the helicopter, wrapped in a thick blanket, given a hot cup of coffee.

Dat's right!

They finish the dance. Doug wants to stay on the floor all night long. Brendan should go, there's really no point in trying to create a relationship when he'll have to leave this city soon, and forever. There is another Jeff, a better Doug, somewhere else. He'll just have to be patient. The man he intends to become will be patient. The new Brendan will not spend so much time wondering what his life would have been like had he had the intelligence and maturity to stay with Jeff. The new Brendan will appreciate happiness as it happens, not look back at it wistfully, recognizing it only in hindsight.

As he heads to the door he's surprised by a young man, perhaps in his mid-twenties, who blocks the trail he blazes through the dense forest of men. The young man's attractive in a non-threatening way: if he's an actor—like some of the men in this club often claim to be—he will get parts in commercials, the young father who nurses his sick children with Vicks Vapo Rub or the newlywed husband whose attempt to fix breakfast in bed is a comical, endearing disaster, so it's off to McDonald's.

The young man puts a hand to his mouth, shouts, "Didn't you used to go with Jeff Moran?"

Brendan frowns. "Who are you?"

"Oh, I'm sorry, I'm Dave. I'm Jeff's partner. I recognize you from some of his old photos."

So here's the younger model, the one from a normal family, no doubt. Brendan looks over at the bar; it's there that he identifies the back of Jeff's head, the skintight dome surrounded by a monk's cap. Jeff's handing the bartender a bill, undoubtedly telling him to keep the change. People get to keep the change when Jeff's around.

Brendan returns his gaze to the young man, who appears eager for this impromptu meeting to go well, for the two of them to be civilized adults. Brendan decides to cast it as a case of mistaken identity. "Sorry, you got the wrong guy. I don't know a Jeff Morgan."

"Moran," the young man says, adding, "oh."

Brendan moves past him but the man places a hand on Brendan's arm, asks, "What was your name?"

As Brendan has been rereading *War and Peace*, he tells Dave, "Pierre. Pierre Bezukhov."

"What's the deal with *that* name?"

Brendan watches Jeff turn around, looking for where his *Dave*, his *partner*, went.

Brendan's running out of ideas. Desperate now, he decides on something scandalous. "What, you looking for a three-way?"

"Of course not! Jesus!" The strategy pays off. As Brendan hoped, Jeff's *Dave*, Jeff's *partner*, almost runs away.

Brendan barely makes it out on the street before he hears someone calling him.

"Hey . . . HEY! Brendan! Where're ya going?"

Of course, it's Doug, not Jeff. Jeff never called him Brendan.

Since Brendan doesn't know where he's going he says truthfully, "Nowhere."

It's a long, chilled, and quiet walk to Doug's car, a green Honda Civic, perhaps seven or eight years old. On its rear bumper is a pink triangle, the little symbol that the Nazis used to identify homosexuals. The car is surrounded by SUVs adorned with *Support Our Troops* and Christian fish magnets.

Before Brendan can take his place in the passenger seat, Doug has to clean up debris, things like ice scrapers, cassette tapes, papers, candy bar wrappers, and plastic bottles containing a few last mouthfuls of nearly frozen spring water. "Sorry," he mutters as he clears a place for Brendan.

They put on their seat belts, and with a grin in Brendan's direction, Doug turns the engine over. He says, "We can go to your place if you want."

Brendan shakes his head; he can't take Doug back to the little room he has chosen for himself in a large Dutch Colonial on Lake Calhoun. He stares out the frosted windshield, says, "Your place is fine."

Doug pulls the car out in the street. In between shifting gears he places a hand on Brendan's knee, saying, "You sure? We don't have to go to my place. We could do something else." But even as he suggests it, his hand slides up Brendan's thigh, and he squeezes the skin beneath his jeans. Brendan leans against the headrest and closes his eyes as Doug's hand continues its exploration, at first tentatively, and then almost defiantly.

Brendan has no idea who this man is.

But then he doesn't know Brendan either.

At a stoplight Doug says, "We're almost there."

Brendan nods.

Doug's apartment isn't all that far from Marv's house, so Brendan will be able to walk out the front door and find his way back without having to stop at some all-night convenience store to ask for directions. Up and down the street are small apartment buildings full of people like Doug, single people, people who can't yet afford homes of their own, who have no one to share them with.

Doug's clumsy with his key ring, he's had too much to drink, and Brendan wonders why he didn't notice it earlier. Once they're in the lobby Doug checks his mailbox, disappointed to find the flyers describing missing people and offering deep discounts, big savings.

Doug nods toward the stairs and they ascend two carpeted flights, the dusty salt tracked in by tenants crunching beneath their feet. Behind apartment doors cats mew, restless, distracted by the sound of footsteps.

When they stop at his door Doug assesses Brendan suspiciously, yearningly. Inside, he flicks on the lights, tells Brendan to make himself comfortable as he heads toward what Brendan assumes is a small kitchen. Brendan takes in the white walls, the parquet floor. He finds a seat on a futon couch, and surveys the unfinished bookshelves, which are largely free of books. Small frames hold pictures of Doug and Doug's friends, men and women whose happy, longing expressions suggest that they are nearly ready to come to terms with settling for less.

When Doug reappears, he holds two water glasses, filled to the brim with red wine. He hands Brendan a glass, and takes a seat next to him as he sips his own so it won't spill. Brendan politely tastes the wine, then places the glass on the floor, away from feet that might knock it over.

Doug kisses him.

When was the last time he was kissed? He doesn't count Marv's grotesque attempt. He searches back in his memory, and there it is, all over again, his last morning with Jeff, years ago now. Jeff wouldn't let him leave without giving Brendan something to remember him by, that's what he told him anyway. He grabbed Brendan's backpack as he was walking away, swung him around with a strength Brendan didn't know he possessed. He drove his lips into Brendan's, like cars at a de-molition derby, and shoved his tongue through Brendan's teeth as if he were punishing him. When it was over, he said, *You can go now. I won't stop you.*

Doug pulls off Brendan's shirt, tosses it onto the floor and its dust bunnies. He moves his mouth down Brendan's neck, to Brendan's chest, sucking one nipple and, finally, the other. It's Doug's hands that make Brendan feel more alive, the way Doug's fingers run all over him, connecting him to another life, not his own. The sensations—gone for so long that Brendan's almost forgotten how to miss them—reassure him that he's human, not so very different from other people, a part of everything.

There's something in Doug's eyes, the eyes he rarely opens, that's deeper than his passion, or is it his desperation? It's his love—his underutilized capacity to love—looking at Brendan with ambivalence, uncertainty, fighting off the pessimism to which it has already grown accustomed.

Doug gasps, the intensity dies. They hold each other, but the serenity slowly disappears, like early-morning mist after the sun has cleared the treetops. Doug's skin, alongside his own, no longer feels the way it did just moments ago. It's the skin of a stranger, of a person unsure of what should happen next. It feels like caution, distance, it's the yellow signal of a traffic light.

What does Brendan's skin feel like to Doug?

They lie there, side by side.

Doug is not his answer; he's not Doug's.

It's time for him to leave, to go back to Marv's house. It's time for him to forget this man's address.

The Babies First offices are closed for President's Day so Brendan meets Cynthia at Good Works. Just two brown middle-aged women work the phones tonight, and Cynthia has stationed them against the wall farthest from her office. She puts down her romance novel when he appears in her doorway. "Right on time," she tells him. "That's why it's gonna work. You're always right on time."

He smiles. When was the last time he showed up for a job anything but late?

She tells him to shut the door. Next, she turns his attention to the short stacks of large manila and white envelopes lying on the floor next to her pressed-wood desk.

He says, "I get it. The white envelopes are cash, the brown checks."

She stands, stretches her arms over her shoulders. "I know you know. We gotta practice opening, sorting, and sealing. You got it? Opening, sorting, and sealing." She tosses a pile of manila and white envelopes at his feet. "Go."

He looks at her, confused. "What?"

"Go!"

He shakes his head as he sits on the threadbare carpet. He rips open a white envelope. Inside is Monopoly money, but just the one, five, ten, twenty, and fifty denominations. He looks up at his sister-in-law, confused. She holds her wrist out in front of her, intent upon her watch. She says, "You're wasting time."

He shoves the Monopoly money to one side, the emptied envelope to the other, and grabs another white one.

Cynthia shouts, "No! No, no, no, no! You put the tens and anything higher in one pile, you put the ones and fives in another, got it?"

He nods.

She drills him for more than an hour, until he can open an envelope with a quick twist, dump the bills, separate the bills into piles of ten and above and five and below. The smaller bills aren't piled up like the larger ones, he shoves these into brand-new unsealed white envelopes, sticking a finger into a bottle of water before he runs it along the envelopes' glue lines, finally pressing them closed. Once she's satisfied that he can open, sort, and seal, she hands him a pen, instructs him to sign all the envelopes full of Monopoly one- and five-dollar bills along their flaps. Each envelope must be signed twice.

He asks, "You want me to sign my name twice on each envelope?"

She purses her thick lips, then relaxes them. Slowly, deliberately she tells him, "No. Not *your* name. Made-up names. There'll be over a hundred volunteers working the registration tables. Just come up with about twenty pairs of names. Then practice signing them so each signature is unique and consistent. That should establish a pattern that'll make them trust your envelopes."

"You're kidding me."

"A name. Come up with a name."

He stammers out, "Alex Supertramp."

"What the fuck kinda name is that? Come on! A name. A Christian, Minnesota name!"

He fumbles with the pen, asks, "Anderson?"

"Good. What's the first name?"

"Erik?"

"Yes, it is!"

And so it goes, Brendan shouting out names for Cynthia to approve or veto. By the end of their time together she's still a bit concerned about how long it takes him to open, sort, and seal, but overall she's encouraged. All he needs to do is pay closer attention and become confident with the plan. She wants to run through the drill again, but he politely refuses. He wants to see Marv before visiting hours are over.

Circumstance has no value. It is how one relates *to a situation that has* value.

He sighs; these are Alex Supertramp's own words, reprinted in *Into the Wild*. He closes the book as he pulls the cord over his head to illuminate the STOP REQUESTED sign that's bolted above the bus's windshield. He tries to think of Christian Minnesota names as he stands.

He's the only passenger to exit, his stop the massive intersection of Northstar Presbyterian, a Super America convenience store, and two older houses, their deferred maintenance on display for the whole world to see. The nursing home's parking lot is nearly empty, and the front entrance glows in the dark like a nightlight, offering a bright trail for his feet to follow.

The temperature soars as he enters the building and his ears fill with bland, innocuous orchestral arrangements of old standards, tunes like "Bewitched, Bothered, and Bewildered" and "I Don't Stand a Ghost of a Chance with You." He recognizes the prelude to "Kalamazoo" as he steps in the elevator.

When he exits the car's open doors, he sings softly to himself, *Kala-ma-zoo-zoo-zoo. . . .* He hums the rest of the song as he heads to Marv's room, but then he frowns, the door is shut tight. He knocks tentatively.

A woman shouts, "Come on in, I'm just getting him cleaned up."

There's something familiar about her voice. He opens the door and that's when he sees her, Cynthia's mother, stooped over Marv, a sterile wipe in her hand. She turns and smiles, but then she frowns. She knows she knows him, but can't quite place him. "Have we met?"

He's barely able to say, "Yes, I come here often."

She tosses the wipe in the trashcan, carefully removes her latex gloves. "No, I haven't seen you round here before. But I know I've seen you."

"I guess I just have one of those faces," he says quietly, bowing his head.

She mumbles, "Now this is gonna drive me crazy. Where do I know you from? You ever been to Chicago?"

"No, ma'am."

She smiles easily, says, "I'll check in on you again in a bit, Mr. Fletcher." She winks at Brendan as she leaves. "You just give me time, I never forget a face."

He almost asks Marv if she always works this shift, before he remembers that Marv can't speak, may not even have any idea who Brendan is. So she remembers him from when he helped Cynthia move, so what? He doesn't recall Cynthia mentioning he was her brother-in-law. She didn't, did she?

He says to Marv, "How are you today?"

The old man says, "Fwahni . . . whuh . . . Fwahni . . ." A tear forms at the corner of his good eye, but it doesn't roll down his cheek, it just lies there, like a stagnant pond.

Brendan takes his good hand, holds it. "Marv, it's going to be alright. Shall we read some more *Harry Potter?*"

Another sound, like the whine of a puppy.

He squeezes Marv's hand gently, places it back on the bed. "It's going to be alright."

Marv closes his eyes, drifts off to sleep, something Brendan won't be able to do himself tonight.

Brendan turns on the television set that's mounted to the wall, muting it so as not to disturb Marv, and hits the UP and DOWN buttons on the remote control. He stops at a channel that broadcasts soap operas at night: a handsome young man is visiting another handsome young man who is behind bars; their expressions are solemn, sober. He recalls his own first visit to see Ian at Rush City.

Jeff was not well pleased by the news that Brendan had found his brother Ian after so many years—well, not by the news that he'd found him, rather by the details of *how* he'd found him, *where* he'd found him. Jeff had initially been curious about Brendan's family: his numerous sets of parents (biological, foster, adoptive) and his two older brothers, both among the missing when he had first met him. But the more Brendan talked about them, the less Jeff wanted to hear. His father's and mother's crimes shocked Jeff, their odd personal lives (here he's referring to his adoptive parents) upset Jeff. It could have only made him wonder in what ways Brendan had been tainted by their influence.

Looking back, he thinks that Jeff was so patient with him out of some sense of guilt. Jeff's own family was unremarkable: parents divorced but friendly, sisters, a brother, in-laws, nieces, and nephews. He'd watch them at the birthday parties and the holiday dinners, amiable, at ease. Their banter came naturally from years spent together, witnesses to each other's successes and failures, the little humiliations and triumphs. Their complete confidence that their group was in fact a family impressed Brendan, the way you might be impressed when an acquaintance reveals a fluency in a foreign language.

Jeff's younger sister, Debbie, was the only one who publicly hinted at what the rest of the family privately thought. Her digs were subtle but they provided him with enough information to know that while the parents resented his gender, the siblings resented him. The complete absence of a family in his own life was at first intriguing: they embraced him, but to console, not to welcome. The comfort they offered was that of a volunteer who had strictly budgeted just one hour per week for good deeds. When he didn't move on after a few months, and then after a few years, the climate changed considerably. His presence among them was no longer a tribute to their tolerance; he was now the lunatic on the bus, the man who mutters to himself while the other passengers pretend not to hear, praying he'll get off at the next stop. Increasingly, Jeff attended his family's functions alone, leaving him with his books.

Jeff had cringed at the news of Ian, his brother's incarceration confirmation of all that Jeff's own family had feared. Jeff had asked: *What did he do?*

Brendan answered: *Talked some senior citizens out of their life savings.*

What else? (Jeff was not stupid.)

I don't know all the details.

Jeff sat him down and held Brendan's hands in his own. He asked Brendan to think, to really think hard, about re-establishing contact with Ian after so many years spent apart. They had known each other as children, now they were adults, people on radically different paths. But Brendan thought then—as he does today—that their paths, Ian's and his own, having drifted apart, were now coming together for a reason. There was some larger purpose to their reunification, one that Jeff, never separated from his own brother and sisters, would never understand.

I'm going to meet him. I'd like you to come with me.

Jeff prepared for the little trip solemnly, as if they were on their way to a funeral. On the drive out Jeff cautioned him not to expect much, telling him that reunions were precarious things. Now he understands that the true purpose of their visit to Rush City that day was to cure him of his curiosity. Afterward, satisfied, he was to return to their home and finally get on with his life.

But seeing his brother failed to have the desired effect. As soon as his eyes met Ian's, something like an electroshock reverberated through his brain and he remembered, with uncompromising clarity, the look on his brother's face when they were separated that day, so many years before. It was the same expression, identical down to the smallest detail: a quiet, childish terror of what lay ahead of them. He thought their reunion a gift, a second chance, an opportunity to set right the wrong that had been done to them, all of them, Steven, Ian, and himself.

Jeff excused himself from further visits, as Brendan had done with Jeff's family. It may have been Ian's size—pumped larger than life from the hours he spent in the prison's weight room—that intimidated Jeff.

Perhaps it was Ian's striking resemblance to his lover. But Brendan suspects it was Ian's manner, the tone of his voice, that lilt of privilege without the money or freedom to back it up. Ian didn't comment on Jeff's absences and Brendan preferred to meet his brother alone. He was free to ask about their parents, their brother, Steven. Ian told him what he could: after their mother had served her brief sentence she regretted terminating her rights; she wanted her children back. Unable to find Brendan because his adoption had been sealed, she fought for his brothers. Her hair, once long and deep-maple in color, was now a short shock of gray, and Ian hadn't recognized her at first during their supervised visits. When she lost her battle for custody she moved on. To where, Ian couldn't say.

His father was dead, the victim of a heart attack that struck as he sat on the toilet in his cell.

But for Brendan, their older brother, Steven, was the most heartbreaking of the three. Before Steven disappeared, he left Ian a note that simply said, *I'm sorry.* Along with that final message was some cash, singles mostly, but there had also been a five-dollar bill in the small stack. It was Steven's good-bye: he ran away from the foster home as Ian slept. This final separation was too much for Ian and it led him, in time, to Rush City.

It occurs to Brendan that most people lead such easy lives and they don't even realize it. They believe that they've had challenges, obstacles, but really what they've experienced are manageable little inconveniences masquerading as tragedies. Tragedies they will speak of for years to come.

He looks at Marv, asleep in the white bed.

He wonders what little inconveniences visit Marv in the night.

Cynthia has picked him up in her new used van. They're parked in a lot along the Mississippi River, just behind a liquor store. When there's a Vikings game at the dome the lot is sold out, but today it's just him, Cynthia, and her secondhand Plymouth Voyager. The engine idles as they switch seats: he's on the driver's side and she, cigarette in mouth, is next to him on the passenger's side.

He's familiarizing himself with the gears, the clutch, the accelerator, and the brake. It's a lot to take in and he wishes that the van had an automatic instead of a standard transmission. Cynthia says very slowly, "Make sure you got it all the way in gear."

He gives the stick a little push. "It's in."

She takes a fast drag, like she's knocking back a shot of cheap whisky to give her strength. "Very slowly, take your right foot off the brake—that's the pedal in the middle . . . and ease your right foot onto the accelerator the same time you ease your left foot off the clutch. You gotta do it just right."

He does as she says. The van pulls ahead hard, maybe a few feet, before it stalls out. He shouts, "Jesus!"

Cynthia's not rattled. She says, "I taught my grandmother how to drive a car when she was sixty, so I can teach you. It just takes time. Chill, you're doing fine."

"This is really confusing with all these pedals and gears and the stick and everything."

"It's cool, it's cool, relax. Now, here's what I want you to do. Put the stick into the center, that's neutral. Put your left foot back on the clutch, that's the pedal on the left, and put your right foot on the brake, that's the pedal in the middle, and turn the key to start the ignition."

He follows her instructions and the engine turns over. She blows smoke out her window and into the unseasonably warm air, says, "Try putting it in first gear again."

The van thrusts ahead quickly, nearly shoving their heads into the dashboard and steering wheel before it stalls out again.

He's embarrassed, and getting angry. Cynthia doesn't help matters when she asks him, "You gotta learn to drive if the plan is to work. Didn't the folks who adopted you teach you how to drive?"

He looks out the windshield to the oak and sumac trees and patches of dirty snow and ice hiding in the shadows on the bank across the river. "My adoptive father taught me how to drive an automatic, but I never got my license."

"Why not?"

"I never earned enough points."

She frowns. "What do you mean?"

"He was a psychologist, so was his wife. They had a point system to try and make me follow their rules. The points were like currency—the more I earned, the more privileges I'd get. Or I could exchange them for candy or books or save them up for things like a basketball hoop. It worked fairly well for the first few years."

"Then what happened?"

"I don't know." He looks over at her and her eyes are sympathetic, encouraging. "I guess I just wanted what I wanted when I wanted it. That's how my adoptive mother put it. By the time I moved out I had accumulated a point deficit I'd never be able to pay off."

"You ever see them?"

He thinks about the face buried in a hat and scarf, the leash in a gloved hand. "No. I haven't seen them in years."

"Do you miss them?"

"No. When they weren't analyzing me they were analyzing each other."

She crinkles her nose as if analysis were some pagan ritual practiced only by savages. She says, "Let's try again. Left foot on the clutch."

This time they make it maybe twenty yards before he stalls them out again, but it's a rush and Cynthia's so excited she's laughing. He scans his memory for any instance he can recall of seeing her as she looks now, happy.

It takes nearly two hours, but he's successfully driven the van in first gear, second gear, and third gear. Fourth gear, Cynthia tells him, is for the highway. He reaches over and hugs her and she lets him.

"Are we going to drive all the way down to Mexico?" he asks her.

"Sure, why not?"

He's on the bus to Rush City for the last time. Today's the day he and Cynthia have been waiting for, the day Ian's released. Cynthia's busy preparing the little apartment that she and her husband will share, a dilapidated place carved out of an old mansion that now finds itself next to a freeway. He'll escort Ian to its front door; leave husband and wife to privately conduct their reunion in their own way. Ian, dressed in blue jeans and a button-down shirt, is, of course, expecting him. Ian looks him in the eye, proud, ecstatic, waiting for the moment Brendan says, "Let's get out of here."

As Ian walks out the doors he becomes emotional. The worst days of his life, or at least what Brendan imagines must have been the worst days of his brother's life, are behind him now. Ian shudders in the cool breeze that shakes the bare branches of the trees back and forth above their heads. They enter a world in which they are both free men for the first time in their relationship as adults. Soon, they'll have the fresh start they need, deserve, and the possibilities that presents make Brendan feel drunk.

They ride the bus together, side by side, heading back to Minneapolis, the city that had sentenced Ian; the news of which, carried in the Metro section of the daily paper, had served to reunite the brothers. All around them are the wives, the girlfriends, and the children of the men they've left behind. Brendan wishes that the little boy whose daddy had killed a communist was on board with his mother; he wants to tell him that one day his father will take the bus back home with him, just as Brendan's brother's doing with him today. Brendan sits back, relaxes, and enjoys the best ride he's been offered in very long time: a family, and soon, enough cash for all of them to start over again, somewhere new.

When they arrive in Ian's new neighborhood, Ian's elated, the prospect of Cynthia's skin almost too much for him to bear. They walk together, arms and legs in sync. The people in the cars that drive by can see them, the two of them together, brothers out for a walk on a warm late winter day, living their ordinary lives. They pass unremarkable houses, ordinary apartment buildings, an anonymous storefront, inside of which checks can be cashed twenty-four hours a day, seven days a week, including holidays. They never close. All of these things—these mundane structures, these everyday sights and sounds—are remarkable to Ian, as if seen for the first time. As Brendan leaves his brother on the front steps of Ian's new home, Ian hugs him, hard. Ian whispers, "I love you . . . Brendan. You've been more than a brother to me and I'll never forget it."

Ian's embrace feels like an old, favorite blanket, soft and worn. It's the warmth of the fireplace, their fireplace, glowing softly as they, Ian, Steven, and Brendan, stared at the lights on the Christmas tree, holding their breaths, waiting for Santa to appear.

After Gail buzzes him into Babies First she winks, says, "Well, look at you, I swear you're glowing! Don't tell me you've met someone?"

Brendan blushes, recalling his one-nighter with Doug. "Of course not."

Now she turns red, too. "Oh, I'm sorry. Of course, it's probably much too soon."

Upstairs, the gals say, nearly in unison, "Well, look who's here!"

He says, "Yes, it's me you lucky, lucky devils."

They titter, charmed by his brazenness.

In no time at all, Ann comes to his table, deposits her bundles. He asks her, "Did you get here early? That's a lot of mail you assembled."

Ann smiles, "I came by on my lunch break. All they talk about at my office are stock prices and tax deductions. I wanted to do something important."

"Good for you."

Ann lingers, says, "I was so sorry to hear about your wife. I mean, I knew that she was in heaven, but I didn't know *how* she had passed on."

As Cynthia had predicted, the story he shared with just one gal, Judy—that Laura had died during a miscarriage—has spread through the ranks. He lowers his head, says, "I'd rather not talk about that."

Ann stammers, "Oh, no, oh, of course not! I'm sorry, that was thoughtless of me."

"It's okay," he tells her.

Ann blushes, slaps herself on the wrist. "Stupid!" Now she whispers hoarsely, "Stupid, stupid, stupid!" as she slaps herself again and again.

"Really, it's no big deal. Please."

Her eyes mist as she says, "I'm so sorry."

Gals glance their direction, wondering what's wrong. He recalls Cynthia's directive: that he had to make them trust him completely. He says to Ann, "Hey, it's not talking about Laura that bothers me; it's talking about how she died. I'm happy to talk about Laura. Would you like to see a picture?"

Ann nods shyly.

He stands up, takes out his wallet, flips it open. There, where a driver's license should be, is a black-and-white photograph of a young woman, perhaps in her late twenties. She's dressed in a high-neck blouse, her hair pulled back, save a few stands that fall over her ears. The soft lips are pursed, in a self-effacing smile. She is his mother, and this picture has always been in his wallet, from the time he first carried one. It was his mother's favorite photo of herself and she had dozens of copies made.

Ann says, "Oh, she was beautiful."

"Wasn't she? I still miss her."

Ann places a hand on his arm, says, "You'll be together in heaven."

Gals strain their necks for a peek.

He says, "It's okay, I don't mind."

The wallet is passed from gal to gal and he hears the soft murmurs, *Isn't she a beauty?* and *What a lovely face.* One gal says, "Isn't it funny how couples look alike? They could be brother and sister." Another gal offers that a black-and-white portrait shows a lot more class than a color one, his wife must have had exquisite taste. The oldest gal, her face heavy with wrinkles, who seems to volunteer more from habit than conviction, smiles warmly at the image he carries, and asks innocently, "What was she like?"

He searches his memory. He sees her in the kitchen during the early-morning hours, squeezing oranges for his father's breakfast. Now she gives Steven, her oldest, a light tap on the back of his head as she laughs at something he did, something wrong, but funny. He hears her English accent, that leisurely voice that so often ended her statements with brief questions, things like *Isn't it?* and *Shouldn't we?* and *Have you?*

He sees her dropping her cup and saucer onto the white carpet.

He says, "She was like nobody else."

His wallet's returned to his pocket and he resumes his duties, placing bound bundles of envelopes into the correct bags. Time passes quickly, the hum of conversation and the sugar from the sweet bars fuel the work. Letters are assembled, sorted, tagged, and bagged.

Three of the gals—Judy, Ann, and one he doesn't recognize—invite him to sit at their table. They're flushed with excitement; something's up. He joins them, politely refusing Ann's offer of another bar, he's already eaten four in less than an hour, two of them just to be polite.

Judy says, "We're going on an action!"

He smiles, confused.

Judy repeats: "An action! A clinic action. We'd love for you to join us."

They wear the giddy looks of people attending a surprise party, the ones who can't wait to jump out from behind a chair or a sofa when the guest of honor arrives. Their invitation is clearly a mark of distinction, he's been deemed worthy.

He hesitates, and they assume it's because he's overcome by their generosity. He says, "I'm not too keen on the idea of getting arrested."

Ann says, "Oh, but it's civil disobedience. I mean, it's illegal, but it's not like robbing a bank or something."

"Let me think about it. Where and when is this action?"

Judy says, "We don't know yet. We get a call and off we go, it's a phone-tree deal."

"Let me think about it."

And he leaves them, confused, disappointed. They had offered to teach him the secret handshake and he had to think about it. Sometimes he wonders what it is that people see when they look at him. He should be pleased that he can pass for a pro-life fanatic; it is, after all, a requirement of Cynthia's plan. But just the same, the ease with which they take him for one of their own is disturbing.

For the rest of evening, he gets beseeching looks whenever he walks by Judy's table. Okay, fine. He'll go on their goddamn action. Jesus, why is nothing easy? And there's still nearly months to go before the Walk.

He takes a seat next to Judy. "I'd like to join you on the action, if you'll still have me."

The gal he doesn't know sniffs and says, "I thought you had to think about it."

He smiles softly at her. "It's just that I'm not sure Laura would have approved. She never took part in any actions herself."

The name of his beloved dead wife shames them, as he hoped.

The power shifted, Ann reaches for his arm and says, "Of course, if you don't want to, that's perfectly alright."

"Yes, yes," Judy and the other woman echo, embarrassed by their thoughtlessness.

But he's a true believer, he will go on their action.

Saturday afternoons are quiet. Ian and Cynthia prefer to keep their own company on Saturdays; Sundays the three of them spend together, for dinner and to go over, yet again, the plan for the Walk, now simply called *the plan*.

Saturdays are his favorite time of the week, spent reading in Marv's den. It's the sheer luxury of it—not just the book but the setting in which he reads it: the room's adorned with rich wood paneling, furnished with a large, powerful chair that could comfortably seat two. This is a sanctuary of a sort, a place where the outside world ceases to exist, the only reality a story told in the pages of book. He stares at the picture of Alex Supertramp on the inside cover of *Into the Wild*. Supertramp sits, his back against an abandoned Fairbanks City Transit System bus, his expression content, satisfied, although "satisfied" seems too weak a word for it. Brendan imagines himself behind the camera, imagines that he's the reason Supertramp smiles as his ankle rests on a knee, his neck itchy from the whiskers of his beard. Brendan sees the two of them reading their books in the Alaskan wilderness, stopping only when Alex says *listen*, and they hear again the cry of a wolf.

An awareness comes over Brendan like a gentle breeze. There's a soft noise, not unpleasant, familiar. The sound of a key in a lock.

He drops the book.

He stands.

Now the click of a bolt as it retracts into the door's frame.

He didn't latch the door. *Goddamn it, he did not latch the fucking door!*

Hinges creak, the door opens. Slow, tentative steps.

He can't move.

He cannot move.

He can't breathe.

A voice, female, calls, "Dad? *Hello?* Dad, are you home? I've been trying to get a hold of you for forever. *Dad?* Hello?"

He cannot make his feet move. They will not move.

The stranger makes her way to the kitchen, where he hears the jingle of keys and the crinkle of a grocery bag as they're placed on a countertop.

Now the sounds of a coat being slipped off, a bag being unpacked, long moments of silent indecision as the cabinets and drawers are surveyed. Hard steps, the *click-clack* of heels, and then cabinet doors open and close, the refrigerator hums louder as items are placed on its shelves.

She finishes, folds the bag. She's talking to herself as she walks down the hall, toward the room in which he stands, helpless. She asks herself questions beginning with *where* and *what*. She nearly walks past him when she makes out his form from out of the corner of her eye.

She stops abruptly, clutches her chest. "Oh my God!"

They look at each other, stunned.

She says, gasping, "I'm sorry, I didn't see you there. Oh my God."

He tries to smile at her.

She recovers, joins him in the den, where they stand facing each other. There's no fear in her eyes; just embarrassment at being caught so totally and completely off guard. She holds out a hand, says, "I'm Kate. You must be Frankie."

He places his hand in hers. A gentle, friendly shake. "Hello."

She laughs, apologetically. "Hope I didn't scare you half as badly as I scared myself!"

"Well, actually, you did. I wasn't expecting you."

She sighs, folds her arms across her chest. "No, I don't imagine you were."

"You have a key?"

She winks. "Dad always puts a spare in the flowerpot. If he knew I knew, he'd stop doing it. Frankly, I wasn't expecting to find anyone home. I would have called and let you know I was coming, but no one ever picks up the phone in this place! I don't even bother leaving messages anymore."

"Marv asked me not to answer the phone, he likes to screen his calls."

"Well, that's my father for you." She looks toward the hallway with a mild hope mixed with a quiet dread. "I don't suppose he's around."

"No, he left this morning. He didn't tell me where he was going."

"Doesn't it drive you crazy? And then, when you worry, he just gets mad."

Brendan laughs softly, the way someone would laugh if he knew what made Marv mad. He says, "He has his own way of doing things, I guess." To end this conversation and get her out of the house, he offers her a little bit of hospitality to refuse. "Would you like something to drink? I could put coffee on, or maybe some tea?"

She doesn't take the hint. "A cup of tea if you don't mind. Don't bother, I'll make it. Will you join me?"

Shit! Shit, shit, shit.

He follows her back to the kitchen, which he gathers is vaguely familiar to her. Her clothes are expensive and do their best to conceal her middle-age spread. The gray she does not color springs out sporadically from her dark hair. She has a look about her, or perhaps it would be better to call it a way about her: an amicable, subdued resignation, a world-weariness much more forgiving and friendly than his own. As the flames lap the kettle, she picks out matching mugs. She plucks the tea bags out of their envelopes, drops them in the cups. She says, "Well, I suppose you're wondering what I'm doing here."

"Belated birthday visit?" His words sting her; he'd only wanted to show her that he was familiar enough with her father's life to know the date of his birth, as Frankie would.

She says, "No. Just visiting an old friend from high school." She adds for emphasis: "She was just diagnosed with breast cancer."

He shakes his head in sympathy.

"Anyway, I thought, since I was in town, I'd take Dad out to eat, catch up a little. Oh, and please, I'm not waiting for an invitation to stay here, I'm at the Whitney. I'm much more comfortable when Dad and I are under separate roofs. But then, I suppose he's told you all about me."

Now, he can tell her the truth. "He hasn't said a word about any of you. There are no pictures anywhere. It made me wonder."

She ages in front of him, her face sinking in on itself, the competent and dutiful grown-up daughter replaced by a somewhat lonely and slightly bitter old lady. But she recovers quickly and he sees again the capable woman, neither particularly young nor particularly old, just arrived to comfort an old friend. She says, "It was just a vain little hope. In case you haven't noticed, the man knows how to hold a grudge."

The kettle rumbles softly. "I have noticed. He's still mad at me for something I did a while ago."

"He's letting you off easy."

"Why is he angry at you?"

She folds her arms again across her broad chest, leans an ample hip against a countertop. She's as desperate for information about her father as he is for information about his children. They begin to trade their commodities cautiously, carefully measuring words like the ingredients of a recipe that's far too ambitious for their marginal skills. She chooses a chatty, casual tone as she begins their exchange, saying, "Boy, he *has* left you in the dark. Truth be told, we didn't react well at first. You have this idea in your head about who your parents are, and then one day . . . Well, let's leave it at that, we didn't react well. At first. He really never mentions us?"

He's allowed more honesty: "Never."

She shrugs. "Stubborn old mule. How is he?"

He tries his best to construct a life for Marv outside the nursing home. "Okay, I guess. It's hard to tell sometimes. He seems happy. He's active with the General Mills retirees."

Her eyebrows rise. "Really?"

"That's what he says."

"He used to say the same thing to my mother. It was during one of their 'meetings' he was arrested in a park."

"Oh."

The simmering stops, the water comes to a boil. With an efficient little flick of her wrist she switches the burner off, lifts the kettle breezily. She pours the steaming water as a housewife would for a neighbor; there's no ceremony, none of the ritualism he imagines women of a certain class employ as they fill the cups of their luncheon guests. She says, in her neighborly tone, "I can't believe I just told you that. Forgive me. It happened long before you arrived on the scene. Now that's he's with a man, I bet you bottom dollar that he's actually going to those damn meetings of his."

He offers another small piece of truth: "He never mentions your mother, either."

She dunks the teabags in the mugs over and over, a sign, he hopes, that she's now as anxious to leave as he is for her to go. "It was an ugly divorce, as you can imagine."

He nods.

She looks at him, meaningfully. "You know, this was a bad idea." She lets go of the teabags' little tags and rubs her eyes, perhaps she wants to cancel this meeting, reschedule at a more convenient time. She says, "It's just never been easy with him. I know you love him, but Christ almighty, it's just never been easy with him. I wish he'd forgive us."

He cues her exit. "He will. One day."

She ignores the prompt, laughs. "It better be one day soon, he's no spring chicken. It'd be hard to try and reconcile with a corpse." She stops, looks at him. "I'm so sorry. I have no idea why I'm saying these things to you. I must be angrier than I thought."

"It's okay."

She hands him a cup, grateful for something to do, she's a woman who can do things: shop for her estranged father, unload groceries in the kitchen of her estranged father, hand a steaming cup of hot tea to a stranger who nearly killed her estranged father. She says, "Here, drink it."

"Thanks," he whispers as he blows on the tea, the scent of orange and spice filling his nostrils. His senses are on high alert, searching for anything—a piece of furniture out of place, some incriminating bit of evidence out in the open—that might tip her off that something is wrong, very wrong, in the home of her estranged father.

She contemplates her mug absently; her impulse to leave has itself gone, vanquished by orange spice. She says, "Do you mind if I ask you a blunt question?"

Saying yes would be bad manners, and besides, she'll ask anyway. "Of course not."

"Why are you with him?"

There's really only one possible explanation she'd believe: *Because he has money.* He says, "Do you want to go for a walk around the lake? It's a beautiful day outside."

She nods, embarrassed—or perhaps she only pretends to be embarrassed—by her boldness. Disappointed, she puts her mug on the counter, another task left incomplete, something else she cannot check off of today's to-do list: *Have tea with the boy toy of your estranged father.*

For today, light jackets will suffice. The temperatures produced by global warming provide Minnesota with a March that feels more like late spring than late winter. The joggers are out in force, along with a parade of other people who walk hand in hand or with babies in strollers or dogs on leashes. He so badly wants a dog. Once this is over, he's going to buy an entire litter of mutts and he'll let them sleep on the bed with him. They'll curl up, eyes and legs twitching as they dream, while he turns a page in one of his books.

After a few hundred silent yards, Marv's daughter says, "I apologize, it was rude of me to ask you that."

"No offense taken."

At the sight of a bench she says, "Do you mind if we sit down for a minute? This is the most walking I've done in I don't know how long."

They sit and she prepares to ask her question again, but presented differently. He pre-empts her: "Marv's not a bad man. He's been very kind to me, and yes, very generous. He offered me some stability in my life when I really needed it."

She stares out at the lake, already alive with geese. "How do you mean?"

And here's where he stops: she may know something about Frankie that he doesn't; confessing to the wrong crime would be disastrous. He says assertively, but not unkindly, "That's between Marv and me."

She says assertively, but not unkindly, "I see." Then she says, "I'm glad we had this chance to chat, Frankie. My brother, sister, and I have been curious about you. We only found out about you by accident, our father slipped up, he never meant to mention you to any of us. If it were up to him, we still wouldn't know you exist."

"Likewise."

At this she laughs softly. She turns her gaze from the water to him. She says, "In the spirit of avoiding any unpleasantness down the road, I'll just put it out there—we're hoping that there won't be any surprises in the will."

An attractive young man walks by, showing off his build in clothes too revealing for the brisk air. Brendan admires him as he considers what Marv's daughter has just said. He's looking for a response that will satisfy her and prevent any more impromptu visits. He says, "Well, you can tell your brother and sister they've got nothing to worry about. All I'm getting is the Oldsmobile."

She smiles sadly, grateful that he's sensitive to the little drama that is their family. His friend now, she says, "I just thought we should clear the air. I'm glad you understand."

Understanding could be mistaken for hospitality, and he can't afford to have her think of herself as a welcome guest. He smiles back at her, saying, "Of course I don't understand. You want the man your father loves to be left with nothing, while you and your siblings take it all. Well, don't concern yourself, I'll be moving out soon anyway, getting a place of my own."

"I only meant—"

He stands up. "I'll be gone by June. I'd appreciate it if you'd just leave us both the hell alone until then."

He leaves her there, fuming on the park bench, appalled that someone like him thought enough of himself to be offended by something she said. That's the way rich people are: their sense of superiority is only a bit sharper than their sense of entitlement.

He walks back to the Dutch Colonial knowing that he well could have been just like her.

He was born rich, really rich, and had a nanny until he was six years old. Even though his parents' money was—as his mother used to say— *new* (but then she would giggle, saying that everything in Minnesota is new), he was accepted into a prestigious private school and won the state grammar Olympics for his age group when he was seven. That was the same year he discovered just how new his mother and father's money really was: they were arrested and sentenced for embezzling millions of dollars from their clients, Minnesotans of Yankee stock who were charmed by his father's English accent and willingly handed over their large portfolios for him to manage.

The county sheriff took everything his parents had, including Steven, Ian, and him. He wound up in foster care, living with three sets of parents until he was adopted at the age of thirteen by a couple who thought they could mold him into a fine young man. His adoptive parents, well into their fifties, couldn't conceive, and Brendan was the youngest Caucasian without a disability available at the time. He doesn't know where Steven ended up. The last time he saw Steven was shortly after their mother and father terminated their parental rights during a jailhouse divorce. Steven and Ian were being re-assigned to a new foster home when Brendan was moved to his adoptive parents' house.

He stops in front of Marv's house. If things had turned out differently, he well could have been like her.

They're canvassing the Walk route, handing out flyers and asking homeowners and shopkeepers to display their sign that reads *ABORTION STOPS THE BEATING OF AN INNOCENT HEART* for the Walk, even though it isn't for another eleven weeks. In ten weeks they will canvass the Walk route a second time in the hope that some homes have changed hands; that some pro-abortionists will have left, replaced by pro-lifers. The responses they get range from confusion to hostility, and only once in a great while does anyone agree to take a sign.

One of the homes on his route flies a rainbow flag. He should pass it by, head to the next one, but he rings the doorbell. Ferocious barking erupts from the other side of the door, as if the dog had spied him approaching and waited until the exact moment he pushed the bell's button to make its presence known.

A man opens the door while attempting to calm the dog down, a mutt that looks like a cross between a German shepherd and a dingo. The man looks forty, or maybe older, not particularly attractive or particularly unattractive, and Brendan is surprised to find himself fighting the urge to put his arms around him, to hold him tight.

The man says, in between shushing his dog, "No soliciting."

Brendan stares directly into the man's droopy eyes with the shallow crow's-feet on either side, like quotation marks. There's a challenging and flirtatious look on Brendan's face that they both seem to question. Brendan says, "I'm not selling anything, sir. Nice dog." He tells himself he needs the diversion, needs to break up the tedium of knocking on the doors of heterosexuals just to have them slam shut on him.

A flicker of interest from the man before he looks down at the dog.

"Don't worry, she just wants a sniff," he says as he releases her. The barking has stopped; she places her nose between Brendan's legs, a canine handshake. The owner says, "How can I help you?"

"I'm with Babies First. Our annual Walk for the Unborn is—"

The man looks back up, a betrayed expression on his pale face. "I know all about your goddamned Walk, you people parade up and down our street every year, like you own the place. Do this neighborhood a favor and go somewhere else." He grabs the doorknob.

"Hey, wait! Wait a sec."

"What?"

Brendan shrugs as he says, "Look, I'm just doing this as a favor for my sister. She's been letting me stay with her since I broke up with my partner."

The word *partner* gets the man's attention. He lets down his guard, says, "Well, I'm still not going to let you put up one of those signs."

Brendan winks at him. "No, of course not. I'd be disappointed if you did."

The man is trying to think of something to say, but nothing comes.

Brendan blurts out the first name that pops into his head. "My name's Pierre. Pierre Bezukhov." The man's sleepy eyes widen at the exotic name. Realizing his mistake, Brendan adds, "Immigrant parents."

Uncertainly, the man holds out his hand. "Sean Reilly. And this," he says, pointing at the dog, "is Maggie."

Brendan takes Sean's hand in his own. Sean's hand feels strong, in contrast to his chin, which is weak. Brendan holds the hand tightly at first, then he glides his fingertips over the palm as he slowly releases his grip. Sean blushes as he says, "Very nice to meet you, Pierre."

Brendan says, "The pleasure's entirely mine, Sean."

He commits Sean's address to memory and leaves him standing in the doorway with his dog.

5

War and Peace

" 'A TALL, BLACK-HAIRED WITCH *in emerald-green robes stood there. She had a very stern face and Harry's first thought was that this was not someone to cross,*' " Brendan reads aloud.

Marv croaks a little, and Brendan imagines him making comparisons between the nurses and the black-haired witch. Brendan smiles at Marv, asks, "Does she remind you of anyone in particular?"

Cynthia's mother enters the room, a plastic basin of hot water in her hands. By way of hello she says, "You shouldn't be reading that to him. The occult displeases God."

He looks at Marv. "He seems to be enjoying it."

She shakes her head disapprovingly. "It's pagan nonsense, and displeasing to God." She nods toward Marv. "Bring him up a little for me, he needs his shave."

Brendan presses a button and the frame hums as it raises Marv's head and shoulders. Cynthia's mother says, "I finally remembered who you are. You helped my baby move out."

He considers denying it, telling her she has him confused with someone else, but instead he says, "You kicked her out."

She pulls a towel out of the closet and gently positions it around
Marv's neck, making sure it's snug enough to catch any stray water. He
thinks of a young girl dressing a doll. He gets up, leans against a wall to
give her room to work. Cynthia's mother says, "She had marijuana under my roof. Have you seen her? Is she still doing drugs?"

"She's fine."

She squints her eyes at him and then she heads to the bathroom.
Her voice echoes against the tiles as she asks loudly, "Did you sell her
those drugs I found?"

"No, ma'am." He looks at Marv, and in case the old man understands, tells him, "Don't worry, I'm not a stoner."

She returns, holding a razor and cream in her hands like a knife and
fork. "How do you know my baby?"

He tells her a version of the truth: "We work together."

She considers this bit of news as she dampens a washcloth in the
basin, creating tiny waves that ripple in all directions. She smoothes
the cloth over Marv's face, saying, "You let me know if that's too hot for
you, Mr. Fletcher." She lathers him and works the razor efficiently, with
quick, smooth strokes. She talks to him as she goes about her task, saying, "The state of this world, all the drugs turning good people bad. So
much suffering, so much evil."

She rinses the razor in the water and begins work on his neck. Now
she moves slowly, cautiously; she's a painter with a brush, a fat old
stroke victim her canvas. "But you know, in spite of all this wickedness,
there's a wonderful future in store for us. One day, this earth will be a
paradise. The lion will lie down with the lamb."

It takes Brendan a moment to understand what she is saying.
"You're witnessing?"

She dips the washcloth in the water, dabs the small puffs of shaving
cream left here and there on Marv's face. She doesn't bother to look at
Brendan when she says, "I think it's a great comfort to him to know of
the everlasting life to come for believers."

"Isn't this a Presbyterian home?"

She gently pats Marv's face dry, applies some moisturizer to his skin.

"It'd be a sin to keep this news to myself. Look at him! If anyone needs to know, he does."

Brendan rolls his eyes. "Don't inflict your beliefs on him."

"I'm not inflicting nothing; I'm sharing the good news."

"I'd prefer that you didn't."

She raises her voice an octave. "Who're you? His wife?"

"I'm—"

"I *know* who you are: Franklin Thompson, *domestic partner.*" She says this like a whiny child might. She adds, "I've read Mr. Fletcher's file."

"Do you want me to file a complaint?"

She shakes her head sadly, motions Brendan next to her with her hand. "Come here. Just come here a minute." Brendan stands at Marv's bedside while she looks down at him like he's her baby, pink and fresh, just placed in her arms by a beaming nurse. She says, "Look in his eyes, I mean really look good and hard."

Brendan sees the pupils, large and dark, the empty black space astronomers study. "What am I supposed to see?"

She says tenderly, "Hope. There's always hope. And you want me to take that away from him?"

Here is where Brendan's ended up then, in the little room of a large nursing home, each compartment occupied by the people who can no longer care for themselves and the ones who take care of them. He sees the old man on the bed, defenseless. He says, "Just give the witnessing a rest, all right?"

She refuses to back down. "He needs to learn about biblical principles, to accept them and uphold them."

He watches in silence as she finishes up. With a soft grunt she picks up the basin, takes it to the sink, and pours the foamy water out. Over the sound of water going down a drain, she asks him, "Could you please tell my baby to call me?"

He stares at Marv, who may be listening, who may not be. "Why don't you call her?"

She braces herself against the countertop now, shoulders slumped.

"I leave her messages every day. She won't . . ." Here her voice cracks and she can't finish.

Marv's eyes search the room. Brendan says, "I'll make a deal with you. You promise to call me the second, the absolute second, he says something intelligible, and I promise I'll get Cynthia to give you a call."

She turns, faces him, her arms crossed across her tiny chest. "I guess you must . . . care about him. In your own way. Okay, it's a deal."

"Just as soon as he says a word . . ."

She closes her eyes, nodding.

On a cool Saturday Brendan takes a walk through the neighborhood known as Uptown, past the teenagers hanging out in the streets, past the cafés full of people. He pauses; on the other side of a coffee shop window are two men sharing a table, and the way they sit tells him they're lovers. They don't speak; they read their papers, occasionally lifting their mugs to their lips, their recently kissed lips.

He wonders how they do it. How they find each other, what their contentment feels like. Perhaps it's like an old pair of worn jeans dropped on the floor by the bed at night, slipped back on first thing in the morning. He wants to know again what coffee tastes like when it's served in a shop where he sits with his lover, the Metro section of the paper in his hands. This had been his routine with Jeff. They would sit silently, happily in the beginning, uneasily toward the end. Jeff had become a nag and Brendan preferred him quiet.

Then, that final morning.

We need to talk, Jeff told him.

Brendan sighed, *Your solution to everything.*

Jeff folded his arms across his chest and stood on one leg, which made his hips uneven. He said, *I've asked you and I've asked you to stop visiting Ian.*

Because your family doesn't approve of my jailbird brother.

No, because I don't think he's a good influence on you. He always plays the victim, like he wound up in there by accident. He's making you think you're one, too. You can't live life like a victim. And you know that my family is your family, too.

They never thought I was good enough for you; Ian just proves their point. They don't know how easy they've had it. I'm doing Ian some good, helping him change his life. That's what family is supposed to do, help each other out. If you think he's such a lost cause, what does that say about me?

Then Brendan zipped up his backpack, which contained nothing of his years with Jeff, and said, *You know what? I was just fine before you came along, and I'll be just fine without you. Spare me your speeches and your oh-so-insightful observations about me.*

When Jeff looked at him just then, Brendan saw the circles under Jeff's eyes, no doubt from a night as sleepless as his own. Jeff shook his head.

So this is it? You're going to leave me for him?

Don't be twisted.

I'm your family. Think about that, why don't you?

He looked at Jeff on that morning, their last morning together. Jeff was showing him that he wasn't afraid, that he was willing to push them until they broke, if for no other reason than to prove that he could be just like Brendan. Brendan was nasty, casting Jeff as a snob, apologizing for his own lack of pedigree, pointing out that Jeff hadn't known bad times, had never seen *his* parents driven away in a police car. Jeff knew his sisters and brother; could pick up a phone and call them, have a cup of coffee with them if there was something serious on his mind or, perhaps, something to celebrate. *Where was Brendan's brother Steven?* he asked him. *Where was his own mother?*

And then Brendan walked out.

He keeps walking now, past the impish leprechauns in the shop windows, their dialog balloons telling him to Come On In for the Saving of the Green! until he sees it, the route with its few signs that demand an end to the slaughter of those waiting to be born. Brendan finds the block, then the house.

He rings the doorbell.

"I don't suppose you remember me," Brendan says. Sean stands there, framed by the doorway, wrapped in a terrycloth robe, his hair wet from a shower, his dog, Maggie, barking at Brendan from the backyard. Sean's skin's so pink that Brendan knows he lingered in the hot spray. Maybe Sean does that every morning, Brendan wants to find out.

"You're Pierre," Sean says, as Brendan hoped he would.

The slick strands of thinning hair are pulled back from his face, and the effect is that of a man younger than the one Brendan had first met, a person less on guard. Brendan smiles and says, "Could I buy you a cup of coffee?" What he really wants to ask for is sex, quick, convenient sex, something to distract him from the gals, from Marv, from all of it.

Sean's eyes consider the offer; consider him, as Maggie's barks give way to the whines of one who desperately wants to be included. Sean nods, says, "Give me ten minutes. I'll be right out." He leaves Brendan out on the stoop next to his morning paper because he's a practical man who doesn't invite strangers into his home.

Brendan sits on the chill cement and thinks. There are other things he should be doing today. He should be visiting Marv. He should go check his books, most of them still in their storage locker. He should beg Marv's forgiveness. He should run as far and as fast as he can. There are many other things he should be doing today, he should not be sitting here, outside the home of a man he just met, a man who really could be anyone, anyone at all, a celebrated artist, a homicidal lunatic, the bodies of his victims stuffed in the corners of an attic.

But this is what Brendan chooses to do today.

"Hope I didn't keep you waiting too long," the artist or the lunatic says as he reappears. The glasses Brendan first saw him wearing are back on, and a thick sweater is wrapped tightly around him. He carries an umbrella in case of rain. He looks older again, not as approachable as the man with pink skin and wet hair.

Brendan says, "Not at all."

Sean leads him to a little coffee shop, replete with old, oversized couches and chairs, beat-up and lived-in versions of the furniture carefully situated throughout Marv's house. Copies of the *Utne Reader* and *Native American News* and *Earth First!* and *Mother Jones* are spread throughout the place. A large, impressive portrait of George W. Bush is painted above the exit, a Hitler mustache on his upper lip, and some graffiti on the interior walls tells visitors to *HAIL TO THE DRAFT-DODGING A.W.O.L. CHICKEN HAWK-IN-CHEAT.* On the wall hangs an Irish flag, directly beneath a banner with the handwritten slogan *CELE-BRATE ST. PATRICK'S DAY, REUNITE IRELAND!* Sean asks after Brendan's sister, whose charity Brendan had paid back by canvassing for the Walk for the Unborn. Sean tells Brendan something of his life, sparing any detail, condensing it all down to its most basic elemental units. He's no Jeff; he's no charmer. He's blunt (there was an alcoholic father who drifted from job to job) and his life has not been easy (his partner died of AIDS more than ten years ago). It gives him an edge, not razor sharp, but hardly dull, either. Or maybe he's just been without a lover too long.

Sean doesn't ask much about Brendan's life and Brendan offers the bare minimum: his ex's name (Tony) and his sister's (Natasha).

When they run out of things to say, Sean asks him, "Why'd you come back?"

Brendan's finally managed to fall asleep for a few minutes in Sean's bed, Sean's arms around him, but now he's awoken with a start. He's had the nightmare again. He's met ex-smokers who told him that they often dream of smoking a cigarette. It's an unexceptional dream, nothing bizarre or curious happens, it's just the ex-smoker puffing on a cigarette. But they awaken terrified, convinced that they have lit up again after so long without smoking. Eventually the panic subsides as they realize they've been asleep.

Brendan's dream is the same; it's unremarkable, save the fact that he's back behind the counter at McDonald's.

Nothing unusual happens. He waits at a freezing bus stop in the pre-dawn hours, half awake, half alive. When he's delivered to the restau-rant he nods at an old man, still drunk after a night of cleaning the floors and tables and restrooms. The manager, about his age, not yet twenty years old, says *Good morning.* The manager's a refugee from Southeast Asia and Brendan wants to ask him whether he's Hmong or Laotian or Vietnamese. He's a handsome man and Brendan wonders what he would do if he kissed him as they worked the freezer, unloading boxes of frozen food, thawing it, cooking it, warming it. It's still dark when the manager unlocks the doors and the two of them drink coffee as they wait for the day's first customers. The manager practices his English on Brendan as they serve people not unlike themselves, truck drivers and janitors and nurses' aides in need of calories before another long day. Brendan recognizes some of the breakfast customers and they greet him by his first name, printed on his badge. By rush hour they're busy, and as usual, some of the teens and seniors scheduled to work don't show up for their shifts. They are forever understaffed, forever training in new people, forever trying to track down employees missing in action.

Lunchtime is the worst. The lines are squeezed side by side tightly; they merge, diverge; people scamper from one to the next like cars trying to outrace the rush hour traffic. The lunch shift usually finds him in the kitchen, no longer standing behind a counter with the little register that tells him what to say and when to say it. In the kitchen lights flash, buzzers sound. They think for him so he will not have to think for himself. They are fundamentalists, McDonald's employees, their bible the company operations manual. The answers to all their questions are to be found in this sacred text, divine pronouncements on how to dress, how everything is to be said and done within this temple of the golden arches. The dream always ends when he hears the fryer's buzzer.

Wide awake now, he inhales and exhales deeply, wipes the perspiration from his brow. He rubs his eyes, grateful for the reality of Sean's bed, the covers, the pillows. From her corner of the bed the dog awakens, tilts her head at him in the darkness. Next, Sean opens his eyes. He smiles warmly at Brendan, reaches out a hand to stroke Brendan's thick hair, which is in need of styling. Sean softly asks, "Something wrong?"

Brendan mutters "No. It's okay, go back to sleep."

Sean's hand wanders down Brendan's neck, down his shoulder, to his chest. "You sure?" he asks, fingering a nipple.

Brendan nods and Sean removes his hand as Maggie lays her head back down with a sigh. Brendan concentrates on his breathing, inhaling, counting to three, then exhaling. He tries to occupy his mind with other things, silly things, like the gals' oversized lemon bars or Cynthia's romance novels. But it doesn't work.

The memory always follows the dream.

The day that he quit McDonald's began before sunrise, as usual; the bus was sparsely populated, as usual. During the ride he tried to read a book, but he was too tired. So he closed it and imagined his future self, a man who was settled, gainfully employed, in love. He had recently dropped out of college, unable to keep up with all the course work and that, in turn, led to a severing of relations with his adoptive parents. He thought it a minor setback; for his faith was strong that his real family was out there somewhere, looking for him, waiting for him to find them. And he would find them, the man he loved at his side.

When the bus dropped him off at the corner he looked up and down the deserted streets, wondering where he was, the man he would fall in love with. He was young and certain that the man he would love was asleep somewhere in the city, unaware that Brendan, the one he would spend the rest of his life with, was about to begin another day of dispensing McMuffins and McChickens and McNuggets while wearing a name badge like a dog tag.

Brendan recalls odd things. He remembers that the parking lot was empty, unplowed from the night's snowfall that was still dropping a handful of flakes on his head. He thought the sparkling white snow beautiful and he was grateful for the way it covered the garbage, the battered cars parked along the street, the ugly evidence that people leave behind. The flakes seemed like a second chance, a clean slate.

He knocked on the door, waiting for the manager to let him in. He stamped his feet, patted his arms against the windchill. He grabbed the door's handle to brace himself as he prepared to pound on the glass. To his surprise, the door swung open. He slipped in silently, searching the tables and stools, looking for the janitor and his mop. He found it strange: the lights were on, the floor clean in that way that makes you crinkle your nose from the smell of the ammonia.

He said, his word a question, *Hello?*

Silence.

He told himself that the janitor had just left; the manager had forgotten to lock the doors behind him. He pulled off his coat, thinking himself quite clever for buying it secondhand at the Goodwill shop. He made his way behind the counter, that wall that separated the uniformed from the masses. That's when he saw him.

His manager was lying behind the counter, playing possum beneath a pool of ketchup carefully squeezed from the individual serving packets they toss in to-go bags. He remembers gasping at the sight, and then the embarrassment he felt for having fallen for the stunt. He thought, giddily, that this was his manager's way of flirting with him. He rolled his eyes as he said, *Very funny.*

His manager didn't move. He crouched down and touched his manager's shoulder.

Next he pushed him, now waiting for the handsome face to awaken and laugh at him. His manager would say, in his best English, *Gotcha,* as he pulled Brendan's face to his own, kissing Brendan the way Brendan had imagined kissing him, the ketchup staining the collars of their shirts.

Instead the manager's body slid in the direction Brendan pushed it.

The triggerman turned out to be a co-worker; Brendan and the gunman had spent a dozen shifts or more in the kitchen together, making fun of anyone who would actually eat the food they prepared. That was the day he quit McDonald's.

"Pierre?"

He looks at Sean, his eyes barely open. "Yeah?"

Sean sits up. "Come on, what's wrong?"

He closes his eyes; focuses on the sensation of Sean's fingers, Sean's palm, as it slowly glides over his face. He takes Sean's hand by the wrist, leads it down his chest, releasing it just below the navel. Sean smiles as he explores Brendan again, searching every square inch of his body, hoping to pinpoint the precise location of his heart.

Brendan reads the last line from chapter eighteen of *Harry Potter* before he looks at Marv and says, "And we'll have to leave it at that, for now."

Marv looks disappointed, mutters something that sounds exactly like *don't stop*.

"What did you say?"

Marv closes his eyes and puckers and unpuckers his lips, a look of deliberate concentration on half his face. Brendan hears: "Down stawpf."

Brendan stares for a moment as Marv's eyes reopen and the lips relax. Brendan says, "I'm sorry, Marv. I promise we'll read some more tomorrow." In spite of the fact that Marv was just changed less than an hour ago, he checks the old man's diaper, which is dry. Next, he arranges the sheet and blankets neatly, placing them by Marv's neck, before hurrying out of the room, down the elevator, and into the lobby. He doesn't want to be late.

Sean and Brendan are going to the movies, and Sean picks Brendan up in the little hybrid with the bumper stickers on back. Sean smiles widely as Brendan takes his place in the passenger seat, complimenting Brendan on being such a faithful visitor to an old, infirm neighbor. The "neighbor" Brendan had to invent to explain the time he spends at Northstar. On the way to the theater, they make a quick stop in St. Paul. Sean's niece turns sixteen today, April Fool's Day, and she's having a six-hour-long party: the first three hours (5 P.M. until 8 P.M.) are for immediate family and extended relatives, the final three (8 P.M. until 11 P.M.) for friends, both female and male. This is a big event, the first time boys and girls will be together by design at her house, and as Brendan and Sean enter the home of Sean's sister and brother-in-law, the niece is the target of much good-natured teasing.

"So how's my favorite little April fool?" an older man asks the niece. "Have your eye on anyone special?"

"What's the lucky boy's name?" a middle-aged woman wants to know.

She smiles grudgingly, counting the minutes until her party *really* starts. When she sees Sean, the relief is palpable. "Uncle Sean," she screams, and pulls free of the less interesting relatives who orbit her.

"Happy birthday, kiddo," he says as he puts his arms around her, and with her pressed tightly against him—her feet don't touch the floor— spins her in a circle.

"Ugh," she says, as he releases her, "you trying to make me barf or what?"

Then, looking at Brendan, she asks, "Who are you?"

Sean answers for him, as if he can't be trusted to give the correct response. "This is Pierre, and be polite. Pierre, this is Eileen."

Eileen says, "Ohmigod, I'm so polite! If I wasn't, I wouldn't care who he was."

Brendan holds out his hand. "Nice to meet you."

She shakes it, her tone letting him know just how uncool such formality is in her world. "And you, too."

Sean waves at a woman who must be his sister; she looks as relieved at the sight of him as her daughter was. He makes his way toward her, occasionally exchanging greetings with the other relatives en route.

The niece says, "I've never met anybody named Pierre before."

"I've met butt-loads of Eileens."

At this she smirks.

He takes in the pile of brightly wrapped boxes and gift bags that overwhelm the small dining room table. "Looks like quite a haul," he tells her.

"I deserve it," she says. "You try being born on April Fool's Day. 'How's daddy's little fool?' 'You should change your name to April Fool.' Blahtey-blahety-blah." She fingers a thin gold necklace she wears over a too-tight T-shirt. She says, "Are you his boyfriend?"

He frowns.

She smiles. "I'm right, tell me I'm right."

She's a pretty girl, and the boys—the straight ones, anyway—are probably in a heated competition for her attention. This must be the main reason she's so obviously looking forward to the arrival of eight P.M. She also thinks of herself as a bit of a rebel, hence the tight clothes, the very public display of affection for her homosexual uncle in front of the other relatives.

He asks her, "How many of his boyfriends have you met?"

"Not many. He really doesn't put himself out there, even though he wants a boyfriend so bad his hair bleeds."

"He wants a boyfriend that much?"

She frowns. "Dude, look at him! What, you can't tell?"

And she's off; a girlfriend has arrived early to help her make fun of her family.

While the other guests will look at him, none will introduce themselves. He wanders into the living room; examines the titles of the few books on display. There are *Chicken Soup* books and thrillers by Grisham, horror novels by King. A biography of Pope John Paul II is next to *The Atkins Diet*. Another biography, *Why Stella Cares*, has a bookmark sticking out of it.

When Sean finally rescues him he says, "Sorry, didn't mean for that to take so long." His arm appears around Brendan's shoulders as he escorts him out of his sister's house. Whether this is designed to make an impression on Brendan or Sean's family, Brendan can't say.

"What did I tell you? Two for one and all the food you can eat!" Ian smiles at his small plate that overflows with chicken wings, barbecued meatballs, and cubed cheese. He holds a pint glass in one hand; another pint glass, empty save some soggy foam that lingers at the bottom, sits on the table between them. Noise and smoke are everywhere: this is a generous happy hour that defies the smoking ban, and therefore, a wildly popular one. The walls are decorated with maps of Minnesota and large old black-and-white photos of local celebrities and has-beens, each signed in black ink. A crowded table of young white men and women are next to them and it's difficult to hear anything except their laughter and flirtations. Brendan's barely made a dent in his own drinks, two glasses of house red.

He asks Ian, "How did you find this place?"

"Word of mouth," Ian tells him, and Brendan wonders what networks Ian has joined since leaving Rush City. Ian's a different man from the one Brendan first met in jail; his eyes are animated and he savors the tastes of real food, genuine alcohol. It seems astounding to him, this world in which he now finds himself, a place where he can eat and drink what he wants, where he can make love to Cynthia, where he can watch television whenever he chooses. The thought that the plan may not work, that he could end up back in Rush City, never occurs to him. Perhaps it's because he's overdoing freedom, every little bit of it, but it's still so new to him, the novelty of it has yet to wear off. He stabs a meatball with a toothpick, pops it in his mouth. What used to be their visiting hours are now happy hours. He invites Brendan to one bar after another, each more affordable than the last, Ian's criteria for selecting them based on complimentary food and deeply discounted drinks.

"How's Cynthia?" Brendan asks him.

He seems to swallow the meatball whole as he tells Brendan, "She's fantastic, absolutely fantastic!" and then he calls Brendan by his old name.

"My name's Brendan."

He winks, says, "Sorry, I do try to remember, you know." Now he takes a bite out of a chicken wing and, chewing, says in a muffled voice, "I'm a very lucky man. Just think, six weeks from now we'll be heading south of the border to start our new lives in old Mexico. A clean slate, just imagine it. We're finally going to get the chance in life other people got, Brendan, the one we were robbed of."

"You're not worried that something could go wrong?"

Ian waves a hand like he's shooing a fly. "Nothing will go wrong. Have some faith, Cynthia knows what she's doing. Come on, *she's Cynthia!* It's *the plan!* You're not having second thoughts, are you?"

"Just a bit worried, is all."

Ian leans in, places a hand on Brendan's wrist. "There's no room for worry. You have to exude confidence, baby brother. When you're with the Babies First people, you have to really be *with* them. You believe what they believe. What's important to them is important to you."

"The things they say . . . I'm afraid I'll make a mistake."

Ian relaxes, leans back in his chair with his hands clasped behind his head. "What do they say?"

Brendan frowns. "They claim to know what happens when we die. They believe there's a hell, where people are tortured for all eternity, with no hope of forgiveness or redemption. It's a disturbing fantasy, but it's one of their core beliefs."

"That bothers you?"

Brendan takes a sip of the house red, which has a bitter aftertaste. "What sort of sadist do they worship?"

Ian smirks. "What else?"

"They take the Bible literally."

"So they're fans, so what? You fall in love with books all the time. Remember how you insisted I read *In the Woods*—"

"*Into the Wild.*"

"Whatever. You told me I wouldn't be able to put it down, but I did."

"It's an amazing story."

Ian points a finger at Brendan. "And that's what the Bible is to them. I want you to think about it in those terms."

" 'The house of the wicked will be destroyed, but the tent of the up-right will flourish.' That's the kind of thing they say to me."

Ian giggles. "You don't believe in pitching your tent? Do me a favor, go get laid, then you'll be in the tent of the upright."

"They say that life begins at conception."

Ian nods confidently. "They're right. Think about it: one set of chromosomes from each parent make the fetus unique. It has its own tissue and blood type. It's not the mother's, it's not the father's, it's the baby's. Life begins at conception."

Brendan stares at him. "You honestly believe that?"

"It doesn't matter what I believe."

Brendan considers his wine. "They say horrible things about gay people."

Ian looks at him seriously. "Use it. Perhaps there's a larger purpose to all this than just money. Think of the satisfaction you'll feel when it's all over."

Shrieks of laughter now from the table next to them. Ian has to shout as he points at the glasses: "Keep up. I'm ready for another round and two-for-one ends in a few minutes."

"Go ahead, I'm fine with what I have."

Ian raises his hand like a schoolboy and the waiter comes over, a thin, pretty young man. The waiter takes Ian's order, all the while looking at Brendan, a question on his face. When he walks away, Ian says, "He seems like your sort. Do you like him?"

Brendan blushes. "I don't know him."

"You can't go on mooning over what's-his-face for the rest of your life."

"Jeff."

"Yes, Jeff. He was so mousy and, really, nothing special to look at. I always thought you could do better. A *lot* better. You're a handsome man, you should enjoy it."

He groans. "I'm not handsome."

Ian shakes his head. "You're my baby brother. There's no one handsomer."

Brendan's been picking up the phone at Marv's for a few weeks, now that he finally has people in his life who need to contact him. He had to change the answering machine's greeting. He recorded an innocuous message that simply informed callers of the number they had reached.

The phone rings; it's one of the gals, the action is on for today, Good Friday, to begin at the exact time it is believed that Christ was nailed onto the cross. They're to meet at the Uptown coffee shop in half an hour. He calls Sean, they're supposed to have lunch, but he gets Sean's answering machine, leaves a rushed message that lets Sean know he can't make it. He calls Ian and Cynthia but no one picks up. Actions weren't part of the plan, but here he is, about to go on one.

The coffee shop's walking distance and he makes the trip alert for any sign of his adoptive mother or father. He counts the years since they last spoke and the total surprises him, what had seemed like just a few is in fact fifteen. With each step he imagines different outcomes for his adoptive parents, some little heartbreak or minor tragedy of their own creation, fodder for their sessions with each other, their *journeys of self-discovery*. He often wondered whether they needed their all-consuming journey to avoid the reality of their lives, whether they preferred the undiscovered to the things that sit in plain view for all the world to see.

He enters the coffee shop and spots his group as they sit around three small tables. With the gals are men, the first men he's seen at a Babies First gathering (with the exception of a few of the administrators who deliver the boxes of materials they sort, stuff, and mail). The men at the tables are as intense as the gals are unassuming; they take themselves too seriously while the women prefer to present themselves as humble, kindhearted. They are men at war, a holy war, and given the times in which they live he wonders if there is any other kind.

Judy waves, points to the seat next to her. He hopes he appears confident, committed, as he joins her under the inspecting eyes of the men. She places a hand on his arm and says softly, "This is going to be big, can you feel it? It makes me so nostalgic for the days when we *really* used to do actions, before the courts ruined everything. Oh, I'm so nervous!"

One of the men leans across the table, solemnly offers Brendan his hand. "You're Brendan, huh? Doing a super job with the mailings, according to the missus."

Brendan thanks him, unsure to which missus he's referring. Brendan can tell that the men consider his contribution women's work, and it makes him suspect in their company. He mentions his dead wife casually during the sporadic conversation. It gets him sympathetic looks from the gals and stiff expressions from their men: he's too soft, too sentimental. Life is hard. People die.

A cell phone rings. Final confirmation, the action is a definite go.

The group joins hands, bows heads. Eyes lowered, Brendan glances around the shop, embarrassed by the spectacle they create. The trendier clientele note their public display of faith, exchange amused looks with one another, as if the men and women praying were children pretending to be grown-ups. One of the men leads the prayer, of course, asking God for the courage of their convictions. Then, with a passionate *Amen*, they stand and embrace, even the men, as they gather their belongings and step out into the street, where a clean white van sits idling in the cool air, waiting for them. They get in silently, begin their journey to a clinic that's only blocks away. One of the men makes several quick calls to television stations and the city desks of the major dailies as they wait for a light to change.

In the few minutes it takes them to reach their target, a dozen of the clinic's own volunteers, called *defenders*, have already gathered by the main entrance. Perhaps twenty of the Babies First protesters are lying down on the sidewalk in front of the clinic; soon they will be handcuffed and pulled away by the police, whose sirens now fill the air. One of the men shouts at Brendan's group and two other vanloads of protesters who hurry to join the protest: "Educate! Educate!" This is the signal to begin chanting as they search the streets for any women who may be arriving for their appointments. Half of Brendan's group is dispatched to the back entrance—Linda, himself, and a few of the others from the coffee shop remain in front.

In the chaos that ensues he forgets the slogans he's been taught. Preachers' bullhorns compete with each other, with the shouting of protesters and defenders, the wail of the sirens, and all of it, all of this noise, is being pushed back down upon them by a news helicopter circling low above their heads. Red and blue and white lights wash over them, the lights of the squad cars, and he feels something, a rock or a bottle, hit him on a shoulder. Teenagers have raced over from the McDonald's down the street and with whatever they can find they pelt the demonstrators, all of them, protesters and defenders alike.

More and more protesters arrive, busloads of them, and they're pushed together, some of them tripping over their own who lie praying in front of the clinic. There are graphic color posters of aborted fetuses held by shouting men and women and children. There are too many of them, too tightly packed; they're out of control. He can't breathe.

"Close the slaughterhouse!"

He can't think.

"Abortion is murder!"

Please stop yelling.

"Give life, don't take it!"

A fat protester leaning into him panics and begs the others to get out of his way as he gasps for air. Now they swarm: a patient's been separated from her defenders, and the protesters are on her, grabbing her, shoving their placards in her face. A wall of people six deep stand between the patient and Brendan and he sees hands pulling her maple-colored hair, the protesters arguing with each other, shoving, shouting. A lone defender staggers near him, her face bloodied, one eye shut.

The patient, or perhaps she's some unfortunate mistaken for a patient, screams.

He grabs the terrified fat man next to him by his shoulders; shoves him hard into the people in front of them. They fall, grunting, then moaning as Brendan walks on top of them—their arms, legs, stomachs, backs, faces—to reach the patient, or the woman they all believe to be a patient.

He wraps an arm around her and makes a fist with his free hand.

Slowly, painfully, the two of them make their way to defender territory.

When the action is over, when the police and the protesters have left, some in handcuffs, the men and women sitting in the clinic's waiting room, silent, terrified, are told by the staff that it's now safe to leave the building. The woman he escorted is with a doctor; hair was ripped out of her scalp and she's badly bruised from all the pushing and pulling. He takes a moment to compose himself before he exits. He's fucked up badly. He wasn't thinking. He doesn't know how to salvage this.

He walks, quickly and deliberately, and when he's again aware of his surroundings he finds himself in a bookstore. He grabs a volume off the shelf of new releases; finds a place to sit out of sight of the other customers, other people. He touches his lip, surprised to find it swollen. He looks at a coat sleeve, discovers a scratch on his hand. He stares at the little wound, the straight line of pink, raw skin that does not bleed. It curves slightly before it disappears into the light flesh tones covered by fine hairs and interrupted by the occasional freckle.

"May I help you?"

He looks up. This is not a cop talking to him; it's the bookstore's security guard. He's a sad-looking man of perhaps sixty.

Brendan must look worse off than he thought. He says, "Just looking, thanks."

The guard says in a tone insincerely helpful, "I think you should go home and get cleaned up. You look like you've been in a fight."

He hates it when people talk down to him.

Perhaps he's shot the plan to holy hell and with it a new life in old Mexico. When Ian asked how the action went, he lied; when Sean asked why he had to blow off their lunch date, he lied. If he sits around Marv's house he'll lose his mind. He considers heading to a club downtown, but instead picks up the phone and calls Sean, who sounds like he's been pouting. Next Brendan catches a city bus to the University of Minnesota campus: a writer whose work he admires is on tour and will be reading there this evening. The writer's a legend, a literary wunderkind who won his first Pulitzer at the age of twenty-three. Now in his sixties—and with a large and diverse catalog of books and collections behind him—he's in Minneapolis to accept an award for a book of literary criticism. Best of all, the event is free.

Sean's waiting for Brendan in front of the performance hall's main entrance, as Brendan agreed. Sean had originally wanted to pick him up so they could ride over together, but Brendan told him that his sister didn't like men coming round her house. Whatever hard edge Sean had when they first met has been shed, he smiles sweetly as he puts his arms around Brendan.

"Hey, hot stuff," he whispers.

Brendan sighs. It's a bit much a bit soon: all the pet names Sean's been storing up, the sexual energy; they're surging like flood waters after the levees have failed. Sean kisses him on the lips before releasing him, a quick peck but still, hardly the type of thing people are used to seeing.

Brendan says, "I hope you won't be bored tonight."

Sean's eyes sparkle as he says, "Well, I've never been to a reading before, but I'm sure I'll like it, honey bunny."

Brendan smiles at Sean, surprising himself with the sincerity behind it. This is probably not due to Sean; more likely it's because of where they are, what's about to happen: Brendan actually enjoys seeing other people if they're gathered for a reading. It feels a bit like a meeting of a mutual assistance association, those small nonprofit organizations immigrants and refugees form to help one another find their way through America. While most of the people who attend readings don't come from abroad, they're a minority in this land and their numbers shrink with each passing year. Judging from the audiences at these events, women of a certain age are now society's guardians of reading literature for the sake of reading literature. These women, along with a few men, are Brendan's fellow travelers in a world that has shifted its attention from the page to the screens of monitors and television sets, a world of video games and reality programs and shoppers' Web sites that confound Brendan.

Audience members sit in the auditorium comfortably; it's as easy to attend a reading alone as it is to arrive with a date or in a group. If Brendan did find someone, someone like Sean (but who won't call him *hot stuff* and *honey bunny*), Brendan would like to think that they'd read aloud to each other every night before they went to bed. Brendan watches as people take their seats; some recognize friends and acquaintances in the audience, and they wave and smile or lean across the aisle to shake hands. A few in the crowd set notebooks on their laps, paper and electronic, and check their pens for ink, their screens for power. All around is the quiet buzz of readers and writers as they settle in for an evening with the elder statesman of their community.

A pudgy Asian man in his late forties, dressed in black and white, approaches the podium. Some in the auditorium applaud, academics and students, no doubt. Brendan and Sean join them, clapping their hands together even though they have no idea who this man is. They discover he's come before them to introduce the person who will introduce the person they're here to see. The man's round face and beautiful hair contrast with his tone, which is toxic. Instead of introducing the person who will introduce the person Brendan has come to see, the man tells stories of his own life, shares the devastating spiritual damage and psychological torment he has endured because he is an American of Japanese descent. As he talks, Brendan scouts the men that are placed throughout the hall, looking for the one with the faraway expression on his face, someone like Alex Supertramp. Brendan notes one or two candidates, but he can't pursue them now, not with Sean sitting next to him like a puppy at the feet of its master.

The bitter, angry man in his late forties finally acknowledges an off-stage cue and quits the podium abruptly. A white and gray academic takes it up. She wears unusually shaped glasses, but her manner is formal, unemotional. She's not someone who begs for approval, she's the person who dispenses it or denies it. A hand to her chin, she raises her eyebrows and scans the audience's faces, seemingly unimpressed. She waits long moments before she speaks, taking her audience's measure, confident that her words will inspire the awe due their famous visitor.

"When I was afforded the great honor of being asked to introduce J. L. Thatcher I hesitated. Yes, it is true. I hesitated. I doubted that I was up to this task; the task that I so inadequately perform for you now, the task of employing mere words to describe the magnificent career of America's foremost man of letters. That I call his work sheer genius should surprise no thinking person, no rational mind, for, as we have all experienced, his words burn in a powerful inferno of passion and intellect, as if a forest set ablaze by but a single strike of J. L. Thatcher's brilliant lightning. J. L. Thatcher's contributions to literature are too numerous and too great to catalog in the brief time allotted me. His wrenching, incendiary depictions of contemporary American lives offer penetrating insights into the spiritual, moral, and intellectual conditions of modern society. He tunnels like a miner into the soul of humanity, his words coming together to compose works of astounding courage. His fearless reflections upon our own inevitable mortality challenge and inspire readers to stare into the endless void of the abyss."

Sean squirms in his seat as she continues.

Finally, she welcomes the man himself, and Sean looks at Brendan tentatively as the audience rises to its feet, the first entirely sincere ovation of the evening. He's here, in this room, J. L. Thatcher in person! He's a heavy man who dresses smartly, though maybe a little too young for his age. He embraces the woman who's introduced him, nods to the crowd. He motions for them to end their applause and resume their seats, but it's hard for them to do. This man has a gift for words, for placing words together in sentences, for arranging sentences into stories that are impossible to forget. He thanks the university, the professor for her remarks about his work before putting his hands together, fingers entwined—save the index fingers on either hand, which he lifts to his lips as he bows his head thoughtfully. He says: "Who am I?" A pause, he asks the question again. "*Who* am I?" Another pause and for the third time, the emphasis changed: "Who *am* I?" A final, lingering pause, followed by: "Who am *I?*"

Sean whispers, "Beats the hell out of me."

Brendan places a finger over his lips as he frowns at Sean.

". . . the savage internal battle declared by an exceptional mind . . ."

Sean sighs loudly.

Thatcher quotes an Inuit hunter who told him ancient truths from the time before time. Thatcher tells the audience how he was humbled—

deeply humbled—to discover that these ancient truths about human nature and mankind's place in the world were nearly identical to the truths
he himself has discovered in his writing.

Sean mutters, "You've *got* to be kidding me."

Brendan ignores the comment.

An hour passes, another standing ovation, and it's time for questions from the audience.

A young woman stands at the microphone in front of the stage and
J. L. Thatcher leans in, studying her intently. She says, "Your work is so
delicately layered, almost as if you are a very rare and precious bird who
lovingly gathers beautiful branches to craft an exquisite and nurturing
nest for the reader."

Sean stifles a giggle and Brendan hisses at him to be quiet.

The young woman asks J. L. Thatcher if the mind of a brilliant
writer is intrinsically a tortured one or if it's the consequence of having
to live and work in a prosaic world. He tells her that she has asked an
excellent question. He shares with his audience a few of his personal
demons: a cold father, a narcissistic mother, which in turn led to three
failed marriages that produced children who, to this day, refuse to speak
to him. Brendan thinks it shameful. Thatcher shouldn't have to put his
heartbreaks on display in a petting zoo, invite his audience to look at
them, stroke their fur, feed them the pellets they can buy for a quarter
at the dispensers. This is beneath him.

Brendan looks over at Sean, who's struggling to keep his eyes open.
Brendan nudges him, irritated yet oddly amused. Sean smiles, says,
"Hey, honey bunny. Let's go back to my place and make out."

Sean wore cologne that made Brendan's lips swell, so Brendan's called
it an early evening. Sean seemed upset until he turned on the lamp and
saw Brendan's bloated mouth. He wanted to take Brendan to the hospital, but Brendan simply had him drive him a block away from Marv's
home.

Sean apologizes again as Brendan opens the passenger's door. "Pierre, I'm so sorry. Are you sure you'll be okay?"

Through puffed lips Brendan says, "I'm fine. I just need to take a shower. Do me a favor and never wear that scent again."

Even in the shadows of the hybrid's interior, he can see Sean turn red. Sean says, "I kind of overdid it with the patchouli oil. I've just been listening to that old Al Stewart song too much lately."

"Sorry?"

" 'Year of the Cat.' "

"I don't understand."

Sean sings, " 'She comes in incense and patchouli, so you take her to find what's waiting inside.' "

"Oh. Good night." Brendan could take a shower at Sean's place, spend the night, but this is getting too real, too uncomfortable.

Sean watches as Brendan walks down the block, disappearing into an alley not far from Marv's home. Brendan presses himself against the side of a garage until he hears Sean's car pull quietly away, a soft whisper in the night. As if on cue, a cat scurries across the pavement, its head bent low, illuminated by the glow of a back porch light. Here it is then: a life on the streets, the cold blocks of cement poured into the ground that separates home from home, family from family. If Brendan were a stupider person, an unluckier person, he would spend tonight darting back and forth between these short buildings, praying that he would elude notice, that the temperature wouldn't suddenly drop below freezing. And that he would find a few moments, perhaps propped up against the weather-beaten post of a wooden fence, to dream of the lives he's only read about in books.

There's a message waiting for him at Marv's house. He hears the voice of Cynthia's mother: "He's started talking and all he does is ask for you. 'Where's Frankie? Where's Frankie?' He does nothing but ask where you are."

He looks at the clock. It's after midnight, it's Easter Sunday. He'll spend it with Cynthia and Ian, going over the plan.

First thing Monday morning he meets with the discharge planner from Northstar Presbyterian in her little windowless office off the main reception desk. He inspects the titles on her shelves, all professional texts in the fields of rehabilitation, gerontology, and health care. She's a coolly friendly woman, somewhere in her fifties, and her light-red hair is casually set. Her manner suggests competence, along with an odd mixture of dispassion and sympathy. Her deep-blue eyes are an exact match with her suit, a simple knee-length dress and blazer, with modest but firm shoulder padding. Her nails are not painted and are cut short. Everything about her suggests common sense, reason, inevitability.

She holds out her hand professionally, competently. "A pleasure to meet you, Mr. Thompson."

He smiles nervously, timidly puts his hand in her own.

She points at a seat across from her desk, asking, "How can I help you?"

He softly says, "I want to take Marv home."

She nods. "Well, that's certainly what we want, as well. We discharge residents after their rehabilitative goals have been met. I'm sorry to say, this isn't the case with Mr. Fletcher. Not yet, anyway. We remain very hopeful, of course."

"Oh."

She opens a file, looks thoughtfully at the papers inside. "In addition, we have to determine what care assistance and special equipment will be needed in the home. And you'll want a home health aide for when you're away from the house."

"I can take care of things. Some of our friends have volunteered to help."

She turns her attention back to him. "Maybe we could set up a trial visit, say for a weekend? That way we can identify any problems that will need to be corrected before Mr. Fletcher returns home permanently."

"What sort of problems?"

"Oh, arranging rooms so that Mr. Fletcher can stay on the first floor, moving throw rugs or small pieces of furniture that he could trip over. He'll need grab bars and seats in the bathroom."

He says hopefully, "That's all been taken care of."

She smiles sweetly at him. "I'd still like to see your home and do a brief assessment before we discuss discharging Mr. Fletcher."

"Everything's ready."

She folds her hands on her desk. "Mr. Thompson, I just have to make sure that you fully appreciate Mr. Fletcher's safety, and his physical and emotional needs."

He tries to impress her with the research he's done, Cynthia's mother being the largest single source of information. "I've lined up a specialist to oversee his care and I've charted all his prescriptions and when he's supposed to take them. I have a weekly menu worked out based on the diet the nutritionist recommended. I know to talk to him even though he can't join in conversations yet. And I know what exercises he has to perform and how often."

She nods, impressed. "Mr. Thompson, I understand that you want Mr. Fletcher back home. That's what we want, too. It's not a question of *if* he should return home; it's a question of *when*. When will he be ready? When will you be ready to have him back? These are the issues."

He doesn't know what else to do, so he says, "Is this because we're both men?"

She blushes, her face a rich rose color, like a Valentine's Day bouquet. Abruptly, and too loudly she says, "Of course not!"

"Then I don't understand what the problem is."

She looks at him seriously. "Let me be blunt. Most people don't find out that they're not cut out to be caregivers until it's too late. You'll be his butler, his valet, his barber, his maid, and his cook, and some days he'll hate you for it because he can't do these things for himself. Are you really prepared for that? It's a tremendous amount of work. People often think they're ready, but when push comes to shove, they're not. That's all I'm saying, it has nothing to do with your alternative lifestyle. I wouldn't be doing my job unless I warned you about what to expect."

Brendan thinks that Marv really would be happier in his own home;

Brendan would be if he were him. And Brendan would be happier with Marv there, where the old man can say whatever he pleases without anyone else to hear. When the Walk is over Brendan will call Marv's daughter before he disappears, let her know that Marv's her problem now. He tells the discharge planner, "I'm ready."

What has he done?

He had the men position Marv in the bed just so, perfectly balanced, Marv's head resting on two comfortably fluffed pillows, the thick blankets and clean sheets pulled up to his shoulders. Brendan addressed Marv like an old friend (he couldn't quite manage to speak to him as if he were an old lover—even he has his limits) as the health aides laid Marv out, and, without a single backward glance, collected their stretcher and walked out the front door.

Marv's awake, active as a toddler, stimulated by being back in his own place. He moves his good arm up and down, side to side, his eyes scan the bedroom, his lips form a delighted half-smile. This is how it goes for the next hour, him flailing in the bed as best he can, Brendan watching, panic-stricken, unsure of what to do next.

An idea occurs to Brendan. He says to Marv, "Okay, you stay here." He holds his arm in front of him, palm out, to make his point: "Stay here. I'll be right back. Stay."

He jogs to the music room and scans the CDs, but there are hundreds, perhaps more than a thousand of them, everything from classical to jazz to rhythm-and-blues to Broadway. He turns on the CD player, presses the EJECT button, and as he hoped, discs appear in the large carousel. He grabs one, runs back to Marv's room, where the old man is stroking the blanket with his good hand, taking in its familiar texture.

Brendan places the CD in the bedroom's boom box, hits PLAY. It feels like minutes, but it's more likely seconds before they hear the keys of a piano, the strum of a bass, the soft beats of a drum. Next, the smooth murmur of a saxophone fills the room and Marv sighs, closes his eyes to savor the resonance.

Brendan discreetly tiptoes away from Marv, from the music, closing the bedroom door tightly behind him. He investigates the three-car garage with its single Oldsmobile. Along the walls are large, deep wooden shelves, piled high with an odd collection of things: a car's spare tire, boxes of old files, bags full of clothes to be donated or left on the curb. He discovers the power tools on a workbench, screws of all sizes and types, and a padlock along with its keys still in their original wrappings. There are also hammers, a wide variety of nails.

He'll install a padlock on the door to Marv's room. He'll drive nails into the window frames so they can be opened only a few inches.

Just as a precaution.

When he returns, he tries to work quietly, but he's unfamiliar and clumsy with tools, and he has to start and restart his project, correcting mistakes as he goes. Marv hears the whine of the drill, the pounding of the hammer, but he makes no sound himself, simply lies there, focusing on the music that Brendan turns up every few minutes in the hope of drowning out the racket he makes. When Brendan finishes, he stares at his handiwork, uncertain as to what he meant when he installed it.

It's just a precaution.

He turns to Marv, dreading his next task. Marv hasn't been changed since before they loaded him on the stretcher at Northstar for the journey home. Brendan winces; the diaper is wet. Marv closes his eyes as Brendan makes his first attempt to change the Depends. Brendan thought he was prepared for this: after all, he had bought a copy of *The Complete Idiot's Guide to Home Health Care*, and reviewed it carefully, practicing the prescribed techniques by miming them as he read along with the text. But the book featured diagrams of pleasant, two-dimensional bedridden people compliantly rolling on one side or the other so their diapers could be changed by equally pleasant caregivers who never lost their two-dimensional patience.

Marv, of course, won't budge.

"Come on," he pleads. "You really want to lie in a dirty diaper all day?"

Marv mutters, forms a few bubbles around his lips. He whispers, "Where's Frankie?"

Brendan pulls on the old man's right arm, the bad one, hoping to roll him slightly, trapping his good arm under his own girth. If Brendan can get Marv on his side he can finish removing the dirty diaper and then roll the clean one up tight against the old man's body, as the *Complete Idiot's Guide* indicates in Figure B-4.

"Ugh, a little help please," Brendan says as he pulls.

He lets go of the arm and the negligible progress he made disappears as Marv rolls onto his back.

Brendan exhales, loudly.

He reaches for the bad arm again, but the good one is free and as he bends over the bed Marv slaps him weakly. It frightens more than it hurts. He cautions Marv: "That was very bad. Don't do that again. Bad." He grabs the bad arm roughly by the wrist and pulls too hard; Marv cries out and so does he, "Jesus! Sorry! I'm sorry!"

Finally, precariously, Marv manages to stay balanced on his side, like snow on the peak just before the avalanche. Brendan moves quickly, grateful for this brief bit of accessibility to the only parts of Marv's body that seem to be in perfect working order. The ammonia smell makes him crinkle his nose, and while Marv hasn't had a bowel movement, there still is something to wipe, and he gags as he works with the paper towels. Quickly he consults the manual, rolling up one half of the clean diaper and placing it tightly against a hip.

"Okay, Marv. We're going to move you onto your back." Brendan kneels on the bed, grunting, as he grips Marv by a shoulder and the waist, pushing him slowly away. With Marv on his back now, Brendan searches for any trace of the clean diaper but it's disappeared under the old man's midsection, a ship lost at sea.

Brendan sits on the edge of the bed, pouting. "You know what?" he asks Marv. "This is just going to have to do for now." He positions a second diaper on top of Marv and tapes it directly to Marv's flesh. He pulls the sheet and blankets up so he doesn't have to see what a mess he's made and he promises himself he'll figure out a better system tomorrow. He gets up, wearily, and heads toward the door saying, "Good night, Marv."

He knows it's a bad idea to leave Marv alone, locked in his bedroom, but he felt that he had no choice. He had to return to Babies First, judge the fallout from the action and its impact, if any, on the plan.

Gail, the new grandmother from Bloomington, doesn't smile at him when she buzzes him in. He says hello, thanks her, but she was at the action and clearly hasn't forgiven him for what he had done. Her eyes, which look directly into his own, tell him that he aided and abetted a woman who allowed a tiny human being inside her—one that can feel pain two and a half months after conception—to be swept away in terror, like a victim of a tsunami.

Walking up the stairs he braces himself; if Gail's reaction is typical he shouldn't have ventured back to Babies First at all. For Ian's sake, for Cynthia's sake, and yes, thanks to the mess with Marv, for his own sake, he has to successfully reinstall the young widower whose wife's name was Laura. If he fails, the plan goes up in flames, and with it, perhaps, his second chance at a real family.

Tentatively, he steps through the doorway and into the mailing room, and the soft chatter of the gals abruptly stops. Most simply glance at Brendan before awkwardly returning to their conversations.

He has fucked up. Yet again.

How will he tell Ian and Cynthia?

He looks at the boxes of monthly newsletters that are stacked along the wall, fresh from the printing shop. Near the boxes is the table that was his, the spot where gals would deliver their bundles which he then tagged and bagged. Linda sits in his spot, half a bar in one hand, and from the looks of it, the other half in her mouth. She chews quickly, forcing the bar down her throat.

He turns to leave.

Linda coughs loudly as she calls his name. He faces her, and as he does, she grabs a cup of water, drinks it down quickly. She wipes her mouth as she says enthusiastically, "Well, look who's here!"

The subdued chatter stops a second time. Gals look at their work, each other. Brendan smiles weakly, defeated.

Linda takes the scene in. Then she says, "Ann, look who's here!"

Ann's stooped over a stack of newsletters. She looks up at Brendan. Finally, the tone of her voice a cold front, she says, "You're late. Linda had to fill in for you."

Now Linda catches Judy's eye. Timidly, Judy says, "Hello, Brendan."

Now gals nod at him or whisper hellos, a few, though, offer him louder and more sincere greetings. He walks to his regular spot and Linda pulls out the chair for him. She points at the mailing bags, the labels, saying, "Hope I didn't mess everything up too badly."

Brendan tries to smile. "I was about to say the same thing to you."

Linda winks, tells him under her breath that actions are for extremists. She's glad he isn't one.

Brendan resumes his normal place and the tension eases a bit. But as he corrects Linda's attempts at bagging, an older gal in a red wig says loudly enough for the whole room to hear, "Honestly, who even does actions anymore? And such a poorly organized one at that. I saw it on the news. Made us look ridiculous, if you ask me."

Ann drops a stack of newsletters on her table with an angry thump, which makes the gals sitting on either side of her sit up straight. "Oh, sure, let's all just sit back and say, 'Excuse me, if it wouldn't be too much trouble, would you not kill babies? If you don't mind. Pretty please?' We're preventing *murder*, get it? Murder!"

The gal in the red wig shoots back, "No, you're not preventing anything. Just making yourselves feel better, if you ask me. The hard work is changing hearts and minds, and you're sure as heck not doing that! The easiest thing in the world to do is just get up on your high horse and shout at people. Honestly!"

A gal murmurs, "Hear, hear."

Now Ann says, "We have to shut these places down by any means necessary. If you do anything less, you're an accessory to murder!"

Some gals gasp, others shake their heads in disbelief, but still others voice approval. Judy says, "Please, let's not fight."

Arguments break out and, as voices raise, one of the younger gals, perhaps Brendan's age, bursts into tears and runs out of the room.

Brendan stands and claps his hands together, shouting over the clamor, "Excuse me!"

Startled, most gals look at him, but others continue to angrily interrupt each other. Brendan claps his hands again, this time nearly screaming, "Excuse me!"

The room's quiet, hostile, and aggrieved faces look at him expectantly. He says softly so they have to lean in, "I'm sorry."

Gals wait for more; a few ask one another, "What did he say?"

Brendan quotes Alex Supertramp: "God, it's great to be alive!"

Gals look at each other, alarmed.

Now Brendan says, "Thoreau said 'No man ever followed his genius till it misled him.' I guess the problem was that I stopped following my genius. I went to the action to please some of you, even though I had my doubts. Well, no, that's not entirely true. You see,"—he pauses, flushed—"you see, Laura never went on actions herself. And she was my genius. I guess that's why I ended up doing what I did. That woman I helped. She looked a bit like Laura. I don't judge those of you who feel actions are the way to go. It's just that . . . I guess . . . they weren't the right thing for Laura. I felt I had disrespected her. I'm sorry if I've disappointed you. I know I've disappointed myself."

Brendan sits back down, places his head in his hands.

There's the quiet murmur of gals summarizing what Brendan has just said for the gals whose hearing is bad. One whispers, "She looked like his dead wife," before repeating, a moment later, "HIS DEAD WIFE!"

Linda stands, says, "You know what I think we should do? I think we should get back to work."

Some gals are still fuming, but they hold their tongues and return to the sorting. Only Judy speaks, maybe to herself: "Poor boy is lonely, that's all."

On his way home he stopped by Ian and Cynthia's apartment. He decided to tell Ian what happened at the action; it was a close call and he needed to talk to someone about it. But now Ian's furious with him for risking his position at Babies First. He stormed off to the tiny kitchen where Cynthia was carefully studying Walk for the Unborn pledge forms, leaving Brendan alone in the claustrophobic living room, strewn with Ian's empty beer cans.

He walked out of their apartment as Cynthia screamed, "He *what?*"

As he got back to Marv's, he set off for the library, afraid to see what had become of the old man in the bedroom. But then he decided he might as well face up to it, find out how Marv has fared on his own.

Marv doesn't look too much the worse for wear. Even so, Brendan decides he needs to do something nice, something kind.

"Guess what, Marv. Tonight you're getting a bath."

Marv shifts his gaze toward him, skeptical.

"It'll do you a world of good," he says to reassure the old man, himself. The bedroom has its own private bathroom, but unfortunately, the tub is rather conventional, small, not like the large Jacuzzi at the other end of the hall. Brendan considers his options, decides that the small tub's proximity makes it the better choice, and turns on the taps. Once he mixes the water to the right temperature, warm but not hot, he adds a generous amount of bath oil from one of the many small bottles that line the sink. Next, he rejoins Marv, wondering how in the world he'll get the old man in the tub.

He pulls off the blankets, the sheet. He relieves Marv of the diaper, wipes Marv a bit so the old man won't stain the carpet. Now he sits on the bed, and though it kills his back, he pulls Marv up by the shoulders, trying to place him in the sitting position. Marv's face loses its ruddiness and glows ghostlike. Brendan gently releases him, encouraging him to sit up on his own, but Marv falls backward with a soft thump. Marv needs a stretcher. Or a wheelchair.

The garage. There's a wheelbarrow in the garage.

"You wait here, Marv, I'll be right back."

It's a challenge to get the wheelbarrow up the stairs, but finally Brendan places it next to the bed, and he lines it with blankets and places a few pillows inside.

"Okay," he tells them both, "let's get you situated."

In truth, he has no idea where to begin. He decides to work the shoulders and the ankles as best as he can, pulling one end and then the other. Marv's body inches toward the edge of the bed. The old man's shoulders are a challenge of the first order; he's too heavy and has a tendency to roll rather than slide. Brendan braces himself, grabs Marv by the fleshy armpits, and tries to pull him along, but all he manages to do is lift the old man slightly as Marv moans, and drop him when his strength gives out.

There has to be an easier way.

Brendan goes back to the bathroom, turns off the taps, sits on the toilet to formulate Plan B. If he wraps Marv up in the fitted sheet, perhaps he can pull the old man like a net heavy with a good day's catch. He puts on a bright face as he enters the bedroom, telling Marv, "I think I know how we can make this work."

Marv scrunches up part of his face in what seems to be an almost hopeful expression. He's not spitting at Brendan, and Brendan grows somewhat confident that the prospect of a real bath has vanquished any opposition Marv might have offered. He pulls out the corners of the fitted sheet, wraps Marv up in it as best he can, tying the ends into a knot just above the old man's shoulders. He twists the corners by Marv's feet together tightly, and pulls.

It works. Marv slides in the direction he pulls him, but the knot over Marv's shoulders tightens into a noose around his neck. He stops; unties the knot, reties it under the armpits in the hope that the massive belly will prevent it from sliding off entirely. Next, he places the wheelbarrow at the end of the bed. Feet first, he drags Marv slowly off the mattress, the old man's legs traveling bit by bit over the wheelbarrow. As Marv's large bottom slides off the mattress it falls into the wheelbarrow's tub with a thump and Marv groans, almost a shriek, which scares Brendan.

"It's okay, you'll be okay," Brendan assures him.

Brendan positions Marv as well as he can in the wheelbarrow, but the arrangement is precarious at best. Marv's belly is pushed into his own legs like a crash-test dummy after the impact. The old man's head and feet dangle over either side of the wheelbarrow. "Sorry, sorry," Brendan offers as he grabs the handles, and with a loud grunt, pulls the wheelbarrow away from the bed and carefully maneuvers it toward the bathroom.

Brendan's so focused on keeping the wheelbarrow balanced that Marv's head and feet hit either side of the bathroom's doorway. Now Marv hisses and spits.

"Shit! Sorry, Marv."

With one hand on a handle, Brendan reaches over, pulls a leg straight up, pushes it over to the other side of the doorway. Marv groans wildly. Now the other leg, and this time, Marv whimpers. Brendan props Marv's head against the doorway, grabs both handles of the wheelbarrow, and shoves for all he's worth.

And finally, they're in.

Brendan's drenched in his own sweat, he may have broken Marv's legs, neck, and back, but they're in.

"Okay, okay," Brendan tells Marv, "It's all good. Almost there." He pulls off his shirt and wipes his face and armpits with it. Marv's eyes are closed too tightly: he's not unconscious, he just doesn't want to see what's coming next or perhaps he's trying to master his pain. All that is left for them is one very short trip and they'll be tub-side. Brendan grunts, points the head of the wheelbarrow at the tub. The only way to get Marv in is to lift the wheelbarrow straight up and gently dump the old man in the water.

Brendan groans, Marv groans, the wheelbarrow groans. Brendan watches as, in slow motion, each frame seeming to last a full five seconds, Marv's body oozes out of the wheelbarrow, the old man's head softly hitting the tiled wall before it submerges, face first, beneath the water's surface. Marv's arms and legs twist around him like a cork clumsily forced back into the bottle.

"Fuck!"

Brendan knocks the wheelbarrow aside and grabs Marv's shoulders but his hands slide right off, thanks to the Moisturizing Magic bath oil. Somehow, Marv's wedged into the tub. Brendan grabs a wrist and ankle and pulls, desperate to get Marv's nose, Marv's mouth, above the waterline.

"Come on, ya fat son of a bitch!"

Marv's face emerges, eyes open, the mouth agape, and Brendan wonders whether he killed him, whether Marv's had another stroke or suffered a heart attack, but then Brendan hears the soft coughing and gasping and he knows that in spite of what he's done, Marv is alive—not well, but alive—and for this Brendan's truly grateful.

Somehow, he gets the old man properly situated in the tub. As he washes Marv he calms down. He sighs as he shampoos what's left of Marv's hair, promising the old man No More Tears.

For the return trip Brendan's a wiser man. He lays a thick blanket out on the bathroom floor, pulls Marv out of the bathtub by placing his arms around the old man's upper chest (he'll need to see a chiropractor if he keeps up this routine), and then lays Marv out on the blanket with a pillow under Marv's head. Brendan grabs one end of the bulky blanket and pulls, sliding Marv back into the bedroom, and though it nearly kills both of them, Brendan squats, sits Marv up, places his arms around the old man's chest again, and lifts. Once Marv's in place, Brendan walks over to the dresser for a can of high-protein drink, shakes it, sets it on the nightstand. "You did very well, Marv, I'm proud of you." He pops a straw in the can as he takes his seat next to Marv. He puts the straw up to Marv's wet lips.

"Have a drink."

Marv stares at the can.

"Drink, please." Brendan wonders what kind of positive reinforcement he can offer to encourage compliance. He comes up blank on incentives save performing a striptease, but he tried that once before and he can see where it's gotten them.

"Please," he sighs.

Marv frowns; refuses to take the straw in his mouth. The old man whispers: "Where's Frankie?"

Brendan says softly, "Frankie's still at Rush City, Marv. He's still in jail."

As if he hadn't heard him, Marv repeats himself: "Where's Frankie?"

"Have a drink, please."

Marv closes his eyes, shuts his mouth.

Brendan blows the hair out of his eyes, frustrated. "You don't want to drink it? Fine, see what I care." Brendan slams the can down on the nightstand and a bit of the Ensure pops up like Old Faithful, splashing his hand.

Gail still hasn't forgiven him. He still thanks her for admitting him, and he mentions Laura's name whenever he can, but these things fail to move her: he has been callow; he has chosen the living he can see over the living he cannot.

He ascends the worn staircase to the bulk-mail assembly room, where the volunteers have gathered. Linda says, "Well, look who's here."

He mumbles his hellos. There's an oddly austere compassion in the responses he receives, a peculiar concoction of genuine sympathy and mock pity. Some of the gals offer him treats, others look at one another knowingly. Linda scowls at the women who would condemn him for escorting a stranger to defender territory. Her expression dares them to say one word against him.

So he sits at his command center, the long table where no one but him, the only man, bags bundles. In order to get a new life he has to let parts of the one he has pass him by, as he's doing tonight. He stares at the zip codes on the envelopes that he shuffles like a blackjack dealer. He looks in the United States Postal Service directory for Healy, Alaska, the town nearest to where Alex Supertramp spent his final days, dying from living the ascetic life so revered by his favorite writers. Healy's zip code is 99743. Brendan writes it down on a scrap of paper: nine-nine-seven-four-three.

They have so much in common, Alex Supertramp and Brendan: affluent starts in life (Alex was raised in suburban D.C., Brendan began his life in Minnetonka), athletic skills (Alex competed in track and field, Brendan played basketball), a disillusionment with college (while Alex finished his degree, Brendan dropped out), the shedding of their birth names, and, of course, a love of reading (it was Alex who introduced Brendan to Russian literature, to naturalist writings). And although Alex rejected his position of privilege as a young adult, Brendan had his snatched away from him as a young boy.

Still, there is one major difference: while Alex severed relations with his family, Brendan has always desperately wanted to re-establish them with his own. In Brendan's fantasy of life with Alex, the boy fated to die in Alaska adopts Brendan's family as his own, and Brendan doesn't worry about being rejected by Alex's family—as he ultimately was by Jeff's—for Alex has already abandoned them. Aside from extended stays with Brendan's mother and brothers, the two men live in a small, remote cabin that has a comfortable bed, a fireplace, two overstuffed reading chairs, and books from floor to ceiling. There are two dogs, abandoned pups Alex and Brendan raised nearly from birth, and they accompany Alex when he hunts for food, kills that Brendan prepares on the woodstove.

Would there be trips to town for supplies? There would have to be. Alex, being the more reclusive, wouldn't accompany Brendan into town to shop for food and secondhand books and clothes. There would be no mail to pick up, as they had officially disappeared (save the visits to Brendan's family), no rude customers to serve since they had no jobs.

Judy delivers a stack of letters for bagging. She says, "You look miles away."

"Sorry," he mumbles.

"Oh no, that's fine. I didn't mean there was anything wrong." She smiles uncertainly and heads back to her table to stuff and fold some more.

During the long winter darkness Brendan would read aloud to Alex from the glow of a kerosene lamp as Alex whittled small gifts for Brendan, bears in mid-lumber, wolves captured as they howl. Each one Alex would present with a shy smile, embarrassed that these tokens are not good enough for Brendan. Brendan would always tell him, *They're perfect.*

There's a message from Sean waiting for Brendan when he arrives at Marv's house. Sean wants to host a dinner to introduce him to his closest friends, and Sean wants to run dates by him. Brendan listens to the message twice. Expanding Pierre Bezukhov's circle seems like a bad idea. He'd prefer a quiet dinner alone at Sean's house, but he already knows he'll say yes to please Sean. Pierre Bezukhov. What was he thinking?

That he'd never see Sean again.

So he sits, facing Marv. This is one of those rare occasions when he actually needs someone to talk to, the distraction of another human being. For his part, Marv is content to listen. Brendan provides the old man precious few details, apart from the fact that he's had a hard couple of days. Then he checks to see if Marv needs changing.

It's a little disconcerting to see what appears to be the beginning of diaper rash on a man of Marv's advanced years. Brendan consults his guidebook, takes corrective measures. On top of the diaper rash, the heels of Marv's feet have turned a bit pink, a sign indicating that bedsores are on their way. Brendan makes a schedule: when he's home, he'll shift the old man's position every two hours. When Marv's on his back, Brendan will place a pillow under the old man's legs (not under the knees, though, as this could reduce the flow of blood to Marv's lower legs). Finally, Brendan will have to invent some little exercises for Marv to do, and somehow (he'll figure this out later) get Marv to do them.

Exhausted, he locks Marv in his room and collapses on the bed in the smallest room. He tries to let himself go, but sleep will not come.

Hours pass. He rereads a short story, an old favorite, "Why I Live at the P. O.," by Eudora Welty:

I was getting along fine with Mama, Papa-Daddy and Uncle Rondo until my sister Stella-Rondo just separated from her husband and came back home again.

It's 3:25 A.M. He's finished the story, and then another, and then another one after that. He has an odd awareness of an eavesdropper poised at his door. He imagines Marv in the big bedroom, just down the hall. He imagines Marv holding his breath, waiting for some audible movement from Brendan's little bedroom: the rustling of sheets and blankets as Brendan tosses and turns, perhaps the sound of footsteps as Brendan makes a groggy trip to the bathroom to relieve himself. Any sound, any noise, would give Marv too much information. Brendan stays frozen in position, stiff on the mattress, his body protesting.

4:14 A.M. and Marv's as still as the grave. He's alive, though, of this Brendan is certain: a death during the night would have announced itself, the gasps, the soft moans and death rattle, the sensation you feel when a spirit abandons its shell. The old man lives on, intent, aware; he has the advantage of a history in this house, he's familiar with its noises and peculiarities. He knows when a creak from the woodwork arrives on schedule; he can easily distinguish between the routine and the unfamiliar sounds of late night. He's unable to lift himself off his own bed, he's locked in that room, yet Brendan is afraid—terrified—of Marv's presence in this house when the lights are out and it is just the two of them, alone, in Marv's home.

5:14 A.M. Marv coughs loudly. Brendan can tell by the way Marv does it that there was an effort to suppress the sounds.

6:10 A.M. It frustrates Brendan, lying there, his table perfectly set for a night of sleep, the guest that never arrives. Today he has to show up for his shift at Babies First, and he'll have to be competent, trustworthy, and likable. But, first, he'll tend to Marv's needs: nutrition, hydration, and hygiene. He will have to move the old man's arms and legs; encourage him to speak. It's unfair. If Brendan thought Marv a smarter man, he'd swear that Marv spends the nights quietly awake to ensure that Brendan gets no rest, to wear him down.

7:46 A.M. Brendan gives up. He showers, shaves, throws on some clean clothes. As he opens the padlock on Marv's door, he says loudly, pleasantly, "How are you," but then he frowns, the room's now thick with the scents of perspiration, urine, and frustration.

Marv glares at him, perhaps aware of how frightening his appearance has become. He needs a shave. His eyes are bloodshot and the red veins create a look all their own, something out of a childhood nightmare.

"How are you?" Brendan repeats.

Marv sighs, his breath rattling.

"I'll get you cleaned up."

Marv mutters softly, inaudibly.

Brendan slides the pillow out from underneath Marv's legs. The diaper Marv wears is soaked through; it smells strongly of ammonia. Brendan cleans him with the wipes; soon, though, Marv will need another bath.

Brendan makes small talk. "Nothing to say to me this morning? You know, I'm truly sorry about this, but it won't be for too much longer."

Marv coughs and then a sound comes from him, a question, "Where's Frankie?" He coughs again, spittle on his lips.

Brendan studies Marv carefully, tells him, "Frankie's not here."

The bundles for mailing arrive at his table fast and furious. An action alert is being sent to Babies First members and friends, urging them to assemble at the state capital in St. Paul for a demonstration in support of funding for an orphanage that's been proposed by the Upper

Midwest's "Mother Teresa," a woman by the name of Stella Cares. She's a local legend, founder of a soup kitchen for the homeless, The Place That Cares, after she changed her last name from Anderson to Cares. Stella herself will be paying Babies First a visit tonight, and the gals want to impress her with their productivity. He reads the action alert:

Is there any better use of our tax dollars than providing a loving environment for children without parents? With Stella Cares's Home That Cares, we will be closer to that day when the abortion industry shuts down for lack of customers. Let your legislators know you want your tax dollars to save lives, not take them!

Judy appears now, a plastic bag of disposable cameras in hand. She had run out to buy them as soon as the executive director stopped in to inform Brendan and the gals of the imminent arrival of their special guest. Gals examine the cameras intently, hoping for a photo opportunity with Stella Cares. All the gals are excited, but the Catholic gals are the most enthusiastic. Stella Cares puts a positive face on their religion, which has suffered from a long list of scandals, all involving children, other than the priest over in Wisconsin who murdered two funeral home workers. But, no, that was related to children, too: one of the workers had discovered that the priest was molesting kids.

"Isn't it wonderful," Judy asks him. "She came and spoke to our church and it was just so inspiring."

"I'm looking forward to meeting her," he says. In truth, he doesn't care, not the least little bit. For Ian and Cynthia's sakes he wants to care, and to care very deeply, but he can't bring himself to do so. His energy is consumed by feigning interest in any of it.

In what seems like mere seconds, the woman herself stands before them. Positioned next to her, the executive director leads the volunteers in a welcoming applause. The executive director smiles efficiently, not too broadly or too thinly, it's the sort of smile that works well for a camera, one that can be sustained without too much effort. When the applause has died down, he says, "I'm honored to introduce to you Stella Cares." The gals applaud again. Unlike Judy, whose hands will soon swell from their beating, Brendan claps softly, politely, the fingers of one hand gently tapping the palm of the other.

Stella Cares is heavy; she has given birth to many, many children. She's dressed simply, in a plain brown ankle-length skirt. She wears a plaid sweater that complements the skirt, her auburn-and-gray hair is tied back in a simple ponytail, and she wears no makeup. She is a large woman, tall and wide. A fashionable dress would be out of place on her frame—like a drunken frat boy at a twelve-step meeting. Her only jewelry is the large crucifix that hangs from her neck like an icicle. It's a Catholic cross; on it Jesus is dying, looking with despair to his father in heaven, who has seemingly abandoned him.

Because Brendan doesn't care, he's the first to offer their guest his hand. He says, "It's an honor to meet you."

Stella Cares pulls his hand to the place just over her heart. She says, "The honor is mine; the glory, His, and He blesses you all for your work." Bulbs flash and he's aware that his expression is wrong; he wears one of shock rather than delight. He places a smile on his lips and bows his head reverently as he timidly backs away. Cameras are thrust in his hands as gals ask him to take a picture of them next to Stella Cares, posing beside her like tourists at a monument, the Liberty Bell or Mount Rushmore. In each shot the executive director finds his way into the frame.

Next, bars and cookies are offered to the special guest, along with praise and awe for all she has accomplished. She dismisses the treats kindly with a small wave of her hand; as much as she would like to, she cannot stay, she must get back to The Place That Cares and her work—her mission, really. The executive director escorts her out.

Judy grabs Brendan's arm after Stella Cares has left, says, "We met a real, live, honest-to-goodness saint!" Then, aware of his bicep beneath her fingers, says, "Oooh, that's big!"

Gals chat amicably. They discuss the campaign that's under way to have Stella Cares canonized during her lifetime. Gals speculate over the likelihood of this happening; they comment on what an honor it would be to have a saint from Minnesota added to the canon. Only Linda looks at him in bewilderment, her face making plain that she doesn't believe in such things as saints or miracles; that these things fall into the category of recruitment tools for the simpleminded. As she drops off a bundle, she says quietly, "We're *all* saints and sinners."

He looks at her, surprised. "You don't believe in the holy saints?"

She clucks her tongue. "I believe in doing what's right without calling a lot of attention to yourself. That's just vanity." She whispers, "Honestly, these Catholics. I mean, I do adore them, but sometimes . . ." Sighing now, she says, "Oh well, I suppose we aren't any better with our Pat Robertsons and Jerry Falwells. Those men are just power-hungry, if you ask me."

She rejoins Judy, who wonders aloud if any places are still open that would develop her film in an hour.

For his part, Brendan leaves a bit early, claiming he doesn't feel very well. The first bus ride back to Marv's comes and goes uneventfully; on the second, angry black men curse each other loudly, shouting *nigger*, and he wonders how he should feel about that.

When he makes it back to Marv's house, he's feeling a bit at sea. When he enters the old man's room, he says, "Hey, Marv."

Marv lies on the bed where he left him, opens his eyes.

Brendan sits next to him, puts a hand on Marv's forehead to check his temperature. Brendan murmurs, "Feels fine."

Next, Brendan pulls the sheets and blankets back, checking Marv's diaper for color.

The old man says, "Where's Frankie?"

Brendan says, "He's not here."

Brendan somberly goes about the business of changing Marv, like an undertaker preparing the body for a wake. Marv shakes his waxy head, says in words that get clearer every day, "Cheer up." In his scratchy, neglected voice he sings: "When the lights go on again all over the world."

Brendan looks at him, stunned. "What's that?"

Marv closes his eyes. "It was . . . popular in the forties. It held out . . . the promise . . . of a better world . . . once the . . . war was over."

"I mean you're talking. Singing. Complete sentences."

Marv shrugs with his good side.

"How long have you been able to talk?"

Another half shrug.

"Say something else!"

He doesn't respond, just closes his eyes. Brendan has to keep him talking, test his memory. "Were you in the war, Marv?"

Eyes still shut, Marv says, "Oh, yes. Yes. Made some . . . of the best friends I ever had . . . during the war. Some of . . . the very best friends." He opens his eyes again, smiles. "Did you know . . . that the night . . . Roosevelt died . . . all the radio . . . would play . . . was " 'Home on the Range' "? It was . . . his favorite, I guess. Funny. I wonder . . . why I remembered . . . that just now."

Brendan says, "Feeling nostalgic?"

"I suppose so. Being here all day . . . gives me nothing to do . . . but think. About things . . . I'd nearly forgotten."

"Like the war?"

He half smirks. "No one . . . forgets a war, Brendan." He rotates his good wrist little by little. "I'd like to . . . sit up. Maybe walk . . . around if I can."

"I don't think that's a—"

"What am I . . . going to do? Overpower you?"

Brendan does as he asks. Brendan doesn't know why—pity maybe, or the need to feel like he's doing something helpful, constructive. As he slowly draws Marv's arms to his sides, the old man moans softly. Gripping Marv's armpits, Brendan grunts as he pulls Marv as gently as he can toward the headboard. Marv leans back awkwardly on a little stack of pillows. Gasping, he says, "I think . . . I'd like . . . to stand up . . . in a minute or two. Not just yet."

Brendan nods.

They sit quietly, Marv and Brendan, in the soft light of the little lamp that sits atop a dresser. It's a comforting glow, casting modest rays in all directions, reminding them how fortunate they are not to have died in a war or found themselves living alone, out on the streets.

Marv asks, "Do you . . . really think . . . I'll get better?"

Brendan crosses his legs, then his arms, tired, comfortable. "Yes, Marv, I do. You've already come such a long way."

There's a vacant look in Marv's eyes, calm, serene. It's almost as if, in this room, confined to his bed, he has found some measure of peace. Maybe Brendan's kept him alive longer than he was destined to live. Perhaps Brendan's spared him a solitary, bitter death. His reflections of the last weeks must have been a reckoning of sorts. He says, "I have children. A boy and two girls."

"I know."

"Grandchildren, too."

"I know."

"It was the only way . . . to get ahead in those days. Had to be a family man."

"Nothing has changed," he tells the old man.

Marv sighs. "Nothing, everything."

And they sit there, the two of them, staring at the lamplight.

Brendan felt he had no choice but to tell Ian about Marv. Well, he did have a choice, but the warm buzz from two-for-one Manhattans had impaired his judgment. And, truth be told, he was tired of the burden of it; it needed to be shared. What few friends he might have told (well, probably not, on second thought) have fallen away, one by one, since he broke up with Jeff.

Anyway, Ian didn't believe him, so he invited his brother over to the house, where Ian walked directly to the bedroom, Marv's bedroom, to see for himself. It feels as though hours have passed when Ian finally joins Brendan in the kitchen, where Brendan's preparing a meal for just the two of them.

Not unexpectedly, Ian's eyes are wide. He looks flush. "You really have him locked up in there," he says as he pulls a chair toward Brendan, turns it around, and sits, his arms resting on top of the backrest.

"It's a shock, I know."

"Are you fucking crazy?"

Ian's right. Brendan's been so distracted by the Walk, his work with the gals at Babies First, that he's failed to appreciate just how far over the top he's gone. He says, "I didn't plan this. I just wanted to live here, but he wouldn't let me."

Ian shakes his head and says, "You should have walked away. Found something else."

Brendan frowns; he doesn't like it when people take that tone with him, even Ian. He says, "Thanks for the hindsight. As soon as the Walk's over, I'll call his daughter, tell her to send somebody over. In the meantime he isn't all that hard to take care of. And he'll be better off for the experience; maybe I've even saved his life. Maybe after all this he won't take some stranger into his home and wind up dead."

They're quiet as Ian takes a pack of matches from his shirt pocket and lights a cigarette. Ian closes his eyes when he takes his first drag, and as the smoke flows from his nostrils he says, "This is serious. They're giving hard time to guys who take over old people's homes. There's three of them up at Rush City for doing exactly this kind of shit!"

Brendan tries to reassure him. "I haven't taken over his home. I feed him, I keep him clean, the biggest gripe he can make is that he's bored. If I keep the house nice and neat and don't steal anything, where's the crime? They're going to lock me up for being his caregiver?"

Ian says, "It *feels* like a big deal."

Brendan mutters, "Says the man who swindled old people out of their life savings."

"What was that?"

"Nothing," he offers.

"What if he dies in there? Then it's murder."

Brendan tells himself to remain calm. Don't give in to the fear, the doubts, the second-guessing. He shakes his head for Ian's benefit. "He won't die; he's received the best medical attention money can buy. He's just getting behind on his rehab for a few weeks, that's all."

Ian concedes the point, in between puffs. "It freaks me out, though. He thought I was you. I was waiting for him to jump out of bed and come at me with a gun or something." But then Ian thinks about it some more, and the panic returns. "Shit"—he calls Brendan by his given name, which Brendan wishes to hell he'd stop doing—"this could fuck up the Walk! What if you get arrested? We need you to drive the truck! They could arrest me as an accessory."

"We'll be in old Mexico soon. This is just one more thing we'll leave behind."

Ian grunts. "Cynthia and I spent months planning the Walk. Months! This," he says as he points upstairs to Marv's bedroom, "on the other hand, just *happened*." He looks at Brendan meaningfully before he continues: "Do you understand that the Walk is just a few hours of a single day? And we've planned, and planned, and planned all over again for just a few hours of a single day. But here, I mean, Jesus! You're flying by the seat of your pants! There's so many things that could go wrong; I don't even know where to fucking begin." Ian's silent for a moment until he barks, "Goddamnit!"

Brendan tries to understand; after all, his brother has only been free such a very little while. But Ian needs to be reminded of his leading role in this little drama of theirs. Brendan runs his tongue over the inside of his cheek and says, his voice steady, "Ian, this was *your* idea. You told me to come here and be Marvin Fletcher's houseboy. Well, surprise, he wanted to fuck me like I was a twenty-dollar crack whore and I wouldn't let him."

"I was trying to be helpful! I didn't tell you to give him a stroke! Shit!"

Brendan sighs. "No, you didn't. Ian, as long as you keep your cool, everything will work out just fine. I'm not going to keep Marv locked up in there forever, just until the Walk. After that we'll be long gone and he'll have learned a valuable lesson about who he invites into his home. Maybe he'll even stop trying to victimize young boys who have nowhere else to go."

Ian says, "Maybe."

Brendan's making headway. "Don't pretend that Marvin Fletcher is some innocent victim in all this. If he had nothing to hide, why didn't he just call the police that first night? Even if worse comes to worst and we're arrested, he wouldn't dare press charges, because he knows he'd be thrown in jail, too. Do you really think that any police officer, or prosecutor, or jury for that matter, is going to come to any conclusion other than that Marvin Fletcher brought this on himself?"

"Of course they would!"

"Spoken like a true heterosexual. And besides, what will the charges against me be? Feeding and dressing an old man who couldn't do it for himself? And on top of it all," Brendan reminds Ian, "I needed a place to live."

"You can sleep on our couch."

"Bit late for that, don't you think? Here, I can keep him comfortable and healthy for three lousy weeks."

Ian, once again in control of himself, says in a hush, "*Maybe* it's not so bad. It's only for a little while."

The timer interrupts with a steady ring. Brendan claps his hands together and says, "Dinner's ready! I don't know about you, but I'm starving!"

As a favor, Ian is watching Marv. Sean's hosting a dinner at his home to introduce Brendan to his friends. Candlelight illuminates the rooms and soft rock fills the house. There's the aroma of burning incense mixed with tomato sauce and garlic, but no meat, for all these people are vegetarians. The only one to eat meat tonight will be Sean's dog, Maggie. This a different set from the one that frequents the downtown clubs; these are men who paired off long ago. They arrived two by two, slight variations on the same theme, as if each pair is really just one couple cloned, their clothes slightly altered from one pair to the next, so that each twosome's appearance is distinguishable from the others'. From the waist up, at least. From the waist down they wear, without exception, blue jeans. On their feet are either tennis shoes or hiking boots. Sean's obviously thrilled as he greets them, for he now considers himself one half of a couple, too. Brendan is *the boyfriend* they have all been waiting for, Sean and his friends, and they are as passionate about everyone finding someone as they are about their politics. These are men who are environmentalists, who write letters to prevent oil exploration and drilling in the Arctic National Wildlife Refuge. They protested both wars with Iraq, both Bushes; they bemoan the fact that big corporations and big money run the country. Two are recently back from Canada, where they were legally married. The men range in age from mid-thirties to mid-fifties, and while amicable company there's an anger beneath their calm surface; rage runs through them like a fault line. The litany of outrages is long and varied: tax cuts for the rich, the GOP, the NRA, homophobia, fundamentalism, racism, global warming, sexism, just to name a few. In between expressing outrage, they compliment Sean on the meal, spaghetti with organic whole-wheat pasta. The "meatballs" are browned tofu and Maggie refuses the forkful Brendan tries to slip her under the table.

None of them talk about books; they are too busy for such things. Registering voters, circulating petitions, volunteering at AIDS organizations, rescuing dogs, these are the things that take up all their time. The dog rescuers get Brendan's attention and they have a pleasant conversation about how much he loves dogs, how he prefers them to the average human being.

"Except Sean," one-half of one of the couples offers. The dinner party laughs. Sean's status as the unhappy bachelor has been quickly buried without comment; the long absence of a man in his life was the one thing throwing this otherwise complete and like-minded set of gay men off balance. Now, with the group's equilibrium finally restored, the couples can relax. Brendan looks at the opposite end of the table where Sean sits, as if he were the last of his class to graduate but still grateful for the diploma. Brendan smiles at him, at all of them. He's been cast as the boyfriend, and for some reason, he relishes the role. He decides against being a star-crossed lover, preferring to act the part of the muscular hero from Cynthia's romance novels.

They're in the middle of a carob dessert bar when one of Sean's friends, a man of perhaps thirty-eight, changes the subject from politics by saying to Brendan, "Pierre isn't a name you hear every day."

Brendan stabs a bit of bar with his fork. He smiles as he says, "I'm the only Pierre I know."

An older man says, "There's the French skunk in the cartoons that always chases that cat."

"That's *Pepé* Le Pew, not Pierre Le Pew," the man next to him says with a laugh.

Another man, about Brendan's age, says, "There's Pierre Bezukhov in *War and Peace*."

Of course Sean has to say, "That's his last name! Bezukhov!"

With a generous helping of disbelief in his voice, one of the men just back from Canada asks Brendan, "Your last name is Bezukhov?"

Brendan nods.

"Pierre Bezukhov," he says. "I don't believe it."

Brendan doesn't know this man well enough to decide if his tone is accusing or teasing but judging from the other guests, he's created something of a stir. They frown at him, not for Brendan's sake but for Sean's. Sean's face is the picture of unease; it's as if he has shown his guests a trophy recently won, only to have them remark that the engraver spelled his name wrong.

Stories come naturally to Brendan, so it costs him no effort to explain, "My parents met in a Russian literature class and they worshiped Tolstoy. They even named my sister Natasha."

Laughter now, and the moment passes. He has a quirky name, but it's the fault of his parents, who fully understood what they were doing when they christened him Pierre Bezukhov. It's a harmless, intriguing little anecdote.

Sean leans forward on both elbows now, his face reveling in the back-and-forth between the people he loves best, and Brendan understands that Sean has fallen completely in love with him. Brendan wonders how Sean could have fallen so fast but then Sean was ready for this, aching for it, it's not Brendan he's in love with, rather it's the idea of being in love with Brendan. When you're aboard Noah's Ark, a singleton in the midst of two of everything, you'll swear that anyone, even someone like Brendan, was made just for you.

Brendan studies him. Sean's not the most attractive man at this gathering, but in spite of himself, Brendan finds something endearing in Sean's expression, the way his eyes let you know just how much he's enjoying himself. Sean catches Brendan looking at him and winks. Brendan rolls his eyes, but this, too, Sean takes as a sign of how much Brendan loves him.

The hours pass and, couple by couple, the company departs in the order they arrived. As they thank Sean profusely they hug Brendan tightly as if he were an old friend. When the final twosome is out of the door Sean collapses on the couch, sighing. Brendan stands in front of him, stroking Maggie's soft ears.

"It was a fun evening," Brendan offers.

Sean holds his hand out to him with a smile. "Come here."

Brendan lets Sean pull him down next to him. Sean's arms squeeze him tight and he grows sleepy.

Now Sean rests his forehead over Brendan's ear, whispers, "They liked you a lot, Pierre. Relax."

It's sweet really, this idea Sean has that Brendan's worried, afraid that Sean's friends didn't approve of him. He's supposed to act relieved, grateful that the dinner went so well. He says, "I'm glad."

Now Sean licks Brendan's earlobe, making him giggle in spite of himself. Sean whispers, "I'm sooo glad you're glad."

Brendan tries to pull away, embarrassed by Sean's silly affections, the way Sean points and laughs at the walls Brendan's built around himself, the ones he's had such confidence in for so long, the straw house he's shocked to find himself living in when he had convinced himself it was made of stone and mortar.

When Brendan kisses Sean, he means it. He says, "Let's leave the dishes for tomorrow."

———

The little scene that awaits Brendan reminds him of when he'd come home late from a party, his father in a robe, waiting up for him (had that ever actually happened?). Ian's gone, having left behind a terse note: *It's late.* The red light of the answering machine is blinking, undoubtedly there are some messages from bill collectors threatening to cut off service, cancel credit. He'll listen to them later. He walks into Marv's room, the lamp alight, the old man's eyes looking at him, expectantly, for some sort of explanation.

He says, "Sorry, Marv. I didn't mean to be gone so long."

Marv coughs, ahems. "Where were you?"

"Out. With a friend."

"Thought you had . . . just the one."

"Did my friend take good care of you?" No sense telling him Ian's name, or the fact that they're brothers, though perhaps he's surmised that already from their striking resemblance.

Marv frowns. "I don't like him."

Brendan shakes his head as he pulls the sheet and the blanket down to check the diaper, which needs changing. The diaper's wet (Marv doesn't move his bowels much anymore, thanks to his liquid diet). Marv's a smaller man than when this all began, thinner, sober.

"Why don't you like my friend?"

"I smelled . . . my scotch on his . . . breath. He looks at me . . . like I'm something he . . . just stepped in."

"You can't blame him for sampling your scotch, Marv, it's good stuff. As for the way he looks at you, maybe he's just trying to figure out what Frankie saw in you."

"What?"

"Nothing, forget it."

"What Frankie . . . saw in me?"

The new diaper's in place. He's taken to dressing Marv these past few days, so he changes the loose T-shirt with a fresh one, pushes a clean pair of sweatpants up Marv's legs. All the while the old man pesters him, asks how Ian knows his Frankie. Marv doesn't let up so Brendan ignores him, preparing the room for the evening walk: the chair is placed against a wall, obstacles on the floor (Ian's empty glass, for example) are picked up and set out of the way.

"He knows . . . my Frankie? How? How?"

"Will you give it a rest?"

"How? How? How?"

"From Rush City, okay? They knew each other in Rush City. That's how I got your name and number. Frankie told my friend and my friend told me."

"I see." Marv is quiet for a moment, but then he gives him his signal, a nod or a sigh, to let Brendan know they should begin. Together, they slide his body closer to the edge of his bed; next, the old man slowly swings his legs out as he pivots as best he can. Brendan reaches under his arms, gently pulls him to a sitting position. Because holding his head up can make Marv dizzy, they wait to see if spots form in front of his eyes before they go any further. Marv catches his breath, swallows. There's a fierce determination in his eyes, as if he's grateful for this challenge. His arms around Brendan's shoulders now, they grip each other carefully, and on the count of one-two-three, they stand.

A short rest before Marv puts his good foot out in front and together they compensate for his bad one. The old man acclimates roughly to this new position, his heart racing from the exertion. Another of his signals and they slowly walk, side by side, around the room. The old man grunts from the effort, from the use of muscles that had been left to decay.

Brendan needs to make this man whole before he leaves.

After Brendan returns Marv to the bed, he puts on a CD. Glenn Miller fills the room and Marv's face relaxes as familiar melodies play. Brendan does this so the old man will reminisce, exercise his mental faculties. Marv says, "Miller never made it . . . to that concert in Paris. Tragic."

An odd collection of memories come back to Marv: redbaiters picketing a Charlie Chaplin film, the birth of his first child, the time the furnace gave out in his second house. Occasionally he talks about his own parents, the father who deserted his family in the thirties, the mother who moved her children in with her sister and brother-in-law and could never afford to move them out again.

The talking exhausts him. Brendan pulls up the sheets like he's tucking a child in for the evening. He says good night to the old man. Marv will fall asleep. Tonight Brendan won't lie awake, convinced that the old man's eavesdropping. Tonight Brendan will lie awake, ashamed of himself for bringing them both to this.

Brendan wishes he could sleep at night.

6

Why I Live at the P. O.

THE PHONE RINGS while Marv is complaining again about the vanilla-flavored Ensure Brendan feeds him. Instead of waiting to hear the caller's voice on the answering machine, as he usually does before he picks up, he rushes to answer it. After twenty minutes or so, he enters the bedroom again.

Marv says, "Do you have . . . a boyfriend?"

That question's unexpected. Brendan says, "Did you finish off the can?"

"Do you have . . . a boyfriend?"

He stares at the old man. "Why on earth would you ask me that?"

Marv half smiles at him. It's an odd smile, not the lustful one he greeted Brendan with when they first met. Brendan tries to gauge its sincerity, but as recent events have borne out, neither of them are particularly good judges of character. Marv says, "You do have . . . a boyfriend. You raced to the phone . . . like a schoolgirl. You're not wallowing . . . in it like you . . . usually do. What else could it be?"

Brendan picks up the can and shakes it: it's empty; Marv's finished the Ensure in spite of himself. "My friend will be around to look after you again tonight. I have to go out."

"So you do . . . have a boyfriend." Then Marv reminds him again: "I hate your friend."

"I know." Brendan cleans up the small mess—the empty can, the used straw and napkin—and puts out a fresh can and straw to serve as a visual cue for Ian that Marv has to be fed. On the chair next to the bed he lays two clean diapers, another reminder for Ian of Marv's bodily needs.

Marv watches the preparations skeptically, says, "He'll spend all night . . . in front of the damn television . . . drinking my best scotch."

"I'm sorry."

"Tell me about . . . your boyfriend. Does he know . . . about me? I bet he doesn't."

Brendan bundles up the dirty sheets; covers the old man with fresh ones. He's chosen plaid sheets from the linen closet instead of the usual white ones; Marv could use a little color. Perhaps he should buy new sheets for Marv's bed, ones with cartoon characters on them, Bugs Bunny or Scooby-Doo, to make the old man look harmless, ridiculous, help take the edge off his little comments. Against bedclothes of pure white he looks pitiable, dangerous, the starkness adds legitimacy to his accusations, the allegations against his brother and him. He tells the plaid, colorful Marv, "You know what? I *am* seeing someone. And no, of course he doesn't know about you."

"If he did I bet . . . he'd run as far . . . and as fast as he could."

"You're right, he would. And that's what I like about him. He's completely normal. What you see is what you get. He's a simple man, there's no mystery about him."

"Sounds dull."

"Unpretentious."

"Same thing."

"Yes, and Frankie was such a complicated man." He starts to say something else but stops. This back-and-forth is something like banter and he doesn't like it. He doesn't like it because he doesn't know which one of them is suffering from Stockholm Syndrome, Marv or him.

Now Marv half smiles his lusting smile. "Is he good-looking?"

He ignores the question; asks the old man, "Did you watch *The Matrix* last night or *Spirited Away?*" They alternate the films every day.

Marv frowns. "The cartoon one."

"Don't you have a DVD club membership somewhere? I wouldn't mind renting you some new movies."

Marv says, as if Brendan should know this already, "But these were . . . Frankie's favorite films. When I watch these . . . I can pretend I'm holding Frankie. I can pretend that we're watching them together."

He puts *The Matrix* in the DVD player.

At last, it's May. But now, with the Walk only three weeks away, his Babies First charade demands more and more from him, time that should be spent looking after Marv or making love to Sean. Tonight he has to share a meal with Judy, who has an unmarried daughter about his age. He knows this because she told him so right after he accepted an invitation to dinner at her home.

He told Ian about it casually, along with his decision not to go through with it. Ian thought it wasn't a problem but when he mentioned it to his wife she called immediately, told Brendan that he absolutely should not, could not cancel. She said she was worried about him. He had made a fool of himself at the action, and now he was refusing a dinner invitation from one of the few allies he still had left at Babies First. If he had any doubts, if he didn't feel he could stick with the plan, he should let them know now and spare everyone a lot of pain. He told her he just didn't feel like sitting through a dinner with holy rollers. *But, if you insist,* he told her, *I'll do it.*

She insisted.

When he told Sean that Natasha, his born-again sister, whose home Scan isn't allowed to visit, had demanded he spend the evening in, Sean said that he understood but Maggie did not.

To get to Judy's house, it's three bus rides on unfamiliar routes followed by a half-mile hike on streets without sidewalks. All the homes look the same, large three-car garages with living quarters hiding some-where behind them. When Brendan arrives at Judy's door she puts both hands on her cheeks, overcome by the small arrangement of flowers he presents to her. Judy's a plain woman; worry lines are her most promi-nent feature, along with the chins that ripple down her neck like the surface of a lake after a stone has skipped across it. There are some peo-ple who confound him, who provide him no clue as to the day, the year, the era he finds himself in. Judy's one of those people; she would look as appropriate in the fifties as she does in this new millennium. You could see a snapshot of her and have no idea from her dress or her demeanor when the photo was taken. Some call this a timeless quality, but not, he thinks, in Judy's case. It's something else, a complete obliviousness to the trends and events swirling around her.

She says, "Oh, you shouldn't have! Oh, look, they're beautiful, just beautiful. You know, I don't think a man has given me flowers since my Hank died."

She calls to her unmarried daughter: "Helen! Helen, come here and look at what Brendan brought us!"

Helen appears in the large entryway that's full of coats, boots, shoes, Judy, flowers, him. She smiles admiringly at the little bouquet. Next, she negotiates her hand around her mother, places it in his. "Nice to meet you, Brendan. Mom's told me all about you."

"The pleasure's mine," he tells her. She blushes slightly, looks down. She is what his adoptive mother would call a *handsome woman*, attrac-tive in a practical way, the sort of person who finds herself invited to functions rather than candlelit dinners.

Judy looks at them, at one and then the other, and her face beams with the possibilities this picture presents. It's Helen who has to say, "Why don't we move into the great room?"

In a cavernous white room, Judy tells them to have a seat, get ac-quainted. She asks him what he'd like to drink and he says a glass of water. He doubts this house has a single drop of alcohol under its roof and, besides, Ian's daily happy hours have put him off liquor. Helen po-litely asks for a diet cola.

The great room feels like a wax museum, a place where time ceases to exist. The knickknacks that line the shelves of a far bookcase remind him of a petrified forest. Helen smoothes out her dress, smiles handsomely. Their anxiety is a large and unwelcome third in the great room, and as it makes itself comfortable for the long evening ahead, Helen asks him if he's originally from Minnesota.

He recalls a favorite Eudora Welty short story. He says, "No, I'm from a little place called China Grove in Mississippi."

"Mississippi? I don't think I've ever met anyone from Mississippi. You're a long way from home."

He smiles. "I haven't lived there in years."

"What brought you all the way up here?"

He makes a small joke: "The weather."

Helen laughs politely as her mother joins them, a tray of drinks in her hands. As she distributes the water and diet colas, Helen asks her, "Did you know that Brendan's from Mississippi?"

Judy stops in her tracks. She looks at him afresh: "Mississippi? I've never met anyone from Mississippi before."

Helen says, "That's what I said!"

Judy says, "You don't have an accent."

He takes a sip of his water, timeless like Judy's outfit. "Oh, I lost the accent as soon as I could. No offense, but you Northerners have a very annoying habit of mocking Southern accents."

Judy finally sits on a large chair outfitted in a floral print, sighing. "Oh, isn't that a shame?"

He talks about his life in China Grove, about his sister, Stella-Rondo, and his niece, little adopted Shirley T, the marvelous blond child. He tells them about his grandfather, whom he called Papa-Daddy, and his grandfather's beard, which Papa-Daddy never trimmed once from the age of fifteen. He tells them about Cousin Annie Flo, who went to her grave denying the facts of life. As he talks, time snaps back on, seconds begin to tick by, then minutes, finally hours. He leaves the two women, mother and daughter, confident that his personal history had made him far too colorful to be suitable husband material.

———————

He exits the third of three buses he had to take to get from Judy's home back to Marv's neighborhood. He has this peculiar habit of sighing whenever his feet are back on the sidewalk after a bus ride, the way he imagines some sailors exhale deeply after landing safely in port after a long voyage. Yes, he knows it's not the same thing, there are no storms or icebergs to avoid on the bus, just the tedium, the noise of cell phones and loud conversations, the occasional crazy person who winds up sitting next to you, a hat made of aluminum foil on the nut's head. He revels in the cool of the evening as he surveys the streets, dark, the light of the streetlamps obscured and diffused by the budding branches of overgrown elms, maples. He hears the occasional car as it slowly passes by and then the more pleasant sound of toenails on concrete, the little *tip-tapping* of a dog out for its walk. He turns to take a look, stroke its fur, ask it questions like *Who's the good boy?*

The dog is small, a Jack Russell terrier, not his favorite breed, but it will do. He kneels down and without asking the owner's permission presents his palm for it to sniff, the *Hello, how are you?* before he can pet its fur, make a fuss. Smiling, his eyes follow the leash to the small, withered hand, and he knows immediately by the slight curve of the fingers, the way the thumb curls around the leather strap, that it belongs to his adoptive mother.

Her eyes water and her voice falters as she says, "Hello, son."

He stays where he is, on a bended knee. He shifts his eyes from her hand back to the dog, who's friendly, probably starved for affection, given its owner. He says, "Good evening, Mrs. Moore."

And there they are, on a dark street.

She wipes her nostrils. "I thought I saw you a few months ago. I tried to get your attention, but I guess you didn't see me."

"Guess I didn't."

"How are you?" she asks, her voice trembling.

He pets her dog under the chin. "Nice pooch. What's its name?"

She smiles, says "Anna."

"After Freud's daughter?"

An enthusiastic nod. "Yes."

He pets Anna and she wags her tail, sticks out her tongue to lick him. "Well," he tells Anna, "I better be on my way."

Mrs. Moore says loudly, dramatically: "Your father died of cancer three years ago this February." By "father" she means her husband. Her voice softens as she adds, "He wanted to see you before he died. I tried everything I could think of to find you."

He lets Anna clean his palm. "I'm sorry for your loss."

"Why did you disappear without a word? We were worried sick."

"I'm gay. I knew how you felt about that."

He feels Mrs. Moore's hand on his head, stroking his hair uncertainly. "Your father went to his grave sorry for how we left things. You dropped out of college, you were gay. We just didn't understand. He wanted to see you so badly."

He asks, "Who did he leave his estate to?"

She stutters slightly as she says, "Well, me."

"And you'll leave yours to . . . ?"

He hears her choke as she calls him by his given name.

He stands with a soft grunt. He takes Anna in, her attentive eyes, her strong ears that move like small radar receivers searching the cold night sky. "Take my advice. Leave it to this poor little dog."

Mrs. Moore whimpers, "Son, please."

He turns away.

After a few moments he hears Mrs. Moore say, "Anna, come." He looks and the dog reluctantly turns around, following her with a regretful backward glance toward him. He sees Mrs. Moore's gray hair cut fashionably short, he sees her delicate hips move up and down as she slowly walks away, her flat buttocks hardly making a dent in her navy-blue slacks. He recognizes her gait, it was the one she employed in malls, school hallways, streets like this one, the walk that would make him shout *Please come back*. As soon as she heard those three desperate little words she'd finally turn, and with her eyebrows raised, a capable smile spread across her lips, hold out her arms to forgive him.

That poor little dog.

When he arrives back at Marv's, Ian's waiting by the door. Brendan smells the scotch on his brother's breath. Ian's face is flushed as he tells him, "About time. I was about to kill that old bastard."

He opens his mouth to ask what the problem is, but he stops. Even from the entryway he can hear Marv: the slow, slurred moans; the soft curses. Alarmed, he asks Ian, "Jesus, what did you do to him?"

Ian flinches. "I didn't do a fucking thing! He was bitching as soon as I walked in the room. 'Stop drinking my scotch. Stop stealing my things.' And then he starts in on me about Frankie. 'How do you know my Frankie? How's Frankie doing?' Blah, blah, blah. So I told him, 'You know what, Frankie was my punk-ass bitch, *that's* how I *know* him.' Then he loses it. He's been screaming for hours."

Brendan mutters *Jesus Christ* and leaves Ian by the door. Ian shouts, "I'm going, okay? I can't take any more of this shit!" Brendan hears the front door slam as he rushes up the stairs and into Marv's room. The light's on, and on the bed, flailing his left side, is Marv himself, on the verge of another stoke.

"Calm down," Brendan says as he sits next to the old man. He grabs Marv's left arm and puts Marv's good hand in his own, holds it tightly. He says, "*Shh,* come on now, it's okay, it's alright, just calm down, please."

Marv looks at him now and spits out, "That bastard! That son of a bitch! He raped my Frankie! He raped him!"

He strokes Marv's pink scalp, says, "*Shh,* take it easy. My friend's no rapist."

"What are you saying?"

He sighs, rolls his eyes. "I'm saying that my friend was probably just horny and Frankie was probably just lonely. Or horny. Or lonely and horny."

"He wouldn't do that to me."

Brendan can't help himself, he giggles, just a little. "Marv, come on."

Marv scowls at him, but then the old man turns his head as best he can. "Leave me alone."

"Don't pout."

"Leave me alone!"

Brendan gets up, checks the windows, which are closed tight. He says, "You sure you don't want me to read to you a little bit before lights out? Some *Harry Potter*? It might help calm you down."

Pathetically now Marv mutters, "Just leave me alone."

So Brendan locks the old man in for the night; checks the box for the mail that infrequently arrives. There's a credit card bill. He opens it, scans the charges from late March through late April and is shocked to find thousands of dollars' worth of charges, all of them made since Marv was moved back home.

"Jesus Christ."

He runs back to the bedroom, unlocks the door, snaps the lights on. He looks at Marv, startled. He says, "What have you been doing?"

Marv stares at him.

"Do you have a phone in here?"

Marv stammers, "No."

He stands over the old man. "Are you lying to me? Because I swear to god . . ."

Fearful now, Marv whispers, "No."

Brendan stares at him, alarmed to find that he can cause such terror. He says, "I'm sorry."

Marv doesn't say a word.

He tells him again that he's sorry. He turns off the light, closes the door, locks it, angry with himself. This is Ian's handiwork, of course, his brother couldn't help himself.

The Walk can't come soon enough.

Cynthia has taken Brendan to the park where the Walk for the Unborn will be held. He had considered telling Cynthia about what Ian had done but decided against it. He'll talk to his brother directly, not through the wife. Cool rain has made the ground slick, so they tread cautiously as the mid-morning sun tries to peek out from behind low clouds. "Over there," she says, pointing with a blueberry-colored fingernail, "is where the bandstand will be. Everybody's supposed to listen to the guy preaching from the bandstand, but other preachers always show up with their own bullhorns and it can get kinda loud."

Brendan tries to picture the rival sermons competing for the attention of the faithful. He asks, "Where do they park the trucks?"

Cynthia nods in the direction of a small parking lot near the pavilion, not too far from the main parking lot where they left the van. She says, "The pavilion parking lot is reserved for the delivery trucks and the media and politicians. Wear some big old sunglasses and a baseball cap in case they're taping interviews near your truck." She frowns as she looks him over. "Cut that mop of yours so the cap covers most of your hair, you're so shaggy right now you're easy to remember. And don't wear shorts. Try to cover as much of your skin as possible, but don't be conspicuous. But wear a Babies First T-shirt, everybody'll be wearing 'em. You want to look like everybody."

He says, "You told me no one could figure out how we did it."

Cynthia gives him an easy smile, the white of her teeth making her skin appear darker. "They won't. Not the day of the event anyway. It'll take at least a couple of days for them to figure out that some money's missing. If they figure it out. And if they figure it out, it'll take them another couple of days to figure out who might've taken the cash. Remember what I told you: they'll probably think it's somebody working registration. I'm more at risk than you are."

This is most likely true.

She places her hands on her hips now, surveys this little piece of greenery like a pioneer in search of a spring. She says, "I know you've got doubts, Brendan. Trust me, so do I. But then I think of what this money could do for us and I take all my misgivings and I offer them up." She looks at him now. "I just offer them up 'cause life's too short not to at least try and be happy. You know what I'm saying?"

He nods with a tiny smirk, barely perceptible to either of them.

She winks at him. "You know, you're a good-looking man. Not as good-looking as Ian, but good-looking all the same."

Shy now, he says, "No, I'm not."

She laughs and he admires her dark hair, which she's had corn-rowed, extenders making it appear as if her hair stops well below her shoulders. She says, "Saying shit like that just makes you all the more adorable. I don't know why what's-his-face ever dumped you."

His shyness evaporates like morning dew in the hot sun. "I left him."

"Whatever."

They stand there, taking it all in. Finally, Cynthia says, "Let's time the route." They walk back to the large parking lot where the Voyager sits alone. Brendan is a gentleman as he opens the passenger door for his sister-in-law before he takes his place behind the steering wheel.

Cynthia lights a cigarette as Brendan turns on the van's ignition. Tentatively, he puts the van in first gear.

"Slow and easy," she reminds him.

They thrust forward in tiny jerks.

"Put the clutch in and shift," Cynthia says. Brendan complies and makes a smooth transition to second gear. Cynthia laughs, says, "Didn't I tell you? If could teach my grandma to drive, I can teach anyone!"

Brendan's pleased with himself, but it's impossible for him not to imagine that he'll screw up on the day of the Walk, the day he's actu-ally driving the truck, impossible not to know he will grind the truck's gears as its engine floods. He can almost see it, the rental truck slowly coasting to a dead stop as he panics, shouting curses and wondering what to do next.

Brendan's relieved as the van joins the sporadic Sunday traffic, he savors the easy transition between gears and tells himself that the de-livery truck will operate likewise, save the fact that it's bigger and he will be seated higher up.

Cynthia directs him in a clipped, matter-of-fact voice. It takes just under fifteen minutes to drive the van from the parking lot to the Ba-bies First office. As they idle on University Avenue, Cynthia says, "Cool, cool. Okay, let's backtrack. Keep your eyes peeled for a good place to unload."

They retrace their route slowly, now unconcerned with the time it takes them. An old water tower catches Cynthia's attention. She points to it and says, "Head there."

The van turns left and goes up a small hill. They investigate the possibilities: the neighborhood is high density, but there's an empty parking lot next to an old school, just below the water tower. Pulling in, Cynthia cranes her neck in all directions. When Brendan draws the van to a halt she lights a cigarette.

"Okay," she says, "on our right is the school building, which'll be empty on a Sunday, and beyond that the park and the water tower. Straight ahead trees and brush, and beyond that some houses, but no clear view of the lot." She sucks in her lips. To their left is more parking lot, and past it trees and a few homes. Behind them more parking lot, a street, and then a few more homes. She says, "This could work. Whadya think?"

He studies the lot and its single Dumpster. Next, he looks into the windows of homes that border it. A person of indeterminate sex walking a small dog appears on the sidewalk that cuts across the lot's driveway, and then quickly disappears. The water tower is an easy landmark. "I think it will work."

Cynthia gives him a quick hug. As he turns the van around she says, "This is gonna work! This is *gonna* work!"

Marv says he can manage by himself, propped up in his bed. He doesn't want Ian to look after him; he'd rather take his chances alone. Brendan has plans with Sean and he hasn't confronted Ian yet about the credit card, so he lets Marv have it his way.

Before Brendan leaves, he outfits the old man with clean sheets and pillowcases. The diaper doesn't really need changing, but it was old, so he dresses Marv in a new one. The final piece to complete tonight's ensemble is an old flannel robe that he wraps Marv in, tying it around the waist in a loose knot. Marv doesn't comment on this new addition to his wardrobe; instead, he closes his eyes as the familiar texture of the fabric embraces him. It seems a welcome surprise.

Brendan doesn't mind the walk to the bus stop now that the scent of lilacs is in the air. Overhead, the leaves glow green from the branches of trees. On Lake Calhoun, he sees Canadian geese hatchlings swimming with their parents. When the bus does arrive, he finds a midsection seat he can have all to himself.

Sean has a surprise of his own for Brendan tonight: instead of a meal at the kitchen table with Maggie at their feet, he's made reservations at W. A. Frost, an upscale restaurant in St. Paul. Brendan's dressed too casually for the exposed-brick-and-fireplace style of the restaurant, but Sean doesn't seem to mind. He insists Brendan select the wine, so Brendan orders a merlot to start, and as the waitress turns to leave, Sean reaches across the small table for Brendan's hand, which he places in his own. An elderly couple across from them flinches and looks away.

"Are you embarrassed?" Sean asks.

"A little," Brendan admits.

"You shouldn't worry about what the breeders think. Just because they act like this is their planet doesn't mean it's true."

It's refreshing, Sean's naïveté. He assumes that Brendan's afraid of other people's bigotry, when in fact it's his own pessimism that frightens him. He knows he'll ruin this, so why bother enjoying it? And really, why does Sean want him? Sean knows nothing about his life save the lies that he chooses to tell him. Brendan wonders who the bigger fool is.

Sean squeezes his hand as he lets go. "I don't want you to be uncomfortable," he says.

They sit in silence, the flames of the fire flickering across the walls, the ceiling. The quiet conversations of the other diners who surround them sound like gentle waves lapping at the sides of a boat. There's something about Sean: an uncomplicatedness, a simplicity that makes him hard when he's without love and soft as Maggie's fur when he's with it. Sean tells him he wants him to meet his parents, who live in a trailer court in Florida. They'll soon be back north to stay with Sean's sister and her family through Minnesota's summer months.

"It's still early days," Brendan says.

Sean grins a stupid grin, says, "You're right. We hardly know each other."

The waitress returns, places a wineglass in front of each of them. She sets the bottle of merlot on the table, produces a corkscrew from an apron pocket. As she twists it into the cork, Sean looks like a little boy, delighted by this magic trick preformed at his very own table.

The cork removed, a small bit of wine is poured in Sean's glass, without any instruction; the waitress has accurately assessed who at her table is the adult, who the child. Approving the vintage, a favorite ritual of Brendan's father, seems wasted on Sean. Sean swirls the glass comically, lifts it to his lips as if wanting to say *between the lips and through the gums, look out stomach, here it comes*. He swallows, says, "Ah!" He nods and the waitress fills their glasses, sets the bottle down between them.

Sean lifts his glass. "A toast."

Brendan holds his glass up as he searches the dining room for disapproving looks.

Sean says, "To us."

Brendan says, "To us," and touches his glass to Sean's.

They drink.

Sean doesn't wait until he's had too much wine to say, "You know, Pierre, I think I'm in love with you."

Brendan reminds him again: "You hardly know me."

Sean laughs, says, "Maybe that's why." Whatever expression Sean sees on Brendan's face tempers his own. He mutters, "Sorry."

"My fault," Brendan tells him. "It's been a long time since anyone told me that they were in love with me."

"Not as long as since I've heard it, I bet."

This, of course, is Brendan's cue. He's been so busy making people miserable—Marv, Ian, Cynthia, himself—that the opportunity to make someone happy shouldn't be allowed to pass. He says, "I think I might be falling in love with you, too."

Sean actually swoons in front of him; the man's a hopeless romantic. An adorable, hopeless romantic.

Marv seems to have bounced back from his discovery of Frankie's infidelity, so now he spends his time reminiscing. It's beginning to affect Brendan. Tonight, during their walk around the bedroom, Brendan told a story he had no intention of sharing with the old man. After Marv relived the excruciating details of his arrest on the banks of the Mississippi, the one phone call he had mistakenly made to his wife, the divorce, all of it, he asked Brendan if Brendan's parents had reacted badly when they found out that he was a homosexual. Brendan's mother and father never had the opportunity to find out, nor did any of his foster parents. Only his adoptive parents discovered the truth, and not from him.

His adoptive mother summoned him to his room one day when he was fifteen years old. She was upset: the three of them—Mrs. Moore, her husband, and Brendan—weren't doing well at the family therapy sessions his adoptive psychologist parents facilitated each Thursday after dinner. Brendan never opened up to them, failed to share anything intimate or shameful. So, in an attempt to crack him open and relieve him of the torment she was convinced was eating him up inside, she made him watch as she searched his room. She was certain he'd reveal the secrets that she was on the verge of discovering anyway: the journal or diary, a pack of cigarettes, some marijuana or pornography.

She began by combing through the dresser drawers; then she moved on to the shelving. She got down on her hands and knees to discover anything tucked away at floor level. Finally—because he was saying nothing—she shoved an arm between the mattress and the box spring, the usual place where shameful things reside.

Her fingers made out pages, the flat texture of writing paper, not the slick, glossy finish of a *Playboy*. It took some effort, but she locked onto the sheets, gently pulled them toward her. She said: *A journal, it must be a journal. Finally, some insight into what goes on in that head of yours.*

It revealed itself to be a tablet of plain white notebook paper, blank save five words scrawled in black Magic Marker across the front page: STAY OUT OF MY ROOM!!!

She looked up at the ceiling and back down at his message.

She said, *You little shit.*

She shoved the pad back impatiently; his taunt had only convinced her to look harder, dig deeper.

She headed for the closet. *Anything you want to tell me?* she asked.

He shook his head.

She rummaged through the clothes on the hangers, inspected the shoes that lined the closet's walls. All the hiding places were empty, the pockets, cuffs, the insides of the sneakers and the more formal footwear. It was then, as she sat on the floor of his closet, defeated, annoyed, that she looked up and saw the ceiling panel that provided access to a crawl-space, which itself gave way to the attic.

She smiled her knowing smile. Game, set, and match.

The closet's ceiling was high; she reached it only by standing atop a six-foot ladder she had dragged from the garage. She pushed the panel up and slid it over. She wasn't tall enough to get her head through the opening, so she searched its perimeters with one hand, the other braced against a wall, helping her keep her balance.

She felt plastic. A plastic bag. She ran the tips of her fingers along its sides. *Magazines,* she announced, the bag contains magazines. She asked again, *Anything you want to tell me?*

He thought, *No, nothing I want to tell you.*

She stood on tiptoe to gain a solid hold on the bag. She almost lost her balance and the shock of the near-fall made her gasp.

The bag appeared. It was orange, the discount color.

She talked to herself: *Easy. Easy. Don't drop it.*

Bag clutched to her belly, she treaded cautiously down the ladder and took a seat on his bed. *How bad could it be? Do you want to tell me or must I find out for myself?* She reached in, hoping to find an old *Playboy,* nothing too graphic or, worse, violent.

She stared at the cover of the first magazine in the stack that sat on her lap. There was a picture of a teenage boy, a very pretty teenage boy, not all that much older than Brendan was back then. The very pretty teenage boy was fully dressed and surrounded by a heart silhouette.

She set it aside. But the next magazine was just like the one before it, just like the one after it would be, just like they all were.

WIN A DREAM DATE WITH TYLER!

She started her review over again with the first magazine; she had obviously gotten something very wrong. She carefully inspected each in turn, one by one.

BRANDON'S SECRET HEARTBREAK!

ARE YOU THE PERFECT GIRL FOR ERIK?

She finished, patted the pile into a neat, tidy stack, and started over yet again.

JOSH'S BRUSH WITH DEATH!

TERRY'S POOL PARTY BLAST!

She sat.

She sucked her lips between her teeth.

She sat.

"And that," Brendan tells Marv as he sits the old man back down on the bed, "was that. We never discussed it again."

Marv looks at him, amused but unsure, as if Brendan had just told him a story from someone else's life. But in fact, Brendan's told the truth. For the first time since the stroke, he has told Marv the truth. Marv regards Brendan calmly as Brendan wishes him a good night. Brendan leaves the old man alone in the vain hope that both of them will be able to sleep through the night.

What Brendan left out of the story was how his adoptive father had reacted when Mrs. Moore told him about the magazines, which she must have done during one of their journeys of self-discovery. His adoptive father was an advocate of tough love. He had forged his modest career on its principles, hence the point system that rewarded Brendan's compliant behavior and punished any original, unscripted thought Brendan may have expressed in his adoptive father's presence. His adoptive father believed that Brendan's attraction to boys was not an intrinsic characteristic; it was either an act of rebellion or a sickness in need of cure. The antidote to both was conversion therapy, conducted every other day for three months in the claustrophobic study. In addition to traditional counseling in which his adoptive father asked questions and solemnly pointed out the greater truths behind Brendan's responses, he showed Brendan photos of beautiful men and women, some taken from the same magazines Mrs. Moore had discovered in Brendan's bedroom. With the photos of women his adoptive father would deliver his comments calmly, kindly, things like *She looks like a woman with a good, kind heart. Someone who could be a caring friend. How nice it would be to wake up in the morning with her in your arms. How comforting to know that you're not alone in the world, that she's there to love and honor you, in sickness and in health, through all of the good times and bad.*

When a picture of a man was shown, his adoptive father's tone became menacing, disgusted. *What a pervert, what a dirty, filthy pervert. He's so miserable that he wants to make you miserable, too. Do you know what he does? He takes boys like you and does awful, nasty, unspeakable things to them. Things that make them cry out in pain, things that make them bleed. And as soon as he's satisfied his appetite, he leaves you. You think you want to touch him? Go ahead, touch him.* When Brendan placed a finger on the photo, where the man's cheek was, he was rewarded with a swift, painful slap across his face. *See? Didn't I tell you?*

The hours spent in the study were visits to another planet, a grim, hostile world populated entirely by saintly women and wicked men. Brendan's only safe passage out of the study and away from the many horrors described in great detail within, was to convert, that is, to feign conversion, to censor his natural instincts and dress himself in the guise of a young man who had successfully made the transition from *immature adolescent infatuations* to *normal adult attractions.* To learn about himself and his immature adolescent infatuations, he journeyed alone to the library, too terrified to actually check out any books about gay men, instead ripping out the pages he needed and stuffing them into his backpack. From there he would study the torn sheets on a park bench, always careful to look over his shoulder for another pair of eyes curious as to what he was reading. Then, when he was finished, the pages would end up in the trashcan where they couldn't do anyone any good ever again.

For the bus ride today he's reading a secondhand copy of *The Collected Works of Willa Cather*. He's reading "Paul's Case," a short story about a depressed and restless (and gay?) young man from Pittsburgh who walks out on his family.

The end had to come sometime; his father in his night-clothes at the top of the stairs, explanations that did not explain, hastily improvised fictions that were forever tripping him up, his upstairs room and its horrible yellow wall-paper, the creaking bureau with the greasy plush collar-box, and over his painted wooden bed the picture of George Washington and John Calvin, and the framed motto, "Feed My Lambs," which had been worked in red worsted by his mother, whom Paul could not remember.

His stop arrives, so he closes the book, stands in the aisle, and prepares to exit the bus with the few other passengers who look out the windows without expression.

The dry hot air slices through the men and women and children as they gather at the capital to show their support for public funding of Stella Cares's Home That Cares. The capital building is imposing, its large dome and columns like something out of ancient Rome. It dwarfs the crowd and Judy's unable to hide her disappointment: there are only about a hundred of the faithful perspiring in the bright sunshine with their signs. Brendan's sign says THE LORD CALLED ME FROM BIRTH, FROM MY MOTHER'S WOMB HE GAVE ME MY NAME. (ISAIAH 49:1)

"Oh, what's wrong with people," she asks him, on the verge of tears. "This is important enough to take a day off from work, after all."

Linda puts a consoling arm around Judy's shoulder. "At least we have a beautiful, sunny, hot day."

At the podium set up in front of the capital's tall, classic columns, the appearance of the Republican governor with saggy eyes and a perpetual smirk charges up the small crowd. He wipes perspiration from his high forehead as he asks his constituents, "So when it comes to providing decent homes for children, where are those big-spendin', tax-raisin', abortion-promotin', gay marriage–embracin', more-welfare-without-accountability–lovin', school reform–resistin', illegal immigrant–supportin' Democrats?"

He doesn't answer his own question, just apologizes for only being able to stop by, and tells God to bless them. Next, a legislator from an exclusive suburb is introduced to wild cheers. She's gained notoriety since spearheading the effort to amend the state's constitution to prohibit gay marriage and civil unions and she has received the state Republican party's endorsement to run for congress. She's thin, white, impeccably dressed; each long, dyed hair is in place. She nods at her audience, thanking them for coming out. Then she looks at them defiantly as she gravely says, "We've had black liberation, and women's liberation, and the homosexual lifestyle liberation. I say it's high time for Christian liberation, what do you say?"

People howl approval.

"We Christians are the ones feeding the hungry, caring for the sick, defending liberty at home and overseas, and providing loving homes to children. It's about time the work we do was supported by the taxes we pay! It's about time we stopped worrying about what the homosexuals think, and what the atheists think, and started worrying about what God thinks!"

More cheers now as her indignation infects the crowd. Brendan looks at the faces around him, some smiling, others full of righteous rage.

"We have to liberate Christianity from its secular chains, expose the myth that divides our *God* from our *government!*"

Linda shakes her head at Brendan, an angry look on her round face. "Yeah, that's the way to win people over; cram it down their throats.

Honestly, she makes me embarrassed to be Christian. We should live Christ's example, not legislate it."

"So why are you here, then?" he asks her.

Linda shrugs, tells Judy and him, "I'm for homes for children."

Judy says, "Still, you want them to grow up right. That won't happen unless they know Jesus Christ."

Flushed now, Linda says, "There's a fine line between living your faith and mandating it."

From behind him he hears, "Franklin? Franklin, is that you?"

He turns and faces Cynthia's mother, who holds her own sign, which says BE A WITNESS TO ALL NATIONS. Judy and Linda exchange glances.

Cynthia's mother says, "You could've knocked me over with a feather when I saw you standing there. I still can't believe it! I thought you people loved abortionists."

Judy asks, "What's that supposed to mean?"

He says, "She's a Jehovah's Witness and I'm . . . Unitarian."

Judy says, "They have Unitarians in Mississippi?"

Linda says, "Why's she calling you Franklin?"

Cynthia's mother says, "That's his name, isn't it?"

He blushes. "You know Brendan's just a nickname. Franklin's my real name."

Judy, who went over his volunteer application when he first joined Babies First, who runs the Bureau of Criminal Apprehension background checks on everyone who wants to join the group, frowns, says, "I thought your real name was—"

He cuts her off: "That's a family name."

Judy says, "I don't under—"

He ushers Cynthia's mother away, saying loudly, "We've got a lot of catching up to do!"

Cynthia's mother frowns at him, says, "Unitarian?"

Still smiling for the sake of the gals a dozen feet away, he whispers, "And what the hell are you doing here? I thought Jehovah's Witnesses didn't go in for politics."

"I'm not demonstrating. Some of us witness here every Tuesday."

The smile never leaves his lips. "Well, you're just everywhere, aren't you? Here, the nursing home, everywhere. I don't need a stalker."

She crinkles her nose. "I'm not stalkin' nobody. What're *you* doing here?"

"Praying for a home for children."

She looks at him suspiciously. "That's good, but you must renounce your unclean ways 'fore you'll please God."

He drops his sign and grabs her firmly by the shoulders, then realizing his mistake, hugs her. He whispers in her ear, his tone that of a man holding up a liquor store: "Do me a favor. Next time you see me, just walk on by, or I'll tell Cynthia that you called her a crack whore."

She pulls back, looks at him, incredulous. "What'd I ever do to you?"

He smiles as he repeats: "A crack whore."

She shakes her head. "You need more help than I can give."

He watches her walk away, talking to herself.

When he rejoins Judy and Linda, they're listening to Stella Cares speak on the example of Christ, of how he lived in a world that worshiped Roman gods, of how he washed the feet of the poor. Now Stella Cares says, "Defend the lowly and the fatherless; render justice to the afflicted and the destitute. Rescue the lowly and the poor; from the hand of the wicked deliver them."

Linda nods approvingly. "Finally, somebody's talking about justice."

When they notice he's returned, Judy says, "Who was that woman?"

He says, "Oh, she works at the hospital where Laura died."

Judy asks, "Why did she call you Franklin?"

"That's my confirmation name."

Linda says, "I didn't know Unitarians were confirmed."

He's in over his head. He says, "If we choose to be."

They look at each other. He needs a diversion. He says, "What do you get when you cross a Unitarian with a Jehovah's Witness?"

Linda smiles, asks, "What?"

"Someone who rings your doorbell and runs away."

The women laugh and then look around, embarrassed, for Stella Cares is still addressing the crowd. With a discreet giggle, Linda says, "Aren't Unitarians supposed to be pro-choice?"

He looks her in the eyes. She's a pretty woman. True, she's fat, but she carries it so well it's difficult to imagine her thin. She could pass for someone years younger. He reminds her, "Laura was pro-life. I'm doing this to honor her."

Linda gives him a hug, says, "This is from Laura."

The weather has gotten even warmer, with high temperatures more typical of mid-July than early May. People are out in abundance, walking and jogging and biking and Rollerblading in all directions. He walks among them, around the lakeshore that's dotted with picnickers and young men playing Frisbee. Some have dogs that wear red bandannas around their necks. One of the dogs jumps six feet in the air, catches a tennis ball. He would like a dog that wears a red bandanna.

He's left Marv alone in the house, wrapped in bright daisy-print sheets, a gesture to the summer weather. To keep Marv company he put on a CD of classical music from among the hundreds of discs that line the walls of Marv's music room. For a moment Brendan had considered walking the old man out into the backyard, letting Marv breathe fresh air, but he decided against it. Marv's adjusted to his convalescence better than he would have guessed; taking Marv outdoors now may cause more trouble than it's worth. Besides, Marv's days spent locked in the bedroom have very nearly reached their end; Marv will have an entire summer to re-establish himself as a free man and decide how he wants to live whatever's left of his life.

Brendan searches the faces of the men and women and children who pass by, looking for the one he'll model himself after. He scans the expressions others wear, some affecting an air of sultry apathy, others stumbling by in confusion or in anticipation of something they so badly want to happen. He's waiting to find one with the right mix of competence and contentment, someone happy to be who they are as they walk around one of Minnesota's ten thousand lakes on a scorching day in May.

A man approaches, his head tilted in uncertain recognition. He believes he knows Brendan from somewhere, but can't quite place him. He's about to offer a wave or a smile when Brendan looks away. This is the man Brendan met in a bookstore, whose skin he briefly grazed, who made Brendan feel so hopeful and then so hopeless. Brendan leaves the man confused, uncertain of what trespass he has committed against him.

Ahead is an Italian-ice wagon, surrounded by a line of children who wait impatiently to place their orders. He joins the end of their snaking line. Today he'll surprise Marv, give him a break from the vanilla protein drink he's been fed. He carries the cup of lemon ice carefully back to Marv's house, ignoring the men who pass him by.

The Italian ice goes over with Marv in a big way. The old man closes his eyes as if in a state of nirvana as Brendan spoon-feeds him the sweet, sticky frost. Marv gasps between mouthfuls, saying, "Oh God, that's so good. Jesus!" The rush of sugar quickly burns off and Marv falls asleep, his system thrown off-kilter by this unfamiliar substance; it needs to recover.

Although the nights are now warm, Brendan decides that he'll build a fire. Sean's told him about his family's cabin up north, and now Brendan's nostalgic for the north woods cabin of his childhood. He wants to relearn the skill he was taught as a young boy at his parents' cabin, how to build a fire. Maybe he'll walk Marv out of his room, let him sit for a while in front of the flames. He grabs a tub off the back porch and heads to the immense stack of firewood.

This was the chore he was assigned by one of his foster fathers, as well: it was Brendan's job to gather wood for the fireplace. It was an easy task when you consider it was his foster brothers who had to do all the shoveling in the winter and mowing in the summer. These foster parents were kind people, but not particularly loving, and he supposes he can understand why: he was just passing through, one in a long line of children they fed and sheltered. It was an odd placement; his foster parents were black, and he later learned that he was sent to live with them to prove a political point during a controversy that had embroiled County Social Services. His foster brothers took to him with mild enthusiasm, Brendan's race a source of interest. In compensation for the cautious affection she gave him, Brendan's foster mother would feed him from morning till late at night. Treats she denied her own sons she insisted he have himself, as if preparing him for an uncertain future by ensuring he had the memory of being sated. Her boys didn't complain; whatever envy they felt for his Twinkies and Ding Dongs passed quickly in the knowledge that they were here to stay, while he was a temporary fixture. Sundays were spent in church, sometimes at services that stretched on for four hours or more as the spirit moved the faithful. Brendan and his foster brothers would get looks from their mother as they passed comments on the other parishioners, laughing at the way someone moved or at the size of an obese woman's ass.

His foster father tolerated the weekly trips to Faith Temple, but when his wife was nursing a sick relative back in Gary, Indiana, for a week in May, he told the boys not to dress up for church. Instead they were to put on their play clothes. He didn't bother to make them swear to keep their trip to Valley Fair, a huge amusement park outside the Twin Cities, a secret; he knew that the elderly women at the Temple would climb over each other to tell his wife that they had skipped the service while she was out of town. Instead, he turned his head to the backseat, where the three of them were strapped in, and said, "Let's whoop it up, boys, 'cause when your mom gets back, there's gonna be hell to pay."

They giggled. He said *hell*.

They rode the roller coaster six times, four of them in the first car after waiting the extra time for the best seats. His foster father would alternate which of them sat in the first car so they'd each get two turns. During that first climb up the steepest hill, the panic Brendan and his foster brothers felt when they peered over the edge gave way to ecstatic joy as they fell, their stomachs in their throats, and as they dipped down low before ascending the next hill, their stomachs in their feet.

At that moment Brendan experienced a wonderful mixture of terror and elation that he thought would last the rest of his life: fear, to be certain, but always tempered by the random rushes of happiness.

When he turns to re-enter Marv's house he sees a grave little man at the back door.

The shock of seeing him stops Brendan in mid-step. Brendan stands there in silence, holding the handles of the tub. The grave little man knocks at the door, now he turns the knob. He shouts, "Mr. Fletcher? Hello? Anybody home?"

Brendan has to say something.

The man will let himself in; he will find Marv. He'll ruin everything.

Brendan has to say something. Instead, he drops the tub to the ground, and the logs roll out in front of him.

The man turns around, startled by the sudden noise. He sees Brendan and says, "Jesus! You scared the hell outta me!"

Brendan says, "Sorry."

The man puts a hand over his eyes; the sun's behind him and as he squints he realizes Brendan's not the one he's looking for. He says, embarrassed by his own sudden fright, "Who are you?"

"A friend of Marv's."

The man takes on a voice of authority, he must make up for his lapse, the scared little jump he does when tubs full of logs fall from the sky and crash into the ground. "Gotta name, friend of Marv's?"

Brendan doesn't like this man. He chooses a name of a character he despises. "My name's Victor."

"Gotta last name, Victor?"

"Komarovsky. Who are you?"

The question's a challenge, and this little man, whoever he is, prefers to be in charge of such things as names, first and last, when they are offered, who offers them. He says flatly, "Ed. Ed Lundeen. I cut the yards for Mr. Fletcher. Do you know where he is?"

"He's staying at my apartment in Manhattan. We swapped homes for our vacations this year."

Ed Lundeen puts his hands on his hips, clearly this is something someone should have had the good manners—not to mention the good sense—to inform him of. "Never said boo about it to me."

Now Ed Lundeen walks toward him, frowns at the wood that surrounds Brendan's feet. Brendan says, "He never mentioned you, either."

This man, this Ed Lundeen, is standing too close to him. Perhaps his name is not Ed Lundeen; maybe it's John Swenson, or Mark Anderson. What if he isn't the man who takes care of Marv's yards, but some local lunatic in search of a victim? Ed Lundeen or the man who claims to be Ed Lundeen studies the face Brendan refuses to flinch. He asks, "You're a friend of Marv's?"

"I'm Marv's lawyer. I represent him on Wall Street. I've never actually met him in person. We conduct our business over the phone. That's," Brendan says as he nods in the direction of the house, "how we arranged our home exchange."

This is credible to Ed Lundeen. He says, "Manhattan, huh? You're a long way from home."

"I love being on the lakefront. It's so beautiful up here."

Ed Lundeen gets to the point, "Well, you can't eat the view. Mr. Fletcher hasn't paid the May fee yet."

"I'll take care of it. How much does he owe you?"

Ed Lundeen smiles. His tone now neighborly, he lies. "Four hundred."

"Wait here."

Brendan leaves the man standing next to the pile of logs. He races to Marv's room. As the old man sleeps, he scours the drawers, the closet, he feels beneath cabinets for envelopes full of cash taped to the bottom. Next the kitchen: he opens the freezer, hoping Marv's eccentric enough to wrap an emergency stash of big bills in tin foil and hide it between cans of orange juice concentrate. The cupboards—maybe in a mug or a teapot. He checks the places he already thoroughly searched during his first week there. If he had time, he'd go through the pockets of Marv's suits that line the walls of the walk-in closet. But he doesn't have that kind of time.

Ed Lundeen's knocking on the door again; he's going to wake Marv up.

"Mr. Coma-ruski? I gotta go now, you got my money?"

Again: "Mr. Coma-rooski?"

Brendan has no choice. He gives Ed Lundeen the money Cynthia's been paying him for the hours he supposedly puts in at Good Works while he volunteers at Babies First.

Ed Lundeen whistles when Brendan hands him the cash. "Wow, you must have a wad stashed in there."

"I don't usually have this much cash on me. Lucky at the casino."

Ed Lundeen laughs as he counts. "Good for you, taking money from those damn Indians instead of handing it over the way I do."

Ed Lundeen's his friend now, someone to ask in for a beer, advice on the best places to drink, eat, get laid. Ed Lundeen waits for his invitation, but when none is offered, he grunts, mumbles, "Okay, then," and heads back down the driveway as silently as he arrived.

Consciousness of food. Eat and cook with concentration . . . Holy Food.

Brendan can't help himself; he's reading *Into the Wild* yet again, hoping for fresh insights. He closes the book, sets it in the grocery bag that sits on his lap, reminds himself to be grateful for the things he eats. He says quietly, drawing the attention of the elderly black man who shares his bench on the bus, "Eat and cook with concentration. Holy Food."

Passengers gasp as the bus comes to an abrupt halt; the driver has overestimated the yellow of a traffic light. With the sudden stop they lunge forward, his fellow travelers and him, holding on to the rails, the seat backs in front of them, trying to keep themselves from falling. Men and women swear softly, a pink baby rolls down the aisle, a delighted look on its face. He hears *Jesus Christ* and *What the fuck* and *Shit!* The old man next to him mutters, "Damn, damn, damn!"

Once the momentum's stopped and they're back in their seats, Brendan looks out the window, stares at a large, black SUV, its lone occupant chatting amicably on her cell phone. He turns back to the man who sits next to him. The man is praying as if they were aboard a plane forced to make an emergency landing. He hears him say, "Help me, Lord, help me, Jesus."

Brendan listens to his mantra until, finally, they arrive at Brendan's stop. In the sunset of a Minnesota spring, he emerges from the bus, carrying his little brown bag and pointing himself in the direction of the ramshackle building in which his brother and sister-in-law reside. He walks with his head down, noting the shattered glass of beer bottles that dot the route, the discarded wrappers of fast-food meals eaten and forgotten.

The small apartment that Ian and Cynthia share smells of Cynthia's spent cigarettes and Ian's stale beer. Brendan volunteered to make a meal for the three of them in order to broach the subject of the charges Ian has made on Marv's credit card. Cynthia sits with him now in the cramped little kitchen, watching the smoke of her cigarette as it reaches the stained ceiling. Her husband is watching the little television set in the other room with a six-pack of Grain Belt in a Playmate cooler. Marv, of course, is locked in a room, the *Matrix* DVD playing silently as he listens to a CD of Dennis Day singing songs originally performed on Jack Benny's radio show.

The main piece of decorating Cynthia has done in the apartment is to hang a huge calendar in the tiny sitting room, crossing out each day that has passed until the Walk. He counts: there are just fifteen days left to go.

The apartment doesn't even have a fan. They should just go to some air-conditioned place to eat, but then Brendan has already bought the food, so he preheats the oven. Cynthia compliments Brendan on his cooking, admiring the fact that a man can actually make a meal. She's impressed by the Shake 'n Bake bag he uses to prepare the chicken and the mixed vegetables that he empties out of a can to boil in a small pot. She sighs, says, "I wish Ian would fix something to eat around here once in a while. I'm the one with the job. What does he do all day?"

"You know he does some odd jobs for the old guy I live with."

She smirks. "How odd?"

He smiles at her, shakes his head. "He's just used to getting his dinner from the prison cafeteria."

She takes a drag, lets the smoke linger in her lungs. As she blows it out, she says, "Jesus, it's hot."

He stirs bits of corn and peas in the water that refuses to simmer. Scenes reminiscent of this one come to mind; the times when his adoptive mother would have him sit at the table and watch as she prepared the family's meal. It was his job to keep Mrs. Moore company as she opened cans and preheated the oven. She would say, *Time to keep the chef from going crazy* as she summoned him from the rec room to the kitchen. She was convinced that if she spent too much time alone she would lose the ability to distinguish between thoughts she wanted kept to herself and those that she said aloud. But it didn't work out that way, and with a roast in the oven she would confide in him, whether she had intended to or not. The kitchen's granite countertops were her confessional; he, her priest. As he grew older he refused to spend time with her while she cooked, no longer interested in or even frightened by the secrets she felt compelled to tell him. After that she had to share her news in the underdone pork loins and cold peas she served her husband and Brendan.

Maybe it's the fact that you don't look the other person in the eye as you work in the kitchen that makes it so easy to bring your most intimate thoughts to the surface. The chopping and stirring offers the diversion needed to ask questions that would crumble beneath undivided attention. He covers the vegetables as he says, "You still love Ian, don't you?"

He expects a shy confession, what he gets instead is a loud "Yeah, I guess so."

He laughs, turns and faces her. "Happy to hear it."

She fans herself with a hand and he notices a thick gold band with a large diamond on the ring finger. She watches him set the table, laying the mismatched silverware on either side of the mismatched plates.

For napkins he carefully folds paper towels, in place of glasses he sets out two plastic *Star Wars* collectors' cups once offered as convenience-store premiums. Ian won't need one; he prefers to drink straight out of the can. Cynthia takes in the preparations, quietly asking him why he goes to all the trouble: Ian will just want to take his meal in front of the TV, and she herself will eat only the chicken's skin, tossing out the rest of the meat along with the corn and peas.

Because Brendan insists, the television is turned off and the three of them sit around a table salvaged from an alley. They eat in silence as they perspire, waiting for the course that never arrives, easy conversation between people who are confident in what the future holds for them.

Once they've finished, Cynthia wants to go over the plan, but Brendan is sick of *the plan* and, truth be told, he thinks he could still have gained the trust of the Babies First crew in just a month or two, not the three he has had to invest. He tells Cynthia he needs some fresh air and then says to Ian, "Let's go for a walk around the block."

Cynthia says, "You gonna leave all these dishes for me?"

He says, "I'll take care of them as soon as we get back."

She grunts, lights a cigarette.

They pass an elderly white man in the hallway who stands by himself, crying. When they make it out to the street he asks Ian, "Who's that?"

"Couldn't say," Ian says with a little smile. "We've got 'em all in this building."

Their steps synchronize as they head to the corner through the darkness. Broken streetlamps loom overhead, and beneath their feet are the cracked sidewalks of South Minneapolis. Groups of small children, some just toddlers, are playing outside in spite of the lateness of the hour. They pass a group of them when Ian says, "What's on your mind?"

He stops, looks his brother directly in the eyes. "I want you to stop using Marv's credit card."

Ian starts to say something, then thinks better of it. When he does speak, it's to ask, "What's the harm? I've thought this through. I think things through, you know. We'll be long gone by the time the collection agencies start pounding on that old bastard's door."

"I don't want to do this to him. I don't want to get into any more trouble."

Ian softly laughs. "Baby brother, you're the one who got us into this mess with that old man. I'm just maximizing the benefits. What difference does it make?"

"It makes a difference to me."

"What, you feel sorry for the guy? You told me he got you drunk and tried it on with you. Think of this as payback."

Brendan sees his books a pile of ashes in Marv's fireplace. He says, "Please, no more. That's all I'm asking."

Ian shakes his head but he says, "Okay, okay, if it means that much to you. I just needed a few things."

Brendan assumes that Ian means the television, Cynthia's ring, happy hours, May's rent, cigarettes, and whatever other "few things" Ian deemed necessary.

Ian says, "No more charges. Scout's honor."

Now what is history? It is the centuries of systematic explorations of the riddle of death, with a view to overcoming death. That's why people discover mathematical infinity and electromagnetic waves, that's why we write symphonies.

The bus arrives at its destination. He closes *Doctor Zhivago.*

He doesn't even completely understand why he agreed to do this, but here he is, back on the Rush City bus. Marv said that it would mean a lot to him—the world to him—if Brendan would go to Rush City and visit Frankie, to see how Frankie's doing. If Frankie's being harassed, if he's having problems with the other inmates, Brendan needs to report it to a correctional officer. Brendan has felt so guilty about what he's done to Marv and by how much time he makes the old man spend alone, that he agreed. It's a bit bizarre, arranging a meeting with a man others have mistaken him for, but for Marv's sake, and perhaps as his own little act of contrition, he gets off the bus and joins the line of women and children waiting to be searched and scanned. It takes a few moments to recognize Frankie, he no longer looks as he once did in Marv's photo album. The short blond hair has grown out; dark roots extend several inches from his scalp. Brendan shakes Frankie's hand; reintroduces himself (their brief phone conversation lasted only long enough to get Frankie to agree to this meeting). Frankie seems confused by Brendan's name and he holds Brendan's hand timidly. Frankie's a weak boy, tall, but so razor thin that his height fails to intimidate. His pockmarked face is a field of detonated land mines.

Reluctantly, Frankie lets go of Brendan's hand as a look of recognition spreads across his face. Frankie says, "Hey, I've really missed you. I was hoping you'd come see me."

Brendan says, "My brother's Ian. It's him you miss."

Frankie laughs, says, "Jesus, you his clone?" They sit across from each other at a small table. Under other circumstances perhaps Frankie could have been a handsome boy; instead he's this frail young man, face scarred from acne, already defeated so early in life. Frankie asks Brendan if he has any cigarettes. Brendan apologizes, he should have thought to bring some.

Now Frankie asks, "How's fat old Marv doing?"

"He's well."

"He never comes to see me, not even once. It's like he's given up on me. I'm not gonna be in here forever, you know."

"I know. He would have come himself if he could, he's been sick."

"How sick?"

"Sick enough to have to stay away."

Frankie looks at him suspiciously, blushing hard. "You his new boyfriend or what?"

"No, nothing like that. Marv wanted me to see you for myself, ask you how you're doing. How *are* you doing?"

Frankie laughs bitterly, looks him in the eyes for the first time since they shook hands. "How the fuck do you think I'm doing? I'm in fucking Rush City. How the fuck would *you* be if you were in fucking Rush City?"

He will tell Marv that Frankie likes to say *fuck* a lot. He says, "Point taken. Well, I've seen you for myself and I've asked you how you're doing. Is there anything you want me to tell Marv?"

"Ask him why he wouldn't hire a lawyer for me. He could've gotten me off, but instead I get a public defender and wind up in here."

"Maybe he thought this was for the best."

"Oh yeah, he's always telling me what's fucking best. 'Get your GED, Frankie.' 'Learn a trade, Frankie.' 'Apply yourself, Frankie.' 'Stop drinking so much, Frankie.' Like he don't drink like a fucking fish himself."

"So I'll tell him that you're angry and you don't want to see him again."

Now Frankie pouts and it has the disturbing effect of making him look like a child. "No, don't tell him that." He broods for a moment before he says, "Tell him to get me outta here. He's loaded, he can get me outta here."

"I'm sorry, but I don't think even Marv can get you released. You have to serve your sentence. If you get out early, that's up to you."

Frankie scowls, slaps his hands against the table so loudly that Brendan jumps. "Gee, thanks, citizen. Must be nice living it up on the outside. Nobody fucking cares about me; they just stick me in here to fucking rot." Then his expression changes, and the sad little boy reemerges. This Frankie, with misty eyes, says, "I can't take it. I can't fucking take it. Will you help me get outta here? Please?"

"I wish that there was something I could do."

Frankie wipes at a tear. "Really? Do you mean that?"

"Sure."

Frankie reaches across the table now, puts his hand in Brendan's. "I like you."

Not that's it's even a possibility, but the grotesque symmetry of having the same man that both Marv and Ian have had makes him cringe. Frankie notices, says, "What? You think I'm not good enough for you?"

Brendan stands up. "That's not the kind of help you need right now."

Frankie shouts at him as he walks away. "What kind of fucking help do I need, huh, bitch? What kind of fucking help do I need? *Bitch!*"

The guard puts his hand on Frankie's shoulder, leads him away as he tells him, "Calm the hell down, already."

There's still another forty minutes before the bus departs. Brendan gets in, takes a seat, and looks out a window. He knows that he has this much in common with Frankie: neither of them is cut out for life behind bars. The misery of the outside is only compounded within the confines of Rush City, Frankie is exponentially more unhappy than when he was with Marv. If Cynthia's plan goes wrong, if Brendan winds up in there, God only knows how long he'd last.

When Brendan arrives back from Rush City, Marv stares glumly at a wall as Brendan tells him of his visit with Frankie. What Brendan says isn't unexpected, but Marv's heartbroken nonetheless. Perhaps the old man had hoped for some jailhouse conversion, not to Christianity certainly, but to some form of self-discipline that would enable Frankie to turn his life around while there's still time.

When Marv finally does speak, he says, "He blames me? He really blames me?"

Brendan nods.

Marv starts to cry. "He has to know . . . that I never wanted this." Marv's voice cracks as he says, "He has to know . . . how much I love him."

Brendan rolls his eyes, reaches for a tissue, and puts it to the old man's nose. "Blow," he says.

He tries to cheer Marv up. "Let's go for a walk around the house today. You haven't been out of this room in how long, now? Maybe you'd like to soak in the hot tub for a little while. Just two weeks and you're on your own again, Marv. We've got to get you back in shape." Truth be told, Marv's beard, along with the weight lost after so long without al-cohol (subsisting on a diet of protein drinks and a single cup of lemon-flavored Italian ice that gave him the runs), makes him look a damn sight better than when Brendan first met him. Perhaps Brendan should try to make his fortune writing a diet book instead of working Cynthia's plan.

Marv shakes his head. "What does it matter? Maybe you did me a favor . . . locking me up in here. I ruin everything I touch. My family . . . my Frankie. My beautiful Frankie."

Brendan stares at him, his captive, an old man miserably in love and a failure at it. There's no clock Marv can turn back. All the words have been said and cannot be unsaid, all the choices have been made, they cannot be unmade. Marv wants to search the house, gather up all the consequences of everything he's ever done, tie them up in a bag, drop it in the Mississippi. He's regret made flesh, and yet Brendan can't help thinking that there is something like beauty in the old man's pitiful expression.

Marv whispers, "I've led my life badly."

Brendan decides that the kindest thing to do now is to let Marv say what he needs to say.

Softly Marv asks him, "Do you believe . . . in life after death?"

"Marv, every atom in your body has been around since the big bang. What more do you want?"

"I meant our . . . consciousness."

Brendan says, "When all this is over you should call your children, build a few bridges."

Marv places his arms over his deflated chest, rubs a shoulder weakly. "I think the . . . kindest thing I could do . . . for them now is . . . to die and let them . . . inherit my money."

Okay, this is all the misery that Brendan can stand for today. He claps his hands together. "Come on, Marv, you old so-and-so, let's take our daily walk. I need you in fighting trim for when I leave."

Marv just sits, the side of his mouth drooping.

"Let's go," Brendan shouts as he pulls him by the ankles, places his feet over the floor. "Put your arms around my neck," he tells him, and the old man does as he says. He pulls Marv up and off the bed so that they're standing, almost in an embrace. "You can let go now," Brendan tells him, but Marv doesn't, he holds on to Brendan, his body trembling as the tears begin again.

He whispers, "Frankie."

Brendan places one arm around Marv's waist. "Come on, Marv, you know the drill. One foot in front of the other. Do it with me, now."

Brendan takes one small step forward, and after a moment, Marv does, too.

"Now swing your other foot around," Brendan says.

And so they begin their walk, a slow pacing that eventually leads them out of the bedroom. Marv's spirits improve as they tour the rooms spread throughout the massive house. Suddenly the old man's a G.I. returning home after the war. There is where he would sit and drink scotch in front of the fire. Here is the kitchen, the modern kitchen with all the latest conveniences; funny isn't it, since he never cooked himself. In the den he runs his hands over the woodwork as if pointing to photos in a yearbook, at the faces of classmates he'd nearly forgotten. He sits behind the oak desk, examines a paperweight with a photo of San Francisco inside. He runs his fingers over the smooth glass as he closes his eyes, and smiling, hums "I left my heart in San Francisco." Brendan lets him linger there, behind the desk, watches as the old man picks up one paperweight after another, watches as the memories come flooding back to Marv, the cities where different choices could have been made, different lives lived.

There's just thirteen days until the Walk, and the team—Brendan, Ian, and Cynthia—is assembled in the small apartment. She says, "You'll meet up where?"

Even Ian has grown tired of the plan. He sighs and says, "The parking lot by the old school beneath the water tower. Do we really have to go over this again?"

Cynthia ignores his question. "Where will you pull up the truck?"

The tiny apartment is sweltering, so in order to get this over with as quickly as possible, Brendan says, "Next to the Dumpster."

She says, "Cool, cool." Then, with a Magic Marker, Cynthia draws a small square directly on the sitting room's worn carpet. Next, she hands the brothers two headlamps, the kind that campers use, small flashlights on headbands that free their hands for the ritual of opening, sorting, and sealing. Next, she tells them to position themselves inside the square for it will be, at most, all the room they have to work with in the back of the truck. This is a new, unwelcome degree of difficulty.

Ian groans. "It's not enough."

Cynthia says, "It's gotta do, baby. You can't work the cans outside. Somebody will see you or a wind'll come along and blow the money away. Or what if it's raining the day of the Walk?"

Cynthia times the men as they open the white envelopes they had dumped from a large white plastic trash can Cynthia has actually stuffed right up to the rim. The full can is heavier than they had imagined: dumping the cans in the small space will be hot, grueling work. She turns out the lights as they point the beams of their headlamps at the envelopes they open that contain the Monopoly money—ones, fives, tens, twenties, and fifties, along with the occasional hundred. The higher denominations are stuffed in black plastic garbage bags (impossible to see through), and the opened envelopes are simply tossed back in the can. Once the can is full of torn envelopes, it will be quickly emptied into the parking lot's Dumpster on the day of the Walk.

Cynthia shakes her head. The look on her face tells Brendan that every single bit of this is taking far too long. She says, "You had the time down last week."

Her husband says, "We had some room to work with last week."

When they shove the smaller bills into new white envelopes Brendan asks, "Shouldn't we bring some sponges for sealing?"

Cynthia smirks. "Stuck in the cargo hold without any fresh air in this heat? Look at you now, you're already sweating like pigs. Use it. Oh, that reminds me, I gotta get gallon jugs of water. You gotta stay hydrated."

The men pull pens from their pockets and begin the task of signing the sealed envelopes over their shut flaps. Cynthia asks Brendan, "Did you come up with a list of names to sign?"

"I will."

She lights a cigarette, irritated. "What the fuck, Brendan? You haven't done that *yet?*"

Ian and Brendan stop, stare at each other. Brendan feels his face heat up as he folds his arms across his chest. Slowly, deliberately, he shifts his gaze from Ian to his sister-in-law.

Ian tells his wife, "It's okay, honey. I'll take care of it. Let's not get upset."

Cynthia exhales a cloud of blue smoke, muttering, "We can't fuck this up."

In a strong, passionless voice, Brendan says, "I am *not* a fuck-up."

She appears caught off guard by his words or perhaps by the expression on his face, which he can't feel. She sucks in smoke, says, "Sorry. I know you're not. I'm just freakin'."

Brendan grunts, "Well, don't."

Ian says lightly, "I'll make up the list. It'll be a laugh. I'll use the names of some of those assholes in Rush City."

In a calmer tone, Cynthia suggests that using the names of people any of them know could become evidence if their crime is discovered. She tells him to just use the white pages, like her telemarketers do.

Brendan and Ian reload the trash can three times, dump it out three times, open, sort, and seal three times. The perspiration makes their clothes stick to their skin. The brothers pick up some speed, but they still have to do better. They must rehearse again. As they clean up their props, Ian says, "I suppose we should try and learn some Spanish."

Cynthia says, "I know 'Yo no permitto fumar.' That means 'I don't permit smoking.'"

Ian smiles, asks, "How did you learn that one, baby?"

She says, "Owner of that taco place on the corner is always shouting it at me."

Ian says to Brendan, "You better pick up some Spanish, too, little brother, if you want to hook up with an *hombre.*"

Brendan blushes.

Cynthia smiles at Brendan, says, "Those Pacos are gonna be all over you."

Brendan shakes his head. "No, they're not."

But Cynthia's certain. She says, "Trust me on this one, dark men eat white meat whenever they can get it."

Brendan and Cynthia laugh but Ian doesn't. He gets up and heads to the kitchen, opens the refrigerator. They hear a lid flip off a bottle.

Sean's niece, Eileen, has volunteered her uncle and Brendan to help chaperone the May dance at the Catholic high school she attends. The common practice is for the parents of each member of the junior class to chaperone at least one dance during the year, but rather than asking her mother and father, Eileen has signed up Sean and Brendan. Sean was eager and Brendan, of course, refused. Because Eileen has so consistently and thoroughly convinced Sean of how much this would mean to her, Sean and Brendan had their first fight.

Brendan told Sean, "This has nothing to do with you or me, she's rebelling. She wants to be cool. Why else ask us to chaperone a Catholic school dance? Do her parents know? Does the principal have any idea?"

The parents, of course, knew: the father didn't like the idea but the mother agreed for both of them. Rather than bar Sean and Brendan from chaperoning, the principal decided not to intervene, saying that a ban was exactly the sort of controversy Eileen wanted to be the star of.

At any rate, nothing rattles Brendan's self-confidence more than winning an argument, so here they are, Sean and himself, standing next to the punch bowl in the St. Nicholas of Tolentino gymnasium. All the windows and doorways are open, and tall fans are carefully stationed to circulate the hot air. Stationed between Brendan and Sean are two female teachers, about Sean's age, obviously assigned the duty of preventing any public display of affection, or, worse yet, homoeroticism.

Which is why Eileen, between dances with her various suitors, runs over to them, and with great excitement, holds both their hands, one in each of her own, as if she is the link, the strong bond that holds Sean and Brendan together in this hostile territory. She wants them to join her and her girlfriends in their little game of ranking the boys on the floor. "Who do ya think's the hottest?" she wants to know. The teachers answer for them. One says, "Eileen, there is more to a person than their looks." The other counsels that "beauty is only skin deep."

Eileen makes a *phhhhht* sound with her tongue and lips. Now she's saying, "You guys should get out on the floor. All the parents dance at least one dance when they chaperone; it's a tradition."

At this the teachers invite Sean and Brendan to dance with them, but Sean refuses the offer and tells Eileen that he will dance with her. Eileen's face falls, but then she says loudly, "Teach me a dance all the gay guys do." And they're off: Eileen leads her uncle to center court where everyone can get a good look.

Brendan's teacher says, "She's certainly full of life, that girl."

He considers her comment, and as he does, he realizes that this newly minted sixteen-year-old really does have a lot of life in her— pettiness, to be sure, but mostly joy, and in abundance. She glistens in the stuffy gym as she moves her body wildly, her face ecstatic, as if she were an old, bitter woman suddenly transformed, given a second chance at youth, to correct all the mistakes made over a lifetime distinguished solely by its sheer volume of bad choices. Eileen is laughing; she closes her eyes and sings along with a Madonna song that was popular years ago:

And I feel like I just got home . . .

Her joy is contagious. Sean throws himself into the techno-beat as well as a middle-aged man who'd rather be in a tent in the woods can. His face tells Brendan he's embarrassed, yet he's enjoying himself too much to let it get the better of him. They're joined by Eileen's girlfriends and by the teenage boys who dream of making love to this sixteen-year-old goddess of beauty who walks among them. To impress her, a tall boy cuts in on uncle and niece and dances with Sean. Within seconds the group pairs off, boys dancing with boys, girls with girls. They laugh and hoot, pantomiming homosexuality as they understand it. Their display doesn't strike Brendan as malicious; it's simply a show of exuberance. The teachers don't seem to be bothered, either, but they're duty-bound to nip this sort of thing in the bud. With a single look directed at the DJ, the music changes in mid-chord, Madonna's pulsating beat replaced by a love ballad. Confident that the boys won't carry the gag as far as a same-sex slow dance in the smothering heat, the teachers help themselves to some punch. Sean rejoins Brendan as the tall boy he had danced with wraps Eileen in his arms, and together they sway leisurely to the music.

"That was a lot of fun," Sean tells Brendan, and means it. Sean's thin hair has wilted and is plastered against his skull. A teacher offers him a cupful of punch, positioning herself between them as she says, "This will help you cool off!"

Brendan and Sean consider it: a slow dance with each other. Brendan wonders what part of a nanosecond it would take for the DJ to change the music yet again, replace the romantic song with some rap or rave number designed to remove arm from waist, hand from shoulder.

They let the moment pass.

Later tonight, after they've completed their duties as chaperones, when it's just the two of them—and the dog—alone in Sean's house, Sean will put on a CD and ask Brendan if he may have this dance. Brendan will roll his eyes, say, *You're such a sap*, and rest his head in the crook of Sean's neck. They'll barely move to the music, just rock slowly back and forth, Sean's fingers stroking Brendan's long hair as Maggie sleeps on the couch, a new red bandanna around her neck.

Cynthia has invited him out to dinner, just the two of them. She said it would be fun to have a nice meal together, but the real purpose of their meeting is to give him a pep talk. She's concerned that with just eleven days left before the Walk he may be wavering. She wants to remind him—again—that her plan is virtually foolproof. Done correctly, no one will even realize that the money has gone missing, at least not for a few days or weeks. They're sitting at one of the Monte Carlo's outdoor tables. The restaurant is renowned for its liberal martinis, which, after some hesitation, they just ordered. He was going to have a pop, but Cynthia said, "Get a cocktail, you need to relax." Cynthia lights up a cigarette as they wait for their drinks, listening to the street traffic. She's changed from distant to cool to jumpy in such a short time that he's reminded again how little he knows her. "Sunday after next," she tells him. "Can you believe it? Sunday after next."

He nods.

She winks at him, says, "This is gonna go off without a hitch, you know what I'm saying? We've got nothing, *nada*, to worry about. See? I've picked up some Spanish!"

"You think I'm worried?"

"I know you're worried."

Mrs. Moore would call that *projecting*. "And you're not?"

"No way."

He looks up and down the tables that line the sidewalk: searching for the man he'll fall in love with is a hard habit to break, even though he'll soon be in old Mexico, even though he's now seeing Sean. There's a candidate sitting by himself at a far table. The man wears glasses with tiny frames and his brown, wavy hair is neatly swept from his face. Brendan decides that he's from out of town, given that he's dressed too warmly. He must be here on business, eating alone and waiting for a co-incidence or some stroke of luck.

The candidate stares at the menu; it's easy to see that sitting alone at a table makes him uncomfortable. He'd rather be back in his hotel room, he should have just ordered room service, opened a bottle of wine and a book. But now a woman joins the man, her expression one of apology, his one of pure delight. Brendan gives Cynthia his undivided attention.

She says, "Are those bible-thumpers getting to you? You know what they'd do to you if they found out you're gay. Those people hate you, Brendan, they despise you, and just because you're different. They don't know how much they hate you, 'cause you're passing."

He smirks. "The Babies First crowd isn't getting to me."

She stares, decides to believe him. "Good. Those people are the like the Taliban; if they get into power folks like you are royally screwed. I mean *totally* screwed. 'Love the sinner, hate the sin.' What kinda shit is that? Those people wanna love people like you to death."

He changes the subject: "I told your mother you'd call her. Have you?"

She laughs as if her mother were a cartoon character, forever having anvils dropped on her head. "Yes. I haven't seen her since she kicked me out, but I did call her. Oh, how I do love that woman, but Jesus H., she drives me crazy."

"How do you mean?"

"Did you know that when I was a girl I had to leave the room when the class said the Pledge of Allegiance? I wasn't allowed to pledge allegiance; it was one of the rules. Imagine doing that to a kid. She had to know I'd get the shit kicked outta me on the playground, but she didn't care. The worst was when she'd drag me with her when she went door to door, witnessing. She'd make me read Bible passages to complete strangers. I think the Witnesses always bring their kids along so people won't yell at them or cuss 'em out."

"Sounds bad."

She sighs in the warm breeze. "No birthday parties and I was always at Kingdom Hall for meetings and study. Other girls would go out on dates or to dances; I'd be home reading *The Watchtower*."

He laughs.

She says, "I guess it's kinda funny. But the thing was, I really believed that shit."

"So do the women at Babies First. Well, most of them anyway. The abortionists are all going to hell."

"Jehovah's Witnesses don't believe in hell."

This bit of news surprises him. "Good for them."

"They believe in Armageddon."

"Oh."

"And it's always just right around the corner."

He smiles. "Well, you have to admit, with the way the world is, they may have a point."

She giggles slightly, but then she becomes serious. "When I was dis-fellowshipped though, that was the worst. I thought I was gonna have a nervous breakdown."

The drinks arrive. Their waitress, a lively, heavyset redhead, swirls the ice in the cocktail glasses, dumps the ice out on her tray, and pours the martinis into them, saying, "This will cure what ails you." She winks as she walks back inside and Brendan wonders whether she thinks they're a couple out on a date or a husband and wife savoring time away from the kids.

Cynthia holds up her glass. "A toast."

He says, "To the plan."

She says, "To the plan."

They clink their glasses, take tentative sips.

Cynthia says, "I'm sure Mom's fine. She's just always mad. She wakes up mad, she watches TV mad, she sleeps mad."

They finish their drinks and the warm buzz of the martini makes him ask her what he's wanted to ask her since they first met: "Why did you marry Ian?"

She smiles at him. "You're kidding, right?"

He shakes his head.

"He never told you?"

"Told me what?"

She reaches for another cigarette. "I was pregnant and we both wanted the kid."

This is news. Ian can talk with great energy and enthusiasm about his successes with the Canadian lottery scam, of how he convinced se-niors to pay him taxes on the imaginary jackpots he claimed would soon be heading their way. But children, family, the years after their parents were incarcerated—these things he doesn't much care to discuss. He asks Ian's wife, "What happened?"

"Never made it to my second trimester. I really wanted that baby, so did Ian. You should have seen him; he was so excited. And then when I lost it, he was good to me, Brendan; I mean the guy was a fucking saint. We kept trying to have babies but the pregnancies would never make it more than a few weeks. Ian stuck by me, though, so I stuck by him when he got sent up."

"I had no idea."

"It's not something he likes to talk about. I've accepted the fact that we're not gonna be parents, but I don't think he has. You'd've thought he was a woman, the way he wanted that baby so bad."

He says, because he's drunk, "He drinks too much."

She says, because she's drunk, "Yeah, I know."

They order their meals and another round. The liquor makes them giddy, and suddenly they're best friends, sharing secrets and making fun of the other diners who surround them. He tells her about the time he read his adoptive parents' psychology books and, as a gag, mimicked the symptoms of schizophrenia for a week, followed by nearly a month of manic depression. They had a psychiatrist prescribe Valium and, since he liked how it made him feel—detached, calm—he overdosed. Next came the tough love: they took him off the drug cold turkey and his withdrawal was the subject of an article they published to much acclaim in a psychological journal. His adoptive parents made his addiction and recovery into a cottage industry, and they would leave him on his own for days at a time as they accepted speaking engagements throughout the Upper Midwest, largely at churches and social-service organizations. He was glad for the time alone, free to read whatever he wanted.

Cynthia laughs until she spills her drink, with a loud "Whoops!"

He feels affection for Cynthia, it radiates from him like signals from a broadcast tower. The more they drink the more she talks and he's happy to listen to her, eager to hear more about her brothers who left the Jehovah's Witnesses for the army, one in Alaska, the other in North Carolina, and their children, who are all doing well in school. She tells him how she suffered as a girl because of her mother's faith, her own mixed race, the obesity she eventually conquered through a combination of cigarettes and speed. She leaves most of her steak on her plate for the waitress to wrap up for her husband. She wonders what forty will be like; she's afraid of getting older. She asks him stupid questions such as *When you were with what's-his-face, who was the man and who was the woman?* He answers with good humor; she is, after all, showing an interest in him and she doesn't mean to offend. In spite of his answers, she's still dubious about his sexual orientation. Of course it's his lifestyle, his right if he chooses it, but she wonders aloud if the right woman couldn't change him.

When they get up to leave she stumbles, and she leans on him to steady herself as they make their way out to the van. They're both too drunk to drive but she hands him the keys to the Voyager, convinced that the ride to his house will sober her up enough to make the trip back to the apartment she shares with Ian. Neither of them is bothered by the fact that he doesn't have a license, and as he slowly drives to Marv's house Cynthia sings along with the radio. He joins in with the occasional *Hell, yeah* or *Dat's right!* When he gets out she leans over, hugs him. The feel of her body embracing him reassures him, reassures both of them that the new lives that await them will be worth the risks they're about to take.

The dominant primordial beast was strong in Buck, and under the fierce conditions of trail life, it grew and grew. Yet it was a secret growth. His newborn cunning gave him poise and control.

Brendan closes *The Call of the Wild*, unsure why Alex Supertramp loved it so, why he wrote ALL HAIL THE DOMINANT PRIMORDIAL BEAST on the wall of the abandoned Fairbanks bus that would become his coffin. Brendan puts the book under his arm, gets off the bus. He's sober, clearheaded. He understands things. For example, he appreciates the fact that he's hanging on by a thread at Babies First. Some of the more observant gals are beginning to suspect that he's making fun of them with his little comments, each one outfitted with a double edge. He's got to be more careful, to make more of an effort. No one said this would be easy.

Except Cynthia.

And Ian.

Not much longer, he keeps telling himself (and Marv), not much longer.

Ann stands, claps her hands together, gets everyone's attention. "Ladies," she says. A long, deliberate pause follows before she says, "and Brendan. Ladies and Brendan."

Some of the gals snicker.

Ann looks around the room meaningfully. "You know what today is?" she asks the ladies and Brendan.

Gals exchange looks.

"The last mailing before the big day!"

Astonished oohs and aahs fill the air, where does the time go, can you believe it?

"All the mailings, all the sign making, all the letter writing, all the canvassing, it's all led up to a week from Sunday. The Walk for the Un-born, the walk for the defenseless little babies waiting to be born. Who'd have ever believed that America would need laws to make a mother's womb a safe place for a child? America's lost her way: deviants have rights, but innocent babies waiting to be born don't! We know what we're being called to do, we hafta make this *one* nation under God. Let's do it. Let's raise more money this year than ever. Let's put an end to the abortion industry. As the Bible says, 'Before he formed you in the womb he knew you; before you were born he dedicated you.' Let us recite together Psalm 139:13–15."

The women say in unison as Brendan silently mimics them: "Truly you have formed my inmost being; you knit me in my mother's womb. I give you thanks that I am fearfully, wonderfully made; wonderful are your works. My soul also you knew full well; nor was my frame unknown to you when I was made in secret, when I was fashioned in the depths of the earth."

Brendan leads the group in "Amen!"

They say their good-byes as they anticipate their imminent reunion at the Walk for the Unborn.

It's then, as he hugs Linda good-bye, that a memory floods over him, quickly, unexpectedly: it's the bell ringing, the rush of little bodies as they escape their desks, the classrooms, the hallways full of open lockers and overflowing trashcans. There's so much joy everywhere, summer is new and not one day of the long vacation has been wasted, it lies out before them, three glorious months of perfect freedom. There will be games with Ian and Steven, the trip up north to the cabin, canoeing around the lake, Hardy Boys books, swimming, tiny frogs he and his brothers will catch and keep as pets, releasing them only when the car is loaded up, their father yelling for the third and final time, *Let's go!*

7

The Biggest Star on Broadway

BRENDAN HAS SPENT MONTHS with the gals, gaining their trust, and long weeks with Marv, keeping the old man alive. He deserves a reward, so when he arrived home—at Marv's—from his volunteer shift at Babies First he called Ian to ask if he would spend a long weekend with Marv. Ian sighed sadly, told him he wasn't sure it was such a good idea. They should spend this weekend going over the plan; after all, the Walk is next Sunday. But then Brendan surprised himself, telling Ian that if he didn't do this one thing for him, he and his wife could go find themselves someone else to drive the truck. The ultimatum stunned them both. Ian promised to spend the afternoons and evenings with Marv, but he refused to spend a single night in the old man's home. So Ian's with Marv and Marv's about as happy about it as Ian is. Brendan tells Marv it'll be fine. He says this because he wants—needs—to spend time with Sean. Besides, Marv is getting better all the time: his speech has notably improved, as has his stamina.

Brendan grabs a bus over to Sean's. Sean waits next to his hybrid car with the TREE HUGGER and IMPEACH BUSH and DRAFT SUV DRIVERS FIRST bumper stickers on it. Inside the little car are grocery bags, books, bottled

water, Maggie, everything they need and more for their trip to Sean's
family's cabin just south of the Canadian border. Sean's a bit irritated
with him because he's late and this spontaneous trip was Brendan's idea,
after all.

Sean says, "Let's go! I want to beat the traffic." As Sean pulls out of
the driveway, Maggie licks Brendan while he opens his book, returning
yet again to *Doctor Zhivago*. When he comes across the passage, he gasps,
delighted:

Oh, how one wishes sometimes to escape from the meaningless dull-
ness of human eloquence, from all those sublime phrases, to take
refuge in nature, apparently so inarticulate, or in the wordlessness of
long, grinding labor, or sound sleep, of true music, or of a human understanding rendered speechless by emotion!

This is the paragraph that Alex Supertramp had starred and brack-
eted. Brendan closes the book, looks over at Sean, who concentrates on
the traffic. The long drive relaxes Brendan. It clears the fog, removes
the self-doubt, keeps at bay the awful things he's recently done. The
sounds of other cars on the highway—soft as they approach, loud as
they drive by, and soft again as they disappear in the horizon—are
calming, hypnotic, they provide purpose. They're two men and a dog
heading somewhere among a few people, scattered here and there, who
are also heading somewhere. This is what people do, they go places,
this is what's expected of them. The normalcy of it reassures him.

Sean reaches for his hand, says, "Sorry if I snapped at you. I was just
anxious to leave."

It's touching, his sensitivity.

They stop near Duluth for a picnic lunch along the shore of Lake Superior. This is Sean's crowning achievement: from out of a cooler he produces an exotic variety of cheeses, grapes, chilled white wine. There is a
baguette and real butter, imported chocolates, fresh strawberries sprin-
kled with sugar. He lays the china dishes out on an old-fashioned red-

and-white checkered tablecloth. For Maggie, he fills a bowl with browned hamburger and rice.

Brendan takes it all in: Sean, the picnic, and the lake. He says, "I was hoping for a burger and fries."

Sean laughs, plucks a grape off the stem, and tosses it in the air for him to catch, which he does, in his mouth. Impressed, Sean says, "Hey, I like that. What other secret talents do you have?"

"They're hardly talents and they're best kept secret."

Sean says, "Not from me, they're not." Sean smiles, pats a patch of ground next to where he sits, cross-legged. The sun's rays illuminate his receding hairline, highlight the large pores on his cheeks.

They talk about the future. Brendan tells Sean he'll begin looking for work once he's made good on his promise to help his sister with the Walk for the Unborn. Sean says he should work in a bookstore, un-aware that Brendan was fired from a Barnes and Noble ten years ago for hiding in the aisles as he read the latest releases, the shoppers searching in vain for someone to help them. Sean suggests putting in a résumé at the human resources department at the University of Minnesota, where Sean works in tech support. There are a lot of positions that don't re-quire degrees, many of them union jobs with decent benefits. He tells Sean he'll consider it as he lies on his back, stomach full, his eyes closed against the late-afternoon sun.

The sound of the waves along the shoreline is hypnotic; each small collision of water and rock a happy ending, one after another, until he believes in such things as happy endings.

They arrive at the cabin.

It's beautiful, in the fading light of day. He takes it in, so unlike the small, battered, and abandoned bus that Alex Supertramp called home. Underneath his feet is a warm, thick carpet that feels snug enough to sleep on. The walls are a mismatch of oak, pine, and maple that sur-round a stone fireplace and comfortable furniture designed for lounging.

The most reassuring sight, however, is the bookcase, filled beyond capacity with old and newer hardcovers and paperbacks, works he's guessing Sean himself has never read but that the family keeps stocked for guests to entertain themselves on rainy days. He wanders through the friendly rooms of the place, a kitchen, a bathroom equipped with hot and cold running water, two bedrooms, and a large deck overlooking the pine forest. Maybe twenty feet below is a clear blue lake, as smooth as carved marble. They watch the sun as it sets, a burgundy curtain that is washed over by a sea of deep, rich blues. Next, the stars appear overhead, millions of them, bright pinholes in the cobalt dome that covers their little world. Tonight they are fortunate sons, the northern lights appear like ghosts on the horizon. They shimmer in phantom greens and purples and he takes this as a sign. Of what, he can't say. He can only hope that it's a good omen, a harbinger of things to come.

After a late meal of grilled brats—the first meat Sean has ever cooked for anyone except his dog—they walk the food off in the cool darkness. Books come back to him, stories about being alone in nature, all frightening and cautionary tales, true and fictitious: *Into the Wild* (of course), *Lost in the Wild*, *The Girl Who Loved Tom Gordon*. Then he stops himself, he refuses to be afraid. He's not by himself, Sean is here with him and this world is familiar to Sean. And, he realizes all at once, to him. He recalls again the tall pines surrounding his family's cabin, the freezing water of the tiny lake.

Back at the cabin now they wrap themselves up in a blanket and sit out on the deck, listening to a wolf pack nearby. Maggie tilts her head as the wolves call to them in the night, the pack's evocative, hauntingly beautiful howls filling Brendan's ears and clearing his mind. The wolves are reveling in the unity of the pack, claiming their territory, and their chorus is full of distinct, individual songs that he begins to recognize like different voices over a telephone's wires. He expects to see a full moon high in night air as they sing, but it's not quite full, in spite of how brightly it shines.

————

Morning.

He slept through the night.

He didn't dream of McDonald's.

The aroma of coffee fills the air as he hears Sean softly singing to himself in the kitchen. When he joins him, Sean looks disappointed. Sean says, "I was gonna bring you breakfast in bed."

"I'm happy to go back," he tells him.

Sean shakes his head, points at the small table. "Sit down. We gotta load up before we head out."

"We just got here."

Sean laughs, sets a mug in front of him. "We're not gonna spend the whole weekend in the cabin. We're going camping, Pierre. Explore a few of the lakes, maybe set up the tent on an island."

"I think we should stay in the cabin."

Sean sighs as he pours steaming coffee into a cup. "City life has made you soft."

That's one way of looking at it.

They eat a hearty breakfast as Maggie stares, enraptured. They do dishes; have sex, Sean's confidence lagging only slightly behind Brendan's own insecurity. All this puts them behind schedule and, as Brendan begins to appreciate, Sean hates being behind schedule. The schedule is like the environment, something to be respected, nurtured, and preserved. The schedule provides order in a chaotic, unpredictable universe.

This is what Brendan tells Sean as he watches him load the canoe. "The schedule," Brendan concludes, "is life."

Sean sets a Duluth pack between—the word Brendan believes is *gunnels*. Sean shakes his head. "Order's an illusion. Anyway, you certainly didn't arrive on schedule."

"Neither did you," Brendan tells him.

Sean ignores the comeback. "I love it this time of year, before all the bugs hatch and ruin everything."

Brendan looks out into the woods, still white with patches of snow.

They're issued their life preservers, Maggie and Brendan. The dog's flotation device fits snugly around her neck and midsection. Brendan also receives a paddle and Sean assigns him to the front of the canoe, the novice's position. From behind him Sean gently issues directions: "Switch to the left side."

On calm water Sean allows them to glide effortlessly, their paddles resting across their knees, the only sound that of Maggie's paws as she rearranges herself for the best view of the shore. Then Sean says, "Paddle on your right," and a second later, "your *other* right."

They arrive on a shoreline with a small, sheer trail barely visible between the trees. Sean says, "Okay, let's go." They land, and Brendan secures the Duluth pack on his back, hugs the cooler to his chest. Sean carries the canoe on his shoulders, which is, as he informs Brendan, the more challenging task. The portage between lakes is steep and the rocky trails are slick from the daily rains and snow. Maggie runs ahead as Brendan stumbles and curses, but they make it to a new shoreline, alive with possibilities.

And so it goes, lake to lake, paddling, drifting, and paddling, while Sean surveys the tiny islands they pass, searching for his ideal setting. As Sean explores his options, the contrast of cold water and bright sun makes Brendan shiver as he sweats. The rocky bluffs overhead engender a feeling of traveling back in time: two more strokes of the oar and Brendan will have never met Marvin Fletcher; twenty beyond that and his parents will have yet to be arrested. Brendan wants to make camp here. He imagines calling his young parents from this spot that sits on a very different sort of map, the wireless connection spanning both space and time. He would tell them to pick up their sons and relocate to New Zealand or Australia or some other Commonwealth outpost far from Minnesota police and aggrieved investors.

Sean splashes Maggie and Brendan with water, snaps Brendan back to the here and now. The dog shakes off the water as Sean tells Brendan that he has already dubbed their elusive campsite Honey Bear Isle.

"And we won't need maple trees on Honey Bear Isle," Brendan replies, "since you'll provide all the sap."

Another splash and this time Maggie barks at Sean, indignant.

The wind quickly picks up, and the tone of Sean's voice changes, his gentle prompts now a short series of sober commands. They face strong, gusting headwinds that form large, cresting waves. They struggle to keep the canoe steady. Occasionally the bow veers a few degrees to the left or right and in spite of their efforts, they're blown sideways. Brendan suddenly understands the danger as the canoe approaches whitecaps broadside, Maggie's whining as she struggles to stay upright, his own hips thrusting one direction and then the next as they ascend a wave, only to abruptly descend. Brendan looks out toward land, the just-budding trees that grow right into the water a reminder that the water temperature's not much above freezing, that death from hypothermia is a real possibility if the canoe capsizes. Sean tries to minimize this risk, tries to keep them close to shore, but they're often blown into the middle of the lake, its depths unknown. They're silent now, their strokes entirely in synch, quartering the waves with the bow.

By the time they attempt to land, they're exhausted, physically and mentally. To get the canoe ashore without crashing it into rocks, Brendan jumps out, dunking himself up to his thighs in the freezing water. The stones beneath his feet are slippery, and he falls into the bitter lake, resurfacing quickly as he pulls Sean and Maggie aground. Maggie dashes onto shore, scouting this new territory for squirrels or chipmunks or painted turtles while Brendan opens a Duluth pack, and changes into dry clothes. Sean investigates a shady spot on the island's highest ground, near but not directly under a patch of trees. From a small bag he produces a tent that he quickly assembles into a tan dome that will be their shelter. As Sean pitches the tent Brendan's tempted to tell him that the house of the wicked will be destroyed, but the tent of the upright will flourish. He resists the urge, Sean wouldn't get the joke, and besides, he came up here to forget all about that nonsense, at least for a little while. Now Brendan unloads a cooler full of food, along with the ceramic filter that will enable them to convert lake water into drinking water. For their time on the island Maggie must make do with dry dog food from the Tupperware containers that serve double duty as her bowls.

Brendan inspects the tent Sean has assembled. "It doesn't look big enough," he tells Sean.

"Size queen," Sean says, and Brendan can see he's relieved that they're alive, not floating facedown in the icy water. They inflate two thin air mattresses not even wide enough for the sleeping bags they lay on top of them.

Brendan grows concerned for the dog. "Where will Maggie sleep?"

Sean says, "With us, of course."

Brendan frowns, but Sean sends him on his way, his task to suspend their food from a tree, well out of reach of hungry bears. Brendan tosses a little orange nylon sack that contains a rock into the air. It's tied to a length of rope, his goal to snare a high branch. But his aim is off; the sack with its long tail falls back to the earth with a loud thump. He tries to snare the branch a second time, a third. He resists his initial instinct to ask Sean to do it for him. He succeeds on his fifth attempt.

The tent is not what Brendan would call a success. Their two-person tent can't really accommodate two grown men, let alone two grown men and a dog, and the air mattress underneath Brendan isn't big enough for his nightly tossing and turning. Add to this the fact that they've arrived during loon mating season, and the birds wake them up at all hours with their extraordinarily loud calls. He hears a loon scream as Sean lies silently; Maggie sprawled on top of Sean's legs. Brendan shifts and fidgets, willing the air mattress to grow and spread into a real bed, like the one they left at the cabin, the perfectly good, warm cabin.

Sean asks, "Can't you get comfortable?"

He looks over at where Sean's face should be in this small world of varying degrees of shadow. He can't see Sean's expression, whether Sean's eyes are open or closed, whether Sean's amused or annoyed.

"Sorry," he offers. He hears rumbling sounds, like raceways or locomotives. He asks, "Did we camp near a freeway?"

Sean's voice snickers as he says, "That's just the wind through the trees."

Maggie growls, something's moving outside the tent, an otter or a beaver. Sean hushes her gently, and in the tone he just used to address his dog, says to Brendan, "You toss and turn a lot."

Granted, Brendan doesn't know all of Sean's intonations yet, but he already recognizes the schoolmarmish voice Sean can bring to some of his observations.

"Sorry," Brendan mutters, aggrieved.

"I'm not complaining, just concerned. You have a lot of nightmares. More than your fair share."

In the safety of this undersized tent, so far removed from his life in Minneapolis, it's tempting to tell Sean the truth—not all of it, but just enough to enable Sean to better understand. A small snippet of truth offered like a cool breath on a freshly brewed cup of coffee, that little gasp before the first tentative sip.

"I'm just worried," Brendan tells the chilly blackness that surrounds him.

"About?"

"The future. After I help Natasha with the Walk I'll need to get my own life in order. I'm thirty-five years old, Sean. I've left things pretty late."

The tone of Sean's voice tells him he's smiling. "We're all trying to get our lives in order, keep them in order. We'll be doing it till we drop dead."

"Still," he tells Sean, "you have your own home, a good job, Maggie."

At the sound of her name, he hears Maggie's tags like wind chimes. She's lifted her head, part of the conversation now.

He hears Sean pat the dog's stomach, saying, "But at any moment I could be the Falling Man. Anyone could."

Brendan leans on an elbow, faces the direction Sean's voice comes from. "Who's the Falling Man?"

"I read about him in a magazine. I was obsessed with him for a while. He was one of the people who jumped out of the World Trade Center. There's this picture of him as he fell. It's got this eerie, graceful symmetry to it because his body was in line with the towers. The papers only ran it one day because it upset people so much; they didn't want to see it."

"I can understand why. Sean, I doubt that terrorists are targeting our tent."

Sean says—for first time since Brendan's known him—with genuine irritation, "Of course not, Pierre, that's not what I meant. I meant that no matter how much we believe our lives are in order, it's an illusion. Nobody knows for sure who the Falling Man is, but he was in the Tower on that day because it was part of the order of his life. And then, from out of nowhere, a bunch of religious fanatics fly a plane into his building, and finally he's forced to make a choice—what to do when the life you knew is taken from you? I fight with my sister all the time about the Falling Man. In spite of herself, she's still such a Catholic. She thinks the Falling Man was wrong to jump. She thinks he should've waited for a miracle. But she's wrong. He didn't wait to suffocate or have a ceiling drop on his head. Yeah, he was a victim, but he took control of his last moments, they all did, all the jumpers. They were left with just a few minutes to decide how their lives would end. I admire them, their courage."

This sudden burst of intensity is unexpected and unnerving. Brendan tries to lighten things up, saying, "You have a very grim side for someone who calls me honey bunny."

"You're not the only one who gets to have a grim side, Pierre. I love you so I'm happy to help you get your life *in order*. But remember, it's just a temporary thing no matter how long it lasts."

"Okay, now you're scaring me."

"I don't think it's scary at all . . . in a way, it's liberating, knowing that the only sure thing is this exact moment, the three of us here in this tent. It helps me tell the difference between what's important and what's not worth my time. It's why I'm such a cornball. It's why I love you. Because it matters."

Another soft clatter of Maggie's tags and her head returns to Sean's sleeping bag with a soft sigh.

Sean says, "You know, my brother-in-law works at the corporate headquarters of one of those rent-to-own chains, the one where people who don't have a pot to piss in rent big-screen TVs. He supervises the managers of delinquent accounts. It's his job to make sure the corporation collects back rent from all those poor saps. Can you imagine? I don't believe in God, but if I did I'd stop. I don't want to worship somebody who puts us on this planet to do something like that with our lives."

After a few long seconds Brendan says, "Still, it keeps Eileen clothed and fed. It's hard to argue with that."

"So she can grow up and do the same thing to feed her own kids? There has to be another way."

"I wish I had your perspective."

Sean reaches over, musses up Brendan's hair. "You will. One of these days you will."

Sean thinks it's funny, but Brendan doesn't: he can't stand it anymore; he has to wash this funk off him. He no longer gives a good goddamn how cold the water is, a day without a shower and he feels primitive, Stone Age. Sean whistles at him as he stands, naked by the water. He remembers the summers at the cabin, the leaps off the dock, the frantic thrashing and screaming as his shocked body took in the frigid water. Those first few minutes in the lake he'd say to himself, over and over again: *It'll get better, it'll get better, it'll get better.*

There's no dock to jump from. He takes a deep breath.

He runs into the water, manic.

Keep going.

It's deep enough, he thinks it's deep enough, *don't think*, dive, dive, submerge. Now he's a Popsicle on a stick, he's making love to a snowman, he's watching woods fill up with snow. *It'll get better, it'll get better, it'll get better.*

It doesn't get better, but he endures it, he scrubs his skin, his hair. He counts to ten, and then he heads back to the shore.

The sun, at last, is useful in its ferocity. He finds a rock, sits, and watches the birds as they glide in midair. He lets the water evaporate off his skin and then there's a new sensation, Sean's hands, massaging his shoulders, working their way further down his body. He turns his head, looks at Sean, the bright rays of daylight illuminating him like a saint, his eyes equal measures of passion and love. This is the moment

Sean lives for, this connection to someone he can care about, care for. Brendan realizes that Sean's handsome in an outdoorsy sort of way; the clothes that make this man are the lakes and forests of northern Minnesota. Sean whispers in a poor imitation of a French accent, "You and me, naked on ze rock, ze sound of ze pounding surf!"

Brendan laughs, something he's never done during foreplay, not even when he was with Jeff. He was always too self-conscious, too immersed in anticipatory fear that he would be found lacking as a partner, that his body wasn't beautiful enough, his skills pedestrian. But now he's laughing so hard he can't catch his breath.

Sean's hands work their way from Brendan's shoulders to Brendan's chest, where Sean's fingertips linger before sliding down the flat stomach. Brendan should be upset, crazed, at his wit's end, for he doesn't know where on the planet he is, he's entirely dependent upon Sean to guide him out of this wilderness as he guided him in. But instead of panicking, Brendan arches his back on the rock's hard surface. He listens to his breath as he inhales and exhales.

He snuck a book into the canoe before they launched and in his blind haste he wound up with *Valley of the Dolls*. As Sean prepares the fire, he opens the paperback at random, picks a line, reads it aloud: "And your Helen Lawson may be the biggest star on Broadway, but she's still a bloated, loud-mouthed broad the moment she steps off stage."

Sean looks at him, confused, but then he smiles and returns to arranging the kindling, trying his best to convince Maggie that it's not a game of fetch.

It's a good sentence; Brendan likes it. Here, alone in the acres upon acres of lakes and trees and rocks, he feels as though he couldn't be any farther from Broadway. He was there once—he recalls it now, for the first time in years—with his parents, Ian, and Steven. They held hands and walked together down the avenue his father called the Great White Way to Times Square. There were people everywhere; the sidewalks were thick with them. They moved over him, around him, a school, a swarm, a herd migrating from the feeding grounds to the breeding grounds. Their sheer numbers intimidated him and he was sad all that night, upset that there were so many people, countless numbers of people, more than he could ever know, more than could ever know him. He didn't want to be one of them, as common as a blade of grass, and he wondered if they felt the same.

They finish their meal of fried fish, and Sean pulls the canoe up to higher ground and turns it over, tying it down securely. "Storm's heading our way," he says. As the sun sets they stow their few items so the winds will not pick them up and carry them off. What felt like a cool breeze becomes a strong gust, rattling the pines and swelling the ripples on the lake into whitecaps.

There's a flash. Seconds later, a clap of thunder fills Brendan's ears, contracts his pupils. They rush into the tent, zip themselves inside. Cold water falls from the sky, pounds against the nylon. For a moment, maybe two, he sees everything clearly: Maggie, Sean, the sleeping bags, the tent's interior, the packs. The lightning strikes are random, violent things, reminders of all the odds stacked against him.

Sean attempts small talk: "Still kind of early for a thunderstorm."

A loud strike, like Judgment Day. He puts his head in his hands. The deafening violence subsides until the next flash of light, heralding a new explosion. A blast and he trembles, defenseless, vulnerable, helpless. The missiles land to the right, to the left, behind, in front. They are tormenting him: this is no accident, no natural phenomenon, it's orchestrated, someone's enjoying his terror, gorging himself on it. The dog gives voice to his panic, whining loudly.

Sean holds him, and sensing his terror, rocks him back and forth. "Hey," Sean says, "it'll be okay, we'll be alright." He enfolds Maggie in their embrace as cold water seeps through the tent's floor, soaking them all.

Brendan opens his eyes.

He's aware of movement, of sound. He hears what must be a

pine cone as it drops. It bounces off the tent, comes to rest on the ground.

He's awake.

He's alive. Wet, frozen, but alive.

He unzips the flap of the tent and Maggie springs to life, bounding outdoors to relieve herself. There are varying degrees of blue outside: the deep, indistinguishable tones of the trees, the lighter shades of the lake and horizon. Sometime he fell asleep. Sometime between the panic and the terror, he spent the energy he needed to fuel his fear; he faded to black. And now, here's the dawn, acting as if nothing's happened. He looks out at the water, the thousands of hard ripples on the lake's surface are gone, and eerily beautiful billows of mist and fog shroud the hills and lakes.

He hears someone say something. It sounds like *hello*.

He hears it again.

"Hello?"

Maggie barks as she squats.

He looks out at the yawning shade on the water. He makes out a canoe, longer than the one that brought them to this island. Inside are what appear to be two figures, a man and a woman, given the tones of their hellos. But then he notices two smaller forms, hears two small hellos. He waves his hand over his head; the man, the woman, the children all do the same. And then they're gone, the shadows they cast blend into the line of the trees.

What amazes him most is the silence. It washes away the ugliness, the bitterness, the world-weary cynicism. It makes him sane, but not the sort of sane that enables people to spend decades working their lives away at jobs they cannot stand, to function in a world overflowing with traffic and products and pre-emptive wars. This kind of sane is the crystal clarity that enables him to spend hours watching the soft ripples of the water as the breeze skims the lake. This is the sanity that savors the lonely call of the loon, the sight of an otter, his eyes aglow at the end of the day. It's the type of sanity that is truly grateful for the simple luxury of a warm blanket wrapped tightly around his body as he stares into the soft embers of the fire Sean has started to boil the morning coffee.

The canoe trip back to the cabin is a short but eventful one. By one lake he saw a wolf as it followed the shoreline, at the next he watched as ravens teased a bald eagle. As they portaged to the next lake, there was a frightening sight ahead of them, a deer, recently killed by wolves. Its exposed ribs were covered in bright reds, a scene out of a horror movie; its head, though, remained untouched, the beautiful eyes shut, as if in sleep. He wondered whether he and Sean had frightened its killers off with their approach. He searched the woods, but there were only ravens perched in the trees, patiently waiting for them to move on. Sean held Maggie back; she was desperate to examine the carcass. Brendan knelt down and petted the fur between the deer's ears, he told her she was good, something that you would tell a dog. He said *I'm sorry* as they left her for the ravens.

The most startling sight was a bull moose among the reeds. He would have thought that an animal so huge could not catch them by surprise, but it did with an ease that was unnerving. The moose lifted his head and watched the canoe glide silently by, Maggie too intimated by its size to bark. He told the moose: *You may be the biggest star on Broadway, but you're still a bloated, loud-mouthed broad the moment you step off stage.* He looked back at the moose, unblinking, as Sean laughed, and for the first time, he wondered what had become of the world beyond this little lake.

They have to stop in Grand Marais for what little gas Sean's hybrid needs, and as Sean navigates the electric car through the small-town streets brimming with outfitters, souvenir stores, and arts and crafts shops, Brendan gets a feeling of déjà vu. He knew that he had been here before, but years earlier with his first family. Looking at the shops, the way the hard rocks meet the tide, brings pieces of it back to him: an image of his mother carrying bread and apples in a white canvas bag as she held his hand; Steven and Ian staring wide-eyed at a horse someone had ridden into town. This is the tiny hamlet where his parents selected live bait and fresh vegetables for their week or two away from the Cities.

More pieces come back to him now, he remembers sharing the backseat with Steven and Ian, over the two-day drive home. They'd spend a night in Duluth (his mother insisted on at least one night in a proper hotel), and eat breakfast in the revolving restaurant atop the hotel. His father, who, with his mother, had emigrated from the United Kingdom to escape their own families, would say to their boys, "See that young man in the apron?"

The brothers nodded, whether they had noticed him or not. When Father spoke, you were to nod.

He said, "Take care, or that'll be you someday. Up at the crack of dawn, pouring water from a pitcher into the glasses of rich people's children."

He remembers thinking at the time: what a wonderful way to live your life, atop a tall building in Duluth, walking across a moving floor, every view different from the next. Meeting people from all over the state, all over the country, maybe even from all over the world. Back then he didn't realize that what he felt about men was contrary to what most males felt. The world was a friendly place, an adventure in every glass of water poured from a pitcher held by a handsome busboy, in every menu he had his mother help him read during the trip back home.

He hates to leave Sean's cabin, hates returning to the messy little reality that is his life. Five hours south there's an old man locked in his bedroom, and the Christians who believe Brendan to be one of their own are in final preparations for the Walk for the Unborn. He should ask Sean to turn around, take them both back to the cabin, where they could live out the rest of their lives together in the wilderness, as he so often fantasized doing with Alex Supertramp. He wonders whether Sean could be happy holding him in his arms in front of the fire or calling with all his might to the pack that would visit them each evening.

What a ridiculous idea. Along the lines of telling Pony Boy from *The Outsiders* to "stay golden" with your last dying breath. He's becoming an even bigger idiot thanks to this man next to him, but it doesn't feel entirely bad. He wonders whether he's happy, whether this—the two of them and the dog in Sean's car—is happiness.

He puts aside the romantic notions and focuses on things like bread and cheese and potato chips for the drive back to Minneapolis. As Sean pulls the car into a gas station he leaves him alone with the pump as he jogs across the street and down to the nearly empty supermarket where just a few husbands are doing the shopping for their wives on Mother's Day.

He pulls a shopping cart out of the stack and he's pleased to find that he's chosen one without a wobbling wheel. He feels so normal, the most normal he's felt in a long time, pushing his cart down aisle one. He does what the other shoppers do, he holds things in his hands, he reads labels, he estimates weight, he calculates the price per pound and per ounce. He hunts for bargains; he searches for products that are limited to five per customer. He's feeling generous with himself, he seeks out guilty pleasures: bags of salty snacks manufactured to taste barbecued; little processed dessert cakes, each one with enough fat for an entire day.

He wheels the cart to the register next to the express lane where people buying six items or less wait in line. He imagines they are people in a rush to live their lives, each one of them terminally ill, with no time to stock up, no life to stock up for. The people in the express line need only six items or less; there are just a few sunsets left for them to see. He inspects the express line, starting at the rear, and diagnoses each shopper: the man has AIDS; the young woman in front of him has breast cancer; the one reading *Soap Opera Digest* has leukemia.

That's when he notices a state trooper with a gut protruding a good foot in front of him, flirting with the cashier. Though this man cannot possibly know what he has done back in the Cities, Brendan grabs the first thing he can find off the impulse rack and buries his face in a copy of *People*. There's a picture of world's sexiest man and his wife. They're divorcing; the critics were right—it didn't last.

He listens as the trooper asks the woman on the other side of the conveyer belt, "You hear about poor old Scottie Thorenson?"

The woman says, "Oh, no, what about him?"

"His family called up from the Cities and asked us to go round his place. Hadn't heard from him in months and they were finally getting worried." He pauses and Brendan glances over to see him leaning in toward the woman, who waits for news of the latest disaster. The trooper says, "Found him at the bottom of a lake pinned under his snowmobile."

The woman clucks. "Oh, no!"

He says, "Oh yeah. Tell you what else, old Scottie had two empty bottles of peppermint schnapps in his pockets."

The cashier scans two Slim Jims, a can of pop, and a bag of chips, saying, "What a shame. It just goes to show you."

"Well, I betcha he died happy. And warm."

She laughs, says, "Oh, that's terrible, don't even joke."

Brendan's cashier waves a bag of chips over her own scanner.

The trooper loudly clears his throat. He says, "I gotta head out and give one of those fancy cabins a look-see. But after that I'm wide open for the rest of the day. You wanna get an early dinner, maybe catch a movie?"

The thought hits Brendan like lightning—does Marv have a cabin around here somewhere? Could this be Marv's family's way of trying to get in touch with their father?

Ridiculous. Calm down.

The woman says, "Oh, Erik, I'm an old married woman. You keep dreaming, mister!"

"Oh, I will. Sweet dreams, and every one about you."

She laughs, says, "Oh, please!"

The trooper could be in the market for a cabin for himself. Brendan tells himself that he's just being paranoid. Remain calm. Never moving his face from out behind the *People* he hands his cashier two twenty-dollar bills.

The return trip to Minneapolis takes them past the exit for Rush City, in another hour they'll be in Minneapolis. In the back of the little car,

Maggie's asleep; the hum of the car's tires a lullaby. He wonders what would happen if he never went back to Marv's, if he just stayed with Sean instead. Would Ian let Marv die or would he release him after enough time had passed, once the Walk had come and gone without a trace of the widowed truck driver, still grieving for his late Laura? Would Marv call the police as soon as he was free or would he walk away quietly humiliated, ashamed of having been a victim?

No, he's got to return to Marv's. This is more of his old irresponsibility; he should have never left Marv alone with Ian. But he wanted this trip so badly. He wanted this: a car, Sean, Maggie, all of them together, on the highway, speeding at eighty miles per hour, heading somewhere new, someplace where he hasn't been evicted from apartments, quit jobs, screwed up relationships. Heading north to the cabin felt like deliverance, as if he'd been saved by this man next to him; Sean's worldview razor sharp, but his heart soft and sentimental. They should turn around, head north to Canada, where Sean's politics would be more in sync with others', where they could be married, start over.

They pass a billboard with a Babies First ad. An attractive, clean white infant is comically dressed, an oversized Minnesota Twins baseball cap on his head (he's a boy, blue is his color). Underneath the giant photo there's a quote: *I WAS AT ALL THE TWINS HOME GAMES THIS SEASON AND I WASN'T EVEN BORN YET!* Surreal, but the point is made: life begins at conception, carry your pregnancy to term, and you'll be rewarded with a healthy, happy, blue-eyed Caucasian male who was as disappointed in the Twins' performance this year as you were.

Sean grumbles, but not at the big baby: Sean has successfully identified and commented upon every vehicle on the road with an American flag sticker, saving his strongest contempt for the SUVs that fly small flags from out their windows. As they pass a Hummer, flags flapping from both the passenger's and driver's sides, its single occupant talking on a cell phone, Sean says, "That's what's wrong with this country. That's what we sent a bunch of kids halfway around the world to die for."

Is this his influence working on Sean, the complaining, the bitterness? Perhaps. But with each new grievance Sean is readying himself for one more petition, another get-out-the-vote campaign, the latest letter to his elected representatives. He doesn't doubt that Sean will continue to agitate, to organize, well after he's died and been cremated (cremation being the only way to dispose of the remains, because, as Brendan now knows, we destroy valuable resources by creating granite memorials to our vanity).

Brendan eats the last of the barbecue-flavored Fritos and Sean's newest objection is to his breath, which is toxic. Brendan smiles at Sean, asks, "Who wants a big, wet kiss?"

Sean laughs, shooing him away as Brendan tries to plant one on him. Sean manages to say, "Cut it out, I gotta concentrate." The traffic's heavy now as more people dutifully depart their cabins and return to Minneapolis or St. Paul, or one of the sprawling suburbs, their Jet Skis, campers, ATVs, and motorboats in tow as if the circus was heading to town.

More disapproval from Sean: ATVs destroy the land, motorboats contaminate lakes, Jet Skis scare away wildlife desperate for places to breed and raise their young. If Brendan pictures Sean and himself years from now, it's in some remote Canadian outpost, old men, Sean scolding him for not composting his own waste, him muttering things under his breath, below the radar of Sean's failed hearing, things like *ehhhh, shaddup ya old fagala* and *can't wait to compost you*. He smiles. What a wonderful way to finish your life, in the company of one who knows you too well, who you know too well, the common history, the fights, the bickering, the companionship, the mutual understanding without a word uttered between you.

Sean reaches over, puts his hand in Brendan's. He says, "I really had a great time. I hope you did, too."

Brendan squeezes Sean's fingers. "Of course, I did. Thank you." Then Brendan places a hand on Sean's thinning hair, pets it slowly.

Hours pass in contented silence. They arrive in Minneapolis, and Sean wants to drive to Natasha's house. Brendan convinces him to drop him off at an anonymous corner not far from Marv's, telling Sean that the sight of the two of them together will make his sister—who has never accepted Brendan's homosexuality—furious. Maggie's awake and anxious to get out of the car, but Sean tells her to sit back down, they're not home yet. At Brendan he rolls his eyes, says, "Pierre, you've got to move out of your sister's place. You're too old to hide your boyfriend from your family."

"I know," Brendan whispers.

Sean pulls Brendan to him, kisses him on the lips. "Move in with me."

Brendan's eyes bulge. "Yeah, right."

But Sean means it. In spite of how little they know each other—how little Sean knows him—Sean's convinced that it's a good idea, perhaps the best idea he's ever had. Brendan tells him truthfully, "I'll just fuck it all up."

"No you won't. We could be happy together, Pierre—"

Brendan cringes. *Pierre Bezukhov.* What the hell was he thinking? How could Sean have bought it? He wonders who the bigger idiot is.

"—you and me and Maggie. Give us a chance. Give yourself a chance, okay?"

Sean's in love, that stupefying love that arrives as a rainstorm after the long drought that produced famine after famine, so he doesn't believe—isn't capable of believing—a single word Brendan says. He ignores Brendan's track record, the fact that Brendan's unemployed.

Sean kisses him again, and Brendan savors the scent of lake water mixed with perspiration, the remnants of smoke from the campfire. A car drives by, its stereo at full blast, the deep bass nearly knocking them over like an unexpected wave. When the noise passes, Sean says, "You don't have to make up your mind right now. Just promise me you'll think about it."

Brendan looks at him afresh; sees the weak chin, the tired eyes, the porous skin that's noticeably pink. He places a hand on Sean's cheek, and he closes his eyes, sighing softly. He's going to break Sean's heart, and the simple idea of it breaks his own. He removes his hand, saying, "I'll think about it. Okay? I promise."

Sean nods, disappointed.

He pats Maggie good-bye and she licks his hand. As Sean and the dog drive off, he wonders what will become of Sean once he realizes that Brendan's left, and for good. When Brendan's in Mexico taking Spanish lessons with his brother and sister-in-law, what will Sean do? Search for a new lover? Or will he have given up on finding someone, Brendan's disappearance confirmation of the fact that he's destined to be alone, a harmless homosexual who performs his job duties well, and is devoted to his niece?

Brendan hesitates in front of the door to Marv's house.

Why couldn't he have met Sean first, before all this mess?

But if not for this mess, he never would have met Sean.

He takes a deep breath, turns the knob.

The temperature plummets as he enters; the air conditioning is operating at full blast. He finds Ian in his usual spot, in front of the television. A bottle of scotch sits on the armrest. Ian looks up at him, smiles. Ian says, "Hey, you're back. How was it?"

He asks: "How's Marv?"

Ian's smile disappears. He shakes his head, mutters, "The fossil's okay."

"I better see for myself."

The bedroom is in shadow. The light he turns on startles Marv, who's lying on the floor in a tangle of sheets. The old man shuts his eyes tight.

He gasps, "Jesus! Are you alright?"

Marv says nothing, just mutters hoarsely. His skin is goose-pimply and dry. The old man's misery is his dead twin, conjoined, the lifeless sibling the doctors cannot remove. And Brendan's a little boy again, daring himself to spend all night out in the woods with monsters, the kind that look and sound exactly like Marv. He says, "Okay, okay, it's alright." *He's going to fucking KILL Ian!*

The sheets appear to be tied together in knots and it takes him long moments to free Marv. Finally, he pulls Marv up onto the bed as the old man moans. He says, "Let me just get you comfortable, you just need a lie-down on a nice, warm bed, You'll feel like a new man."

Marv glares at him as he grabs a fresh diaper: in addition to falling out of bed, Marv has wet himself. Marv holds out his good hand for the Depends, saying, "Let me do it."

"Marv, that's not a good—"

"Let me do it!"

Marv needs to be appeased; he needs to appease him. "Okay, okay."

It's odd, watching the old man perform a task he's done for him dozens of times. He resists the urge to help, to correct, to show Marv the most efficient way to rid himself of a wet diaper. He brings Marv a glass of water, which the old man drinks manically. To spare Marv further humiliation, he turns his head, focuses on the wall, the white noise of the television Ian watches down the hall. Marv groans, and he hears the tape of the Depends, a soft thud, and then the sounds of hands and knees on carpet. Marv is crawling to the closet like a dog with only two good legs.

He sees the old man, naked, save the oversized T-shirt, creeping along the floor, gasping for each breath. Marv's desperate to get to the closet that's full of clothes, his own clothes, not the sweatpants and oversized T-shirts that Brendan's been dressing him in. On the other side of the closet door hang suits in variations of black and gray, power colors, the wrappings of the executive he once was. This old man, this old homosexual man, this ancient closet case, wants the armor from days gone by, the high-flying uniform of the businessman, the family man, the normal man, the one he should have been all along.

He has to know that the exertion will kill him. He's performing the last rites; he's trying to pull his own plug. Whatever peace he has or has not come to pushes him forward. Brendan admires and fears it, this decision of his. Of course, it's not one that Marv has the right to make. Brendan's future will *not* begin with Marv's death hanging over his head: the old man will survive this, better off for the experience, as horrible as it's been. Brendan counters Marv's drama with lightness, says, "Whoa, hang on there, cowboy, where do you think you're going?"

Marv doesn't stop; he keeps pushing his body across the carpet, sideways, like a crab, struggling for every inch. Marv gasps, "I want to wear my own clothes! I want to wear my black suit!" Marv looks as if he's about to die as he gasps, "I want to look like a man . . . when they come to collect my body . . . not this ugly mess you've turned me into!"

Brendan's levity was a mistake. Brendan walks over to the closet, alarmed. "Marv, calm down, please, calm down. I'll get your suit for you. You can wear it today, but then we'll have to go back to loose clothes. You won't be very comfortable wearing a suit in bed, now will you?"

He meant for his tone to be comforting, reasonable, but it only upsets Marv more. "I can do it myself! I'm a grown man! I'm a man!"

Marv's words sting and he backs up, watching the old man's achingly slow progress to the closet, his bulk, although lighter than when they first met, threatening to stop him in his tracks. What has Brendan done to him? Jesus, what has he has done to him?

Marv's crying hard now, from anger or frustration, but most likely this is part of the plan, he's working himself up into such a frenzy that his heart will have to give out, or there'll be another stroke, ending this ordeal for both of them. Brendan says, "I'm sorry, Marv." What should he do? Why won't someone tell him what to do? He says, trying to be affectionate, "Just let me know if you need me to help you get dressed."

Now Marv's laughing and crying at once, the old man's trying to push them both over the edge.

Ian enters the room, the warm buzz from the scotch he's drunk making him rock where he stands. Before he even notices Marv, he asks Brendan, "What's going on?"

Brendan says, as calmly as he can, "Marv would prefer his black suit today."

Ian frowns, not understanding what Brendan's said, but then he catches sight of Marv inching his way to the closet door, huffing and puffing and blowing the house down. Ian leans forward, which nearly makes him fall over, but he catches himself on the doorway. He gasps, "What the hell?"

The practical thing for Brendan to do would be to walk out the front door and never come back. But someone needs to be the voice of reason; someone needs to de-escalate this latest crisis. He counts to ten and tells himself that Ian will eventually sober up and Marv will eventually regain his composure. He says to Ian, "Why don't you go back to your television show? I'll talk to you about this later."

"I can help."

"No, you can't."

Marv surprises them both by making it to the closet. Brendan sees him pull a suit down from its hanger and onto the floor; it lands with an unexpectedly heavy *thump* that's almost drowned out by the old man's thick and chaotic breathing. Brendan says to Ian, "Go on, I'll handle this. You're in my way."

Ian sulks for a moment or two before he finally leaves.

Brendan walks to the closet, where Marv has propped himself up against a dresser. The old man's trying to reach a T-shirt, but his arms are nearly useless. Marv looks up at him in frustration. All the old man says is "Please."

He pulls a crisp white undershirt from a drawer. The shirt is too big for Marv now, but the ill fit doesn't bother the old man, the feel of the clean fabric seems to soothe. Brendan stands and looks at the button-down shirts hanging in a neat row, arranged by color. He asks Marv, "Which shirt would you like?"

The old man's breathing is more even now as he whispers, "A simple white one."

He looks at the group of whites, most decidedly unsimple. Each has a slight variation that distinguishes it from the ones next to it. He holds a shirt he believes to be the purest white in front of him. "Will this do?"

Marv nods slightly as he slowly, carefully runs his fingers over the armbands of the clean undershirt that now covers the dirty one. Brendan kneels down beside him and pulls the old man slightly toward him. He says, his voice encouraging, "Can you hold your good arm out for me?"

Marv sticks the arm out quietly, and Brendan works the sleeve up to the armpit. He adjusts the shirt, bringing it around Marv's back, and then he gently takes the old man's bad arm by the wrist and places it in a sleeve.

"This is a beautiful shirt," he tells Marv.

Marv smiles a very little bit and says, "I had them all custom made."

"Your tailor does excellent work." Like the undershirt, it's too big for Marv now.

Finally breathing evenly, Marv says, "I wish I had someone to leave them to. If they were your size, I'd give them all to you."

Brendan works the buttons on the cuffs. "That's a lovely thought, Marv, thank you."

Marv says, "You're welcome." The old man's composure returns, one piece of clothing at a time. "After all, you're the last person I'll ever talk to in this life."

He reassures Marv. "We both know that's not true." He tugs on the shirtsleeves and they fall into place, just at the wrists. He says, "Very handsome. Very handsome indeed." And then, because it's the truth, his voice cracks as he tells Marv, "I'm sorry for all this. I really am. I wish I could take it all back. I wish it never happened."

Marv looks at him now, his mouth gaping. Whatever desire, then fear, then hatred he has felt toward Brendan dissipates. His face softens as he says, "No, I owe you an apology, Brendan. I shouldn't have treated you the way I did. I should have been more understanding."

He whispers, "That's sweet of you to say. But I really fucked up and I'm sorry."

The old man almost sounds happy as he says, "Cufflinks, please. There are some gold ones in the top drawer."

Brendan sighs; not anymore, there's not. No doubt Ian helped himself to them along with anything else of value. Brendan closes the drawer, saying, "Let's try it with only the buttons first and see how you like it."

Marv takes his meaning.

After nearly fifteen minutes Marv's nearly dressed like *a man*. Brendan reaches for the finishing touch, the suit coat that lies on the floor, still on its hanger, but Marv stops him, saying, "Let me do that myself." In spite of the air conditioning, there's a film of perspiration on the old man's skin, making him appear as if he's melting. The dark fabric of the suit pants completes the picture of a dead man nearly ready for viewing. Brendan wants to help Marv stand up, but Marv insists he will do it himself.

Brendan asks, "Shouldn't I get you back to bed now?"

"No! You're always taking care of me, it's not fair. Send that miserable friend of yours in. I want him to *carry* me to bed. I want to ask him where my gold cufflinks went!"

Brendan pats Marv's shoulders, the latest crisis nearly over. "Now, there's the Marv I've grown so fond of. You had me worried there, for a little while. You sit right here, I'll go get that miserable old friend of mine."

Marv nods as Brendan leaves.

Ian's in the easy chair, remote in hand, surfing the seemingly end-less number of channels, always lingering on one program just long enough to decide that he must be missing something better on another station. Brendan wishes that the notice that the cable was to be shut off had arrived a week earlier. Brendan very nearly shouts, "What the hell do you think you're doing?"

Ian doesn't look at his brother. He mutters, "What?"

"You could have killed him. He's an old man, Ian."

"What do you mean?"

"Tying him up in sheets! And he fell out of bed!"

Now Ian looks at him. "I tied him down with sheets so he *wouldn't* hurt himself. And so I could get a moment's peace and quiet. He's fine."

"Why the hell did you do that?"

"Soon as you were out the door he's trying to get out of bed. By the time I got here this morning he'd gotten himself free somehow. Found him lying in the middle of the room, the old fuck."

"He doesn't do that when I take care of him!"

Ian snaps, "Well, then, *you* take care of him!"

He tries to keep his tone dispassionate. "I will. But right now he's asking for you."

"Why me?"

"Because," he begins, explaining it to Ian as he would a child, "there's something he'd like to discuss with you. A certain pair of gold cufflinks."

"What? He doesn't know what he's talking about."

"After your stunt with the credit card, I thought we'd agreed not to steal his things. And I swear to God, Ian, if you hit him . . ."

Ian switches off the television and turns around to face him. Ian's hurt, humiliated by his kid brother, who's acting like he's the one in charge. "I took good care of him. And I tied him down so he *wouldn't* get hurt . . . stumbling around in the dark. . . . Why are you being like this? I did you a favor. A big favor. What's the matter; didn't you get any this weekend?"

Brendan starts to say something, but stops himself. In as calm a voice as he can manage, he says, "You tied an elderly stroke victim to his own bed."

Ian looks at him, dumbfounded. When Ian can speak, he says, "Yeah. But he was fucking elderly when I got here. He had had the fucking stroke when I got here. He had been locked in his fucking room when I got here." Ian calls Brendan by his given name before he says, "Don't take this out on me, little brother. Don't you dare take this out on me."

Brendan fumes. Ian's the one who sent him to Marv's in the first place. Ian has conveniently forgotten that the plan rests entirely upon Brendan's shoulders: his older brother's getting worse instead of better, perhaps—though he hates to admit this—becoming more of who he really is every day that he's on the outside. Ian's letting his body go soft along with his mind. Brendan finds himself regretting, for just a moment, ever re-establishing contact, just as Jeff had warned. The six-packs of beer Ian seems to consume hourly are making his center thick, his mind weak.

Ian looks like he might burst into tears as he turns the TV back on. Whatever Brendan would like to say would be fairly meaningless to Ian right now so he leaves him, planning to patch things up later. Brendan walks down the hall to discover that he's talking to himself. He pauses outside of Marv's bedroom, trying to remember what he just said. He shakes his head, frustrated, like Ian, it will have to wait.

Brendan tells himself to lighten up as he steps through the doorway to Marv's bedroom. He hears a sound, a pop, like a firecracker. His brother Steven used to make him cry when he'd steal one of his Matchbox cars and blow it up with a firecracker.

How odd to remember that just now.

He wonders whatever happened to Steven.

He looks down at his stomach. His shirt's wet, a dark stain spreading across his torso. He frowns, confused, but then he understands. He looks up at Marv, who is standing unassisted in his black suit pants, white shirt, and black suit coat. Brendan says, "Oh, God, I'm bleeding. Look at me, I'm bleeding."

Marv lets a gun drop from his withered hand and onto the floor. He stutters, "I, I didn't mean it, Brendan. I thought you were him! Oh my God . . . I thought you were that monster who raped my Frankie! I'd never shoot you!"

Brendan rubs his stomach and his palms turn red. He raises a hand up to his face and examines it closely, like he's seeing blood for the very first time. Then it's no longer his hand he sees, but tiny spots in front of his eyes. They swirl as they breed, until they're everywhere in the room and the force of gravity's too much for him to bear. He falls to the floor, not so very far from Marv's gun.

Ian's here, screaming. Before Brendan fades to black he sees Ian on top of Marv, his brother's fists a blur, his mouth a stream of profanities.

Things, people, come and go, wander in and out of his consciousness. There's the familiar feel of Cynthia's Voyager, then bright lights overhead, faces above him, looking down. Sounds are off in the distance: voices, urgent and stern, the beeping of electronics, the hum of machines.

Then nothing.

———

How long was he . . . ?
Nothing.

Something.
He's aware of something.
Ian.
He tries to focus. He looks around, he concentrates.
Ian sits next to him in a crowded little room where men lie on gur-
neys, another on the floor, atop a thin blanket, placed flush against a
wall. Ian holds his hand as he smiles sweetly at him. He says, "Jesus
Christ, you scared the hell out of me. . . ." (That other name again.)
He looks at Ian, he doesn't know—can't feel—what expression he
wears on his face. The numbness is comforting, peaceful, the feeling of
not being able to feel. But then there's Ian's voice intruding again:
"We've got to get out of here. They told me you're lucky, the bullet
didn't hit anything vital. Can you sit up?"
Speak. Ian wants him to speak. He tries to shake his head; at least
he thinks he tries to shake his head. Perhaps he is shaking his head.
Perhaps he did shake his head. Maybe the end comes now.
Ian shoves an arm around his shoulders, another under his knees.
"Come on, we *have* to get out of here. For me, please, come on." Ian
lifts him up and into his arms with a stifled grunt and now Brendan's
wide awake and he really, really wants to die because he's never been in
so much pain. He must have cried out, for Ian's big face looks down at
him, panic-stricken, and his brother whispers frantically, "Jesus, be
quiet! You want me to go back to Rush City?"
Maybe this is how he was destined to die, in Ian's arms.
They're out in the streets; it's after dark and chill. He knows because
he faces the sky, he sees the streetlights, the peaks of buildings that surround him on all sides. Ian carries him, like too many groceries he can't
put down. The pain's in Brendan's head now, just behind his eyes. It throbs

to a set pace, the regular ache of indecision, of living or dying. He feels his body oozing out of Ian's grip like hot wax. He tries to scream when Ian bobs him up in the air for an instant, readjusting his hold on him.

He's fading. He says very tenderly to Ian, like it's a kiss, "Where?"

Ian shushes him, as if he's a colicky baby, as if keeping him quiet will stop the pedestrians around them from staring.

He wants Sean. They could have gone to Canada.

He would have liked to have gone to Canada. There men can get married.

There's a sound, it's loud, irritating. There and gone, there and gone, there and gone.

"Thank God! She's here! She's here! Cynthia! Over here!"

The wind vanishes, the temperature soars. He slips away in the backseat of his father's car, his head in Steven's lap, on the seemingly endless journey from the cabin up north to their home in the Cities.

He's beginning to understand pain like never before.

His vision focuses on a ceiling fan and a faded white stucco ceiling adorned with sparkles. The fan is still, a light hangs beneath it, dark, dusty. He rolls his head to the right and he sees a few wooden crates. In-side are stacks of romance novels and magazines. He's at Cynthia and Ian's apartment.

He moves his head to the left and there's Ian, asleep in a chair, his heavy breathing tense and drawn. Brendan feels oddly safe with Ian next to him. And then he's gone again, floating in the blackness until Marv pays him a visit, his bad side healed, demanding Ensure and a new Depends and his gold cufflinks.

Is it hours later or just minutes? Seconds? He can't tell.

It's still dark, but there's a change in the hue that lets him know that dawn is coming. Ian's beside him and he has a vague recollection of a loud noise, of his own blood, of fists pounding on flesh.

———

He opens his eyes again.

Darkness, but it's a new darkness, one just beginning. How long has he been lying here? The romance novels and magazines are still to his right, but to his left sits an empty chair. He should sleep; this must be the hour when people take to their beds, eyes heavy after another day of doing whatever it is they do. He wants to stand, to walk to a window and look out on the world, to see if it's changed for the better or the worse. He has to call Sean; he knows that Sean will be worried. But he can barely lean on an elbow before his body screams out in protest.

He lies back down and waits. He smiles, in spite of the needles and pins that prick him over and over again. Was this what Marv felt like? When the old man claimed that he thought Brendan was Ian, was he lying? Did Marv know who he shot, and offered that excuse to make it easier for Brendan? (Why make it easier for someone you hate enough to shoot?) Maybe Brendan's losing his mind.

It's then that he hears it, the vaguely muffled sounds like little grunts and heavy, stunted breaths. One voice he knows to be Ian's, the other, Cynthia's. Words arrive and depart his ears like planes at a busy airport. Some are frantic, desperate, words like *shit* and *no* and *Jesus*. Some words line up together to form sentences; others do not.

I fucked it up for all of us.

It'll be okay, baby, it'll be alright. We just gotta make it through the Walk.

Jesus, I fucked it all up.

He did this to us! Nobody told him to! We just gotta make it through the Walk.

But I'm the one who sent him to that old man.

8

Family Happiness

BRENDAN'S AWAKE.

He has been for what he would guess to be an hour now. He's spent this time, eyes shut as if in a coma, playing and replaying the events of the past months back and forth in his brain. It's time to let Ian and Cynthia know he's woken up. Ian arrives first and runs a hand through his dirty hair, tells him of the prayers and the bedside vigil; it makes him believe that Ian's sheer will alone was what pulled him through. He's grateful, humbled by the depth of Ian's devotion. After all, at the end of the day Brendan was the one who got them all into this mess. He's the one who's put the plan at risk.

Cynthia tells Brendan not to worry; they can go ahead with the plan once he's fully recovered. He has about seventy-two hours to do so. He promises her he'll be able to drive the truck. He owes these people.

He spends the hours lying on a mattress, playing out a hundred different scenarios in his head: new cities, new identities, new lovers. But then he sees Sean, sweet, sappy Sean, he hears Sean tell him that he loves him (well, who he believes him to be, anyway) and he imagines the two of them leaving this city and heading north, to Canada, where

Sean can always be beautiful in the wilderness and where Maggie can stalk squirrels and deer and Brendan can shed the identities of Franklin Thompson and Pierre Bezukhov like dead skin.

Ian hasn't said a word about Marv, but the old man must at last be dead. How could Marv not be? He saw Ian on top of him, Ian's fists pummeling the old man, the blood rushing out of Marv's nostrils, ears, eyes. How could he rid himself of that? How is there any forgiving that?

No. He tells himself that Marv's alive. Alone but alive, no harm done.

Sean. He has to call Sean.

And tell Sean what?

Lying here with no painkillers is making him insane. Ian and Cynthia smile sweetly and bring him food, drink, and warm clothes. Cynthia tenderly cuts his long hair with a pair of sewing scissors, assuring him that with a baseball cap on, no one at the Walk will be able to remember the color of his hair. She holds a mirror up to his face, and he sees her sloppy work, the uneven length of the strands, the bits of scalp here and there.

For now his brother is helping him walk, but for Sunday, he will have to walk under his own power. Their route is not unlike the one he took with Marv, a continuous loop from bed to doorway and back again. Ian medicates him with alcohol; discount vodka from a plastic bottle. Ian slips it in his tea, a cola, anything that makes it more palatable. Still, he can taste it, can see the big plastic Phillips bottle next to a cracked wall.

"You're doing fine," Ian tells him as they shuffle across the floor, his steps meager, timid.

"I'm sorry you have to do this."

Ian stops their slow progress, squeezes his shoulders hard. He offers a prediction as fact: "You're going to be just fine, so stop apologizing. What's done is done."

"I don't know."

Desperate, Ian says, *"What's done is done."*

He doesn't answer; he focuses on walking, one foot, then the next. As they revolve in a tight little circle, smaller than the small room, he imagines Ian alongside him for all eternity, setting the pace, telling him what to do. He has to get to a phone. He has to call Sean. Sean will be worried, upset; he'll think Brendan doesn't want to live with him. Brendan wants to live with him.

Brendan whimpers, "I need to make a call."

Ian says again, "Cynthia took the phone."

"Could you walk me down to Ali's Market? They've got phones."

"For Christ's sake." Ian decides he needs to rest. Ian sits him in a chair salvaged from the alley. Ian gets a beer, snaps it open, drinks. Brendan studies Ian as he sits on the mattress, looking for signs of their father, their mother, Steven. He asks Ian, "Don't you think it's odd, the way we've turned out?"

"Is there something wrong with the way we've turned out?"

"I didn't picture this, that's for sure."

Ian studies his beer can. "Things happen."

"We had a better start in life than most."

Ian ignores the comment, drains his beer, gets himself another. Self-recrimination is not his pastime; what has happened, what will happen for that matter, are distant, foreign places to him. A man named Marv has probably died (this Ian finally told him today, along with the fact that he left Marv unconscious under a pile of sheets and blankets), but Marv is not dying at this very moment, money will be stolen, but they are not stealing it right now. Right now they are, the two of them, brothers, in a little room where Brendan's learning how to walk again, where Ian is drinking his second beer of the early afternoon. Brendan knows what will happen next: Ian will bring him a cola laced with vodka, then Ian will drink more beer, Cynthia will come home from Good Works, and finally all three of them will again rehearse the plan. He knows this, it happened last night, it will happen again tonight, but Ian, he thinks, only suspects what will happen, has only some vague notion of the routine they find themselves in. Brendan wonders how Ian does it. Part of him envies Ian: no past to regret, no future to fear. Ian doesn't notice as he does that Cynthia's terrified, may in fact be preparing to leave Ian, because she's not leaving him right now. The plan can't go wrong, because for it to go wrong, Ian has to witness it as it goes wrong.

Brendan says, "I think we should try to find Steven. And Mom. Maybe they could help us out of this mess."

Ian sighs. "Steven's long gone and Mom's probably dead by now. Besides, there's no mess as long as we keep our cool."

"I just think that maybe things would be different if we were all together again."

"After the Walk you can search for Steven if you like. With our luck, he's probably a cop."

Brendan doesn't know why, but he's getting emotional. His voice cracks as he says, "I think we should try to find Steven."

Ian looks up at the ceiling. Then he looks back at him.

Brendan begs now: "Can you *please* tell Cynthia that I need to use the phone?"

Ian, mutters, "Yeah, okay? For the last time, I'll tell her. Jesus." Ian finishes his second beer, and on his way to the tiny kitchen for a third he turns on the small black-and-white television set. A woman appears on the screen in a high neckline and pearls. She speaks to Brendan, telling him of disasters domestic and foreign, and then a new face appears, holding a microphone. This reporter is outside and Brendan recognizes the odd angle of the old maple tree behind him. Now the reporter introduces a taped report in which a grim little man is being interviewed. Brendan knows this man from somewhere.

He cuts Marv's yards. He's Edward Lundeen.

Edward Lundeen discovered Marv's body hidden under a pile of bedding. Concerned by the victim's long absence from the property, he had let himself in with a spare key the victim kept hidden in a flower pot.

Brendan's heart stops beating, time stands still. He understands several things at once, including the fact that the authorities must be looking for a man in his thirties who goes by the name of Victor Komarovsky and claims to be a lawyer from Manhattan.

It's on the verge of sunrise, he can tell, the birds have begun their songs. The pain in his side has kept him up nearly all night, fueling the little scenarios that he plays in his mind, fallout from the description Edward Lundeen has surely given the police.

Part of him still can't believe Marv's really dead.

Sean. He has to call Sean.

Now that Ian has taught him how to walk he slowly rolls his body—his side killing him—to the edge of the mattress. He slides himself onto the floor. It's then that he notices it, hidden behind a stack of romance novels. It's difficult, but he gets to his feet, grunts and moans his way to the crate upon which sits an old peach-colored Princess phone.

He hasn't heard it ring once during his time here, there is only the occasional beeping of Cynthia's cell phone. But he takes it on faith that this phone is live, connected, that it will carry his voice to Sean, deliver the news that, yes, he will move in with him, yes, he will do the right thing and drop out of Cynthia's plan (but no, he can't, he owes his brother and sister-in-law a new start), yes, he will live his life differently from this moment on.

Dead. Like Marv, the fucking phone is dead.

He lies on the floor, the tears forming in his eyes, watches the first pinkish hues appear in the deep blue of morning. This was the hour his father would rise, and with no effort to conceal his steps, descend the stairs of the house for his daily jog. Next, Brendan's mom would awaken and head to the kitchen, where she would brew coffee and squeeze the fresh orange juice her husband always insisted be waiting for him upon his return. Some mornings Brendan would join her, and it would be only the two of them, Ian and Steven would sleep till noon if you let them.

Brendan rarely spoke as she sliced the oranges and squeezed out the juice by hand. It was enough to watch her, to see the delicate twists of her wrists, the look of simple concentration on her face. If he ever did want to talk, she would tell him to get on with the job she'd invented just for him, changing all the cups on the shelves from upside-down to right side up. For this he would have to kneel on the countertops and focus on keeping his balance, afraid that something as soft as a word exiting his lips could have enough force to knock him off the edge and onto the floor.

She preferred to do the talking and his questions made her impatient. So, as he turned one cup over, and then another, she would tell him about where she and his father used to live, in London. They had a spacious flat on Red Lion Square, not far from the British Museum. There were cats, two of them, and she missed them. The flat was not a place they could ever go back to, so she would visit it again with him in the kitchen of her Minnesota home, detached with a three-car garage. He was not allowed to ask why they had left England, why they had decided to move to Minnesota. There was to be no discussion of aunties or uncles, grandparents or cousins. These questions would only make her answer him with one of her own, *Aren't we family enough for you, little prince?*

When his father returned, gasping and sweating, he would look at Brendan's mother, and then at Brendan, and ask, *All the cups in order then?*

Some mornings the nanny would join them. She was a young, pretty North Dakota girl who loved to grab him by a wrist and an ankle and spin him through the air on what she called plane rides, until he grew too big for such things. His mother didn't like her. Looking back he's often wondered whether his nanny was also his father's mistress or whether there was some other unforgivable source of his mother's contempt. Even during those mornings when the kitchen was full of the four of them, Mom, Dad, the nanny, himself, it was a silent place, as if a sacred temple where even words softly spoken were blasphemous. Nanny was gone a week after his sixth birthday, and her departure, like grandparents and cousins, was not to be discussed.

How odd that he and Ian should follow so sloppily in their father's footsteps. Dad was a gentleman bandit, entertaining clients at elegant dinner parties hosted by his wife as he brought his own particular brand of bookkeeping to their accounts. And look at his sons, both of them ending up as dependent upon Cynthia and her own accounting system as they were as children upon their father and his.

He wears a baseball cap like the big baby on the billboard along Interstate 35, and large sunglasses as he stands with the men, the gals' men. He shifts the light backpack on his shoulder, the only thing inside is a change of summer clothes and some toiletries for later. Today is the Walk for the Unborn and the morning crew who set up the tables and tents gives the drivers the keys to the trucks, along with warnings about particular vehicles, which gears stick and how hard to lean on the aging brakes. The men aren't friendly; they haven't forgiven him for his performance at the action, for causing controversy. Only one of their number will have anything to do with Brendan; he's new, the son of a gal, not the husband of a gal. As they receive their instructions Brendan sees Cynthia listening as one of the gals chats with her at the registration tables. She wasn't able to speak to Ian and Brendan this morning, only utter unintelligible words as she hung her head over the toilet, her nerves eating her insides out. When he asked where her cell phone was he was rewarded with a deep retch and the sound of vomiting echoing in the bowl.

He was the only one to ask if they really wanted to go through with it. Ian merely quoted his wife from the final pep talk she had given the night before: *If we do this right nobody's gonna know that the money's gone missing.* So here they are, pulled along by their own momentum: Cynthia's at the tables, the husband Brendan suspects she's preparing to leave is nearby with the Voyager; and Brendan, the screw-up both of them still need, leans for all he's worth against the truck that is the linchpin of the plan. People are arriving in great numbers; whole congregations empty out of church buses to walk as groups. Walkers greet each other enthusiastically; some close their eyes and hold their hands over their heads to offer praise. Picnic lunches are everywhere, and everywhere children bow their heads and pray along with moms and dads before biting into pieces of cold fried chicken. Preachers compete for audiences, and petitions are circulated for an odd collection of causes, everything from school vouchers to opening up the Boundary Waters Canoe Area Wilderness to Jet Skis and ATVs.

After the coordinator of the volunteer drivers offers a brief prayer, and after the son of a gal ogles some teenage girls, Brendan spots a phone near the pavilion.

Each step Brendan takes toward the pavilion rewards him with a fresh bit of misery, but he is careful to keep a neutral expression on his face. He's just a few yards from the phone when he hears voices shouting his name. His truck is already full; it's time to make his first delivery. He stares at the telephone receiver, the small buttons on which single digits are printed, numbers that, like words in a poem, can be arranged together, can connect him to something much larger than himself.

The team captain hollers now, his tone demanding: "Brendan, you're all set to go!"

Of course he is.

He smiles, waves, somehow manages to get in his truck, which the volunteers have filled with trashcans. He should just make his deliveries as promised. Here is what he should do: get out of this truck, go pick up that phone, call Sean. But instead, he drives, timing his exits carefully, ensuring that the truck won't wind up in a caravan of other Walk trucks whose drivers could witness his brief detours and ruin everything.

He can't believe he's actually doing this, he can't believe it's actually happening. He can't believe that Marv is dead or that he was shot. It's his disbelief that makes it all possible. His adoptive parents often talked about *disassociation,* how people are able to remove themselves from the events around them and even from their own actions. Perhaps it's a talent, something that evolution selects for: people with the capacity to do what must be done, because they refuse to accept that they are doing it.

In traffic, he's surprised by how accommodating people are. They see a U-Haul truck and they follow from a respectful distance. They assume he's under stress, fearful that he may make a wrong move, ending their lives or his own. But it's a very disingenuous sort of thoughtfulness, the kind he's come to expect from people since the moment a very short and pretty white woman with a briefcase informed him that his mother and father had terminated their parental rights.

That they had given him up.

He's giving in to bitterness; he needs to adjust his attitude. He should simply review the facts: he's driving an old, orange and silver truck. Stacked to the roof behind him are trashcans, white ones, brown ones, cash and checks. He looks for other Walk trucks before he makes his quick turn and he soon ends up in the parking lot of the old elementary school, named after an unfortunate young man killed in the Spanish-American War. There's the van parked alongside the Dumpster, Cynthia's Voyager. Ian's behind the wheel, one of his wife's generic cigarettes between his lips, a large flask of what Ian calls Dutch courage carefully placed on the dashboard in front of him.

Brendan frantically waves at Ian as he puts the truck in neutral; pulls the emergency brake up.

Ian's outfitted like his brother, in a Minnesota Twins baseball cap and large sunglasses. Ian opens the van's door and nearly trips over his own feet as he carries dozens of empty white envelopes and a box of black garbage bags to the truck.

Brendan shouts, "Come on, come on, let's go."

Ian says something under his breath as he joins him in the back of the U-Haul. As soon as Ian's inside and they've taken off their caps, and stuffed their sunglasses inside, Brendan pulls the cargo door shut. They put on their headlamps in the darkness and then the brothers dump the contents of a white trashcan in a space even smaller than Cynthia had predicted. Their arms and shoulders touch, bump into each other. Brendan rips open white envelopes, placing the larger bills in the trash bags while Ian packs the small bills, the ones and fives, in the new white envelopes that he seals with the sweat pouring from his face.

Ian stares at a sealed envelope, whimpers, "Name, I need a name."

Brendan looks at him, astonished. "Didn't you make a list?"

"I think I left it at the apartment. I think that's where it is."

Brendan grunts, perspiration stinging his eyes. How's he going to explain the fact that he's drenched in his own sweat when he arrives at the Babies First office? He'll say he hosed himself down to cool off and if he comes across one, he will actually do it. Brendan says, "Christopher McCandless."

"Chris Mick what?"

Brendan tries again: "Chris McCain."

Brendan stuffs a garbage bag like it's autumn. Ian stammers, "Name, I need a name!"

"Pierre Bezukhov."

"What the fuck kind of name is that? You *want* us to get caught? Jesus, help me!"

"Pete Bushmill."

A few seconds later: "I need a name!"

"Toni Bushmill."

Again: "A name!"

"Leo Tilson!"

They finish, dump out another white trash can, and Brendan realizes they won't be able to get to all the white trashcans without unloading and reloading the truck. What they can reach will have to do. Whenever Ian opens the cargo door to throw the torn white envelopes in the Dumpster, the cooler air renews them. Still, Brendan can hardly see, not for lack of light, but because of the salty sweat that runs down his brow. The air is thin, and the brothers' fear has a temperature all its own, like something inside a volcano or on the surface of the sun. His jeans cling to him and he wipes his face with his shirt. He looks at his watch, barks, "One minute!"

Ian says, "Hang on, hang on!"

"Ian!"

They open, sort, seal; open, sort, seal, but Ian is lagging as Brendan shouts, "Time!"

Ian shines his flashlight in Brendan's eyes. "I'm not ready, Jesus, I got all this shit left to go."

Now he points the beam of his light at the truck's floor and Brendan sees the small mounds of ones and fives and even ten-dollar bills that surround Ian on all sides. Brendan can't show up at the office with a single loose bill. He says, "Go, go, take the bags, I'll do it myself."

"But . . ."

"Go!"

Ian pulls open the cargo door and for a moment Brendan feels a cool breeze, breathes in fresh air. He shouts Ian's name and points to his own headlamp. Ian frowns, but then he gets it. He takes off the headlamp, retrieves his cap and glasses. Then he quickly slams the door shut and Brendan ignores his pain, takes in the money scattered around; there's too much of it, he needs a broom, a dustpan, a fireplace. He stuffs it in a spare garbage bag, considers tossing it in the Dumpster, or why not just put it in the van along with the rest? The sorting is a waste of valuable time anyway.

The plan.

Thirty thousand dollars just for Brendan.

His brother and sister-in-law are liars or idiots, but most likely both. But then so is he. *How the hell* did they think they would fit all that money and three people in a van and just drive it across the Mexican border?

The plan! Jesus!

He finishes up, removes the headlamp, puts the cap and glasses back on. He opens the cargo door, limps out the back of the truck unsure of what to do with the bag full of small bills. He tosses his headlamp to Ian, saying, "Be sure and turn it off."

The bag of small bills, the bag of small bills . . . Shit, he'll just keep it, stuff as much of it as he can in his backpack when he gets the chance. He watches Ian, desperately arranging garbage bags in the van. Ian jumps at the sound of the U-Haul's engine turning over, but then grabs his flask, raises it, and drinks to Brendan's health as his brother shifts into gear. Brendan heads down University Avenue, toward the Babies First office, where the true believers wait patiently for what's left of his delivery.

He glances at the black bag next to him that glistens with his sweat.

He has to call Sean.

And say what?

He turns off University Avenue and onto a side street. After a few blocks he finds a gas station and pulls in; turns off the truck's engine. At the edge of the station's tiny parking lot is a pay phone. He shoves a hand in one pocket, and then in the other: no quarters. He's hauling thousands of dollars and he doesn't have change to make a phone call. He punches the bag, tells himself to calm down. He'll just have to go in the station and get change.

He rips open the bag next to him, grabs two fives. He opens the cab's door. He makes his feet move.

Inside the station's little store a cashier sits opposite him behind a thick, dirty pane of bulletproof glass. Displayed in back of her are candy bars: Baby Ruth, Nestlé Crunch, Oh Henry!, Heath, others. Above her head, within reach if she stands up, are packs of cigarettes in neat vertical rows, the generic kind favored by Cynthia, the high-tar, high-nicotine brands that Ian loves.

He should take up smoking. He's heard smokers say that cigarettes reduce stress, help them manage crises. This is a crisis, he tells himself. And he can finally afford the habit.

He tells the cashier, who's thoroughly engaged in a conversation she's having with a friend at the other end of the office's phone line: "Hi. Pack of Marlboros, please."

She says to the phone, "Hang on; hang on a sec." At him she glares, grunts, "What?"

He repeats, "A pack of Marlboros," dropping the *hi* and the *please*.

She sighs. "Longs or shorts?"

"Shorts."

"Regular, medium, or lights?"

"Surprise me."

At this he gets her undivided attention. She looks at him suspiciously, uncertain as to whether he's flirting or threatening. She decides on the latter. She pulls down three packs of cigarettes, lines them up on her side of the glass, and with an impatient mumble, orders, "Pick one."

He really hates it when people talk down to him.

From his side of the bulletproofing he points to the first pack on his right. She reaches for it, but then he slowly moves his finger back and forth along the row as he says, "Eeniee, meenie, minee, moe, catch a tiger by his toe—"

Now he says, his pace quickening, his finger a blur in front of the red and white packs "—if he hollers let him go, eeniee, meenie, minee, moe!"

She folds her arms across her chest and gives him a look.

He says, "Moe. I'll take a pack of Moe today." He slides the bills in the little slot that connects their two worlds, saying, "Make it all quarters." She makes his change, picks up the phone, and continues her conversation as she shoves the coins and cigarettes across the border and into his territory.

She turns her back to him as she says, "You wouldn't believe the assholes that waltz in here—" and he slaps a hand against the glass. She jumps, drops the phone to the floor.

He shouts, "Have a nice day."

She stares, wide-eyed. When she can talk, it's to say: "Fuck off, asshole!"

A flash of memory now: in high school he played basketball, and while he was a quiet kid, the team consisted largely of bullies, loud and tough boys who loved to get into fights. In an effort to end this, players were taught peer mediation to resolve conflict. But if tempers continued to rise and violence was likely imminent, they were supposed to just walk away.

Even if they're laughing at you? he asked.

Yes, even if they're laughing at you, the coach said.

But if we walk away, they'll think they're right even if they're wrong. They'll think they've won. You want us to walk away then?

Especially then, the coach sighed. *You'll know you're doing the responsible thing, the adult thing.*

What his coach didn't say was that one day he'd get tired of being the one who walks away insulted, wronged, the names he'd been called ringing in his ears. He smiles at the cashier, says for her: "Thank you, come again." And he walks out.

He plugs a quarter in the phone. What does he say to him? How does he explain his disappearance?

He misses Maggie. She's a sweet dog.

"Hello, you've reached Sean Reilly. Please leave a message and call the White House to demand they bring our troops home." *Beep!*

"Sean? Sean? It's me. I . . . I was in an accident but I'm better now. Please call me—"

At Marv's? You fucking idiot!

"No! Don't call, I forgot, the phone's been disconnected . . ."

Because?

". . . because my sister got behind on the bills."

Now *that* sounds likely.

"I'll call you as soon as I can."

It's then that he notices it: another truck full of Walk donations. Inside is the son of a gal, a perplexed look on his acne-scarred face. He pulls his truck to a stop alongside the curb and Brendan sees the indicators flash their hazard warning. The son of a gal leans over to the passenger side window and shouts, "What are you doing?"

Brendan shouts back at him, "I just needed a bathroom break."

The son of a gal frowns, reminds him that they're not supposed to stop anywhere but the park and the office.

Brendan appears contrite now, places a hand over the pain in his side, his wet shirt sticking to the skin. He says, "Breakfast went right through me. It was either stop or make a nasty mess in the truck."

The son flinches. "Why'd ya come here?"

The little bastard has been following him. He lies some more: "Reflex, I guess. This is my neighborhood."

The son considers this. One of the cars now lined up behind his truck honks its horn, but he isn't moving. Finally, he shouts, "If this is your neighborhood, why not just stop off at home?"

Brendan smiles, yells, "Turned out I couldn't make it the extra few blocks. I didn't want to shit my pants, all right?"

The son shouts, "Follow me. We better stick together in case you have to make another stop. We're not supposed to leave the trucks un-attended, ya know?"

"I'm fine now," he tells him, "I'll see you at the office."

The beeping behind the son's truck has become a chorus, drivers stick their heads out car windows, cursing:

Move your fucking truck, asshole!

This isn't a parking lot, asshole!

Move it or lose it, asshole!

Brendan looks at him for long moments, and then the son shifts his gaze to Brendan's truck, the driver's-side door still open. The son gets a clear view of the garbage bag, of the bills sticking out of the hole Bren-dan ripped in it. The son puts his own truck in gear. As he pulls away drivers speed up and pass him, flipping him the finger.

Brendan doesn't know what else to do, so he leaves. He tosses the bag into a garbage can at a red light. He ignores his pain, sticks to the plan, opening, sorting, and sealing with Ian. He times his departures and arrivals in order to avoid the son of a gal.

Another pass and Ian empties his flask as Brendan tries to figure out how to fit more garbage bags into Cynthia's van. That's when he hears it, the beep of a cell phone.

He looks at Ian. "You have a *phone?*"

Ian nods sloppily.

"You had a fucking phone all this time?"

Ian frowns, pulls the cell phone out of the van's glove compartment. Ian listens to what Brendan assumes must be Cynthia's voice from the park. She tells Ian, who tells him, that the majority of walkers are well on their way; that the pledge drops will now be fewer and far between.

Or, to put it another way, they're done.

They've pulled it off. Just as Cynthia said they would.

All he has to do is drop the truck off at the park while Ian heads back to the apartment with the van. In another hour, they'll be dividing up the cash and Cynthia and Ian will be heading to Mexico together or maybe they won't. And he'll be on the bus to Sean's house, his share in a backpack and suitcases, and once Sean opens the door Brendan's going to put his arms around him, and after that he doesn't know what will come next. His arms around Sean; that is the only thing he is certain of, and for now it will have to do.

Ian takes off his shirt, which is drenched in sweat and his milky white skin glows in the bright sunlight, highlighting every flaw and imperfection. They might as well be twins for the identical blemishes. Ian pulls a joint out of his wallet, lights it.

Brendan gasps. "Jesus! What the hell are you doing?"

Ian inhales so deeply he nearly collapses. Smoke pours out of his mouth as he says, "I just need to calm down. It's my little tradition after a score."

"Somebody's going to smell it and call the cops."

Ian snaps, "Nobody's around, and I *need* this."

"You're the one always going on and on about confidence. Where's yours?"

"I can't get behind the fucking wheel until I've fucking calmed down, yeah?" With the joint dangling from his lips, he holds his arms out in front of him. "Look, my hands are shaking!"

"For Christ's sake, somebody might see you! Hide yourself if you have to smoke. Jesus, Ian! I mean, *Jesus Christ!*"

Ian slinks away like a boy who's been caught masturbating. He makes his way to the tall bushes and thick elms that grow on the hill of the small park across the street from the school. It becomes Ian's own little magic forest, the kind that elves and leprechauns might live in. Maybe he'll be lucky enough to catch one, maybe it will grant him a wish, maybe he's lost his nerve to go through with this, maybe Brendan's losing his mind. Their new beginning as a real family could be going up in smoke.

Brendan walks to the parking lot's driveway, on the lookout for witnesses. He sits on the steps to the school's front entrance, counts to ten.

He looks across the street at a small church, a reconciled church, one that welcomes all, gay or straight. It's positioned alongside the school building near the bottom of the small hill, hardly a hill at all. But even so, at its humble summit, this hill is the highest point in the city. From the top of the hill, you can see for miles. He looks up the avenue that ascends Minneapolis's Mount McKinley, and that's when he spots it: a police car. A second one pulls up alongside the first.

He limps back to the van, frantically, loudly whispering: "Ian? God fuck it! Ian? For fuck's sake get over here! Now!"

Nothing.

"Ian!!!"

Nothing.

He drags himself back to the lot's driveway, crouching low to the ground, and risks another look up the hill. A cop has gotten out of his squad car and is talking to a woman who's walking a dog. A second figure emerges from the backseat. Even from this distance he recognizes the son of a gal.

He makes it back to the van. "Ian?! God fuck it! Get over here!"

Birds are singing, for the first time he hears them, chirping as loudly as if it were dawn. He's allowed a moment to focus. He sees Ian, stoned to the gills and stumbling through the tiny forest, trying to follow the sound of Brendan's voice, which must seem to him to come from all directions. Instead of making his way down the knoll to the parking lot, he lurches, walks to his left and then his right. Brendan swears silently, gets in the van. They have one bit of luck anyway: Ian's left the keys in the ignition. He turns the engine over. From his vantage point behind the steering wheel, he sees Ian slip down the tiny slope, emerging on a sidewalk. Ian's drunk, stoned, lost; he's staggering along the street that separates the park from the school. Brendan pulls the van out of the parking lot. If he makes two sharp lefts, up the hill, then down, he can pick his brother up, get them both out of there with the money, and leave the police nothing but an orange rental truck full of heavy brown trashcans and lighter white ones.

Brendan makes the first left, telling himself that Ian, as their father would say, is all *mouth and trousers*. "Exude confidence," Ian told him, and look at Ian now, struggling to put one foot in front of the other. Brendan thinks back to their first reunion at Rush City, recalls the joy of seeing Ian again, the hope that they could become the family they were always meant to be.

Brendan makes the second left and that's when he sees a police car slowly following his brother. The son of a gal is riding in the backseat, his arm extended, his finger pointing at Ian, who looks so much like Brendan—that is, if you've only seen Brendan in a baseball cap and a pair of sunglasses. But it's the expression on Ian's face, not its features that Brendan recognizes as his own: the confusion, the bewilderment. All at once Brendan wonders whether those seniors were really fooled by Ian, by the quaver in his voice when under pressure, or did they simply feel sorry for him, pretending to be fooled as they sent him their checks so he wouldn't starve? Brendan sits in the van, its engine idling. He whispers, "Ian. Ian, come on, big brother, come on, don't let me down. Please."

The police car stops, and two officers emerge, motioning toward his brother. Ian shrugs his shoulders at the cops and awkwardly continues on his way.

The policemen look at each other, wondering what they should do next, but then the bigger one grabs Ian and forces Ian's arms behind his back as the smaller one cuffs the wrists together. Brendan's eyes swell as he hears himself moan softly, "Jesus, Ian. I mean, Jesus fucking Christ, Ian."

He pulls into the driveway of someone's home, kills the engine, slides down in the seat, and waits. Perhaps only a few minutes have passed, or perhaps an hour, or perhaps a lifetime when he turns the key in the ignition and leaves, alone, his only company a van full of black garbage bags.

He pulls the Voyager out into the traffic of University Avenue, the main route connecting Minneapolis to St. Paul. He's not far from the campus when he sees some college boys jogging in a little group. They're like migrating geese, keeping a tight formation and making loud noises as they bounce along the sidewalk. Life is so easy for some people it just makes him ill. He bets their mommies and daddies pay their tuition and plan to give them cars when they graduate.

He tells himself to stop it, he's got to concentrate. North. North. North. Just keep repeating the mantra, the one he made up as he pulled out of an anonymous driveway.

Oh God, what the hell has he done?

He opens the glove compartment, looking for a map and he sees it, a gun, Marv's gun no doubt, the one the old man shot him with, stashed away by Ian, he guesses, his brother's little insurance policy in case things went wrong.

He drives right past the entrance ramp to I-35 North.

He curses himself, makes a U-turn to get back to the ramp but he's on a one-way street and now drivers curse him from their cars and the little tanks they love to drive. He leans on the horn and steers against traffic; fuck 'em anyway. *His life has been very hard,* so excuse him if he makes one goddamn wrong turn! Don't act like it's some crime against humanity! This isn't Iraq! Nobody's died!

Except Marv.

Calm down. Concentrate.

He nearly skids into a woman driving a pickup. She yells obscenities, they all do, they all honk their horns and scream at him. He could grab Marv's gun; he could shut them all up.

Stop it.

The ramp, he finally makes the fucking ramp.

Review. Let's review. If his assumptions are correct, Cynthia and the rest of the registration volunteers will soon be picked up by the police as witnesses. She may play dumb for a while, but eventually she'll crack wide open and provide them with all the details, she's not as strong as she'd like to think she is. Ian. His poor Ian. What has he done to his brother, to Cynthia? They were his only friends, his only family. They'll tell the cops everything, why shouldn't they? Including—and he's counting on this—their plan to head to Mexico.

The freeway is fairly clear heading north and he breathes deeply, relieved to be just another anonymous driver, no longer the lunatic he was moments before, barreling the wrong direction down a one-way. He looks across the median; it's the southbound lanes that are busy, full of families heading back from their weekend at the cabin. There won't be many weekday residents around the lakes, at least not for another few weeks, a good thing.

He's calming down.

He's not losing it.

He centers himself by focusing on the speedometer and keeping the needle as near to the Day-Glo 55 as he can. He concentrates on his breathing, inhaling deeply like a smoker, and exhaling through pursed lips. It's then that he notices the van's other needle pointing to E.

It's pointing to E.

Stupid fucking Ian is so fucking stupid that he forgot to put stupid fucking gas in the stupid fucking van! Goddamnit! He's so fucking stupid!

Now he has to find a service station fast. He's made it only as far as Forest Lake, maybe forty minutes north of the Cities. He takes the exit and as he drives down what looks to be the main drag, he finds himself immersed in a sea of cars, fast-food restaurants, and gas stations. His closest option is a Super America. He pulls the Voyager in slowly, try-ing to remember which side of the van the gas tank is on.

He's surrounded on all sides by SUVs, their drivers pumping gas as they speak into cell phones. They're talking to their husbands or wives or children or parents, barking complaints or commands like *I told you to do that an hour ago* or *Set it for channel three and hit the* RECORD *button, it's not that hard.* Their complete absence from where they physically are reassures him. The more engaged they are in what's going on where they're not, the less likely they'll be to notice a panicky man standing next to an old Voyager packed to overflowing with garbage bags.

He fills the tank too much and the van spits up a little gasoline. He replaces the nozzle and regrets that he left the sunglasses and baseball cap in the truck. He's reluctant to leave the van alone, but he locks it securely and trusts that the other people buzzing around the pumps lack the curiosity or the nerve to investigate the load he's hauling. Inside the little store, there's a line five deep for the single cashier who's stumped by a request for a money order. She keeps looking behind the customers, waiting for someone to appear, someone competent in the ways of the money order. She smiles nervously at all of them who wait impatiently but silently, too polite or too shy to complain.

A man comes into view from the back of the store. He's Native American, his brown complexion and long black hair a stark contrast to the heavy white people all around. He exchanges hushed tones with the other cashier before he sorts out the mess, freeing his co-worker to deal with the simple transactions, payments for gas or purchases of a bag of chips. For some reason Brendan doesn't mind the delay; standing in the midst of people who don't know him and have no idea what he's done gives him some measure of confidence that re-inventing himself may not be as hard as he thought. But as he says "Pump six" to the cashier, his nerve falters. The smile she gives him makes him wonder whether she's going to pick up the phone and call the police as soon as he's out the door. It's stupid, really, but as he leaves he coughs, bending over so far that his true height can't be measured by the exit, its frame clearly marked in feet and inches.

He stops in front of the van, holds his side.

He should have bought something to eat.

He takes the risk of being seen at the Forest Lake Super America and he doesn't even bother to buy food for the road. If he goes back inside now he really will be memorable.

In his frustration he drops the keys and as he bends to pick them up, hits his head on the van. He curses loudly and a heavyset woman across the service island from him looks up from her cell phone, shoots a disapproving glance his way, and then returns to her conversation.

He tells himself to calm down; tells himself he's acting like a fool.

He opens the door slowly, he sits down carefully. He places his hands on the steering wheel and holds them there, focusing on the feel of the ribbed plastic beneath his fingers. *It's okay, it's okay. Drive.*

He decides to pick up a meal from one of the countless drive-throughs, but they're all backed up with Jeep Cherokees and Chevy

Suburbans and Ford Explorers. He changes his mind and heads back to
I-35. He can't afford the wait and he needs to feel the wheels turning,
delivering him from the Twin Cities and all that's happened there.

The cell phone on the dashboard rings. Jesus, the cell phone is ringing. He picks it up, presses buttons until he finds the correct one. Hys-
terical now, he shouts, "Ian!"

It's Cynthia: "Where the fuck are you guys? The Walk's over!" He
hears her burst into tears, and she sobs, "Come get me. Please. Where
are you?"

He can't help himself, he starts to cry. "They got him, Cynthia,
they got Ian!"

She screams, "Who? Who's got Ian?"

"The police, the police have him, oh fuck, they have him, Cynthia,
they fucking have him."

He watches cars pass him, their drivers looking over, alarmed that
he can't seem to keep the van in a single lane. "I'll come get you, you
still at the park? I'll come get you. I can be there in a half hour, I
just . . ."

Long moments pass without a response. When she does speak, it's to
tell him, "No, you go on. You go."

"What are you going to do?"

Calmly, slowly, her voice defeated, she says, "I'll call you later. I gotta
get out of here *now*. I'll call you later, we can meet up in Chicago."

"But I'm not—"

And she hangs up. He drops the phone on top of the bags on the
seat next to him, puts both hands firmly on the steering wheel. His
mind wanders back to the Super America and the man who knew how
to issue a money order. The man didn't look that much older than he is
and he wonders what it would have felt like to run his fingers through
the man's long hair. He wonders whether the man's an artist making do
at the cash register until he sells his first work. He wonders whether the
man will be discovered, acclaimed, if his art will be revered for genera-
tions to come.

He wonders if the man would save him if he had the chance.
He wonders if Sean will.

He makes it to Duluth before the adrenaline wears off. The vast expanse of Lake Superior shimmers under the sunset and groups of
teenagers wander up and down the streets waiting for something to
happen. His backpack sits next to him on a bucket seat, atop a garbage
bag. Zipped up tight inside are the sweaty clothes of earlier today.

He's famished. He needs to lie down. He wants a checkered tablecloth by the lakeshore that's covered with glasses of wine and plates of
cheese.

He has to find a drive-through; he can't leave the van unattended,
stuffed full of unmarked bills. He makes his way through Duluth's
downtown and toward the northern outskirts, where he finds a
McDonald's. He had promised himself the day he quit McDonald's
that he would never eat at one again, but as there's no line of cars, he
pulls in.

A muffled adolescent's voice squawks from the menu board's
speaker: "Welcome to McDonald's, would you like to try an extra-
value meal?"

He's disoriented from the drive, the Walk, abandoning his brother,
his sister-in-law, the entire day. "No, thank you. Just give me a Big Mac,
large fries, and a large Coke."

The teenager is like the Wizard of Oz, a disembodied voice speaking
though all kinds of machinery. Brendan's the Cowardly Lion, doing his
best to stay put and not flee in sheer terror. The voice tells him how
much he owes, that he has, in fact, ordered an extra-value meal in spite
of himself, and that he should pull up to the second window. His side
aches from the stress and from its own recent experience playing host
to a bullet. A scrawny boy opens the pickup window. (Are they now
manufacturing boys for McDonald's like they do the fiberglass arches
and the menu boards? They all look the same to him.) He rips open one

of the garbage bags and from the pile of bills that fall out, he hands the boy a twenty.

He almost laughs, he's such an idiot.

As the boy hands Brendan his change, he drops some of the coins onto the curb between them.

The boy says, "I'm sorry. Do you want to count what you have in your hand and I'll give you the difference?"

He shuts his eyes tight, willing them to rehydrate, to come back to life. This is taking too long, he's making too many mistakes; he's got to get out of here. "Keep the change, I just want my goddamn food."

Now he's offended the boy, which will make him all the more memorable when the kid's questioned by the police. The media can report that not only is he armed and dangerous, but also unnecessarily rude. He says, "I'm sorry"—he squints as the boy's badge—"*Randy*, my mother died very suddenly this morning. I'm not myself."

Randy hands him the bag and a large cup, and he can tell by the look on Randy's face that he has now successfully emblazoned himself into this kid's memory for all eternity. Randy offers him his condolences, saying, "I'm very sorry for your loss, sir."

He stares at the bag that Randy holds just outside the van's window. For some reason he thinks that McDonald's should make his order complimentary, in view of the recent death in his family. It should be a "Sympathy Meal"; a picture of Ronald McDonald dressed entirely in black on the bag, a look of benevolence painted on his face. Instead of a toy, a handkerchief and half a Valium inside. Maybe he could hold the viewing at a McDonald's, the corpse laid across a counter, the mourners passing sadly with trays that they will bus themselves.

He's got to put some miles between this boy and himself.

He strains to keep his focus as he heads north up Minnesota's Arrowhead. He frets about his destination, Sean's cabin in the north woods. What if he can't locate it in the pitch blackness? What if Ian gets back at him by claiming that he was the one who killed Marv? What if Sean has found out what he's done?

He tries to put at least five more miles behind him before he allows himself to think about anything. But this route and the vast expanse of trees recall the summer days spent at his parents' cabin. He and his brothers would swim in the lake, no matter the temperature, until their lips turned blue and their mother called them back inside, where she poured hot toddies down their throats to warm them up and put them to sleep. Theirs was the only cabin on the little lake. If it still exists, and if he can find it, and if it hasn't been opened up for the season yet, he could stay there instead of Sean's cabin.

Sean.

He has to talk to Sean.

He reaches for the cell phone, turns it back on. Through glazed eyes he tries to make out the illuminated buttons, the ONE and the POUND sign and the little star that glows green. He stares too long; the van drifts over the highway's shoulder. He turns back to the road, corrects his course. He needs to pay attention. He needs to *multitask*, the way he was taught to do at Target. He keeps his focus on the road, glancing at the phone as he pushes its tiny plastic bumps. He hears ringing, then a voice, Sean's voice, nearly drowned out by the thick static of their weak connection.

"Sean! It's me! It's Brendan!"

"Brendan?"

"It's Pierre—we have a really bad connection. I'm sorry."

"Pierre? Pierre! What happened to you? I got your message and was worried sick!"

A coursing of static now; powerful, impossible to ignore. "Sean? I'm okay now."

"You're okay now?"

"I'm okay now."

"Hello? Pierre? Are you there? Can you hear me?"

"Yes! Yes, I can hear you!"

"Pierre?"

"I hear you!"

"Pierre?"

And the connection dies.

He hasn't been multitasking so now he's lost. He panicked, he ran too fast and too scared, and now he doesn't know where the hell he is and he *has* to sleep. He feels like crying as he pulls the van off to the side of a two-lane highway and turns off the lights, the engine. There's no room for him to lie down so he leans against the pile of garbage bags on the seat next to him, so exhausted that it feels like a feather mattress.

He can tell it's early, maybe not even six A.M. The sun is low and its light comes through the van's windows at a sharp angle, a glare that makes him squint. The air is full of birdsong and the grass is covered in a soft, frosty dew. He can smell pine on the swift breeze that finds its way into the van through a window he failed to roll all the way up. The temperature dropped overnight and he wakes up hugging his knees to his chest. He needs warm clothes, hot coffee, a solid plan. He has none of these things. And why not? He's smarter than that. At least he used to be. Or at least he used to think that he was.

He opens the van's door and, shivering, teeth chattering, he steps out into the new morning, his body sore and tight and begging for a real bed to rest itself on. He wraps himself up in his arms and he tells himself that, yes, he made a mistake by not thinking far enough ahead, by agreeing to Cynthia's plan. Yes, he should have never picked up a phone and called Marvin Fletcher. At a minimum, at a bare minimum, he shouldn't have locked up an old man in a bedroom, he should have walked away, but then again, where would he be right now if he had? A shelter? A soup kitchen? If he hadn't done this he wouldn't have met Sean.

He thinks he's in love with Sean. Or maybe it's just his desperation trying to convince him that he is. Sean's in love with him, he's told him so. This can work; they can leave Minnesota behind with the money from the Walk, start new lives in Canada. No, Sean would never do that.

Now he tells himself firmly and without qualification: *Stop it. The situation is salvageable.* All it requires is unemotional, rational thought, something he once thought himself quite capable of. Working to his advantage are several factors: first, that nobody knows where he is, and second, that he has ample resources to discreetly buy what he needs.

He rotates his shoulders and spreads his legs, stretches his back to work out the kinks. He does all this carefully so as not to aggravate his wound. The little crumbling highway is empty, and there are no plowed fields or farmhouses, just trees as far as his eyes can see. He reaches for his toes and groans; he wonders how he would appear to a stranger passing by in a pickup truck. The driver would see a man, a van. The man might be in trouble, the van may have stalled, run out of gas, a tire could be leaking air. The stranger in the pickup would slow to offer assistance, but, no, the man waves the truck on, a smile on his terrified face, his panic a second skin of no recognizable shade, it sets him apart, it's a warning, a plea.

That is how he would look to a stranger passing by in a pickup truck.

He's losing his mind. This is how it is to lose your mind; it's terrifying because you're a helpless witness as it happens, until you become an amnesiac with no recollection of how you used to function among the ordinary, the everyday.

No, he's exhausted, that's all. It's the fatigue that tries to convince him he's about to cross some point of no return, that persuades him he's standing on the edge of a pit, a dark, bottomless pit, about to tumble in. He will not stumble in; he will not spend his life in free fall. There is no stranger in a pickup truck offering to help, he has no second skin, his flesh is white, and his expression calm.

He orders himself back in the van. He thinks, *Warm your hands over the heating vents; your fingers are frozen through.*

The Voyager starts, the engine warms, the hot air brings his body back to life. He takes Marv's gun and stuffs it in his waistband. He takes the cell phone, stuffs it in a pocket. He runs his fingers through his choppy hair, willing it into place. He says to himself: *First things first. Drive, find a place to get some breakfast, buy a thermos full of strong coffee, and figure out where you are. Next, plot a direct course between that place and Sean's cabin. Finally, go there, take a hot shower, and get into bed. This tired and dirty, you're bound to make avoidable mistakes, and one of them could send you to Rush City, lock you in a cell next to Ian's.*

And stop referring to yourself in the second person.

He asks himself: *What sane person does that?* He remembers Alex Supertramp referring to himself in the third person, writing in his journal: *Two years he walks the earth. No phone, no pool, no pets, no cigarettes. Ultimate freedom.* It was only when Supertramp was dying that he returned to a first-person voice, and his given name, Christopher McCandless.

"Okay," Brendan says out loud as he pulls back on the road. He's a man who knows what he's doing, has a list of tasks. He will start with the most important one, cross it off his list, move on to the next. The list will keep him in motion, keep him sane, until he finds the place where he can rest.

The list steadies him. It clears the fog, removes the self-doubt, and keeps the pit at bay. He thinks clearly, he realizes that somehow, as he raced out of Duluth he wound up on Route 4 North and spent the night in the Cloquet Valley State Forest.

At a gas station in the town of Markham he fills up the tank, buys a thermos, coffee, sports bars, candy, sandwiches, a hat, a souvenir T-shirt, and a gallon of spring water. The old man with an accent so thick that Brendan has to use all that's left of his powers of concentration to decipher what he says, tells him that the easiest way to get to Grand Marais, the little town on a great lake, is to take 16 East to 15 East to 61 North. Brendan buys a map and has the old man mark the route for him. The shopkeeper shakes his head as he plots Brendan's course, and Brendan suspects that he's quietly amazed at how stupid folks are these days, so dumb they can't follow the simplest of directions.

Brendan thinks he'd like a job at the old man's little store. Sean and he'd live in a small apartment above this place, nights spent with books, Maggie, days spent pulling out maps for lost people, directing them to where they want or need to go. He would be good at it, he thinks, tending shop in some remote part of the country, setting his reading aside at the sound of tires on gravel so he can ring up a tall bottle of orange pop, a map full of destinations, or a brightly colored bag of potato chips.

As the old man hands him the map Brendan says, "Thanks."

The old man nods, says, "Oh-tay, den." Brendan's the most recent in a long line of people in search of something, maybe he'll find it, maybe he won't, the old man's done his best, made it as clear as possible.

Brendan sits in Cynthia's van, nearly scalding his throat with the coffee. After some sleep, a shower, a shave, he'll be a new man, a confident man, the one who will call Sean again, tell him this time, *If you truly love me you won't ask any questions. You'll put Maggie in your car and join me here at your cabin and together we'll head north to Canada. You said it yourself: order is an illusion.* And it will be Sean's love and Brendan's newfound confidence that come together to create their new lives.

This will work out.

Just in case some of Sean's family are visiting the cabin, he hides the Voyager in a clump of trees alongside the main road and painfully makes his way by foot. He doesn't want them to see the van full of garbage bags.

That's when he spots it: the trooper's vehicle outside the cabin.

Fuck. Oh, fuck.

He crouches behind a lush young tree; he makes out the form of a police officer on the other side of the guest-bedroom's window. The trooper moves from room to room and when he's done with his inspections, heads out the front door.

Brendan pulls out Marv's gun, the barrel of the Smith and Wesson pointing straight ahead. It takes the trooper longer than he would have guessed to notice him.

"Ha-low," the trooper shouts, a hand covering his eyes. "I didn't see you there."

He doesn't answer him.

The trooper makes out the shape of the gun in Brendan's hands. He says, "Official business, friend. No need for that thing."

He doesn't say a word.

Now the trooper smiles wide, a condescending look on his face. "Let's talk about this, okay? Just lower your weapon, and we'll talk this through. You don't want to do something you'll regret, do you?" As he asks his questions he moves his free hand to his holster. He's about to kill Brendan.

Brendan severs the connection between his brain and his fingers. The gun that he holds in his hands fires. The bullet whizzes past the trooper, closer than Brendan would have liked. The man falls to the ground, cursing.

What the hell is he going to do now? *Remain calm.* Brendan shouts, "Stay down! Stay the fuck down!" The man lies on his side. "Facedown, asshole!" He watches the trooper struggle; sees him spread his arms out in front of his body. Brendan asks him, "Jesus Christ, what have you done? What have you done to me?"

"Nothing, friend, I've done nothing. Now let's calm down, let's not do something stupid."

"I am *not* stupid!"

"No, no, you're not stupid, that's absolutely right, you're absolutely right."

Brendan stands over him now, the gun just feet from the trooper's head. "What am I going to do? What the hell am I going to do now?"

The trooper says, "Well, you don't want to kill me, for one thing."

Brendan laughs. How long does he stand there, his gun aimed at the man's skull, the trooper twitching in anticipation of his death? A decision, Brendan needs to—has to—make a decision about this man, this man's life, his own. Why has this happened? Why does disaster follow him wherever he goes, even here to this little cabin lost among the pines of northern Minnesota? Why is this man trembling at his feet?

He focuses on his breathing. He squats down next to the trooper, empties the man's holster of its weapon. His captive breaks their silence, saying in a voice that's too normal, too reassuring to be believed, "I think you should let me go now, don't you?"

But Brendan doesn't answer him, he just stares at the short brown and gray hair on the man's head, at the thick, heavy neck. He wonders how wrong it would be to end this man's life for him. He wonders whether he's the type of person capable of putting a bullet in a man's brain. He wonders whether there's a point to any of this. Should he put the barrel to his own head and fall, bloody and lifeless, on top of this terrified man? What is the better thing to do? Who needs this the most?

He says, "Where's Sean?"

The trooper takes that tone again, says, "I don't know a Sean. Are you planning to meet someone named Sean? Is he a friend of yours?"

He feels his eyes water. "I guess not."

He sits next to the trooper as the sky dresses itself in the soft pinkish hues of sunset. The temperature drops, the air chills. It will be dark soon, cold. The trooper pleads with him softly, there is a wife, children. The trooper's oldest is in fifth grade; she wants to be a nurse when she grows up. Another girl, this one in second grade, possesses an extraordinary gift for math. More questions from the trooper now, questions about actions and consequences, about the short term and the big picture. These are meant to be helpful, to guide Brendan to a conclusion that will spare both their lives.

Brendan asks him, "What's your name?"

He says, hopefully, "Erik."

"Erik, my name's Paul. Where are you from, Erik?"

Softly: "Silver Bay, originally. You?"

"I'm from Pittsburgh."

Erik says, without the slightest trace of irony, "Well, Paul from Pittsburgh, I'm pleased to meet you."

He sighs. "Wish I could say the same, Erik, how I wish to hell I could say the same."

That's when they both hear it, the sound of wheels rolling over hard dirt and stone. Another car is heading toward the cabin, another state patrol car, this one with two men inside.

Erik from Silver Bay says, very seriously, "I think it's time to put the gun down." Then he calls Brendan by his given name and Brendan almost drops the pistol in surprise.

The car stops, idles in front of them, and then the motor is turned off. The men inside point their guns at Brendan's head as they reach for the doors.

Brendan whispers, "Where's Sean?"

One of the men, from behind the car's open door, shouts, "Put your weapon down and place your hands on top of your head."

Erik suggests helpfully, "Let's do as he says."

From the cabin's window he sees Sean's niece, Eileen, her young, beautiful face unbelieving, her mother pulling her away from the glass.

Epilogue

IT'S VISITING HOURS. During his first few weeks in Rush City Sean would come see him, but just, as Sean put it, *for closure.* Sean's little circle of friends has been his rock through this whole ordeal and now they've begun fixing him up in earnest, the way other people give a grieving dog-owner a new puppy to distract them from their loss. Brendan imagines Sean's family of choice demanding to see identification, birth certificates, and proof of employment from the men they consider matching Sean with. He sees interview committees during which the couples inform would-be suitors of Sean's recent trauma, his big heart, and his ability to make anyone—even someone like Brendan—happy. Their schemings must have worked; Brendan never sees him anymore. He had hoped to work Sean's need for closure to his advantage, put a romantic notion in Sean's head of standing by his man as Brendan repaid his debt to society, and then, together, make a new start. During what Sean told him would be the final visit, Sean apologized for what had happened, how the police had called him, after they had examined Marv's phone records. For the fact that he had said *Who?* when asked if he knew a Victor Komarovsky. How, after recognizing Brendan's face from the police sketch drawn from Ed Lundeen's single meeting with Mr. Komarovsky, he had said, *That's Pierre.* How he told them of their trip to his cabin. For what it's worth, Sean told him, he had believed Brendan when Brendan testified that it was

Ian who had killed Marv. Now that Ian's plea-bargained to a lesser charge, Brendan's been vindicated, at least as far as murder's concerned. Sean said he knew from their short time together that Brendan was incapable of doing such a thing. But even as the words were leaving Sean's lips, that look of incomprehension Brendan had noted at their first reunion passed over Sean's face; the sheer bafflement at what Brendan *was* capable of.

Brendan asked after Maggie, Eileen, Sean's friends. He apologized for scaring Sean's niece up at the cabin. As Sean got up to leave, Brendan told him that he was in love with him. Sean just said, *Good-bye, Victor Hall,* calling Brendan by that other name, his legal name, the one given him by his parents, one last dig. But even now Brendan doesn't know if Sean was criticizing him by using that name or if Sean was chastising himself for being so taken by someone whose true name he never even knew.

So, Sean's gone for good. And now visiting hours come and go, just bundles of empty minutes for Victor Hall, AKA Brendan Wolf, AKA Franklin Thompson, AKA Pierre Bezukhov, AKA Victor Komarovsky, AKA just Paul from Pittsburgh. His life is like an old, beat-up directory, full of addresses friends have left, numbers no longer in service or reassigned. When someone actually does show up to see him, it's almost worse than if no one did. For his only visitors now are Ann and Judy, the gals from Babies First. He's their prison ministry project. They bring him odd things—rosaries, Christian magazines and newspapers, and pamphlets: "What Every Christian Needs to Know About Homosexuality" and "Freeing Yourself from the Chains of Homosexuality." The tapes they give him begin and end with contemporary Christian rock and they are desperate for him to decide on a favorite song, for any evidence that their work is making headway.

And, of course, they bring him bars: lemon, chocolate, and coconut. Judy had said, *Bars for your time behind bars!*

He tells them at each weekly visit that they insist upon making, that they are idiots. And if he fooled them once by pretending to be a pro-life fanatic, how could they ever be certain that his hoped-for jailhouse acceptance of Jesus Christ as his personal lord and savior would be any more sincere?

Faith, Ann always tells him.

They're so damn smug that way, Christians.

The bars he gives to the other inmates in the hope of avoiding a fight or worse. If he gets lonely, there's Frankie, everybody's girlfriend, but he feels sorry for Frankie, who drifts like a ghost, bruised and battered, through the corridors, with a swollen lip on his gaunt face. Brendan's sister-in-law has vanished and his brother is incarcerated at Oak Park, the prison for Minnesota's hardest-core offenders, the cumulative severity of Ian's crimes now making him *a threat to public safety*. The only thing that might possibly have been considered a silver lining, a letter from his oldest brother, Steven, ended up being more disturbing than the arrest or anything that has happened since.

Dear Victor,

How long I have prayed to be reunited with my beloved brothers, and how heartbreaking *it is to find you are both in prison. I know Mom and Dad were no role models, but their crimes were not your legacy to inherit. I hope you don't try to absolve yourself of what you have done by blaming them. They were who they were, but you and Ian are who you* choose *to be. We are not imprisoned by the circumstances of our birth. And it is not too late, for you can still choose to change your life.*

In the hope that you will soon find yourself on the one, true path, I enclose a book that will point you in the right direction. If you read it with a sincere *heart (I cannot overemphasize this), and ask the Lord if it is true, He will answer you through the Holy Ghost. He will invite you to become a saint, and you will be glad. Please,* listen *to the still, small voice of the Lord. You will hear it if you only allow yourself to.*

I became a saint at the age of twenty-five. Believe me, I had been a lost, bitter, angry young man, angry at our parents, angry at the world, and even angry at God. I had an excuse for every single sin I committed and nothing was ever my fault. I told myself my life would have been better if only our parents had never been taken away. If only I had not ended up in foster care. I was killing myself with cheap alcohol and cheap women who didn't give a damn about me. I was working dead-end jobs and moving every few years in the hope that a change of scenery would do me good. You know that old saying, Go West Young Man? Well I kept heading west, living in Sioux Falls and then in Cheyenne and then in Provo. But the old adage is true: you can't run away from yourself. *Wherever you go, there you are. But Victor, we are so fortunate that the Lord has a plan for us. When I was getting ready to pull up stakes again and try my luck in Reno, I met a wonderful gal who taught me how to truly love and how to believe and we've been married ever since. We stayed on in Provo for a while, but moved by Truth, we settled in Colorado City, where we live the one True faith. Oh, the* happiness *we have known here!*

If you and your brother were different sorts of men I would be happy to have you know your nieces and nephews and grandnieces and grandnephews, but the article I read suggested that you are a Sodomite and stated that Ian had taken a woman of negro lineage as a wife. These were the most painful *things to learn, far more painful to me than the crimes you have been convicted of. I must tell you that in purer, more righteous times, the penalty for you and your brother would have been death. So, yes, I was* distraught *by the deviance of my siblings, but I accepted the news as God's punishment for reading a Gentile magazine, the very one that reported it all, in ugly detail.*

But I gain strength from the knowledge that it is possible for you to return to the presence of God and for our family, yes, even Mom and Dad, to be united for all eternity. *This is my heartfelt prayer, one that, with the grace of God, you can help answer. You were a spirit child of God before you were born, and you were sent to this world to learn and to progress. Don't you know that* the fact that you are alive is proof you have already accepted God's plan? *You must try to remember! Rejoice that God knows how we fail here on earth, each and every one of us, which is why He gave us Jesus Christ, to make it possible for our* sins to be forgiven!

Read *this Book I give you.* Study *it. Yes, even* question *it. I know I did before I finally* accepted *it. And once you have accepted it, write me.* But not one second before. *Today is but a moment, eternity forever.*

Your Brother,

Steven

Even though Brendan is hungry for books, he could not stomach the Book of Mormon that Steven had sent. He read Steven's letter once, and then once more, and then one final time, before ripping it to shreds and dropping the tattered bits into the cell's toilet. His cellmate had scowled at him when he did this, but then his cellmate's face rarely offers him any other expression.

The cellmate is a strict Muslim, the successful product of a form of conversion that's vigorously encouraged among the black inmates. The cellmate faces Mecca, reads the Koran, and best of all, he doesn't speak to Brendan, because Brendan's a *white devil* and a *pervert.*

So Brendan occupies his time with books, as he always does when left to his own devices. On the city bus routes his books served him well, the open pages a pre-emptive strike against anyone who might consider harassing him or attempt to engage him in conversation. With his books there's no eye contact to avoid, he's shielded visually and psychologically from others, men like him who find themselves in exile, quarantined by a society that rightly—and occasionally, wrongly—wants nothing to do with them. Their prison terms are vacation days for their fellow citizens, who bask in lives temporarily free from their impulsiveness, their stupidity, their aimlessness.

Desperate at first, Brendan quickly devoured the small classics section in the prison library and was rewarded with a raised eyebrow from his cellmate while he was reading *The Autobiography of Malcolm X.* He's beginning a new stack, recently donated by the Books for Prisoners Project. Today he's excited to read yet again an old friend he's found among the charity books, a work he was introduced to by Alex Supertramp—*Family Happiness* by Leo Tolstoy. The events of his life, recent and

otherwise, have led him to believe that Leo and he are now of the same
mind on what should make a person happy.

I have lived though much, and now I think I have found what is
needed for happiness. A quiet secluded life in the country, with the
possibility of being useful to people to whom it is easy to do good,
and who are not accustomed to having it done to them: then work
which one hopes may be of some use; then rest, nature, books, music,
love for one's neighbor—such is my idea of happiness. And then, on
top of all that, you for a mate, and children, perhaps—what more can
the heart of a man desire?

What, indeed?

So this is how he'll measure his sentence, in books, just as he once
measured his books in sentences. He has to teach himself to read
slowly, make each book last; they are, after all, the only little piece of
freedom he has, his only escape, however short-lived. The prison library has only a few hundred books—real books, that is. He doesn't
count the manuals on how to get a GED, be a good father, conquer your
addictions, and manage your anger. With the meager number of titles
available to him he must savor each word, weigh it carefully, and measure it precisely. He must give each book an exploratory sniff, breathe
in its bouquet, swirl the first paragraph in his mouth, and then nod quietly to himself, thinking, *Yes, this will do, I will read this book.* Still, he'll
have to read each volume many times over, even the ones he doesn't
particularly care to revisit. Ahead of him will be hours spent with fine
wines in exquisite bottles as well as time with fermented grape juice
drunk directly from a twist-top jug.

This cell, then, must serve as the *room of one's own*, shared with a car
thief. In this room there are the odors of cleaning solutions and human
biology instead of the fragrant must of old books and worn slippers; there
are the sounds of men shouting obscenities, threatening lives, groaning
ejaculations. This is a sordid existence; grown men living in the oral and
anal stages of development, being fed concoctions that make them turn

their heads, infants refusing the spoons their mothers place in front of their lips. They eat, they shit, they piss, they jerk off. They wait, passing the time with curses, threats, fights. Their world's elemental table is comprised of just five units: piss, shit, sweat, blood, and cum. When they speak, it's to say *motherfucker* or *motherfucking*, their vocabulary list of two, so simple that they're all on the dean's list.

Sometimes they sleep, but not all of them, and not every night. For Brendan, sleeping is the best part of his Rush City existence, head and shoulders above his books. Tonight he won't dream of what happened today in this prison or what happened years ago at a McDonald's in South Minneapolis. Tonight he'll dream of a spring picnic on the shores of Lake Superior, of a dog eating hamburger and rice out of a china bowl, of grapes gently landing in his mouth.

When he wakes up, his capacity to hope refueled, he'll imagine the possibilities beyond this small cell with its religious fanatic, its basin, and its toilet. There are lives out there, lives that are clean, simple; that are noble in their cleanliness and simplicity. A life he will lead once he's served out his term.

When that day comes he'll need a new name.

He's considering Alexander.

Alexander Supertramp.

About the Author

Brian Malloy's debut novel, *The Year of Ice*, won the American Library Association's Alex Award, was a *Booklist* Editors' Choice for the "Best of 2002" and a finalist for the Ferro-Grumley Award and the Violet Quill Award. His first novel for young adults, *Twelve Long Months*, will be published in 2007. He has taught creative writing at the University of Minnesota, the Loft Literary Center, and Emerson College.

Visit the author's Web site at www.malloywriter.com.